Exercise in Alchemy!

Jenk removed the black cloth, revealing a glass vessel about the size and shape of an ostrich egg.

Caleb leaned forward to examine the egg. It was filled with a viscous fluid, a dull clouded liquor, but Caleb was just able to make out a tiny, doll-like figure suspended in that fluid. It appeared to be a perfectly proportioned little man, no more than six inches high, accurate in every detail, right down to the fingernails and eyelashes, utterly realistic in every way, but for his minuscule size and the grey-green pallor of his skin.

"Six and thirty days ago," said Jenk, "this was a mandrake root crudely fashioned to resemble a man . . ."

Don't miss Teresa Edgerton's *Green Lion Trilogy*:

Ace Books by Teresa Edgerton

THE GREEN LION TRILOGY

CHILD OF SATURN
THE MOON IN HIDING
THE WORK OF THE SUN

GOBLIN MOON

GOBLIN MOON

TERESA EDGERTON

ACE BOOKS, NEW YORK

This book is an Ace original edition,
and has never been previously published.

GOBLIN MOON

An Ace Book / published by arrangement with
the author

PRINTING HISTORY
Ace edition / February 1991

ISBN: 0-441-29427-8

Ace Books are published by The Berkley Publishing Group,
200 Madison Avenue, New York, New York 10016.
The name "ACE" and the "A" logo
are trademarks belonging to Charter Communications, Inc.

PRINTED IN THE UNITED STATES OF AMERICA
10 9 8 7 6 5 4 3 2 1

Acknowledgments

The Whensday People, as ever, provided invaluable critiques and insights while this work was in progress: Ellen Finch, Joy Oestreicher, Dani Vitro, Delores Beggs, Mike Van Pelt, Alis Rasmussen, Ed Muller, Rich McKenzie, Dean Stark, Kimberly Rufer-Bach, Leslie Lundquist, Jeanette Hancock—Bob Levy taught me everything I know about rowboats, Kevin Christensen plied me with innumerable books and resources, and Beth Gilligan helped me in so many ways that I could not begin to list them all.

Special thanks are due to Tad Williams, Patron Saint of Fledgling Novelists, and to my "research assistants," John Edgerton and Ann Meyer Maglinte.

Finally, I would like to thank my editor, Beth Fleisher, and my agent, Jane Butler, for patience and tolerance above and beyond the call of duty.

GOBLIN MOON

Of The Goblin Moon

A quaint Superstition still current in the Rustic Villages and indeed among many Ignorant Folk, personifies the full Moon as a Loathsome Hag with a prodigious Appetite, who, roaming the country lanes and byways, Devours all whom she meets: Men, Women, Children, Horses, Cattle, Sheep, Goats, &c., all without Discrimination and sometimes at a Single Gulp.

This Superstition, our Colleague, Dr. Finsbury, hath traced back to the days of Dark Evanthum, and indeed, it is well known that Moon Worship was a feature of all the Ancient Religions. Whereas the Enlightened Pagans of Panterra worshipped the Moon Goddess as a stately white Woman, the Magicians and Adepts of Evanthum depicted her as a ghastly Giantess who, swelling ever greater at the time of her Monthly Approach, and her Appetite increasing in proportion, required to be Propitiated and her Blood-Lust sated with divers horrid Sacrifices, Rituals, and Ceremonies—the which neglected, her Anger was Terrible, and great Mutations, Quakes, Fires, Tempests, Deluges, and all manner of Disaster both Natural and Civil the Inevitable result.

Such Upheavals are not unknown in Our Own Day, but Modern Philosophers attribute them to another Cause, which is: to the Magnetic Attraction between the Earth and the Moon, whenever that chilly orb draws Nigh.

From *Magica Antiqua, a Complete System of Magical Philosophy, containing both the History and the Principles of the Art, along with many Curious Anecdotes concerning the Beliefs and Practices of the Ancients* by Horatio Foxx, F.G.G., Doctor of Alchemy, of Natural and Occult Philosophy, &c., &c.

Printed for Darrington, Dover, and Zabulon, at Porphyry Lane, Lundy, Imbria

1.

In which a Discovery is made.

The moon wallowed, pale and bloated, on the horizon. The tide, running abnormally high even for this time of Iune's near approach, had turned; no longer reversing the river's natural flow, it swelled and accelerated the headlong rush of waters down to the sea. Oars creaked in rusty oarlocks as a flat-bottomed rowboat carrying a grizzled old man and a sturdy youth headed across the current, pulling for the dark western shore.

The old man sat on the stern thwart, scanning the river, while the boy rowed. At first glance, they might have been mistaken for sea-faring men, for they dressed much alike, in cloth caps and long full-skirted coats of some rough fabric so worn, patched, and stained that it could no longer be identified; they wore their hair in short tarry pigtails, sailor-fashion. But their pale faces gave them away, and their wide dark eyes, like the eyes of some nocturnal bird of prey. They were river scavengers, Caleb Braun and his grandnephew Jedidiah: men who slept by day and worked at night, rowing out on the river after dark when the fishing scows, barges, and pleasure craft that plied the river Lunn by day were all tied up in dock.

Near the middle of the river, Caleb reached out with the gaff hook to snag a piece of floating wood. It proved to be a piece of decorative molding depicting one of the Seven Fates, a gilded figure like to a naked man with outstretched eagle's wings sprouting from its shoulders. The gold paint was beginning to flake away, giving the features a leprous cast, but the wood was still sound. With a grunt of satisfaction, Caleb dropped the molding in the bottom of the boat.

When they reached quieter water near the shore, Jedidiah rowed upstream, turned the boat, and started across again.

"Upriver!" Caleb's hoarse warning barely allowed Jed time to reverse the stroke of one oar and turn the boat so that the bow

3

took the impact. There was a dull thud and the boat rocked wildly as something heavy glanced against the bow and scraped along the side. Jed caught only a glimpse of a blunt-ended shadow riding low in the water and a gleam of moonlight on ornate brass fittings, before the current caught the coffin and sent it bobbing on ahead.

"Pull, lad, pull," Uncle Caleb called out. "Blister me, we'll lose it, you don't move sharp!"

Jed plied the oars frantically, spinning the boat one hundred and eighty degrees, then rowing with all his might to get downstream of the coffin. Then it was Caleb's turn to move swiftly, using the gaff hook to draw the long black box closer and tying ropes through two of the handles.

With the coffin securely in tow, Caleb sat down again, rubbing his hands on the sides of his thighs. "Ebonwood, by the look of it, and see them fancy handles? Some fine country gentleman, or a baron or a jarl inside, maybe. Should be money and jewels as well."

Jed nodded glumly. If not gold coins or a jeweled brooch, the long black box would likely contain something of value. Yet at the thought of opening the coffin and claiming those valuables, he could not repress a shudder.

"You got no call to be so squeamish," snorted Caleb. "You was bred for this life, which is mor'n I can say for some of the rest of us. You got no call to quake and rattle your teeth at the sight of a box of old bones."

Jed knew it was so. Just about as far back as he could remember, he had been accompanying his granduncle on these night-time expeditions. But even before that (as Caleb was fond of reminding him) he had been a dependent of the river and the tide. The very cradle that had rocked him as a baby was constructed of planks from the wreck of the *Celestial Mary;* his first little suit of clothes—in which he had amazed the other urchins, in velvet and lace—his mother cut from the cloak of a drowned nobleman. And much of the food and drink which nourished him since had been purchased with deadman's coin.

Old Lunn, she was a capricious river, as Jed well knew: restlessly eroding her own banks, making sudden leaps and changes in her course, especially upriver in the country districts where there were no strong river walls to contain her. Swelled by a high tide or by the rains and snow-melt of Quickening, she swept away manors and villages, churches and farmhouses,

4

crumbled old graveyards and flooded ancient burial vaults, dislodging the dead as ruthlessly as she evicted the living. No, the Lunn respected no persons, either living or dead, but the crueler she was to others, she was that much kinder to men like Jed and his Uncle Caleb.

For by river-wrack and by sea-wrack brought in by the tide, off goods salvaged from water-logged bales and salt-stained wooden chests, by an occasional bloated corpse found floating with money still in its pockets, the scavengers gleaned a meagre existence year 'round, and—especially when the full moon brought high tides and other disturbances—were sometimes able to live in comfort for an entire season off the grave offerings of the pious departed.

Despite all that, Jed always felt a cold uneasiness robbing the dead.

"Willi Grauman opened a coffin once—found the body of a girl inside: her hair down to her feet and the nails on her hands mor'n a foot long, and the box all filled with blood—Willi says she was fair floating in it." Jed spoke over the continued creaking of the oars. "It weren't a *natural* corpse at all, it was a bloodsucker. Willi slammed the lid down, and—"

"Willi Grauman is a liar. I thought you knowed that," said Caleb, speaking with calm authority.

Jed hunched one shoulder. "Erasmus Wulfhart ain't no liar. He says his granddad opened a box once, and there weren't no body at all, just a white linen shroud and a great heaving mass of worms and yellow maggots—one of them worms crawled out and got into old Wulfhart's clothes, and while he slept that night that worm ate a hole right through his leg: flesh and bone and all. Erasmus seen the hole hisself, or the scar, anyways, and the old man limped to the end of his days."

"I heard another story how Karl Wulfhart lamed his leg, and it weren't nearly so romantic," Caleb replied coolly. He reached into a pocket somewhere inside the capacious folds of his coat and removed a long-stemmed pipe. Reckoning it was time for a change of subject, he said: "Heard there was a quake up-country. Mayhap we're not the only ones in luck this night."

When Iune drew near the earth in her elliptical orbit, the unstable country upriver was prone to seismic tremors and quakes, and sometimes it was the agitated earth, not the river, that leveled cities and towns and forests, or, in a ghastly reversal, swallowed the living as it spewed forth the dead.

5

"Oughtn't to speak of luck afore it's been proved good or ill—nor afore we've learned if our fine country gentleman took a notion to curse his grave goods," Jed muttered. He remembered a time twelve weeks past, in the season of Frost, when old Hagen Rugen had come into possession of a pair of solid silver candlesticks, the grave offering of a rural parson, and died not three days later of the Horrors.

"Superstitious foolery," said Caleb, as if he could read Jed's thoughts. "Hagen Rugen was a drunkard and guzzled *hisself* to death on the money he made off them candlesticks. 'Deadman's coin is no worse than any man's,'" he quoted.

Jedidiah set his jaw. Uncle Caleb was a fine one to scoff at superstition. Wasn't it "superstitious foolery" that brought Caleb so low in the first place—him and that old madman at the book-shop?

"Aye, I know what powers there be to bring a man to ruin—and how he may bring his own self low with foolish schemes and crackbrained notions." Caleb spoke again as if guessing where Jed's thoughts were leading him—which in all probability he did, having a knack for that sort of thing. "What man knows better than me?"

Caleb stuck the pipe in the corner of his mouth. "I've lived off this river for nigh fifty years—a hard life, some would call it, but I never took no harm from it, though I took silver and gold from the dead as often as I could. No, and I never seen any bloodsuckers or bonegrinders, neither. But when I lived in a fine mansion, having a respectable post as servant to the family of a jarl—and was more than a servant, was friend and *confeedant* to the son of that noble house—then I knew something and experienced something of Powers and Intelligences, and all the evil things that can blight a man's heart, and twist a man's soul, and dog a man's footsteps wheresoever he might choose to go, and all with no other object than to bring him down to Ruination!" Caleb nodded emphatically, took the pipe out of his mouth, and tapped it on the side of the boat as if for further emphasis. "When you've seen and done and suffered as much as I have, lad, then you'll be fit to say what's superstitious foolery and what's just plain TOM-foolery. Until then, you'd do well to let yourself be guided by wiser heads."

Jed said nothing, but continued to row.

• • •

Jed tied up at a wharf on the eastern bank, just below a tavern known as the Antique Squid. The upper stories of the tavern were dark, but the windows on the lower floor cast forth a welcoming glow of orange firelight, and the strains of a lively jig played on the fiddle and hurdy-gurdy drifted through an open door.

Jed scrambled out of the boat and climbed nimbly onto the stone pier. Caleb followed, his movements slow and stiff. They used a stout rope and an ancient winch to haul the coffin out of the water.

At the patter and scrape of approaching footsteps, Jed whirled around just in time to spot two furtive figures emerging from the shadows near the river wall. He reached for the gaff hook, ready for a fight. But then a familiar voice hailed him from the direction of the Squid, and two burly figures in dark cloaks and tricorn hats came out of the tavern. The footpads melted back into the darkness, at the approach of the Watchmen.

"Seems we're in luck." Matthias, the taller of the two constables, a big, coarse-featured redhead, nodded in the direction of the coffin.

The men of the Watch claimed a share of everything the scavengers brought ashore in Thornburg, offering in return their protection against the thieves and ruffians who inhabited the wharf at night, and also against the hobgoblins and knockers who lived in warrens inside Fishwife Hill and crawled out through the sewers when the moon was full.

This same Matthias, Jedidiah suddenly recollected, had claimed a silver-plated figurine from the ill-fated Hagen Rugen—which argued in favor of Caleb's contention that deadman's plate and coin were as good as any man's. It stood to reason that if the parson had cursed the candlesticks, he had not neglected the rest of his hoard, yet here was Matthias, as big and as ugly as ever, a full two seasons after Hagen's demise.

Caleb began to unfasten the latches and bolts that sealed the coffin. Still thinking of all the gruesome tales he had repeated earlier, Jed felt that cold feeling grow in the pit of his stomach. Walther and Matthias, each at an end of the ebonwood casket, lifted the lid.

"Sol burn me black!" Walther exclaimed, but the others stared silently, rendered speechless by surprise.

The body of a man in antique dress, and what appeared to be a perfect state of preservation, lay inside. He was just past his

7

middle years, with dark shoulder-length hair and a neat beard streaked with grey. His eyes were sewn shut and his limbs decently composed for burial, but a faint bloom was in his cheeks and a fresh color was on his lips, and the whole effect was so entirely lifelike that it seemed he could not be more than hours dead; yet he was dressed in the style of a scholar of the previous century, in a dark velvet tunic and breeches, a black silk robe, and a wide collar of delicate white lace. A pewter medallion lay on his breast, attached to a broad scarlet satin ribbon around his neck, and instead of the usual grave offerings of gold and silver, he had been buried with his books, ancient volumes bound in crumbling leather, with curious symbols stamped in gilt upon the covers. On one appeared the same mysterious sigil that was stamped on the medallion: a two-headed serpent devouring a fiery disk that might have been meant to represent the sun.

"Burn me!" Walther exclaimed again. "If that ain't an ugly jest—to tog a man in fancy dress, pack him up with a load of dusty old books, and tip him into the river apurpose!"

Matthias, recovering, made a sign against bad luck. To rob the dead was one thing—an act, arising as it did from sound financial motives, which was instrumental to the advancement of the living—but to make a mockery of the rite of burial and with no discernible notion of profit . . . even to men as rough and profane as the two constables, this was a shocking impiety. And by the look on Caleb's face, the expression of a man in the grip of some tremendous emotion, it was evident he was as shocked as the others.

But Jed had conceived another idea entirely. "Look here, I don't reckon 'tis a corpse, after all. Only a wax doll like the figures they sell at Madam Rusalka's."

Indeed, the waxen transparency of the skin, the lifelike color, argued that the body could not be made of any ordinary mortal clay. Yet no one could bring himself to put a hand inside the coffin and put Jed's theory to the test.

Matthias laughed uneasily, rubbing the red stubble that grew along his jawline. "A wax doll . . . aye. Dwarf work by the look of it. It may be worth sommat to somebody. Them velvet togs, too, and that lace collar, they didn't come cheap—they'll bring a pretty price of themselves, if no one wants to buy the figure." He turned to Caleb. "Them old books, too . . . reckon we could sell them to your crony, old Jenk the bookseller?"

With a visible effort, Caleb tore his gaze away from the coffin and its contents. His voice shook and his body still trembled with a violent agitation. "Gottfried Jenk . . . aye, he'll want to see the books—and mayhap the rest as well. Run along, lads, and fetch us a cart. I've no coin for you now, Matthias, but I've a notion that Jenk will pay us well for this night's work."

2.

Of Gottfried Jenk, his History, and the Temptation he was subjected to that same night.

Jenk's bookshop was located at one end of an ill-lit cobblestone street, in a decrepit building with a high peaked roof and a gabled front. The shop occupied the lower floors, while the bookseller lived in a tiny suite of rooms under the eaves.

When the moon-faced grandfather clock down in the bookshop struck the hour of midnight, Jenk had still not retired. These nights when Iune was full, strange fancies plagued him, making sleep impossible. He sat at a queer little desk in his bedchamber, reading by the light of a single candle: a high-shouldered old man in a snuff-colored coat and a powdered wig, bent over an ancient Chalazian manuscript he was attempting to translate. Every now and then, he passed a pale, trembling hand over his forehead.

His head grew heavier and heavier; his eyes watered and burned. The characters he was trying to decipher began to move, to hump and crawl upon the page, to slide off the edges . . . With a cry, he pushed the manuscript away. He rose and began to pace the floor.

A hollow-eyed figure in a tattered frock coat sprang up to block his path; Jenk threw out a hand to fend it off. The wraith rolled a bloodshot wolfish eye, tossed back its head, and howled at him, pawing its narrow chest as if in mortal agony. Jenk gasped; for the pain was in his own breast, a devouring heat that ate through flesh and muscle and bone, leaving a dark, burnt-out cavity in the place where his heart had been.

"Naught but a shadow and a mockery," Jenk whispered to himself. With quaking limbs, he returned to his chair and col-

9

lapsed. "A shadow and a mockery, which I may banish and be . . . whole." At his words, the apparition faded and was gone, and beneath his clutching hands the old man felt solid flesh and bone, the pounding of his heart—indeed, it leapt about and banged against his ribs so frantically that, for a moment, he feared it must burst.

"I am whole," the old man repeated, not to himself this time but to the room at large. In all the dark corners, hobgoblin shapes groped and squirmed, struggling to acquire tangible form. Even when he buried his face in his hands, he could not block them out. Visions of his past . . . old hopes, old fears, old loves, old hates, all of them grotesquely changed, grown strange and terrible in their altered shapes.

He shook his head, as if by doing so he might clear his mind. He knew he must remember . . . must remember who he was and what he had been . . . must separate the true memories from the false. In that way only could he hope to move beyond the tangle of dreams and visions.

He had been . . . a young man of good family, the youngest son of a jarl, with a modest fortune of his own. A brilliant, bookish youth, his name recognized far beyond his native Marstadtt, beyond the principality of Wäldermark, known in all the capitals of Euterpe . . . a man admired, courted . . . his only liabilities (or so he thought them then) a pretty, spoiled wife and an infant daughter. Through a series of startling philosophical essays which he wrote and saw published, he gained the interest of an aged scholar who bequeathed to him certain rare books on alchemy and magic.

In those books, he discovered spells and formulas, diagrams, scales, magic squares: the tenets of a secret doctrine going back more than eighteen hundred years to the days of Panterra and Evanthum. Not all that he read there was new to him . . . he had some prior acquaintance with natural philosophy and knew of the Spagyrics, who claimed the pure, unblemished tradition, and of the Scolectics, who sought knowledge as power, often to their own destruction. He knew the dangers, but he had not been warned. Because those books promised him . . . ah, to be sure! What did those books *not* promise him? Wealth, fame, even immortality, could be his, but most of all the higher knowledge . . . knowledge of the universe in its innermost, intimate workings. He sought that knowledge and lusted after that knowledge as ardently as ever man desired woman. And what was the price of this thing he craved with almost a physical longing? A few short

10

years of study and various expenditures . . . laboratory equipment bought, salts and acids and metallic compounds purchased . . . the fire in his athenor consuming . . . consuming fuel day and night . . . and the expenses mounting until, his substance gone, he applied to moneylenders, ran up an enormous debt . . . and ruined himself in a fruitless quest for the Elixir of Life, the secret of transmutation, and the mystical stone Seramarias.

A distant kinsman in trade had provided the money for him to open this bookshop, and here he still lived and did business nearly a half a century later. He led a quiet, orderly, scholarly existence, punctuated the last five years by these periodic fits of disorientation and confusion, when the teeming products of his troubled brain threatened to overwhelm him.

As Jenk moaned and writhed in his chair, the sound of creaking cartwheels and scuffling feet down in the street attracted his attention. It seemed to him that there was something . . . something enormously portentous in those sounds. With an effort, he rose and crossed to a window. He was just unfastening the casement when someone knocked on the door below.

Jenk opened the window and stuck out his head. The moon had set behind Cathedral Hill; the lane was lit only by dim, flickering street lamps set at uneven intervals all down the street, and by a lanthorn which some demented person seemed to be waving about under his window.

As his eyes adjusted, Jenk made out the familiar figure of Caleb Braun, hopping about with uncharacteristic energy and doing a kind of impatient dance before the bookshop door. At his side, young Jedidiah held the lanthorn in one unsteady hand, while he attempted, with the other, to restrain Caleb's impatience. Farther down the street, two burly constables pulled a spindly cart, loaded with a huge black casket, up the hill.

For a confused moment, Jenk thought the coffin had come for him, and that Caleb and Jed constituted his funeral party.

Then his mind cleared. Perhaps it was the damp weedy air rising up from the river, perhaps the sight of his old friend helped to restore him. Jenk clutched the windowsill to steady himself and called out softly, just as Caleb raised his fist to knock again, "I am here, Caleb. I will come down and let you in."

The stairs leading from Jenk's attic rooms to the ground floor were so narrow and steep that he had to descend sideways like a crab, with the candle in one hand and his back against the wall. The bookshop smelled of dust and mice and decaying scholarship.

11

From the foot of the stairs, a narrow passageway led between high shelves crowded with old books and manuscripts. Jenk had acquired a notable collection of rare and valuable volumes, though many were there on consignment: *The Mirror of Philosophy* with its bizarre tinted woodcuts; Tassio's *Reflections;* one of five known copies of *The Correction of the Ignorant;* and (the pride of the collection) Antony's *The Fool's Paradise* bound in crumbling indigo leather with leaves edged in dull antique gold and but three minor errors in transcription.

At the front of the shop, the hands on the moon-faced clock marked the hour of three. Jenk balanced his candlestick on the top of the clock-case and crept to the door. With trembling hands, he unfastened the latches, lifted the bar, turned the handle, and peered out around the edge of the half-open door.

The cart pulled up in front. Jenk eyed the coffin mistrustfully. "Why do you bring me this? I've had no dealings with the dead these five and forty years. And why do you disturb me at this unconscionable hour?"

"It's books, Gottfried . . . books with the mark of the Scolos on 'em," Caleb whispered hoarsely. "Books and sommat else . . . You'll understand what it means better'n me, I reckon. But let us come in, Gottfried. You'd not want the neighbors to see what we've brought, or talk of it later?"

Reluctantly, Jenk moved aside and allowed the others to wrestle the coffin off the cart, maneuver it through the door, and set it down in one of the narrow aisles between the shelves. Caleb lifted the lid of the casket, and Jenk brought his candle over, the better to view the contents.

There was a serenity, a sort of blissful, dreaming peacefulness, on the face of the corpse that Jenk could not but envy. He felt a familiarity, a sense of inevitability to this moment, that sent a cold chill down his spine. "You found this in the river?" he asked, struggling to maintain his composure.

"Aye . . . floating on the river, just after the turn of the tide."

Despite Jenk's best efforts, the hand holding the candle began to shake; a splash of hot wax fell on the rim of the coffin. "This may be a gift of the sea, then, and not of the river."

Caleb lowered his voice again. "Could be . . . but it weren't in the water long; you can see by the condition of the wood. And however it come to us, it weren't no accident."

Matthias cleared his throat uneasily. "Young Jed, here, reckons 'tis one of them wax figures the gentry set up in their parlors. But

12

the eyes, now, that's an uncommon touch. Morbid, I call it . . . if it *is* a wax doll.''

Jenk forced himself to smile benignly. ''The gentry—and more particularly, the nobility—are addicted to morbid conceits. There is a fashion for mock funerals—all the rage, so young Sera informs me—whereby women whose husbands are still quite hale and whole don widow's weeds and stage elaborate demonstrations of grief—declaring it were better to mourn their menfolk, if only symbolically, in advance, than to risk being overtaken by their own mortality, and not live to do the thing at all. I believe,'' he said, more to himself than to the others, ''that these reminders of the fragility of human life and the wanton caprice of the Fates add a certain piquancy to present good fortune. And a 'corpse' in the parlor, as I take it, may be the newest fad.''

As only Caleb stood in a position to see what he did, Jenk reached down and gently lifted one of the hands. The texture of the skin and the flexibility of the joints convinced him that he was not holding the hand of a wax figure. Though the flesh was as cold and as lifeless as clay, this thing had once been a man.

He felt the smile stiffen on his face as he continued: ''And yet . . . perhaps not. The guilds use effigies in some of their more obscure ceremonies. I observed one such ritual myself, when I was a young man—though in that instance the figure was made of cloth and straw.''

He set down the hand and picked up one of the books; a section of the leather cover crumbled and fell as a fine dust into the coffin. He wondered if the continued preservation of the ancient volumes might not depend on their proximity to the corpse.

Jenk carefully returned the book to its place in the bottom of the casket. He turned toward Jed and the two constables. ''But whoever is responsible for this curiosity . . . I am grateful, yes, most particularly grateful that you thought to bring it to my attention. For I am, as you must know . . . quite fond of curiosities.''

Walther and Matthias bobbed their heads vigorously and grinned at him—no doubt expecting more than his thanks in recompense. And Caleb sidled closer to whisper in his ear. ''Don't worry about Jed—he'll keep quiet for my sake. But pay the others well. We don't want them spreading no tales.''

''Indeed yes,'' Jenk agreed loudly, for the benefit of the others. ''The Guild . . . if it was one of the guilds . . . might resent any inquiry into their mysteries . . . purely scholastic on my part, I do assure you, but perhaps to be taken amiss. We had best keep the

13

matter quiet . . . for all our sakes. If guildsmen put the effigy in the river, no doubt they expected it to *stay* in the river and might conceive some lasting resentment against those who brought it here.''

Crab-wise, Jenk ascended the stairs to the second floor. In a dark corner near the back of the building stood a dusty oak cabinet once used as a wardrobe. Now it was stuffed with old letters, with ancient deeds and legal documents decorated with wax seals and faded ribbons. Placing his candle atop the wardrobe, Jenk removed a ring of heavy iron keys from a pocket in his breeches, unlocked the cabinet, and removed a little wooden box stowed away at the back behind a pile of yellowing papers.

The box contained a scattering of gold and silver coin, a handful of wrinkled bank notes: the savings of many years, intended as a dowry for his granddaughter, Seramarias. If he meant to make use of the books, Jenk knew, his expenses would not end with bribes to the Watch.

And yet he was convinced that Caleb had spoken truly, that the books and the body had not come into their hands by accident. Of all the men who worked on the river—ignorant, illiterate men most of them, who knew nothing beyond their daily struggle for existence—that the casket had come to Caleb Braun, who alone among the scavengers would recognize the symbols on the books, who alone would realize the other implications of the discovery as well . . . no, it was too great a coincidence. Caleb had been fated to make the discovery, just as he was fated to bring it to the attention of Jenk himself.

"And yet . . . to what end?" Jenk wondered aloud. "It may be that the books were sent for our consolation—that we may gain back all that we have lost."

He thought of the long years of poverty and struggle, of the wife who deserted him, and of the daughter he had hardly known until, disowned by her mother's kin, betrayed and abandoned by the man she married against their wishes, she came to the bookshop to live for a short space, to bear a daughter of her own, and die. The child she bore, at first an intrusion on his solitary existence, the bookseller grew to love—and suffered his poverty doubly through all young Sera was denied.

Sera was eighteen now, a handsome, spirited girl. Five years ago, he had reluctantly sent her to live with her wealthy relations. Oh, yes, he knew full well how her pride must suffer as the recipient of Clothilde Vorder's condescending favors. But it was

14

of Sera's future he had been thinking, and of the wealthy men she would meet in the Vorders' house—one of whom might have the wisdom to recognize the value of her beauty and intelligence, to ignore the paltry size of her dowry, and ask for her hand in marriage. Now it came to him that the hope was a vain one, and that his beautiful and accomplished Sera was doomed to dwindle into a dreary old maid, little better than a servant in the Vorder household . . . unless he could find a way to mend his fortunes.

"But . . . how if the books were not meant for our worldly benefit, but for our spiritual redemption?" Jenk moaned softly to himself. "Caleb and I know the danger in possessing such volumes. It may be that we were meant to destroy them, to save some other poor fool from ruin. A final expiation for past sins, here at the end of our lives." He put a hand to his forehead. His brow burned as with a fever, but the palm of his hand was cold and clammy. Yet his mind remained clear, remarkably clear—indeed, he was impressed by the coherency and logic of his own arguments. "It may be that the Fates cast them carelessly our way, merely to see what we would make of them. Or it may be that the Intelligence which ordained our ruin so many years ago has not finished tormenting us yet."

Were he to beggar himself a second time, Jenk told himself, Sera would not be materially affected; but the public disapprobation, if the nature of some of the activities he contemplated became known—that she must feel keenly.

And yet . . . was he strong enough to resist the sheer entrancing *mystery* of the thing . . . the allure of forbidden knowledge? If he and Caleb were to discover the secret that maintained the body of the sorcerer, entirely uncorrupted, these hundred years and more, that discovery might lead to other, even greater secrets as well. At the thought, Jenk felt a cold thrill pass over him, the first stirrings of an old excitement, far beyond any pleasure the flesh had ever offered him.

"May the Father of All forgive me," he whispered. "I believed myself cured, but the old passion, the old hunger, returns, even stronger than before."

With shaking hands, Jenk unlocked and opened the box. If Sera would suffer his disgrace only obliquely, he told himself, she would enjoy the full benefit of his success. Fine silken gowns he would bestow on her, velvet slippers and ruby bracelets, page-boys and serving maids to wait on her every whim, and a dowry sufficient to ensure a brilliant marriage.

With his head full of these and other pleasant fancies, Jenk counted six silver coins into his hand. Then he replaced the box, locked the cabinet, picked up his candle, and descended the stairs.

3.

Concerning the Morbid pleasures of the Wealthy. The Reader is introduced to Miss Seramarias Vorder.

Thornburg-on-the-Lunn was a sprawling sort of town, a great, irregular, many-limbed town, shaped rather like a starfish, spraddled out on either side of the river. Indeed, it might be said that the Lunn gave Thornburg its character, for it was a capricious sort of town, a town of many contrasts, ancient and young, rollicking and cruel.

River port and market town combined, that was Thornburg, where pink-cheeked farmers and their daughters sold their fruits and vegetables side by side with hoarse-voiced fishmongers crying their wares and dark-skinned foreign peddlers hawking painted fans, cockatoos, and "diamond" necklaces made of pinchbeck and paste. It was a cosmopolitan place where men and dwarves and gnomes lived amicably side by side; a shabby-genteel sort of town, where taverns and warehouses and tiny crowded shops, crumbling old churches with belltowers and medieval guildhalls with clocktowers, were all tumbled together with parks and public gardens and elegant neo-classical villas.

At the center of town was Cathedral Hill, where the streets were narrow and steep, and crowded at most hours of the day with a constant traffic of foot travelers, carriages, carts, and sedan chairs. But behind the cathedral existed an unexpected haven of peace, a quiet old graveyard hidden behind iron gates, where the grass grew long and green among crumbling marble monuments and mossy gravestones, and dandelions and daisies sprouted in the cracked flagstone pathways.

16

Twenty years and more had passed since the last bodies were buried there. The elegant mausoleums were falling into disrepair; many of the statues and gravestones had tilted or tumbled and were not put aright. So it came as some surprise to the shopkeepers who did business on Church Street, one bright afternoon in the season of Leaves, to see a fashionably dressed funeral party trudging up the hill. At a stately but inexorable pace the procession came, and not only the shopkeepers took note. The busy wives of the town, the gentleman loungers, and the country girls in bright calico gowns who came into Thornburg at this season of the year to sell tame rabbits in wicker cages and baskets of painted eggs . . . all stopped what they had been doing to stare and to wonder, for this procession was remarkable for two very curious facts: the absence of a corpse, a coffin, or a bier; and a group of white-stockinged serving men who stalked on ahead of the sable-clad mourners, bearing hampers and baskets bulging with foods and wines, linen cloths and fine crystal. The servants entered by the imposing iron gates, and proceeded to lay out an elegant picnic repast among the gravestones.

"Such a pity Count Xebo could not attend his own funeral." The speaker, a stout matron in an enormous powdered wig, seated herself on a low cenotaph and lifted her gauzy black veil. "He left town on some business, you know (his country estates are sadly encumbered), and what was the poor Countess to do with the invitations already sent, and all the arrangements made?"

"A great pity," agreed her companion, a middle-aged dandy in high leather boots like a cavalry officer. Except for the boots there was nothing military about him. He wore his hair unpowdered and neatly clubbed at the back, but the front hung loose in dark golden lovelocks; his garments were laced, fringed, and beribboned to a remarkable degree; and he carried a tiny black fan. To many a susceptible maiden, he was a perfect figure of romance.

He spoke, moreover, with a foreign accent and a slight hesitation, which lent weight to his words, creating an impression that everything he said, no matter how trivial or commonplace, was the product of deep thought. "But we may comfort ourselves with the thought . . . that at some future event held in his honor, the Count will be beyond all concern for his estates . . . and shall certainly be present."

"Very true," replied the lady, accepting a crystal goblet filled with red wine from one of the servants. " 'Tis unlikely that a man of such venerable years will disappoint us a second time.

17

"But do tell me, my dear Jarl: what do you think of my daughter, Elsie?" she asked, nodding in the direction of a stand of dark yews, where two young women—one of them slight, pale, and golden-haired, the other a statuesque maiden with glossy dark brown curls—were strolling arm in arm.

"Your daughter is exquisite," Jarl Skogsrå replied warmly. "And yet there is something . . . I do not know how to say it . . . a quality of fragility, perhaps, that while it enhances . . ."

"My Elsie has never been in the best of health. She suffers dreadfully from a number of mysterious complaints." The lady spoke complacently, as though she believed she gained consequence by the possession of a sickly daughter. "However, we may see an improvement very soon. The dear Duchess has recommended a new man and a new course of treatment, and I am certain it will do poor Elsie good."

The Jarl murmured a few words expressive of sympathy, and the fond mother, apparently satisfied with this exchange, sipped her wine and turned her attention to the delicacies offered her by a footman in black and silver: quails' eggs, boiled snails, cheese tarts, pickled samphire, and other dainties, all tastefully arranged on a bed of dandelion leaves.

"But I am curious about this other young woman I see always in Miss Vorder's company," said the Jarl. "Her cousin, I believe?"

The lady selected a pigeon pasty. "A distant relation only. The orphaned daughter of a profligate kinsman; my husband insisted on bringing her into our household as a companion for Elsie. An obstinate, headstrong girl, but my daughter is so passionately attached to her that it would be cruel to separate them." Mistress Vorder selected another pasty and swallowed it at a gulp. "To do her justice, she takes great care of Elsie, and after all, she is more convenient than some wretched gin-swilling nurse, and entirely presentable besides."

The Jarl heaved a soulful sigh; he took her hand (it was a little greasy after the meat pies) and kissed it. "And this—this toleration of an interloper in your home—is but one of many sacrifices, I believe, which you have made for the sake of the precious ailing child."

The lady turned pink, flattered by his air of sympathetic respect. "I could not begin to list them all. You little know what I have suffered on Elsie's behalf. I believe we have seen every doctor, apothecary, herbalist, and chirurgeon in Thornburg, and the tor-

18

ments they have inflicted on my poor child are truly heart-breaking . . . the bleedings . . . the vile medicines . . . the horrid diets. I vow, I am a woman who has endured much.''

On the other side of the cemetery, in the shade of the trees, the object of Mistress Vorder's motherly concern relinquished her companion's arm and seated herself, with a weary little sigh, in the long grass.

The dark-haired girl sank down beside her. "Shall I send a servant for your powder?"

Elsie shook her head. "Please, Sera, no. I don't feel ill, only a little tired and breathless. Let us sit here in the shade for a time, until I feel stronger.'' She allowed Sera to remove her hat for her, an elaborate affair decorated with black velvet roses and a vast quantity of spotted black tulle, and set it down on the grass.

"I was thinking . . ." Elsie added dreamily, as she stripped off her black net mittens and dropped them into her lap, "that when I die, I would like to be buried in an old graveyard like this. So very peaceful, don't you think? And the statues in the new cemetery are so . . . so immense and ugly, they frighten me a little.''

When her cousin spoke so, Sera found it difficult to answer, difficult to speak around the painful constriction in her throat. Yet she forced herself to reply briskly, scowling as though she were merely cross and not sick with apprehension. "I don't approve of these morbid fancies, and I wish you would not make these 'death-bed declarations.' You are two years younger than I am, and shall most likely live to bury *me*.''

Elsie smiled her sweet, fragile smile. "*Your* death is something even *I* daren't contemplate. You are so strong and so stubborn, dear Sera, I almost believe you will live forever.''

The other girl's dark-browed face softened. "Then learn to be as strong and obstinate as I am, my darling, and spend eternity with me. How could I bear the prospect in any company but yours?''

Sera untied the black ribbons under her chin and removed her own plain, flat-crowned straw, which she immediately proceeded to use as a fan to cool both herself and Elsie. As Elsie's natural delicate coloring returned, Sera felt a cold wash of relief. *I am the one growing morbid*, she scolded herself. *Elsie has only to sigh, or turn pale, or say she is faint, and I am instantly convinced that the awful moment has come . . . her doctors have finally succeeded in killing her. But I must not allow myself to think such things . . . must not allow myself to dwell on them . . . or else I*

19

shall grow so foolish and wicked there is no telling what *I might do.*

"I certainly don't care for the company here," she said aloud. "Or for the occasion—so precisely calculated to encourage sick fancies. I can't imagine why Cousin Clothilde insisted you attend." She fingered the skirts of her black bombazine gown. "And these ridiculous weeds, so warm and uncomfortable on a day like this—why should either of us wear deep mourning for Count Xebo, who is no kin of ours, and rather more to the point, is not even dead?"

"Mama insisted that I come because she knew Jarl Skogsrå would be here," said Elsie. "I believe she is match-making again. I see you frown, and I don't blame you. He was perfectly charming to me, and I confess I liked him, but not when I saw how rude he was to you—not even asking Mama for an introduction, when we all rode in the same carriage to meet the Countess!"

Sera made an airy little gesture, dismissing the Jarl's discourtesy. "His rudeness to me is nothing; I am accustomed to these slights. I don't regard it, and neither should you. In general," she added thoughtfully, "I believe I prefer a man who is at least honest in his cruelty, better than the sly insinuating sort who hints at all kinds of horrid familiarities and supposes I must be flattered by his attentions simply because I am poor."

As she spoke, Sera chanced to encounter the glance of a pasty-face youth in a preposterous wig, a certain Mr. Hakluyt, who, on the occasion of a previous meeting, had whispered a vulgar piece of impertinence in Sera's ear and then slithered off before she was able to reply. He was watching her now with what could only be termed a speculative gaze. Sera returned his stare with a scorching glance of her own and hoped that would be sufficient to wither his pretensions.

Elsie remained innocently unaware of this little exchange. It was plain that she was strongly attracted to Skogsrå, but her loyalty to Sera was even stronger. "In general, you say . . . yet it is easy to see you have conceived a violent dislike of the Jarl. Well, I won't like him, either—though he *is* so very handsome and speaks with such a delightful accent—for you see people more clearly than I do, and your judgement of character is better than my own."

Sera experienced a sharp pang of remorse. She had a habit of conceiving strong prejudices, sometimes on the strength of a word or a gesture; it was a habit she deplored, but was unable to overcome. "No, no, you mustn't say so," she protested. "Indeed, I

20

know nothing against the man. Any animosity I may feel toward Jarl Skogsrå is purely personal and . . . rather puzzling, for I haven't seen or heard anything to make me doubt his intentions or his character.

"Perhaps I am only jealous because you were so instantly and so strongly attracted," Sera added softly, smoothing her cousin's disheveled golden curls with a gentle hand and a fond smile. *Jealousy . . . yes . . . and perhaps a little envy. How can I be so spiteful?*

"I am so selfish," she told Elsie, "that I am bound to resent any man who appears to be a serious rival for your affection— but you must not reject the Jarl on that account, indeed you must not."

Elsie took her hand and squeezed it affectionately. "Perhaps I will allow myself to like him a *little* bit, but that is all. I could not love any man who didn't value my Sera as much as I do."

The afternoon grew warmer. Sitting in the long, sweet-smelling grass, the two girls began to feel drowsy. Sera continued to wave her hat in a desultory manner. Elsie stifled a yawn and looked around her for another topic of conversation.

Mistress Vorder still sat perched on a marble slab, deep in conversation with the Jarl. The other picnickers were scattered about the cemetery in pairs or small groups, seated on the ground, or strutting among the gravestones, like a flock of crows come to feed among the crumbling mausoleums and mournful statues: Countess Xebo . . . Lord Vizbeck and his aging mother . . . two barons and their baronesses . . . the pale Mr. Hakluyt with his eternally roving eye . . . the Duchess of Zar-Wildungen . . . representatives of a number of wealthy but untitled families . . .

"How odd," said Elsie, with a mischievous sideways glance at her companion. "I made certain he would be here . . . just precisely the sort of occasion to appeal to a gentleman of—of a poetical sort, don't you think?"

"I really couldn't say," replied Sera. She felt her face suddenly grow warm and an uncomfortable fluttering begin in the region of her heart. "That is . . . I suppose you must be thinking of Lord Skelbrooke. But he is such a will-o'-the-wisp, always appearing and disappearing when one least expects him, it is virtually impossible to determine in advance where and when one is likely to meet him."

• • •

21

As evening approached, the servants began to pack up the baskets and the hampers, and a long procession of sable-draped carriages and sedan chairs lined up outside the cemetery gates.

"And so it is arranged," said Jarl Skogsrå, as he escorted Mistress Vorder to the carriage which had conveyed them from Count Xebo's town house earlier. "I shall call on you and your so charming daughter tomorrow morning."

"Indeed, I depend on you." Mistress Vorder leaned heavily on his arm, for she had eaten and drunk more than was good for her, and the combination of the sun and the wine made her head buzz unpleasantly. "I am delighted you have taken a fancy to my Elsie, sir, for I believe you are just the sort of man who can make her happy.

"But it is not my opinion alone—or her father's—that Elsie will consult in choosing to accept or reject you," she added, as the Jarl handed her up into the carriage. "You must exert yourself to please elsewhere. I hope you are not too proud to do so?"

The Jarl smiled a curiously feline smile. "I understand you. It is for me to win the favor of Miss Sera as well . . . to court her friendship as ardently as I woo the beautiful Elsie. It is not beyond my power to win her, madam, I do assure you. I have had some . . . acquaintance with young women of her sort in the past—poor but proud, yet not immune to the persuasions I know how to exert."

Mistress Vorder tittered obscenely. "Use what blandishments you will to win over young Sera. But as for those *other* young women . . . you will have to give them up, you know, if you are going to marry my Elsie. I won't permit you to break her heart."

"I am a passionate man, a man of single-minded purpose," said the Jarl, putting one hand on his heart, clicking the heels of his high, military-style boots, and bowing deeply so that the loose golden curls obscured his face. "And I take leave to assure you that the woman I marry shall have no cause to complain of any neglect!"

4.

In which Jedidiah falls in with Respectable Company.

Early one morning, when the shadows were long and the street lamps on every corner burning low, Jedidiah left his ramshackle lodgings by the river wall and set out at a brisk pace. It was that weird, plastic hour when night mutated into day, and the town of Thornburg took on a whole new character: when the prostitutes, footpads, and assassins who freely roamed by night returned to their back-alley hunting grounds or their ill-lit dens; when shop-keepers unshuttered the windows of their shops, and bakers, butchers, and greengrocers drove their rattling delivery wagons through the narrow streets of the town. It was that hour when the river scavengers tied up their little boats and headed for the nearest tavern to dine on peas-porridge, herring, and ale.

But Jed's habits had drastically altered during these last eight weeks. Without explanation, Uncle Caleb abandoned the river and went to work for Gottfried Jenk. *"Find another partner, or find other work—ain't that what you always wanted, anyways?"* the old man insisted. *"You never did care for the river, and that's a fact. Think you'd be grateful I finally cut you loose to do exactly as you please."*

Which was all very well and good, Jed countered, except for one small thing: he knew no trade but the one he'd been born to—supposing you could dignify it by the name of trade—and he was years too old, at the age of seventeen, to offer himself as a 'prentice and learn anything new.

Six weeks later, Jed was still looking for work. Finding it increasingly difficult to live on the wages the old man earned at the bookshop, Jed and Caleb had long since been reduced to a diet of gruel and hard-tack. This morning, Jed headed for Antimony Lane, where a colony of dwarves had settled and opened up shop, as glassblowers, potters, and purveyors of fine porcelain. He had heard that one Master Ule, a prosperous dwarf who owned

23

a bottle factory, wanted a boy to sweep up and run errands—menial work, better suited to a lad much younger, but by now Jedidiah was willing to take any job that would enable him to pay his rent and buy a little salt pork to go with his morning biscuit—any job that did not involve a return to his former occupation and his old disreputable way of life.

The Thornburg Jed knew best was unmistakably a riverside town: a town of docks and bridges, ships and sailors; of crooked streets with wet-sounding names, like Dank Street, Tidewater Lane, and Fisherman's Alley. But to reach Antimony Lane on foot, Jed left that Thornburg and ventured into the "respectable" part of town, where thatched roofs gave way to slate, stone chimneys to copper chimney pots, and the architecture revealed a tendency toward antique columns, decorative stonework, and wrought-iron gates.

Jed followed Tidewater for about a mile, until it became Church Street and climbed Cathedral Hill. Even at that early hour, the traffic was dreadful. Jed felt something bump up against his knees and glanced down to see a self-important gnome, in a tall black hat adorned with an immense silver buckle, glaring up at him.

"Beg your pardon," said Jed, stepping to one side—gnomes were terribly careful of their dignity, as Jed well knew, and like to take serious offense when taller folk blundered into them. But in doing so, he put himself directly in the path of a stout dowager in a goat-drawn vinaigrette, who pulled up just in time to avoid running him down.

Jed decided to escape the crowd by ducking down Mousefoot Alley, but he soon lost himself in a bewildering maze of narrow streets and tiny squares and courtyards, where the buildings were all of stone and brick—by which he knew he was in the dwarf quarter, though he had lost all sense of direction: no respectable dwarf consented to live inside wooden walls. Jed was debating whether to stop a passerby and ask for directions, or enter into a china shop and inquire, when a familiar voice called out his name.

Glancing back over his shoulder, Jed spotted an open carriage on the other side of the square, parked outside a goldsmith's establishment. There was no driver in evidence, only a page-boy in a powdered wig and scarlet livery to hold the heads of the horses; Jed did not know the boy, but he did know the passengers. One of them, a dark-haired girl of about his own age, in a gown of dull green poplin and a countrified bonnet tied with primrose ribbons, nodded at him and gestured imperiously.

24

Jed heaved a sigh, thrust his hands into the pockets of his old frieze coat, and walked across the square with dragging feet and a dim hope that some distraction might present itself and claim the young lady's attention before he reached the carriage.

The hope was a vain one, as Jedidiah might have known. Sera Vorder's fingers were doing a brisk, impatient dance on the side of the carriage when Jed finally arrived.

"Fine morning for a drive," he said, ducking his head sheepishly, and studiously avoiding the gaze of Elsie, who looked prettier and more fragile than ever in a gown of white muslin figured with cabbage roses and a big leghorn hat. "You ladies lost your coachman? Why don't I scout around and see if I can find him?"

To his relief, Sera's frown vanished and she burst out laughing. "Don't be nonsensical, Jed—and don't you bow and scrape to me! Our 'coachman' is Jarl Skogsrå, and he and Cousin Clothilde are inside the shop. I expect they will return at any moment, so don't be difficult—just offer me a hand down, because I have something particular to discuss with you and I won't tolerate interruptions."

Jed heaved another sigh. Sera had such a decided way of making a request, it was difficult to resist her. He opened the door of the carriage and helped her to alight. But he could not resist a sidelong glance at her companion. Catching Elsie looking back at him, he blushed to the roots of his hair.

"I hope you know I don't put her up to this, Miss Elsie."

Elsie smiled at him. To Jed's mind, she was the prettiest girl in Thornburg, with her fair, almost translucent skin, and her soft golden curls, but there was always a tentative quality to her beauty, a kind of delicate expectancy in her smile, that brought a lump to Jed's throat.

"I know you don't, Jed," said Elsie. "But when did Sera require encouragement to stand by old friends?"

Sera took his arm and shook it impatiently. "Come along, Jed, before Cousin Clothilde returns. I'm in no temper for another lecture on the impropriety of being seen in low company—either from her *or* from you. I've heard it all too many times before."

Even as she spoke, the shop door opened, and Mistress Vorder stepped out into the street, accompanied by a limping, foreign-looking dandy in high boots. From the grim look on Clothilde Vorder's face as she approached the carriage, it was plain that Sera was in for a scolding and that Jed himself would likely come in for more than his share of the blame. Wishing to avoid a scene

25

(and reckoning that Mistress Vorder, in her grotesque curled wig and her outsized hoop, was a sight too unwieldy to effectively pursue them), he turned tail and ran, dragging Sera with him: around a corner, down a long alley, and into another open square.

When he thought it was safe, he released her arm. Pulling off his cap, he used his sleeve to wipe his forehead. "I ain't accustomed to all this running about in the heat of the day," he said, leaning up against a cool brick wall.

"Really, Jedidiah." Sera righted her straw hat, smoothed her skirts, and readjusted the drape of her flowered silk shawl. "Cousin Clothilde will suspect the worst now. And what of Jarl Skogsrå? They will imagine an elopement at the very least. I hope you are prepared to do the honorable thing and make an honest woman of me."

Jedidiah glared at her. "When I *do* marry, she won't be a sharp-tongued piece like you, that I promise you. She'll be someone sweet and gentle, someone like . . . ."

But now Sera was laughing at him again, which brought such an irresistible alteration to her dark-browed face that Jed could not help laughing along with her. And over her shoulder he spotted a canted signpost whose weathered lettering read: *Cairngorm Court/Antimony Lane*. If Sera had led him astray in one sense, she had at least set him straight in another.

"Anyways," he said, replacing his cap and adjusting it with a pull and a tug, "your Cousin Clothilde don't suppose nothing of the sort, nor Jarl what-you-may-call-'im, neither, I'll wager. But you don't tell me what this is all about, *I* might begin to suspect sommat of the sort."

Sera's smile faded. She was an attractive girl with a pink and white complexion and a head of thick dark curls like a Gyptian, and Jed thought she might have been prettier still were it not for the lowering brows and a habitual look of discontent, as though she could never quite forget all she had lost through her grandfather's folly and her father's wickedness.

"I called at the bookshop last week, and I heard—I heard that Caleb Braun has abandoned his old occupation, to spend his days minding shop and running errands for my grandfather. As for Grandfather . . . he is so secretive about his activities, I can't help but wonder if the two of them have embarked on something ill considered . . . even dangerous. What does it all mean, do you know?"

Jed shifted from one foot to the other, cleared his throat, tugged

26

at his cap, and tried to think of a way to save himself. Not for the first time, he cursed himself for his promise to Uncle Caleb. "*All for the young lady's sake, not to go aworrying her for naught,*" the old man had said, swearing him to silence and extracting a particular promise not to mention the coffin or the books to Sera. Without thinking the matter over carefully (for that was before his granduncle announced his decision to abandon the river) Jed had agreed.

"Ask Walther Burgen or Matthias Vogel—I've reason to suppose they might know sommat about it," Jed temporized.

Sera regarded him with patent disbelief. "I . . . ask Walther Burgen or Matthias Vogel? What an idea!"

Jed heaved a profound sigh and rolled his eyes heavenward; he had not really expected any other reply. "You know your own business best—or always say you do, anyways. I tell you what I *can* do," he said, wiping his sweating hands on his coat and trying another tack. "I'll keep a close eye on Uncle Caleb—and your grandfather, too. I see or hear anything different from what I already . . . that is . . . I see or hear anything I reckon you ought to *know* about, I'll send word."

From the way Sera bit her lip and tapped her slippered foot on the cobblestone street, it was ominously evident that she suspected him of withholding information. She looked like a young woman who was going to speak her mind in no uncertain terms. Jed braced himself to weather the storm.

But an unexpected diversion rescued him: a little gilded carriage, so small it might have been meant to carry a child, which came down the street at a sedate, not to say dignified pace, pulled by six fat beribboned sheep. The passenger was a dainty blonde woman, as exquisitely formed as a fairy, in a gown of pearl-grey satin and fluttering cobweb lace, and her coachman was a rotund gnome, no more than three feet high, with exceptionally large taloned feet and a fine pair of curving horns. Chained to the seat beside him was a sad-faced miniature indigo ape with a jeweled collar. As she passed by, the lady in the carriage nodded at Sera and raised a tiny hand in greeting.

"Better than a circus," said Jed, goggling appreciatively.

"Don't be impertinent," replied Sera. "That is the Duchess of Zar-Wildungen, if you please, and a most particular friend of Cousin Clothilde's. Her tastes are somewhat eccentric, I grant you, but she is known for her wit and intelligence as much as her fashionable affectations, and has gained considerable conse-

27

quence. I should tell you, as the patron of many prominent doctors and philosophers.

"Which reminds me," Sera added, with a sigh, "that I really ought to go back to poor Elsie. She is to see Dr. Mirabolo this afternoon—the Duchess's current favorite—and I am determined to support her during that ordeal."

Jed drew his breath in sharply. "Has Miss Elsie been ill again?"

"Oh, Jed, she is practically never well." Sera's expression turned suddenly tragic, and she made a little convulsive movement with one hand, clutching her shawl. "And her symptoms are so many and—and so varied, you would almost suppose she was shamming, though I am convinced she is *not*, and with every new physician who attends her, poor Elsie develops a new complaint."

Jed stuck his hands back into his pockets and made a rude but expressive noise at the back of his throat. "Every new quack, it sounds like to me."

Sera nodded sadly. "Yes, I fear you are right. And I have tried to convince Cousin Clothilde—however, you know how stubborn she can be! She says . . . well, she says a good many cruel and condescending things about my birth and my prospects which do not seem to address the subject at all. I haven't convinced her yet, Jedidiah, but I assure you that I mean to keep on trying until I do."

Jed took his hands out of his pockets, folded his arms, and scowled most horribly. "Seems to me your Cousin Clothilde takes a considerable pleasure in quacking Miss Elsie. Seems to me there must be some doctors in Thornburg who know what they're about."

"I believe there must be, but Cousin Clothilde will have nothing to do with them," Sera admitted. "She only seems to care for . . . for fads and miracles. And the Duchess of Zar-Wildungen encourages her.

"I can only suppose that the Duchess means well—so sweet and generous as she is," Sera added, with another sigh. "But from what I have heard of him, I can't help thinking that this new doctor of hers—this Dr. Mirabolo—is bound to be immeasurably worse than any of the rest."

5.

In which Elsie Vorder suffers in Mind and Body.

Dr. Mirabolo was a fashionable physician who had gained a reputation treating fashionable women for fashionable complaints, by soaking them in tubs of saltwater, applying leeches to the soles of their feet, and by exposing them to the "healing influences" of large chunks of magnetized iron. In order to receive those treatments, it was necessary to seek the doctor at his consulting rooms in a narrow building on Venary Lane, an establishment he had modestly dubbed the Temple of the Healing Arts. The "temple," as Sera soon discovered, was really a second-story suite, sandwiched in between a music school and a fencing academy. It could only be reached by climbing a long flight of steep stairs.

"If Dr. Mirabolo were in the habit of treating the truly ill—and not an assortment of hypochondriacs and hysterics—it seems likely he would rent other rooms, no matter what the expense," Sera whispered in Elsie's ear, as she supported her up the stairs.

She glanced back over her shoulder, at Elsie's mother, who, huffing and puffing, and leaning heavily on Jarl Skogsrå's arm, followed behind them. "As it is, I suppose many of his patients derive considerable benefit from the exercise."

Elsie giggled a little breathlessly. "Poor Mama. I don't think she had any idea what was in store for her."

By the time they reached the doctor's gilded reception room, Elsie and her mother were both on the point of collapse, and Jarl Skogsrå's limp was more pronounced than ever. Nevertheless (and with an elaborate show of courtesy), he found a fragile-looking chair for Elsie to sit on, sent a servant after a sturdier seat to accommodate Mistress Vorder, and pulled up another frail gold-painted chair and offered it to Sera.

This unexpected attention on the part of the Jarl, Sera barely noticed. She was too occupied with Elsie's fan and vial of hartshorn and trying to attract the eye of a somber-looking serving

29

man, who was offering tea in shell-like china cups to a sallow matron in plum-colored satin and her three spindly, blue-haired daughters.

"I wonder if I might be of assistance?" said a quiet voice behind her, and Sera turned. The voice belonged to a slender gallant in lilac taffeta with foaming white lace at his throat and wrists and knots of silver ribbon on either shoulder.

"Lord Skelbrooke," she said, and suddenly discovered she was as breathless as Elsie.

"How do you do, Miss Vorder?" Lord Skelbrooke removed a dove-colored tricorn liberally decorated with ostrich plumes and silver braid, and bowed over Sera's limply extended hand.

Francis Skelbrooke did not paint his face as some of the other dandies did, for he had a fine fresh color of his own. He elected to wear his own hair, immaculately curled and powdered at the front, tied back in loose white curls at the back. But he always wore a tiny black satin patch in the shape of a five-pointed star high on one cheek, and he made liberal use of the scent bottle. *I despise effeminate men,* thought Sera. But much to her annoyance, she felt her heartbeat accelerate and the palms of her hands grow damp.

Cousin Clothilde spared her the necessity of a coherent reply. "We've been here this age," said Mistress Vorder, "and that dreadful serving man has not offered us any tea."

"Allow me to rectify his neglect." The young Imbrian nobleman bowed once more, tucked his hat under his arm, and strolled off to speak to the servant. Sera sank down into the chair which the Jarl was still holding for her, and waved her fan frantically in a futile attempt to cool her face.

Strong tea and dainty white sugar cakes did much to revive Elsie. "And if you had eaten a decent breakfast as I begged you to," Sera whispered over the teacups, "I am convinced you could have made the climb easily. Dear me . . . I don't doubt that I should have dizzy spells and swooning fits myself, if I started the day with a half a biscuit and a draught of vinegar!"

"But you know that Mama doesn't like me to eat before noon," replied Elsie. "Dr. Gustenhover told her that a large breakfast would overheat my blood."

Sera sniffed disdainfully. "Overheat your blood indeed! When your hands and your feet are always cold as ice." She resolved to smuggle some sausages or boiled eggs up from the kitchen tomorrow morning and coax Elsie into eating them. *What Cousin*

30

Clothilde does not suspect, she cannot forbid, and if she asks no questions, I shan't be obliged to lie.

"You dislike Lord Skelbrooke—I can't imagine why," Elsie was saying. "He is not either kind of man that you described to me before: neither cruel and haughty nor insultingly familiar. There is not a more courteous man in Thornburg."

Sera herself did not understand it. Proud men and dissolute men did nothing to ruffle her composure; she could ignore the discourtesies of the one sort just as coolly as she crushed the pretensions of the other; therefore, it was a mystery to her (and the cause of great resentment) why Francis Skelbrooke, with his soft voice, his faint Imbrian accent, his speaking grey eyes, and his gravely respectful manner, never failed to discompose her. This did not, however, prevent her from inventing an excuse for Elsie's benefit.

"Francis Love Skelbrooke is a poet . . . and what is more he is a visionary. To be one or the other is to be no more foolish or impractical than most young men, but the *combination* of 'visionary poet' is one that any rational being must find positively intolerable."

Far from being shocked by her cousin's vehemence, Elsie stifled a giggle. "Dear Sera," she said sweetly, "I do believe that I love you best when you are being completely unreasonable."

Lord Skelbrooke reappeared a short time later, this time escorting the Duchess of Zar-Wildungen. They made a pretty pastel pair, the Duchess and Francis Skelbrooke: she in grey satin and cobweb lace, he in lilac and silver, and both of them so small and neatly made. Sera felt uncomfortably conscious of her extra inches and her matronly bottle-green gown.

"You see I arrive in good time to accompany you," the Duchess said, in her clear, childlike voice, as everyone rose to greet her. "I cannot conceive how I have gained a reputation for always arriving late." And she smiled so irresistibly, gave them such mischievous, piquant glances, that no one gainsaid her, for all she had kept them waiting for nearly an hour.

Standing on tiptoe, the Duchess kissed Elsie on the cheek. "And how fares my godchild today?"

It was another of the Duchess's affectations to address Elsie as her godchild—though this, Sera was convinced, could hardly be true. The usual number of godparents was twelve: twelve sponsors to appear in church the day an infant was named, twelve godmothers and godfathers to send gifts every year on her birthday.

31

Sera could name every one of Elsie's twelve, and the Duchess of Zar-Wildungen was not among them—nor had she, as far as Sera remembered, ever sent any birthday gifts. Still, it seemed a harmless fiction, and afforded both the Duchess and Elsie considerable pleasure.

The Duchess had just seated herself, in the chair Sera vacated, when a servant came to usher their party into the inner precincts of the temple.

The matron and her three cadaverous daughters preceded them into the treatment room, and there were other fashionably attired visitors as well: the men in bag-wigs, sausage curls, and enormous pigeon-wings, the ladies in large, picturesque hats. Dr. Mirabolo catered to an exclusive clientele.

The inner sanctum was decorated in a rich foreign style, with potted palm trees in every corner and brass statues of sphinxes, griffons, and winged lions to either side of the door and between the floor-length windows. In the center of the room stood a large covered vat, oval in shape, encircled by more of the gilded chairs.

The doctor was a short, spidery, lively little fellow in a curly dark wig, a black suit, and a pair of gold-rimmed blue spectacles. He greeted the Duchess with effusive deference. "Always a pleasure, Gracious Lady, always a pleasure and an honor. And so you have brought this precious child to see me?"

He took Elsie's soft, cold hand in his dry parchmenty one and eyed her sharply through the tinted glass. "Yes, yes, I see by looking at her. An infection of the blood, there is no doubt, and magnetic treatments are the only cure."

"But we have already tried magnetic treatments," said Mistress Vorder. "Dr. Lully prescribed them for Elsie, along with a diet of barley biscuits and vinegar, and under Dr. Gustenhover's care she consumed so many iron filings that I vow and declare 'tis a wonder to me the poor child did not grow as heavy as lead."

"Drs. Lully and Gustenhover are admirable men—indeed, I have the highest regard for them both. But sadly behind the times, madam, sadly outdated in their techniques." The doctor spoke solemnly, shaking his head. "The magnetic tub is the latest, the very latest medical advance, and as you shall see, extremely efficacious."

"Mama," said Elsie, in a stifled voice. "You said that we had only come to *consult* with the doctor."

"Of course, of course," murmured the doctor, rubbing his hands together and shifting about from one foot to the other in so lively a fashion that his resemblance to a scuttling black spider was more pronounced than ever. "I shall explain the technique to you in detail, and you shall see these others experience the benefits. I make no doubt you will be so delighted with the demonstration, you will be impatient to begin your own course of treatments."

He skipped over to the vat in the center of the room and lifted the lid. Sera moved forward along with the others, to see what the tub contained. Corked bottles containing a clouded fluid covered the floor of the vat. "Magnetized saltwater," said the doctor proudly, "and the medium surrounding them is fresh water treated with certain minerals, along with a judicious mixture of ground glass and iron filings."

Cousin Clothilde appeared suitably impressed. "And how do you administer the benefits of this device?"

"Through a human agency." The doctor replaced the lid of the vat, reached into a coat pocket, and produced a short iron rod. "I have many trained assistants—men and women of the first quality, I can assure you—who, possessing the required gift, donate their services to relieve the sufferings of their fellow beings." He bowed in the direction of Jarl Skogsrå. "Perhaps you were not aware that your gallant escort is among them."

Mistress Vorder eyed the Nordic nobleman with surprise and a little resentment. "You told me nothing of this, sir," she said coldly. "I had no idea you were one of the doctor's magnetizers."

"But dear lady, I had no notion of deceiving you," replied Skogsrå. "Indeed, I believed my connection with this establishment well known. It is the very reason why I insisted on accompanying you. The Duchess knew of it, certainly." He limped over to Elsie and raised one of her hands to his lips. "I hope, in the future, to play some small part in effecting your cure."

As they spoke, more people came crowding into the room through the same door. The atmosphere was growing close. Sera knew that Elsie had difficulty breathing when the air was bad, so taking the younger girl with her, she maneuvered a path through the crowd, heading for the nearest window. After a futile struggle with the casement, she concluded that it was sealed in place. But at least the air was a little cooler near the glass.

"It is time for the demonstration to begin," the doctor announced. A number of men and women, including the matron's three gaunt daughters, seated themselves around the vat. Several others, including Jarl Skogsrå, produced iron rods similar to the

33

doctor's and positioned themselves between the chairs, with the rods extended horizontally in front of them.

"You understand," said the doctor, speaking for the benefit of the Duchess and Mistress Vorder, "that my assistants have a marked affinity for the magnetic waters, which they have helped me to magnetize, as well as possessing a natural sensitivity. For this reason, they are able to direct the healing influences into and through the rods, and thus effect a cure."

As he spoke, those in the chairs reached out, each grasping the iron rods to either side. The effect was almost instantaneous. Some closed their eyes and began to breathe harshly; others threw back their heads and fastened their gaze on the ceiling, moaning as if in pain. Most stared straight ahead, as if into some imaginary distance, their faces etched with expressions of the most sublime ecstasy.

"This is the most appalling nonsense I ever saw or heard of in my life," said Sera, reaching instinctively for Elsie's hand. Several people turned to glare at her, but Sera continued on boldly, "Magnetic influences, indeed! I daresay in most of these cases the cure just as much as the complaint is entirely imaginary."

"I feel certain you must be right," Elsie whispered. But then she felt the blood rush out of her head, and she was barely able to force out the words: "Oh, Sera, do look!"

Two of the girls began to twitch spasmodically; a white foam appeared on the lips of one of the ecstatics. As Sera and Elsie watched with increasing horror, three women went into violent convulsions.

"Sera," said Elsie, "I think I am going to swoon. Please take me out of here."

Sera tore her gaze away from the twitching figure in the nearest chair. Elsie trembled as though stricken by a palsy, and her eyes were wide and dark. *This is monstrous . . . they have made her really ill. Why, oh why, had I not the wit to remove her earlier?*

She offered her cousin the support of an arm and led her toward the door.

Elsie clutched Sera's arm convulsively. "Here comes Mama—I know she is going to insist that we stay." Mistress Vorder was bearing down on them, as if determined to cut off their escape.

Sera hardly knew which way to turn. While it was essential that she remove Elsie from the hysterical atmosphere present in the room, a bitter public argument between Sera and Clothilde was calculated to do almost equal harm. *If she boxes my ears before all these people, I shall certainly lose my temper and strike her in return . . . but no, I mustn't. For Elsie's sake I must bear whatever comes.*

"I think," said a pleasantly accented voice in Sera's ear, "that I may really be of some use here." And Sera discovered Francis Skelbrooke at her elbow, with an expression of grave concern on his sensitive face. "Allow me to escort Miss Vorder from the room while *you* deal with her mother's objections."

Before Sera had time either to accept or reject his offer, he took Elsie by the arm and whisked her away. This ploy had the desired effect, for Mistress Vorder, taken by surprise and momentarily confused as to her objective, hesitated just long enough for her daughter and Lord Skelbrooke to make good their escape.

Sera watched him lead Elsie through the crowd and out the door, with a mixture of gratitude, relief, and resentment—though she had little time to contemplate either his convenient intervention or his cowardice in leaving the more unpleasant task to *her*. Cousin Clothilde was soon upon her, red-faced and indignant, demanding an explanation.

Before Sera could offer that explanation, Mistress Vorder launched into a long lecture on the impertinence of young women in general and the ingratitude of orphans in particular. Sera listened as patiently as she could, replied as temperately as her pride would allow, and left the room at the first opportunity.

6.

Which is largely Concerned with the Manufacture of Glass.

By following Antimony Lane, Jedidiah eventually returned to the river, at a spot where the meandering Lunn all but doubled back on herself in a wide, shining loop. Master Ule's Bottle Factory was located at the end of the street, where the lane ran downhill to the river and ended in a set of broad stone steps. It was a large red brick building of uncertain age—not very dirty, considering the clouds of grey smoke issuing through a number of stacks on the roof and its proximity to the damps of the river.

As a prospective employee, Jed went around to the rear of the building. It had, as he had suspected, a wharf of its own at the back, a weathered but sturdy-looking pier. On the wharf, two broad-shouldered dwarves were loading crates onto a barge, while a third dwarf, in a rough brown coat and a waistcoat of robin's-egg blue, supervised and made notations in a little book. Jed's spirits dimmed. Most wichtel (as the dwarves were called) were gregarious and seemed to enjoy the society of Men and gnomes, yet one did hear of the rare dwarf who refused to employ any but his own kind.

But in response to Jed's inquiry, the dwarf in charge readily put aside his book and offered to take him to Master Ule.

Jed obediently followed the dwarf into the factory. He had never seen the inside of a glassworks before, and the bustle of activity immediately impressed him. He was relieved to note that at least half of Master Ule's workers were full-sized men. An immense circular, brick furnace with a domed roof dominated the center of the factory. Two large fellows were busy stoking it with mighty logs of pine and oak. All around the furnace, at glowing arch-shaped apertures, the glassblowers and their assistants worked: Men and gnomes and dwarves, shaping the molten glass into bottles.

Jed had only a moment to observe all this. His escort whisked him through the factory and through a series of passages and storerooms. At last they arrived in a bright, high-ceilinged chamber with windows facing on the street, which apparently served both as storeroom and counting-house. There, the dwarf took leave of him.

Two young dwarves sat busily writing at two small desks near the door. A larger desk in one corner of the room was piled high with ledgers and accounting books and papers, all tumbled together in what appeared (at least to Jedidiah's untrained eye) to be an entirely random fashion. Sitting behind that desk was an elderly dwarf in a grey tie-wig, a plain suit of clothes, and a leather apron, sorting through the books and papers, muttering to himself, and tugging at his wig with an air of great distraction.

"Blast young Polydore! Scorch and blister him! *He* can make sense of it all . . . can put his hand on the very paper immediately. But when he is away, I cannot find a thing, not a blessed thing!"

This, Jed surmised, must be Master Ule.

Neither of the younger dwarves looked up to acknowledge his presence, so Jedidiah made bold to approach their master. "Begging your pardon, sir," he said, removing his cap, "I've come about the job."

The dwarf glanced up. Abandoning his accounts, he looked Jed over with a pair of piercingly bright eyes. It surprised Jed the way he could shift his attention like that: absorbed in his books and papers one moment, then examining the boy so shrewdly he gave the impression he could see right through him. "I fear you have come to the wrong place, young man—I advertised for an errand boy. And in any case, that position has already been filled."

Jed's face fell. Seeing his disappointment, the dwarf said kindly, "I can assure you that the position would not have suited you. The boy I hired was half your age. I feel certain you can find something better."

"No, sir, I don't reckon I will, saving your worship." Jed could not help sounding a little bitter. "And as for not being suited . . . any honest work I could find would suit me proper."

He turned and started back toward the door, wondering how he was going to find his own way through the maze of rooms and passageways. But the dwarf called him back. "See here, my lad, I take it you've been out of work for some considerable period of time?" Jed nodded. "Well, I may be able to find something for you, after all. What can you do—what skills have you learned?"

Jed blushed and shook his head, "No skills to speak of . . . but I'm powerful strong, I ain't afraid of hard work, and I learn real quick."

The dwarf continued to stare at him with those disconcerting dark eyes. "I can see you are strong, and I must confess that I like your face. You look to be a bright lad, and an honest one. All this being so: how is it that you were never apprenticed to any trade?"

Jedidiah shuffled his feet uneasily. He knew that most folks looked on river scavengers as little better than thieves, but he couldn't help that. Nor did he like to lie—even supposing (which did not seem likely in the present instance) that he could get away with it. "I used to work with my granduncle off the river, but he . . . well, he retired in a manner of speaking, and I never did care for that line of work."

Master Ule nodded sagely. "I quite understand. A somewhat uncertain livelihood, I take it?"

"Yes, sir. It was, sir." Jed was amazed to hear the dwarf take

37

the matter so lightly. He wondered if Master Ule had misunderstood, taking him for a fisherman or a bargeman. "But it weren't the money, sir . . . I'm willing to work cheap."

The dwarf made an airy gesture. "Well, well, we needn't worry about that. I do not pay my workers starvation wages—and I pay at the quarter moon as well as at the full." By which Jedidiah understood that the dwarf had *not* misinterpreted him. "Now then . . . let me see what I can find for you to do."

It did not take long for the dwarf to find something. For the next several hours, Jed worked hard, moving crates of glass, restacking firewood, and at a variety of other tasks. But as the day wore on he began to wonder about the value of his work, and whether Master Ule was inventing things for him to do.

That thought troubled Jed. He did not like to accept charity, no matter how discreetly offered. But when he tried to broach the subject to Master Ule, the dwarf waved him off with a good-humored grin. "Nonsense, my lad, nonsense. We are a little slow in getting out the orders this week, with Polydore absent, but when he returns there will be plenty for you to do."

Polydore was Polydore Figg, Master Ule's nephew (as Jed had gathered by now), and he was normally in charge of the warehouses and the counting-house; he had been out seven days with a chill in his lungs, and his lengthy absence had created considerable confusion within his domain.

But in the factory Master Ule reigned supreme, and there the making of glass bottles proceeded with great energy and efficiency, for Master Ule was everywhere, overseeing his workers, lending a hand or a piece of advice wherever it was needed, as well as attending to those special tasks which were specifically his as Master of the Glasshouse, like preparing the batch: the mixture of sand, ash, and other materials of which the glass was made. This last called for considerable skill, Jed learned, for the quality of materials varied, measurements could not be exact, and the proper mixture was only achieved by that combination of experience and intuition which distinguished a master glassmaker.

Moreover, several different varieties of glass were manufactured at Master Ule's, and each kind required a different sort of sand, a different sort of ash: hard sand and oak ash, high in salt and soda, for the so-called black glass bottles (really a dark green) that were used to store wine, ale, oils, scents, and medicines; fine white sand, crushed from pebbles, and the ash of barilla or glasswort for the clear glass bottles that would later be painted with

38

bright enamels or etched with acids, and eventually grace side-boards and supper tables in the homes of the wealthy.

Catching Jed watching him, in an idle moment, Master Ule set him to work pulverizing cullet, which was the broken glass the journeymen used to top off the huge pots of red clay in which they fused the batch.

But he was back in the room at the front, an hour later, re-stacking a pile of crates—the arrangement of which had not entirely satisfied Master Ule earlier—when the glassmaker rushed into the room and began searching among the ledgers and papers on the large desk.

"Here now," the Master said to one of the clerks, a stout young dwarf with ruddy cheeks and a moleskin waistcoat, "do you know where the bill of lading for the alehouse consignment might be?"

The younger dwarf declared that he had no idea.

"Begging your pardon . . ." said Jed, glad of an opportunity to be of real use, "ain't that the paper you're looking for over there on that box?"

Master Ule crossed the room and picked up the sheet that Jed indicated. "It is, thank the Powers." But then he gave a little start and examined Jed all over again with those disconcerting dark eyes. "Did you see me put this down here earlier?"

"No, sir," said Jed. "Leastways . . . I don't remember that I did."

"Did anyone tell you what this paper contained?"

"No, sir," said Jed.

"Then how on earth did you know what it was?"

"Don't it say so right at the top . . . 'The Moon and Seven Stars, Tavern and Brewery'?"

"It does indeed," said Master Ule. "But tell me this, my lad . . . do you actually mean to tell me that you know how to *read*?"

It was then that Jed realized his mistake. In the country districts, literacy was high, for there was no end of parish schools and energetic parsons to take the children of laborers and farmworkers in hand, but in towns like Thornburg there were few charitable institutions, and many, many more poor boys and girls in want of an education, so that only the children of the *genteel* poor were ever chosen. The result was almost universal illiteracy among men of Jed's class. That Jed himself was an exception to this rule, his associates on the river treated as something of a joke—his betters, when they learned of it, regarded his abilities as a mark of presumption.

39

Jed blushed and hung his head, wishing he'd had the sense to keep quiet. "I ain't no scholar," he protested.

"But you *can* read?" Master Ule persisted. "In the name of the Father and the Seven Fates, it is nothing for you to be ashamed of! But where on earth did you happen to acquire that skill?"

"From Gottfried Jenk the bookseller." Jed made the admission reluctantly. "I used to take lessons along of his granddaughter, Miss Sera Vorder, but she always got on better than me, coming to it all naturally, as you might say."

Master Ule handed him a ledger bound in green leather. "Read something to me . . . choose any page you like," he demanded.

Somewhat hesitantly, Jed read off a page of names and figures.

"And I suppose . . . but naturally, this schoolmaster of yours— what did you say his name was?—taught you to write as well?"

As Master Ule already knew the worst of him, Jed saw no reason to conceal the truth. "He taught me to write and to . . . well, there was history, and geography, and all manner of other lessons in them books he taught me to read, and I couldn't very well help learning them along of my letters, now could I?"

"Show me," said Master Ule, and provided him with pen, ink, and paper. This, however, was rather more difficult. Even without books, Jed was always unconsciously reading things: street signs, and shop signs, and handbills pasted up on walls. But since abandoning his studies with Gottfried Jenk he had never had occasion to set pen to paper.

Using a crate for a writing desk, Jed laboriously wrote out his name and the day of the year.

"You are somewhat rusty, I perceive," said the dwarf, examining this effort. "But with a little practice I believe you might write a very fair hand. I suppose you can add up a column of figures?"

Jed replied that he could, and proceeded to demonstrate.

"But my dear good lad, did it never occur to you to seek employment as a clerk?"

Jed shook his head. It certainly had not. Young men who dressed and spoke as he did were not employed in counting-houses and offices.

"Well, perhaps not . . . Your appearance is somewhat rough, and your speech leaves much to be desired. But with a little polishing . . . with a little polishing we might put you in the way of a very good position."

"Yes, sir," said Jed, rather stunned by this proposition, though by now he began to perceive that he had fallen into the hands of a sort of dwarf philanthropist.

For the rest of that day, Master Ule set him to copying accounts from one ledger into another. When he had a moment to think Jed wondered, privately, how the absent Polydore Figg would react on learning that Master Ule had hired such an unprepossessing new clerk. Much to his surprise, the other clerks did not seem to mind at all, and continued on with their work, ink-stained and cheerful, as though it were nothing out of the ordinary for them to work, virtually side by side, with a ragged boy from the river who filled the room (Jed knew he was no garland of meadowflowers) with an odor of tar and saltwater.

"See here," he finally gathered the courage to ask the others, "am I of any use here at all?"

The stout young dwarf put down his pen, tipped back his chair, and appeared to consider. "You've given Master Ule the opportunity to do a good and generous deed—which there's nothing he likes better. That's useful, anyway. And if you work hard and learn all that you can, why then, he'll find you another position just as he promised, and there you *may* be of use, as well as affording considerable satisfaction to the kindest heart in Thornburg."

Jed thought that over. "I take it," he said, "I ain't the first piece of river trash Master Ule's taken up and tried to make into something better."

"You're the first in the counting-house," said the other dwarf, looking up from his work. "But half the fellows in the glasshouse were once 'trash' (as you are pleased to call yourself) and now they are all worthy and useful members of the community . . . thanks to Master Ule. Oh, I don't say he hasn't taken a scoundrel or two in by mistake, but he's a very good judge of character and most of his charity cases turn out well.

"We don't mind taking our turn and helping you to get on," he added. "Why should we? We are all Master Ule's beneficiaries, in one way or the other. Work hard and learn all you can—that will please the Master—and if you please him, you please us as well. But if you are too proud or too lazy to take the opportunity he has offered you . . . why then, you will disappoint us all."

With the matter presented to him in that light, Jed could only conclude that he would be a bit of a scoundrel himself, did he refuse Master Ule's help. He went back to his ledgers with a good will, and a firm resolution that he *would* work hard, learn all that he could, and prove himself one of the deserving ones.

When evening came, Master Ule took his hand and pumped it vigorously. "You are a hard worker, and a very good boy. I am pleased to employ you."

Under the circumstances, Jed felt uncomfortable bringing up the subject of money—but gratitude and good resolutions notwithstanding, he could not afford to work for nothing. "We never did come to no agreement on the matter of wages."

"No more we did," said the dwarf. "I thank you for reminding me. Now, let me see—you have been out of work for some time now, so I think I may safely assume that your financial circumstances are . . . somewhat embarrassed?"

There was no denying that, but Jed was still reluctant to take advantage of the dwarf's good nature. "There ain't been any talk of throwing me and Uncle Caleb out of our lodgings . . . not yet, anyways."

Master Ule considered for a few moments more. "What do you say to fifteen shillings a week—the first fortnight in advance? In that way you may pay off some of your more pressing debts, as well as buy yourself a new suit of clothes."

Jed was too dazed to answer. Fifteen shillings a week, thirty a fortnight . . . that was close to a season's pay for his gleanings on the river, except when the moon and the tides were particularly generous.

Master Ule continued on: "In general, we begin our day here an hour after sunrise, but you needn't trouble yourself about arriving late tomorrow. I expect you will wish to spend the morning settling your affairs and visiting a tailor."

When Jed arrived home that evening, he found Uncle Caleb waiting up for him, in the little room they shared above a grog shop, seated in the one good chair the room could boast of: a rocking chair pulled up by the tiny fireplace. Even at this season, nights by the river were often cold and damp, so Caleb had lit a little driftwood fire on the hearth and set Jed's evening bowl of porridge on the hob to keep warm.

"We can save the porridge for morning and fry it up in grease," said Jedidiah, unwrapping a brown paper parcel he had carried in and arranging the contents on a little table by the fire: a side of bacon, six sausages, a pot of fresh cheese, and a loaf of bread.

The room was not an elegant one, but it possessed a certain broken-down charm. Besides the rocking chair, there was a foot

42

stool and two or three other, less reliable chairs. The walls had been papered some fifteen years before—during a period of comparative prosperity following the sale of a jeweled brooch—in a pattern of blushing gillyflowers and curling green ivy on a pale cream ground, but the paper was scarred now, the gillyflowers and the ivy faded, and a large oak sideboard (the result of another windfall) was filled with mismatched china in blues and roses and antique golds, most of it chipped or broken.

These amenities had been purchased to please Jed's mother, who had abandoned the family roof three years past, to live with Jed's sister and her sea-faring husband, declaring that neither the sideboard nor the wallpaper was conveniently portable, and she supposed young Belinda had equally nice things of her own, anyways.

As for the other domestic arrangements, they consisted of two bunks built into the wall, two patchwork quilts in colors as faded as the wallpaper, two ancient mattresses and a pair of striped pillows, a hammock suspended from the ceiling (which accommodated Jed's nephews when they came to visit), a frying pan and a stewpot, some bent silverware, an oak bucket, a wooden spoon, a wash tub, and (a final relic of Mistress Braun's residence) a rag rug lying on the floor by the fireplace.

Jed took his chances with one of the chairs, sat down, and began to relate the events of the day. Much to his surprise and chagrin, Caleb greeted his new position and his prospects for the future, not with delighted approval, but with a burst of outrage.

"A bottle factory? Blister me if the boy ain't gone and thrown his lot in with the d----d Glassmakers!" Caleb pounded his fist on an arm of the rocking chair. "Didn't I never warn you about the Glassmakers Guild and all their tomfool rituals and mummery?"

"I guess you have," Jed replied, with a sigh. "I guess I remember it all pretty well, you being so particular about telling me. What I *don't* understand is what it—"

But Caleb was not about to spare him another recital. He folded his arms, rocked his chair, and fixed Jed with a beady black eye, so fierce and full of fire, the boy knew there was no use continuing until Caleb had had his say.

"Them *other* guilds is mostly harmless," said Caleb. "Does they dress up in fancy robes on festival days and chant nonsense? Yes, they do. Does they carry on between times with secret handshakes and passwords, all real mysterious? They do that, too. But the difference is: it's mostly play-acting, just calculated to impress ignorant folk like you and me, to keep us in awe of the all-mighty guilds and their all-mighty craft mysteries, which even the guildsmen they don't hardly none of them know what they're about. The words and the rituals has all lost their meaning, and you ask me: 'tis all for the best. But them Glassmakers are different, they take it more serious than most. Yes, and they got good reason, because *they know what the ceremonies is for, they remember the magic and the mystery at the heart of them.*"

By now, Caleb was rocking his chair so hard that the floor boards creaked in protest, and the cups and plates on the sideboard rattled and jumped, 'til it seemed likely that the old man would bust them all.

"What they don't know—or won't know—it don't make no difference," Caleb continued, "is the danger in what they do. They're dealing in mysteries they don't rightly understand, and I know for a fact them guildsmen has been tampering . . . *tampering with things they had much better leave clean alone.*"

But by this time, Jed's patience was wearing pretty thin. "Yes, but I don't see what none of that has got to do with *me*. I ain't been *apprenticed* to Master Ule or nothing like that."

"*They ain't all of them glassmakers—I told you that afore,*" thundered Caleb. "There's gentlemen . . . bookish gentlemen, done joined the Guild as well, hoping to be let in on some of their secrets . . . think them guildsmen is some kind of magicians, and if'n they join the Guild, why, *they'll* become magicians, too."

"I think you've gone plumb crazy," Jed told him frankly. It was not his way to give his granduncle any sass, but Caleb had pushed him beyond all endurance. "Magic! You're obsessed with it, you and Mr. Jenk. But I was there at the bottle factory all day long, and nobody said nothing about your magical rituals. They was all too busy making bottles or shipping them out—and there's naught mysterious or magical about any of that!"

"Hmmph!" sniffed Caleb, though it was obvious Jed had given him pause. The old man became thoughtful; the rocking and the rattling gradually ceased.

"Aye . . . well, I reckon not . . . not likely they'd make you a 'prentice nor let you in on any of their secrets, you being related to me and all," he sniffed resentfully. "But didn't it never occur to you, lad, that this Master Ule of yours took such a shine to you just because he knew you was my grandnevvy? Didn't you

44

never think he might be curious to learn what Gottfried Jenk and I been doing at the bookshop?"

Jed was aghast. "Here now . . . you don't think it was Master Ule and the Glassmakers who put that coffin with the wax doll into the Lunn?"

"Put the coffin . . ." Caleb did not immediately remember the story Jenk had concocted for the benefit of Walther and Matthias. "No, no, it ain't nothing like that. I meant to say that word might have got around, that Walther and Matthias might not be keeping mum the way they promised. There might be folks who got questions about the . . . wax figure . . . and what it all means."

Jedidiah shook his head. "If Walther and Matthias blabbed, we'd know it. And anyways, I just remembered: Master Ule didn't have no idea who I was when he hired me. No, he never asked my name until the day was half done. And even then . . . why should he guess—or care—that I was *your* grandnevvy? There's a hundred men named Braun in Thornburg."

Jedidiah did not mention that Master Ule had taken a greater interest *after* Jed mentioned his connection with Gottfried Jenk. He knew that Caleb was bound to make more of it than was sane or reasonable. As for himself, Jed had no doubts in the matter at all; after spending a day in Master Ule's bottle factory and speaking with his clerks, he was firmly convinced that the dwarf was not capable of conceiving anything so sinister as an ulterior motive.

"Aye . . . well, maybe so." Caleb began to rock again, but more gently this time. "And after all, this Master Ule of yours ain't nothing but a bottlemaker. That's a simple craft. I don't reckon he stands high in the counsels of the Guild."

He rocked a little more and thought a little longer. "As long as the pay is good and he treats you well, I don't see no harm, if you want to go on working for him."

Which was just as well, Jed thought. He knew he was on to a good thing working for Master Ule, and he was not about to toss it all aside just to satisfy Uncle Caleb and his wild suspicions.

7.

Wherein Gottfried Jenk accomplishes the Miraculous.

Not far from Venary Lane, where Dr. Mirabolo held forth at the Temple of the Healing Arts, was a street paved with blue-grey cobblestones, lined with seedy little thatched-roof shops: apothecaries, herbalists, and chemists for the most part, though an occasional taxidermist, lensmaker, or purveyor of scientific instruments lent a little variety, while maintaining the philosophic "tone" of the neighborhood.

To that part of Thornburg came Gottfried Jenk, one breezy afternoon, late in the season of Leaves. Plainly but meticulously dressed, from his carefully powdered wig to the polished brass buckles on his blunt-toed shoes, the bookseller walked briskly, displaying a nervous energy quite remarkable in a man of his years.

He entered a shop meaner and dingier than any of the rest. It resembled a taxidermy shop: the shelves displayed a collection of pelts and bones, fins, feathers, antlers, tusks, and horns, and other odd bits and pieces of brute creation in various stages of preservation. And it had something of the barber-surgeon's establishment as well: yellowing teeth (human, and dwarf, and gnome) collected in glass jars, hanks of braided hair suspended from the beamed ceiling. But it *smelled* like nothing so much as a slaughter-house.

The proprietor, a Mr. Prodromus, was no more prepossessing than his establishment. A big man with a walleye and a mane of wild dark hair, he was very dirty and very jaunty. He wore a dingy red kerchief around his neck and a gold ring in one ear.

"Back so soon, Mr. Jenk?" the shopkeeper inquired, with an insolent grin. "Hope you ain't got no complaints against the goods I sold you. Or was it more of the same you was wanting?"

"I wish," said Jenk curtly, "to purchase more of the same."

The shopkeeper's leer became considerably more pronounced, and he winked broadly. "That's the way, Mr. Jenk—no need to

46

be specific. No need for you to go naming out loud what I shouldn't *have* nor you shouldn't *want*. I like a man as knows the value of discretion.''

He led Jenk into a grimy little room at the back of the shop, where he opened a tall cabinet so deep and narrow that it reminded Jenk of the coffin back at the bookshop.

''Well, now . . . ain't that a shame and a pity?'' said Prodromus, after searching the shelves for several minutes. ''Seems I sold the last of that lot, and I can't rightly predict when there'll be a fresh supply.'' He shook his head mournfully. ''It's these new laws, Mr. Jenk, they'll be the ruin of me yet. There ain't near so many private executions as there once was, and bribes to the hangman is very dear. But look here . . . I got sommat else as might please you.''

Prodromus dived back into the cabinet and emerged holding a glass jar. ''The hand of a Farisee, pickled in brine. A rare item and a fine specimen.''

Jenk eyed the bloated contents of the jar with extreme distaste. The hand was losing its shape; the brine had acquired a yellowish tinge. Either it was very old, or it had been inadequately preserved. ''Thank you, but I have no use—''

''It don't matter,'' said the shopkeeper, with unimpaired good humor. ''Just take a look at this.'' He returned to the cabinet, replaced the jar, and came out holding something shriveled and leathery, about the color and size of a dried apricot.

''The mummified ear of an Yndean prince,'' he proclaimed proudly. ''Forty wives, this one had, and two hundred little uns.''

''Mr. Prodromus!'' The bookseller could not contain his outrage. ''I am a widower these seven and thirty years, and a man of sober habits. If you cannot provide what I ask, I must bid you good day.''

Jenk left the building in some little haste; he was not sorry to emerge into the light and air. He made several more calls that afternoon, and a few small purchases—as could be seen by the odd bundles, wrapped in brown paper, which distorted the pockets of his full-skirted coat—but his energy dissipated as the day wore on and he trudged back to the bookshop in the early evening with a grey face and a discouraged step.

As Jenk walked through the door, a silver bell tinkled to announce his presence. The shop was dimly lit. The diamond-paned windows were filled with glass so old and dark they permitted no light to enter from without, and the smoky old lanthorns hanging

47

from the beamed ceiling did little to penetrate the gloom. In a corner at the back of the shop, in a chair tipped backward against the wall, sat Caleb Braun, with his cloth cap pulled down over his eyes and his stubbled chin resting on his breast, snoring lustily.

Jenk stood for a moment looking down at him. In his faded and patched blue coat, with his bearded cheek and his grizzled pigtail, Caleb little resembled the brisk, ambitious young footman who had entered the Jenk household fifty years before. Memories of that younger Caleb made the bookseller gentle as he touched the old river man on the shoulder and softly spoke his name.

Caleb pushed back his cap, opened his bleary eyes. "Had ye any luck in obtaining the tinctures?"

Jenk shook his head, drew up a high stool, and sat down with a weary sigh. "No, Caleb, I had no luck today. The prices Koblenz and Jakob demanded were beyond all reason, and Mistress Sancreedi—who might have been moved to lower her prices had I offered a convincing plea of poverty—was unwilling to sell me the tinctures at any price, unless I would reveal to her my entire purpose."

At the name of Sancreedi, Caleb shuddered elaborately. "I'd as soon we had no dealings with that woman. There's sommat uncanny about her . . . them big yellow eyes like a cat or an owl, and never a sound when she enters a room."

"Uncanny indeed; 'tis said the Sancreedi's have Farisee blood," Jenk agreed. "And yet they are not to be despised on that account—far otherwise. Like all fairies, they have an exaggerated sense of justice. And it is just because Mistress Sancreedi is so painstakingly scrupulous in all her dealings that I was unwilling to confide in her now."

Caleb removed his cap and rubbed his grizzled head. "We're in too far to back out now."

Jenk took a watch out of a pocket in his waistcoat, opened it up with a flick of his thumb, and stared numbly at the time. The watch case was skull-shaped, done in white enamel, with pansies and Spagnish lilies painted on the face. It was one of the few fine and fanciful things Jenk still owned; he expected to be buried with it. "I have no desire to beggar myself a second time, either by ill-conceived actions or by a failure of nerve. I have considered (and really, I do not know why I should be so reluctant—for pride is a vice I can ill afford) . . . I have considered writing to the Duke. He was always a generous man and his antiquarian leanings are well known. The books from the river are old, and the mysteries

48

they treat of even older; I believe they might serve to pique his interest. In truth, had I not been too proud and too secretive to accept his help before, I might be a wealthy man today.''

Caleb grunted. ''Zar-Wildungen? I thought him dead and buried these ten years or more.''

Jenk smiled thinly. ''Buried, in a manner of speaking, but not yet dead. He lives much retired at the Wichtelberg, his country estate, having abandoned all but the quietest and most scholarly pursuits, for his health is not good—indeed, I believe he must be well past ninety—while his Duchess remains in town leading a life of fashionable excess. Yet even Marella Carleon could not exhaust the Zar-Wildungen fortune, and if we can gain her lord's patronage, why then . . . we should have no difficulty meeting Jakob's price.''

Jenk closed his watch, put it back in his waistcoat pocket. ''It grows late,'' he said. ''You may close up shop if you wish. And when you are done you may join me in the laboratory. I have something to show you which may prove of interest.''

While Caleb barred the front door and shuttered the windows, Jenk took down one of the lanthorns, went to a low door at the back of the shop, and drew out his iron ring of keys. The door was padlocked with an ancient brass lock. Jenk sorted through his keys, found the one that he wanted, and opened the door.

The airless room on the other side boasted but a single window set high in one wall, and that was shuttered and barred. The furnishings were sparse: a chair, a bench, a stool, and two long tables constructed of scarred planks. A fireplace in one corner had been bricked in to form an athenor, or alchemical furnace, and a copper still was joined to the furnace by a bulb and a glass pipe. The rest of Jenk's laboratory equipment was arranged on one of the tables: flasks and retorts; aludels, crucibles, and balaenium, and the monstrous bronze mortar in which the alchemist ground his herbs and his powders with a great iron pestle. On the second table rested the long ebonwood coffin.

Jenk hung his lanthorn from a hook in the beamed ceiling and lifted the lid of the casket. When the coffin first arrived, it had smelled of the river, damp and weedy, but as the wood dried the river odor faded, to be replaced by another that was dark and pungent, like a mixture of camphor and hemp. The odor was not precisely unpleasant, but it was pervasive, clinging to Jenk's skin and to his clothes long after he left the room.

49

But the body in the casket did not change, not in any particular—as many times as he examined the corpse, Jenk was surprised anew by the incorruptibility of the flesh, and by the uncanny preservation of cloth, leather, and paper which pertained to the corpse's immediate vicinity.

For the sake of experiment he had placed certain items in the bottom of the coffin: a bouquet of violets, a loaf of bread, and a bowl of fruit. Each was just as sweet and fresh, when Jenk came to remove it, days or weeks later, as when it first entered the coffin. As another experiment, he cut a small square of velvet from the sorceror's tunic—the cloth had decayed and fallen into dust in a matter of hours.

And yet . . . to what end had the body been preserved? What value did it possess, once the spirit of the former occupant had fled? Was the spell one of the sorcerer's own devising, or was he the subject of an experiment initiated by an even mightier magician? These and other questions continued to puzzle and excite Jenk. The only clue (and he could not be certain that it *was* a clue) was a little piece of narwhal ivory he had discovered clutched in the corpse's left hand.

But the books, not the body, drew Jenk to the coffin now. The books were old, older by far than the body, most of them written in an archaic hand and a dead language. They were so fragile that their pages disintegrated rapidly if removed from the coffin. To make use of them, Jenk always did as he did now: he took up the volume he wanted and placed it open on the chest of the corpse.

He opened to a page near the middle of the book, took a pair of spectacles out of his pocket, and placed them on the end of his nose.

"There is a Stone called Seramarias which does not occur in Nature," Jenk read. *"Its properties are Marvelous, for it neutralizes Poisons, attracts other Gem-Stones as a Lodestone attracts Iron, and gifts the One who wears it with the power of Prophecy. Many other Applications, equally Remarkable, have been ascribed . . ."* The bookseller shook his head. To compound the stone Seramarias had been his dream for many years, but without the tinctures he was helpless.

He turned another leaf, scanning the page until he came to the proper passage. Then he walked over to the other table and unloaded the contents of his pockets, unwrapped the brown paper parcels.

Caleb shambled into the room and glanced inside the coffin.

50

He paused to examine the open book. "*To Make an Homunculus or Little Man . . .* " he read aloud. "Blister me! That ain't what you're about now—tell me I'm mistaken."

"It is," Jenk replied calmly. "Why should I not attempt it, after all?"

Caleb shook his head. "But you tried it afore those long years past—again and again you tried it, and never had no luck. Doomed to failure, you said. It can't be done no way at all. A fable, you said. A mad fancy. You said all that, and *I* don't forget it, even if you do."

"I wonder that you should remember words spoken so carelessly, so resentfully," said Jenk. "I spoke out of disappointment because I could not effect what other men had effected before."

"Not nobody we ever knew . . . no, not one of 'em could ever boast of that," Caleb reminded him.

"But the Ancients possessed the art—we have that on the very best authority," Jenk insisted. "The formulas I attempted before were faulty, they were all of them incomplete, though many of them hinted at a process . . . Well, well, you will remember how it was: I believed I might divine that process, that the answer to the riddle, while not explicit, was at least implicit in the formulas themselves . . . I had many theories, but all of them failed me."

He gestured in the direction of the coffin. "Imagine, then, my astonishment on opening that volume, to find the whole art written out in careful detail. Naturally, I was skeptical at first, just as you are now, but you shall see how far I have succeeded."

He directed Caleb's attention to a curious construction at one end of the table: an object draped in black cloth, resting on an iron tripod. A lighted candle in a glass chimney (evidently meant to direct the heat of the flame upward) stood under the tripod. Jenk removed the black cloth, revealing a glass vessel about the size and shape of an ostrich egg.

Caleb leaned forward to examine the egg. It was filled with a viscous fluid, a dull clouded liquor, but Caleb was just able to make out a tiny, doll-like figure suspended in that fluid. It appeared to be a perfectly proportioned little man, no more than six inches high, accurate in every detail right down to the fingernails and eyelashes, utterly realistic in every way, but for his minuscule size and the grey-green pallor of his skin.

"Six and thirty days ago," said Jenk, "this was a mandrake root, crudely fashioned to resemble a man: rudimentary arms and legs, no more than a suggestion of the other features. I washed it in blood, in milk, and in honey. I made a slit in what might be termed the belly and inserted the white of a boiled egg treated with *sperma viri*, whale oil, and other—rather more arcane—ingredients. Then I sealed it in this glass egg, where I have been incubating it over a gentle but steady heat ever since. During that time, it has slowly increased in size, becoming what you see now."

Caleb took a deep breath, then exhaled it slowly. "You're telling me . . . this little poppet you done carved out of a root . . . is *alive*? That it's agrowing and achanging right there in your crystal egg, like a seed in the earth or a babby in the womb? You're telling me . . . you done fathered a *child*?"

"It is certainly alive," said Jenk, "though beyond that . . . you perceive it does not move, it does not struggle to breathe, it has not *quickened*. As we see it now, it has no more life than a plant—which indeed, it was from the beginning."

He readjusted the spectacles on the end of his nose, the better to view his own creation. "What it may yet become, I do not know—beyond the fact that it will certainly not be a human infant . . . not in the sense that we would define the term. You can see it more closely resembles a tiny mannikin. Should it eventually become a sentient being, I believe it will emerge from its egg fully mature—ignorant, certainly, in need of tutoring—but mentally and spiritually mature."

Caleb put out a shaking hand to touch the crystal egg, then drew back again, as if regretting the impulse. "You're mighty cool, Gottfried. Think you'd be excited . . . and mor'n a little afraid."

"But you see, I have been watching the process develop for many weeks now," Jenk replied, with a shrug. "I have had ample opportunity to temper my elation . . . and my apprehension. I admit that sometimes, in the watches of the night, I still wake and wonder what terrible thing I am creating here. But that is vanity, Caleb, sheer sinful vanity, for I am not creating a new thing at all, only following in the footsteps of the Ancients."

Turning his back on the marvel he had created, Jenk went back to his brown paper parcels. But Caleb could not tear his fascinated gaze from the tiny figure in the glass egg.

"It is too early, of course, to term this experiment a success," Jenk was saying. "The creature, if one might term it such, may never be more than what we see now. Yet no man living has carried the process even so far. So today I purchased a second mandrake root, in order to repeat the experiment. Perhaps I shall send the result to the Duke, along with my plea for funds. I cannot but think he will be suitably impressed, and respond most generously.''

But Caleb had passed beyond any interest in the Duke of Zar-Wildungen or his gold. "Gottfried . . ." he said, in a trembling voice. "Where did you come by the *sperma viri*?"

Jenk turned on him a look expressive of the utmost disgust. "Surely you do not suppose that *I* . . . ?"

Caleb shook his head. "No, Gottfried, no, I didn't think nothing like that. You've fathered a child; she's dead, but you've got young Sera to take her place. But I . . . I'm fond of Jed and the girls, but they ain't my own.

"It weren't through any—any disinclination that I never wed, you know that," he continued earnestly. "I just never had nothing to offer a woman, not until Joss's little widder come along with her three hungry babbies, worse off even than I was. I was glad to take them in, to play pa to her, and grandpa to the children, but it weren't nothing like having little ones of my own."

As his former servant spoke, Jenk's expression had softened considerably. "I know, Caleb, I know," he said gently. "And I know, too, though you do not reproach me, to what extent I was responsible for your poverty, the ruin of your early hopes. But even supposing that your seed were still vital—which is by no means certain, my friend, for you are no longer young—it will be a freak, an artificial creation, with no more humanity or claim on humanity than an ape or a four-legged brute. Were that not so, I would not think of sending one so casually to the Duke . . . Were it not so—"

"Send this one to the Duke," pleaded Caleb. "It's plain enough you don't care what comes to it. And I don't reckon it has no father likely to take an interest."

Jenk pulled up a chair, sank wearily down on it. "Its father—if you might term him such—was a felon, a gallows-bird. An involuntary reaction at the moment of death and a man hired to stand beneath the gibbet and collect the semen while it is still fresh—"

Caleb waved this explanation aside impatiently. "Well then . . . your little man, he's got no living father. And *you* ain't inclined to own him, I can see that plain. Send him to the Duke, to do with as he likes, but the other one . . . we could keep it ourselfs, we could treat it kind."

Jenk put a gentle hand on his old friend's arm. "You would

53

be dooming yourself to almost certain disappointment. The mandrake may not quicken. And even if it does, and we bring it to term . . . it may know nothing of human affection, naught of joy, or fear, or any other emotion.

"You might acknowledge the homunculus as your own—but would the bond between you mean anything at all to the creature itself?"

Caleb did not reply at once. Then he gasped and gave a startled cry. "It moved. I seen it move!"

Jenk started to his feet. But then, common sense returning to him, he shook his head and resumed his seat. "I believe you are imagining things, my friend. You want so much to see it come to life . . ."

"I seen it move," insisted Caleb, clutching his arm. "Look for yourself, you don't believe me."

Jenk bent forward, peered into the egg of glass. The homunculus was utterly still, giving no more sign of life than it had before. And yet . . . and yet, it almost seemed to Jenk that the color of the skin had changed, had acquired a more lifelike hue than—

"It's moving now . . . you can see for yourself," breathed Caleb.

As the two old men watched in astonishment, the little creature began to stir, to move sluggishly as if awakening from a long slumber. His skin assumed a rosier hue, and a pulse of life passed through his tiny frame. The little head moved slowly from side to side, and the eyes fluttered and opened.

Caleb was shaking from head to foot. "You done it," he said. "You done created a thinking creature."

Gazing into the face of the homunculus, Jenk could only nod in wordless agreement. The little man stared back at him with wide-open eyes—eyes which revealed neither the blankness of an idiot nor the innocence of a child.

Jenk struggled to master himself, to force out the words. "May the Father of All forgive me," he whispered hoarsely. "I believe I have created something unspeakable."

54

8.

In which Sera falls into the Clutches of a villain.

Once or twice in every fortnight, Sera paid a visit to her grandfather at the bookshop and spent a pleasant afternoon drinking tea in his little sitting room under the eaves. If the weather was fine, Sera walked; if it was wet, she stayed at home, or spent her meagre pocket money on a sedan chair rather than risk Clothilde's displeasure by requesting the use of one of the carriages.

On the thirty-first day of the season of Leaves, Sera dressed carefully, donning the old gown of black bombazine which she had recently refurbished with yards of white lace. She wished to appear happy and prosperous, lest she give her grandfather any cause for concern.

She paused to study her reflection in the long mirror over her dressing table. Even with all its fresh trimming of lace, the gown was sadly out of date. *But Grandfather knows nothing of feminine fashions, and I've nothing else suitable for an afternoon call except for the bottle-green poplin.* There was nothing to do but to make the best of it.

And with white net mittens . . . and the flowered shawl . . . and her Sunday bonnet with red silk roses . . . and a little gold brooch nestled in the lace . . . the black bombazine did not look so ill. Sera picked up her reticule and left her bedchamber.

She met Elsie and her mother on the stairs, just coming in from an afternoon call. Clothilde Vorder came first, stalking up the stairs with her head held high and a look of vexation upon her florid face, while Elsie trailed dismally behind.

At the sight of Sera, dressed to go out, Mistress Vorder bridled. "And where do you suppose that you are going, miss?"

For Elsie's sake, Sera tried to control her temper. "To visit my grandfather . . . You said that I might."

"I do not recall," said Cousin Clothilde, "anything of the sort. I had counted on you to write the invitations for my supper party.

55

Indeed, I distinctly recall telling you—''

''—that you required my services tomorrow afternoon!'' said Sera. ''It is no use pretending otherwise, for Elsie was there, and so was Cousin Benjamin, and rather more to the point: my grandfather is expecting me.''

Clothilde's hand twitched, rather as though she would have liked to slap Sera, but Cousin Benjamin's study opened on the landing above, and the door stood ajar. Though Benjamin Vorder was, as a general rule, too lazy and too neglectful to take issue with Clothilde's bullying mistreatment of his kinsman's daughter, both women knew well that he would not countenance any physical abuse.

''You are a bad, insolent girl,'' said Clothilde. ''Do not suppose that we shall not speak of this later. And just see that you are home before supper, or it will be the worse for you!'' And she continued on her way in high dudgeon.

Sera put out a hand to stop Elsie as she walked by. ''My dear, what is it? Have you quarreled with your mother?''

Elsie nodded. At first glance, she looked sweet and fresh, in a dainty white dimity gown and a wide straw hat trimmed with velvety pansies and pale Spagnish lilies. (*Like a bride . . . or a corpse*, thought Sera—then scolded herself for being so fanciful.) A closer examination revealed an unnatural glitter in her eyes and a hectic flush on her cheeks. To Sera's mind, she looked feverish.

But that was Clothilde Vorder's way: to exhaust Elsie by dragging her along to teas and afternoon calls and routs and picnics when she was genuinely ill and ought to be resting, then to torment her with doctors and unnecessary medications when she was otherwise perfectly well. *She parades Elsie and her infirmities as some women make a show of their gowns, their jewels, and their carriages*, thought Sera.

''I told Mama, in the carriage coming back, that I did not intend to visit Dr. Mirabolo ever again,'' said Elsie. A second visit to the establishment on Venary Lane had been as shocking as the first, and far from benefiting from the demonstration, she had spent the next three days in a state of nervous collapse.

''And so she is cross with you . . .'' said Sera. ''Never mind it, my dear. She can rail and plague you as much as she likes, but she cannot force you to go there against your will.''

Elsie looked at her doubtfully. ''Can she not? I think that she might. Mama has such—such a forceful character.''

Sera took her hand and squeezed it. ''You are sixteen years of age and no longer a child. She cannot whip you, or lock you in your room. And we live in a civilized country; you are not the daughter of some wicked oriental potentate. Your parents won't immure you in stone, or cast you out for undutiful behavior—well, I suppose they might disown you, at that . . . but not for anything so trivial as this. You would have to do something particularly dreadful. And I cannot see Cousin Benjamin in the role of tyrannical father . . . No doubt he would find it too strenuous for a man of his sedentary habits.''

Elsie smiled weakly at Sera's attempt at humor. "No, I am not like to be cast out, or anything so dramatic as that. But she might . . . Sera, she might send *you* away, as a way of punishing *me*."

"Yes," Sera agreed, with a sigh, "she might do that." The threat was a very real and present one. Whenever Sera spoke or acted to disoblige Cousin Clothilde . . . whenever she supported Elsie in resisting her mother's wishes . . . always there was the risk that Clothilde would send her away, that she and Elsie would be parted. "But to do that, she would also require your father's permission, and I do not think that Cousin Benjamin would be willing to oblige her.

"And anyway," she added, tossing her head, "I would sooner *be* sent off, sooner go to live with my grandfather—which I should not mind at all, if it did not mean parting from you—rather than stay on to be used as . . . as another means of making you docile."

Sera left Elsie lying down in her bedchamber, with a book in her hands, and a shawl of Mawbri silk cast over her like a blanket, and a maid-servant in the room to look after her during Sera's absence. She left the house and set off at a brisk pace, for the walk was a long one and she had delayed too long already. She knew that Cousin Clothilde would find a way to punish her if she came home late.

It was a fine day, and the cobblestone streets were crowded with sedan chairs and open carriages, horsemen and pedestrians, costermongers and peddlers of all sorts. Those who rode in carriages and chairs did not scruple to hold up traffic by stopping to examine the goods or to make a purchase. But Sera enjoyed the bustle, the color, and the variety.

The season was nearing its end. The country girls, who had been selling rabbits four or five weeks earlier, were now selling caged mockingbirds and goldfinches. Sera spotted an old man selling the tiny wooden dolls in white dresses, which, adorned

57

with rosebuds and scarlet ribbons, would accompany the young girls of Thornburg into church on the first day of Flowers, ten days hence. Rose-Brides, these dolls were called.

Sera had no time to visit her godmother, Granny Harefoot, as she had originally planned. Granny Harefoot sold curios and other odd bric-a-brac in a little establishment three doors down from Jenk's bookshop; the old dwarf was a friend of Sera's and—being something of a force in the neighborhood—was an invaluable source of information concerning the comings and goings, the doings and the general well-being, of all her neighbors. Sera decided to postpone her visit to the curio shop, but she did stop to buy buns and cider cake from a street vendor in a calico apron. She did not like to arrive at her grandfather's empty-handed.

A long procession, apparently one of the guilds, blocked her progress at Church Street. Sera was forced to wait, with rising impatience, until after the parade passed. By that time, the traffic was so dreadfully snarled, it seemed best to take the long way around.

There will be no time for a proper visit . . . Oh, dear, why did I leave so late? If I hadn't been there when Cousin Clothilde came in, I wouldn't be in such a dreadful coil now.

She was walking on Dank Street, which was blessedly empty, when a carriage pulled up beside her and a familiar voice called out her name. "Good day, Miss Vorder. Out for a little stroll, are we?"

Sera looked up to see Lord Krogan, an intimate of Cousin Clothilde's—a gentleman of that sly, insinuating sort which Sera so particularly disliked. Yet there was no point in being rude when the question had been civilly phrased.

"I am going to visit my grandfather, sir. He is expecting me for tea."

Lord Krogan flourished his whip. He was fat, middle-aged, and (so Sera had been informed) as bald as an egg under his wig, but he fancied himself something of a sportsman and dressed accordingly. "Perhaps you would care for a lift, Miss Vorder. We appear to be heading in the same direction."

Sera opened her mouth to decline, but then she reconsidered. She was late . . . she was already growing tired . . . Though she disliked Lord Krogan too much to go driving with him under ordinary circumstances, there could be no harm in accepting a ride in an open carriage. "You are very kind. I would be very much obliged."

58

Lord Krogan stopped the carriage and leaned over to offer her a damp hand up. Sera allowed him to assist her, then settled down in the seat beside him, with her reticule and her bag of buns and cider cake in her lap. She gave Lord Krogan the direction of her grandfather's bookshop and explained the shortest way to get there.

"A fine day," Lord Krogan said politely, as he snapped the reins and the carriage began to move—then he spoiled the effect by leering at her suggestively and adding, "And you, if I may say so, appear in fine form as well."

Sera ground her teeth and did not reply. At the rate they were bowling along she would not have to endure the man's company for very long.

They continued on in silence for several minutes, until the Viscount whipped up his horses and took a corner at high speed, almost oversetting the carriage in the process.

"My lord," Sera said breathlessly, "perhaps . . . you have mistaken my directions. This is not the way to my grandfather's."

Lord Krogan grinned at her and made no answer, except to touch up the horses again. As they rounded another corner, Sera clutched the side of the carriage, in order to avoid being thrown out.

They continued on at the same breakneck speed, for some time. Sera gradually realized that Krogan had never intended to take her to her grandfather's at all. *Good heavens, what can he mean by this!* She had heard many wild tales of dissolute gentlemen and helpless maidens, but she had never given these tales any credit. Yet, as fantastic as it seemed, she could not escape the conclusion that Lord Krogan was actually attempting a daylight abduction.

"Lord Krogan," said Sera, as steadily as she could. "I demand that you stop at once, sir, and permit me to alight."

Her abductor threw back his head and laughed. "You have accepted my invitation, Sera. It is much too late for you to back out now."

Sera, by this time, was genuinely frightened—but she stiffened her spine, lifted her chin, and replied sternly, "I have not given you leave . . . sir . . . to address me by my given name. And if you will not *stop* . . . I shall certainly be obliged to *jump*."

Lord Krogan only leered at her. "I do not believe that you will. You are a sensible girl . . . dear Sera . . . and you must be aware how shockingly dangerous that would be."

With a sinking sensation, Sera realized that what he said was true: they were traveling at such a rate now, that any attempt to

59

leap from the carriage would certainly entangle her with the back wheel.

Sera tried to think. *He can't mean to take me out of the town, for he would be obliged to slow down passing through the gate, and I could jump. Merciful heavens! We must be heading for some bagnio or—or a brothel. Can he possibly suppose that I would actually consent to accompany him inside?*

"Lord Krogan," she said severely, "if this is intended as a— a romantic escapade . . . I beg that you will not flatter yourself by supposing . . . that I will cooperate with you in any way."

It was then that Lord Krogan made a serious miscalculation, by turning onto another narrow lane much busier than the streets they had been traveling. As the Viscount reined in, Sera braced herself, ready to take action at the first opportunity. Then a stately berlin rumbled around a corner and pulled in front of them.

Lord Krogan hauled in on the reins, and Sera saw her chance. She gathered up her skirts and leaped out of the carriage. Landing badly, she twisted an ankle beneath her and dropped her purse and her package. But she was up in a second, gathering up her possessions and limping down the street as swiftly as she could go.

Lord Krogan, declining to abandon his carriage, gave her up for lost and did not give chase.

9.

Which finds Sera in no better circumstances than the Former.

Sera looked around her, with considerable disfavor. This was no part of Thornburg she knew, no place where she cared to linger. The street was so narrow, the overhanging second stories of the crooked old houses actually met in places, forming a dim, winding tunnel between ugly, sooty buildings: tenements and taverns and gin shops. An occasional lanthorn lit the way, swinging from a rusty chain, but there was no room to accommodate a sidewalk, forcing Sera to walk in the street, which was muddy and ill paved.

60

The people were shabby and dirty; the neighborhood reeked of garbage, poverty, and cheap spirits. Sera gathered her flowered shawl more closely around her and set out briskly in what she fervently hoped would prove to be the right direction.

Men like Lord Krogan should be boiled in oil! thought Sera, as she limped down the street. *They should be forced to swallow white-hot stones. They should . . . Oh, dear, I fear I have been dreadfully sheltered—I don't know any punishment that is harsh enough!*

At first, she could not understand why she attracted so much attention, why the women stared resentfully as she passed, and the men made such rude remarks. But then she realized that it was the way she was dressed. Her stiff black bombazine (so shabby a gown among the Vorders and their intimates!) . . . her white gloves . . . her flowered bonnet and her silk shawl . . . Sera was suddenly conscious of how she must appear to these ragged and ill-fed people: the pampered daughter of a wealthy family, who had never lacked for anything in her life. *Little wonder if they hate me,* thought Sera. She lowered her eyes and walked on, as swiftly as she dared.

But when she passed a signpost, she glanced up, hoping to gain some sense of direction. It was difficult to read the faded lettering, in the twilight between the overhanging buildings, but she was just able to make out the name.

Capricorn Street, said the sign, and Sera felt a chill snake down her spine. Capricorn Street . . . the name was certainly familiar— it had all the familiarity of a recurring nightmare.

"*Don't you never go down Capricorn Street, for you'll never return again!*" The old warning came back to her, a memory of childhood days in the old neighborhood. Spoken by the mothers and fathers, the older brothers and sisters of Sera's friends, those terrifying words prompted the younger children to imagine all kinds of horrors. On Capricorn Street there were cannibal witches . . . warlocks with wooden feet and staring glass eyes . . . feral dogs and yellow demon cats . . . a whole collection of frights and bogey-beasts designed to strike terror into childish hearts.

If Sera knew better than that by now, if she knew that Capricorn Street was nothing more than a narrow dirty lane leading from her own shabby-genteel neighborhood into a perfectly ordinary slum . . . yet some of the old superstitious terror remained. *And if there are no witches and warlocks, there is crime and vice and*

61

every form of human degradation—and that's quite terrible enough.

But at least she knew for certain which direction to go.

As Sera continued purposefully on her way, she passed many groups of ragged children: dreadful little wraiths, with pinched-in faces and knowing eyes, who conducted their games with a sort of heartless, down-trodden weariness, that suggested a duty rather than a pleasure. Even their laughter sounded shrill and hysterical. Sera could not bear to look at them. She wished that she dared to cover her ears, so she would not have to hear them.

One of their songs, set to a peculiar jangling tune, followed her all along the street:

> *Sally go 'round the stars*
> *Sally go 'round the moon*
> *Sally go 'round the chimney pots. . . .*

Both the words and the tune had a haunting quality that disturbed Sera very much.

As she walked, she grew increasingly aware that someone followed her . . . a man, most likely, and almost certainly drunk, by the sound of his shuffling footsteps and the leering remarks that greeted his progress all along the dreary lane.

"Here now, missy . . . seems you've got yourself a fine gallant," someone called out in a rough voice.

"Don't you take no for an answer, cully. She ain't so proud as she looks!"

Yet Sera knew better than to increase her pace. *If I run, he will only give chase.*

"How do you do, Miss Vorder?" Sera was startled to hear her own name spoken by a voice that was gentle and cultured, and somehow familiar—and even more surprised to note that the footsteps following her suddenly ceased, and everyone on the street fell just as suddenly silent.

Sera glanced up. A tiny white-haired woman in a long grey cloak fell into step with her. "Mistress Sancreedi!" said Sera, recognizing the only one of Elsie's many doctors who had ever done her a bit of good.

"My dear Miss Vorder. What on earth has caused you to stray into this part of the town?" Mistress Sancreedi was not much taller than a dwarf, and more daintily built than the little Duchess of Zar-Wildungen, yet she possessed a natural dignity about her

62

which commanded instant respect. Though no longer young, she was still a handsome woman, for old age had treated her kindly, refining her beauty rather than spoiling it. The one jarring note in an otherwise lovely face was a pair of yellow eyes, as unusual in size and expression as they were in color.

"I come here *not* by inclination," replied Sera, "but by . . . by misadventure. I am going to visit my grandfather. And if it isn't impertinent for me to ask: what brings *you* to Capricorn Street?"

The little apothecary made a dismissive gesture. "In the course of my professional duties I come here often. Indeed, I am well known in every part of Thornburg and move about quite freely. Allow me, Miss Vorder, to extend that 'safe conduct' temporarily to you, by escorting you to your grandfather's."

Sera was more than happy to oblige. "You are very kind," she said.

They walked on in silence for some time. Though Sera knew it was rude to stare, she could not help stealing a sidelong glance at her companion, every now and again—for truth to tell there was something decidedly eccentric about Mistress Sancreedi's attire.

Over an antique gown of mossy green velvet she had laced a stiff black bodice, and she wore, besides, a wide ruffled collar of white lawn edged with point lace. Her big straw hat had been embellished with wax fruit and fresh flowers, but rather more startling were the two live birds, a robin and a jenny-wren, that perched on the crown. She was carrying a covered basket, which (by the sounds issuing forth, and the occasional emergence of a striped paw or a white-tipped grey tail) seemed to contain kittens.

She is undoubtedly the oddest woman that I have ever met, thought Sera. *But I know her to be a good one.*

They passed another group of children, trudging a dreary circle and singing the same song that had disturbed Sera before. "Mistress Sancreedi," she said aloud. "Do you know what game these children are playing? And the verse that they sing: I feel I know the words, though the tune is strange to me."

"But it is not a *game* they are playing," the little woman replied. "Rather, they are weaving a kind of a spell. Nor is it surprising that you should know the words, which are based on an ancient invocation to the sun and the moon, a spell of protection against the terrors of the night.

"You frown, Miss Vorder, as though you disapprove," she added. "Will you tell me why?"

63

Sera shook her head, uncertain how to express what she felt. "These children . . ." she said at last. "Their circumstances are so wretched, their condition so miserable . . . I cannot imagine anything worse than the lives they already lead. What need have their parents to—to invent bogeymen with which to scare them?"

"No need at all," said Mistress Sancreedi. "These children are quite capable of imagining their own bogeymen. You are shocked by what you have seen here. The condition of these children moves you to pity and disgust. But to see them at their worst, you would have to come here at night.

"These children," said Mistress Sancreedi, "know nothing of pillows or clean linen. They spend the nights huddled together with their equally wretched brothers and sisters in a pile of filthy rags in some draughty corner. Rats are their frequent bedfellows, and the violent squabbling of their drunken parents a familiar lullaby. More often than not, these children go to bed hungry. Is it any wonder if they sleep lightly and their dreams are more often nightmares? But worst of all, perhaps, is their fear of hobgoblins, whenever the moon is full."

"It is very sad," said Sera, with another shake of her head. "But there is nothing supernatural about hobgoblins, you know. They are just—just vermin. And they only come out when the moon is full because subterranean tremors make their tunnels unsafe."

"As you say," Mistress Sancreedi agreed. "They are only vermin . . . but they possess a rudimentary intelligence. And unlike rats and other vermin, they have clever little hands which enable them to unfasten latches and pry open windows; they have a hundred different ways of gaining entrance to these old, tumbledown houses. Moreover, they run quite mad above ground, and their bite is poisonous.

"You would say that the poison is a mild one, and the wound not serious if treated properly," the apothecary added, when Sera opened her mouth to speak. "But rosewater and oil of clove are quite beyond the means of these folk. That little lad over there . . ." Mistress Sancreedi indicated an emaciated urchin, not more than six years old, who leaned on a crutch and stumped along on a wooden leg. "He was bitten by a hob before he learned to walk. His mother did not send for me until the poison had spread from his foot to his leg. I came in time to save his life, but not to save the limb."

Mistress Sancreedi gave a weary little sigh and changed the

subject. "But tell me something of your cousin, Miss Vorder. Has her health improved at all?"

"It has not," said Sera. "I do wish that Cousin Clothilde had been more reasonable and not dismissed you!" Yet it was not to be wondered at that Mistress Sancreedi's prescription—a sensible diet, moderate exercise, and mild herbal draughts to aid Elsie's uncertain digestion—had not found favor with Cousin Clothilde.

"I fancy," said the apothecary, "that the Duchess had something to do with my dismissal. Marella Carleon has done a great deal of good in this world—indeed, I believe she is universally regarded as a great philanthropist—but she also has much to account for."

As they continued on their way, through the dirt, and the garbage, and the gloom, Sera launched into a long story of Elsie and all her ills, which somehow became an account of her own wrongs and ended with Sera telling Mistress Sancreedi all about Lord Krogan and his disgraceful behavior.

"And I simply do not know what I should do. If I complain to Cousin Clothilde, she is certain to believe whatever lie Lord Krogan chooses to tell her; he will be able to convince her that I said or did something improper to encourage his attentions. As for Cousin Benjamin . . . it is likely that he would believe me, but what steps could he take besides challenging Lord Krogan to a duel and almost certainly getting himself killed? Yet if I say nothing, and Lord Krogan himself spreads the story about—"

"Oh, but I do not think that he will do that," said Mistress Sancreedi. "A foiled abduction is nothing to brag about. His intentions were wicked (which some people may actually admire), but his execution was fearfully inept (which no one will admire at all). Your own actions, on the other hand, were quite remarkably courageous."

Sera, however, was not convinced. "I don't see that. There is nothing remarkable about jumping out of a carriage which is hardly even moving. Indeed, upon reflection, it strikes me as rather a hoydenish thing to do. I ought to have been able to quell Lord Krogan's ardor by—by the dignity of my bearing or . . . or somehow taught him to respect me as he ought."

Mistress Sancreedi threw back her head and laughed. "But my dear Sera, I believe that is precisely what you *have* done. In any case, you have earned my respect, and that is not easily won."

• • •

Mistress Sancreedi took her leave outside the bookshop. "Indeed, Sera, I have long wished to better our acquaintance . . . and regretted, on that account, that I was not better friends with your grandfather. I should have liked to be there when you were named." With which mysterious pronouncement she touched Sera lightly on the cheek and went on her way.

Sera entered the bookshop at a quarter to four, feeling unusually uplifted, remarkably at peace with herself and with the whole world. *If I were inclined to be fanciful, I should imagine there was something almost magical about her . . . something in Mistress Sancreedi's voice or her touch, a spell against anger, resentment, and envy. But it is only that she is so very good—so sensible and so wholesome—that one is instantly inspired to become better oneself.*

Her grandfather, as Sera soon learned, was out. "Went off an hour or two past on some errand—no, I *don't* know where he might be," Caleb said irritably. "I reckon he'll be back afore long, if he knowed you was coming."

With spirits undimmed, Sera bade Caleb a surprisingly dulcet good afternoon and climbed the two flights of stairs to her grandfather's living quarters in the attic.

She removed her hat, her shawl, and her mittens, and draped them over a ladderback chair. Sera moved about the attic with easy familiarity, lighting a fire in the red brick fireplace in Jenk's little sitting room, hanging a kettle of water over the flames to boil.

Humming a half-remembered tune under her breath, she arranged plates, cups, and saucers on a table, found a dish for the cider cake and another for the buns. She searched a cupboard until she found a loaf of dry bread, cut off two slices, skewering them on long-handled forks, and arranging them in a rack on the hob to toast.

By this time, the kettle was only just beginning to steam, so Sera opened the work basket which she kept at the bookshop, rummaged through the contents until she brought forth a frilled shirt of her grandfather's. It was so old and fragile that it was coming apart at the seams. Seating herself in one of the two wing chairs by the fire, she threaded her needle and set to work.

So she was when Gottfried Jenk entered the sitting room a short while later. The old bookseller paused, unnoticed, on the threshold, enjoying the pretty scene of comfortable domesticity thus presented. In the heat of the fire, the wild roses in Sera's cheeks were more vivid than ever; her glossy dark head was bent in concentration as, with tiny careful stitches, she mended the ancient shirt.

He had only a moment to observe her, before Sera looked up and saw him standing by the door. "There you are, Grandfather. You have come just in time. The water is boiling, and the teapot is warming on the mantel."

Jenk moved slowly across the room, bent stiffly to kiss her on the forehead. "You look tired, dear Grandfather," said Sera. "I hope you aren't ill?"

"I have not slept much of late," Jenk told her. He walked over to the open cupboard, took down a small painted chest of eastern design, and set it on the table. The box contained a black tea from the Orient, blended with dried raspberry leaves.

"No, no, I assure you—I am not ill. Nor am I . . . of an unquiet mind," he added hastily, as Sera's dark brows came together. "It is only that my . . . studies . . . occupy so much of my time." As he spoke, Jenk moved slowly about the room, preparing the tea, taking down a crockery jam pot and putting it down on the snowy tablecloth. "I am old, my dear, and I have not many years ahead of me. Therefore, I wish to learn as much as I can, in the time that remains."

Sera looked up from her mending, hesitated a moment before speaking. Mistress Sancreedi's influence was fading, and she was beginning to remember certain conversations and observations that had worried her before. "When I came to see you two weeks past, I stopped in to visit Mistress Harefoot and Mistress Leer along the way. In both of their shops I heard a story . . . a most disturbing story—I didn't like to ask you about it before, when Caleb Braun was present. You have not—please tell me that you have not begun dissecting bodies, as they say. The risk of disease, especially to a man of your years . . ."

Jenk sank down wearily in the other chair. "The dissection of the human body," he said, with as much dignity as he could muster, "is illegal. Or rather, it is an act forbidden to all but members in good standing of the College of Chirurgeons, who perform their experiments under the Prince's warrant."

"Yes, yes, I know that," said Sera. "But I know, also, that the men of the Watch may be bribed to overlook—"

Jenk cut her off with an imperious wave of his hand. "I am not dissecting bodies, Sera, or indeed, engaging in any other activity of an illicit nature. It is true that I maintain a primitive

67

sort of laboratory in a room down below, but if you wish to examine it, in order to set your mind at rest . . . why then, you are welcome to do so."

As he had anticipated, Sera shook her head; she would never question her grandfather's word. *How easily* (thought Jenk) . . . *how easily I have learned to lie to her. Yet is it not entirely for her own good?*

"If you say that you are doing nothing wrong, dear Grandfather . . . then naturally I must believe you," said Sera.

When the tea had steeped, the old man poured a small amount into his own cup and an equal amount into Sera's. He smiled at his granddaughter over the teapot. "Do you remember . . . but of course you will recall . . . how you used to see pictures in the tealeaves? You used to amuse me with your—predictions, one might almost call them . . . for they were often relevant to things which actually occurred afterwards."

Sera felt an odd, fluttering sensation in her stomach. She remembered those "predictions" very well—for all she had labored so earnestly to forget them—as she remembered, also, certain terrifying childhood experiences, which this conversation with her grandfather had already brought to mind.

She recalled, with particular horror, a series of recurring nightmares, in which, seeming to rise from her little bed in the attic and walking barefoot down to the bookshop, she had seen her grandfather, in a strange dark wig, bending over an open coffin which contained a putrefying corpse . . .

Sera shuddered, remembering the livid face of the dead man, the sickening stench of the decaying flowers that lined the casket. Sitting up a little straighter, she resolutely put the memory out of her mind. "I fear that I was a dreadfully fanciful child! How fortunate that I've grown wiser with the years."

Her grandfather smiled at her, a smile both wistful and quizzical. "Wiser, my dear? I wonder. Had you chosen to train your intuition instead of suppress it, it is possible you might have been capable of great things."

But Sera would not—could not bear to—give any credit to her disquieting childhood fantasies. "You know I put no faith in intuition . . . or in anything of the sort," she said firmly.

Rather than disturb her further, Jenk allowed the subject to drop. He poured another cup of tea for himself, brought the toast to the table, and spread it with damson jam. Between sips of tea and bites of cider cake, Sera went on with her sewing. When she finished mending his shirt, she folded it neatly and brought out the work basket again.

"I really do not know how you manage to mistreat your handkerchiefs so badly," she said, displaying a particularly disreputable specimen for his inspection. "And here is one that is even worse—" she began, then broke off with an exclamation of surprise and dismay. "Why . . . it—it looks exactly like a tiny shroud."

For a moment, Gottfried Jenk struggled to find the words. He opened his mouth as if to speak, closed it, shook his head, and passed a trembling hand over his brow. Then he managed to collect himself.

"You are acquainted with Mistress Vogel, who comes in to scrub for me? She was here with her niece but a few days past. The child brought a family of wooden poppets and her bits and pieces of sewing; she was making a gown for a little Rose-Bride. It *is* that time of year, is it not?"

"Yes . . . it is that time of year," said Sera. But she had not failed to notice Jenk's temporary confusion. A faint doubt crept into her mind, the first doubt she had ever entertained as to her grandfather's veracity.

Though she instantly and resolutely pushed that doubt to the back of her mind . . . yet it remained with her. And it would emerge again and again to trouble her, in the weeks to come.

10.

Which the Sensitive reader may wish to Omit, but Ought to be read, nevertheless.

The tavern known as the Antique Squid was a great untidy elephant of a house, built of grey stone and half timber, with dormer windows and cupolas and chimneys starting out of the roof and the upper stories in unexpected places. It was a crazy old house, all curves and odd angles, with shutters hanging loose on broken hinges, doors that regularly jammed (or refused to close at all), and a slate roof carpeted in a patchwork of shaggy green moss and ruddy houseleek.

The taproom at the Squid was long and narrow, rather resembling an attic lumber room for its low, beamed ceiling and the number and variety of its furnishings: scarred oak tables, upholstered armchairs with broken seams and horsehair sticking out in wiry tufts, benches, settles, stools both high and low, trunks, and packing crates. In addition, the taproom boasted two fine fireplaces, each with a cozy inglenook, a dozen or so clocks (some of these even kept time), and a number of dim old paintings done in oils. Perhaps the most striking feature was the many-tentacled sea-creature preserved in formaldehyde in a bottle behind the bar, the antique squid for which the tavern was named.

The tavern had a reputation for solid comfort combined with a convivial atmosphere. Folk came to the Squid for good brown beer and well-aged cheeses, for steaming bowls of purl or mulled wine, for demon fiddlers who could play all night long with scarcely a pause, and for comely, good-natured barmaids.

It was customary among the Watchmen who nightly patrolled the eastern bank to meet at the Squid and drink a tankard of ale or porter before walking their evening rounds. Matthias and Walther, Oderic and Theodor, Abel and Thaddeus: big men with loud voices, they dominated the crowded taproom with their presence.

They had met as usual, one particular evening near the end of the season, and claimed an inglenook for their private use. The ale was excellent, a fine fire blazed on the hearth, and the fiddlers were just tuning up. But conversation lagged, largely due to Theodor, who sat in a shadowy corner of the nook with his tricorn pulled down over his eyes, and answered the sallies of the others with grunts and disspirited monosyllables.

After about a quarter of an hour of this, Oderic gave his partner a friendly shove. "You're in a black mood this night, cully. Another squabble with your old woman, was it?"

Theodor put down his tankard with a thud. "Molly's all right— I got no quarrel with her. Tell you what: I'm surprised the rest of you ain't a good deal more sober, seeing what night this be."

The others exchanged a puzzled glance.

"It's the thirty-seventh," said Theodor. "And the Gentlemen is always active around this time. And when I think of finding another dead girl, like the one we discovered last year this same time . . . well, it makes me sick, and I ain't ashamed to say so."

70

The other constables all moved uneasily in their seats, unnerved by this unwelcome reminder. But Matthias spoke out loudly and heartily—perhaps a little too heartily, to disguise his own discomfort. "That may be—but two seasons has passed since the boys on the west bank made *their* discovery—and that was just one of the Gentlemen themselves, with his tongue cut and his throat slashed . . . not one of them poor sacrificed girls. Seems to me as if the Knights of Mezztopholeez has turned their hands to less bloody-minded mischief than they was inclined to afore."

Theodor shook his head glumly. "Not likely—not bleeding likely, cully. Those as have a mind to them *amusements* ain't inclined to take satisfaction in no milder entertainment. They'll be up to their old tricks soon—if they ain't already—and when they does . . ." Theodor did not finish the sentence, but he did not have to. They were all familiar with the handiwork of those "gentlemanly" blackguards the Knights of Mezztopholeez, and it was not a subject that any of them cared to reflect on.

Particularly not Matthias, who pushed back his chair and rose to his feet. "There, now—you've infected us all with your foul humor. It may be as you say, but I for one ain't inclined to spoil my whole evening, adreading of something that may never come to be. Come along, Walther, we got a job to do."

With an apologetic glance in the direction of the others, Walther followed his partner out of the tavern and into the street.

The night was damp and windy, and the moon was thin but waxing. Not a comfortable sort of night, thought Walther. He felt all jumbled and jumpy inside; he started at every moving shadow, and whenever a wisp of cloud passed over the moon, a chill of fear crawled down his spine.

Matthias, on the other hand, was set on maintaining a bold front. As he and Walther walked their rounds, the big red-head swaggered on ahead, humming a tune under his breath and swinging his nightstick jauntily—a performance that did not fool his partner and only served to increase Walther's nervous jumpiness.

When Walther hesitated at the mouth of an ominously dim and malodorous alley, Matthias snickered nastily. "You're an old woman, Walther, and I never knew it."

"And you're a braggart and a blowhard!" his partner countered. "You can hum your songs and flourish your nightstick but I ain't fooled. You're sick right through to the marrow of your bones, just the same as me, thinking what we're like to find."

"Maybe I am, and maybe I ain't," said Matthias. "But if I

am—where's the sense in brooding on it?"

"I can't help but think on it," said Walther, with another shiver as a cloud passed over the moon. "Them poor butchered girls. I lived among violent men all my life, and I can understand a deed of passion or revenge. But the Knights and their d----d heathenish rituals. It's wicked, Matthias, it makes my skin crawl. Why does they do it? No one knows. No, nor no one knows who they be—not until one of them turns up dead. And no one knows their number neither. There could be a hundred of them, and nobody's wife or sweetheart safe, no man's sister, and no child's mother."

"Mostly it's whores," Matthias pointed out. "The last five girls they found was—"

"Some of the nicest girls I know is whores," Walther retorted.

Matthias shrugged that one off, just as though he were not on a first-name basis with half of the girls on the streets. He turned and entered the alley, swinging his truncheon as before and humming that same annoying tune.

After another moment or two of hesitation, Walther hurried to catch up with him. His eyes slowly adjusted to the deeper gloom of the alley—just in time to see the shadowy figure of Matthias go down right in front of him, cursing fit to raise the dead.

Walther stood where he was, extended a groping hand into the darkness below. "You all right, Matthias?"

"I ain't busted nothing," came the reply. "But I twisted my ankle and scraped my hands."

"What made you stumble?"

"You know d--n well what it was made me stumble. You been talking of nothing else since we left the Squid." Matthias rose painfully to his feet. "Help me to drag the body out into the light, so we can see what we got here."

Matthias took the shoulders and Walther searched around until he found the feet. He was pleased to discover that the corpse had thick ankles and was wearing a pair of men's shoes. They carried the body out of the alley and down a wider street until they came to a circle of yellow lamp light. The corpse landed with a heavy thump as it hit the cobblestones at the foot of the lamp post.

"Just as I thought . . ." said Matthias, squatting down on his heels, the better to examine the corpse. The dead man wore a well-cut coat of crimson velvet; diamonds sparkled in the bloody lace at his throat and on the buckles of his shoes. Evidently he had been a man of some consequence. "Tongue cut and throat slashed from ear to ear." Matthias removed a purple velvet mask

72

covering the upper part of the dead man's face. "And his brow marked with the sign of a traitor, written in blood. One of their own they feared might blab ... pity they got to him afore he was able to speak out. We'll take the pin for ourselfs—it won't be missed—and leave the fancy buckles for the Chief."

Walther removed the diamond stickpin—gingerly, so as not to touch the clotted blood staining the lace. But then he made a discovery: "Look here ... over his heart: a powder burn and a hole in his waistcoat. Shot with a pistol, he was! That ain't regular—that ain't the usual thing at all."

"No more it is," agreed Matthias. "No need to shoot a man once you've cut his throat. And as for plugging him first and cutting him afterwards ... I never knew the Gentlemen to be so merciful."

It seemed a more thorough examination of the body was in order, so the two constables set distastefully about the task. In a pocket of the dead man's flowered waistcoat they found a scrap of bloody parchment. Four words were written there, in a flowing aristocratic hand. Neither Walther nor Matthias could read, but those four words they recognized, for they had seen them before under similar circumstances: *The Knights of Mezztopholeez.*

Walther straightened up. He removed his tricorn and scratched his head. This was a puzzle and no mistake. "But maybe it weren't the Knights, after all. Maybe it was an ordinary murder, made to look like ... no, not likely. There ain't many know the proper signs, except for the Watch and the Gentlemen themselves."

"Well, it ain't for us to worry our heads over, anyways." Matthias pushed himself up off the ground. "Leave that to the Chief Constable and the lieutenants. All we got to do is bring the body in. You stay here and I'll go for a cart."

Matthias limped down the street and disappeared around a corner. Walther—not best pleased at being left alone with the corpse—leaned up against the lamp post.

Matthias reappeared much sooner than his partner had expected—and without the cart. Hobbling as fast as he could go, he gestured wildly. "Leave that there ... come see what I found."

Walther sprang away from the lamp post and followed Matthias around the corner.

"Blister me if it ain't another corpse!" breathed Walther.

"Shot through the heart, then slashed and marked, just like the other one," said Matthias grimly.

Walther shuddered profoundly. "Two in one night, that ain't

regular neither. Theodor was right: they took so long between killings, they've busted out worse nor ever. I don't like it, Matthias—I don't like the feel of it.''

"No more do I," said Matthias. "I reckon there'll be worse mischief afore this night is done.''

11.

Containing Scenes rather more Adventurous than Revealing.

Had the Knights of Mezztopholeez known, at that very moment, all that Matthias Vogel and Walther Burgen knew, the men of that secret brotherhood might have echoed their apprehension. Men of violence though they were, the bloody deaths of two of their brethren formed no part of their plans for the evening.

The Gentlemen (as they were called) were members of an ancient brotherhood with a lurid history of black magic and bloodshed—a history far more terrible than the people of Thornburg guessed, because the Chief Constable and his immediate predecessors, partly to prevent a panic, partly to prevent a public outcry against their own inability to unmask the Knights and bring them to justice, had veiled their deeds in a dark shroud of secrecy. Yet word leaked out, and rumors about these nobly born rascals and their activities were rife. Everyone had heard of the Knights of Mezztopholeez, but not everyone believed in their existence; of those who did, only a few outside the Watch knew the full extent of their wickedness.

They met in a certain old house, in a blind court at the summit of Fishwife Hill. Though the exterior of the house looked weathered and shabby, the interior was furnished in a luxurious oriental style conducive to the drinking parties, the orgies, and the other decadent amusements which kept the Knights occupied and out of worse mischief during most of the year. But there was a large chamber at the back of the house all draped in purple velvet and black satin, and in that room was an altar consisting of a long marble sarcophagus supported on two gilded pedestals, where the

74

Knights of Mezztopholeez practiced their demonic rituals.

They were met in the altar chamber in full ceremonial attire: jeweled masks, elaborate curled wigs in the style of the previous century, and hierophantic robes embroidered with stars and suns and planetary emblems and other mystic signs. Though they claimed to model their ceremonies on archaic fertility rites, these latter-day druidicals were far more devoted to the *form* than to the original intent of the rituals—which more often than not centered around the death and mutilation of a beautiful young woman.

They had selected as victim a young prostitute, not more than seventeen, who lay now upon the altar, as still and as pale as death. She had come into the house bound and drugged, and though her bonds were gone, and her dirty rags had been replaced by an expensive gown of cream satin and blond lace, the effects of the drug had not worn off. The Gentlemen had dressed her, taking their time about it; they had powdered her, and perfumed her, and tenderly combed out her long golden hair, all in preparation for the sacrifice.

So secret was the brotherhood that members never met but when they were masked, and each man's identity (at least in theory) was known only to three others: the Grand Master and his two original sponsors. Each new member was recruited by abduction, led hoodwinked into the altar chamber, and offered the choice: join or die. Most joined, for the brotherhood chose its initiates carefully; occasionally, however, they misjudged their man. In that case, the candidate suffered a sudden (and invariably fatal) attack of scruples, and the body was marked with the sign of the apostate and left for the Watch to find.

By now, all was prepared and ready for the sacrifice, save that three members of the brotherhood had not arrived: Gentlemen rejoicing in the pseudonyms Avarice, Debauchery, and Mortal Sin. The appointed hour had come and passed and the girl on the altar began to stir in her sleep and make little sounds indicating that she was about to revive.

At last the Grand Master lost all patience. "May the Hag swallow them up . . . we'll wait no longer!" he proclaimed, striding toward the altar.

He nodded to his acolytes. "Bring me the athame, the bowl, and the chalice."

Being thus provided, the Master unsheathed the dagger and spat upon the blade. "I consecrate thee in the name of Mezztopholeez and all the dark spirits of the earth."

75

Just then, there was a stir of movement by the door. The Master looked up to see a willowy figure, in a gorgeous robe of sapphire satin and a tremendous white wig, entering the room. The man known as Mortal Sin stopped and looked around him with a great affectation of surprise. Then he bowed a deep and elaborate bow. "I do crave your pardon for the interruption. It would appear that I have mistaken the hour."

The Grand Master grinned at him, baring even white teeth beneath his green velvet mask. "I had thought, perhaps, a failure of nerve."

"No indeed," replied the newcomer. "I do assure you—I would not have missed these festivities for all the world." As if to confirm his words, he moved closer to the altar and peered over the Master's shoulder with a great show of interest.

"Such a delicious little thing as she is," he murmured. "Do you know?—it seems almost a waste."

As he spoke, the girl awoke and looked around her. Her eyes widened in disbelieving terror, as she took in her surroundings, the circle of masked sybarites, and the long gleaming knife.

"Ah, yes, my dear," the Grand Master assured her, "you have fallen into the hands of the Knights of Mezztopholeez. This is no nightmare, but grim and earnest truth, and the fate that you fear shall indeed be yours."

He raised the dagger and began to chant the sacrificial hymn. The others moved closer in anticipation.

But: "I think not," said a light affected voice in the Master's ear, and suddenly there was the barrel of a tiny hand pistol pressed against his left temple. The soft voice took on a steely edge. "If you cut the girl . . . make a move . . . or speak a single word, I will blast your brains out."

The Grand Master froze obediently in place.

"Very good," said Mortal Sin, removing a second pistol from a pocket somewhere inside his robe. "And of course, should any of you others decide to play the hero, I will shoot you dead as well, for the filthy dog that you are."

It appeared this caution was unnecessary. They were not men of an heroic stamp, not ripe for martyrdom. Not one of the Knights so much as shifted his position; not one of them displayed the least inclination to sacrifice himself for the sake of his brethren.

When the slim figure in blue satin addressed the girl, his voice lost some of its edge. "If you feel well enough to rise, madam,

76

I wish you would do so—incidentally placing yourself outside of this gentleman's reach.''

When she did as he told her, he nodded approvingly. "I perceive that you are a very brave girl, and that my efforts on your behalf are not wasted.''

And then, without warning, he calmly pulled the trigger, blowing the Grand Master directly to Perdition.

The Knights watched in rigid silence as the body of their preceptor crumbled to the floor and lay at the foot of the altar in a spreading puddle of blood and brains. Entirely unperturbed by this gruesome sight, Mortal Sin let the blood-spattered gun fall from his hand and fastidiously wiped his fingers on the purple velvet altar cloth.

One of the Knights finally gathered the courage to speak.

"Traitor . . . you'll suffer for this,'' the man known as Malice whispered hoarsely. "There are still two among us who know your true name, and you have but one shot left.''

For answer, Mortal Sin reached again inside his robe and produced a third pistol.

He spoke to the girl: "Have you ever handled a pistol like this before?''

"Aye, sir.'' Her voice was low but steady. "Leastways . . . I had a lover once, he was a trooper; he taught me to shoot off his horse pistols. I suppose it was much the same?''

"You will find these much lighter and easier to handle,'' he said. "You can oblige me by taking these pistols and keeping them trained on my good friends here. You are doing excellent well. I see that your hand is steady, though you are still rather pale. Take a deep breath but do not close your eyes. Now, if you feel able—and without turning your back on the rest of us—walk across the room and stand in that doorway over there.''

When the girl stationed herself according to his directions, he reached inside his robe once more. Everyone watched curiously, to see if he would produce yet another pistol. Instead, he brought out a tiny gilded box and flipped open the lid.

"Snuff . . . this will never do,'' he said, with a slight shake of his head. "It is the wrong box.''

He closed the snuffbox and replaced it in his pocket, searched through the garments underneath, and eventually came up with another box, this one inlaid with ivory and pearls. "Sleep Dust,'' he explained, lifting the lid to reveal a fine crystalline powder.

"It is very potent . . . the contents of this box tossed into the air should be enough to send you all into a deep slumber. Ah . . . you are kind to be concerned on my account but you have no need, no need at all, I do assure you.''

''Curse your bones!'' exclaimed one of the acolytes. ''I suppose you mean to tell us us that you are immune to the mother-fornicating stuff?''

Mortal Sin sketched a tiny formal bow in his direction. ''I regret to inform you that I became addicted to the powder at a very early age. Yes, yes, it is a filthy habit and you are right to condemn it—but one that serves me well in the present circumstance, you must admit. It would take a very large pinch, inhaled directly, to make *me* so much as drowsy.''

He poured the powder into the palm of his hand and blew it into the air. So fine and light was the Sleep Dust that it rapidly dispersed throughout the room. ''You will all indulge me by taking deep breaths.''

He spoke to the girl: ''If I catch one of them trying to hold his breath, I will say the word, and you must immediately shoot him.''

Already, the Knights were growing drowsy. Despite their struggles to remain standing, they began to fall, one by one.

''Oh . . . and about my name . . .'' some of them heard the voice of Mortal Sin, just before unconsciousness overwhelmed them. ''. . . my sponsors—our esteemed friends Avarice and Debauchery . . . unable to join us . . . in all the excitement . . . neglected to make their apologies. I do beg your pardon. They were unavoidably detained . . . unavoidably *permanently* detained.''

Outside on the dark street, he retrieved his pistols from the girl.

''Begging your pardon, sir, but . . . what happens now?'' she asked breathlessly.

''What happens next depends on you,'' he said, concealing the guns in some inner pocket. His voice and his manner had changed; all the elegant affectations were gone; he was now brisk and business-like. ''You must run in search of the Watch, bring as many of them as you can back here with you. No, I cannot accompany you. My continuing ability to function effectively would be hampered were I to reveal my name and my purposes to our stalwart constabulary. Your testimony, along with the circumstances and surroundings under which they shall discover these gentlemen, ought to convince them that an arrest is in order.

''After that . . .'' He shrugged his shoulders. ''After that we can only hope that the Chief Constable will know what to do. If he is wise, he will deal with them secretly and efficiently, rather than run the risk of a public trial. Otherwise . . . my former colleagues are all of them wealthy men, and most of them, I believe, are men of some position in the community; such men might use their influence to win their freedom.''

The girl took a deep breath. "The man with the knife—the one as you shot, sir—I knew him. I recognized him as soon as he spoke. He was . . . was a steady customer of mine.''

The man narrowed his eyes behind the mask. "You do not surprise me,'' he said. "For a man of that sort, *knowing* you in advance would increase his enjoyment of the entire situation. You may also be known to some of the others . . . which is not a comforting thought, for it places your safety directly in the hands of the Watch.''

He was silent for a moment, as if considering what to do. "We may hope that the Watch will prove wise enough to rid us once and for all of these insidious rascals—but were I in your place, I should not depend on it.'' He reached inside that capacious robe of his and withdrew a small money purse. He extracted a large note and pressed it into her hand.

"Once you have summoned the Watch, try to slip away home, gather together anything of value that you may own, convince anyone whom you hold dear to accompany you, and leave Thornburg for good. But should none of this be possible . . . if you find yourself in desperate straits . . . a message left with any Glassmaker in the town directed to me under the name of Robin Carstares will eventually find me.''

"Yes, sir. Thank you, sir.'' The girl accepted the money he offered her, tucked it down the neck of the ivory gown. "But . . . I don't see how I can tell them constables any sort of believable tale, without I tell them all about you. And then they'll be wanting a description. What do you want me to tell them?''

"As to that,'' he replied, "I will leave that up to you. You must reply as your conscience dictates.''

The girl took another deep breath. "All very well—and I hope you won't think me ungrateful for asking, for you did save my life—but . . . you wasn't really one of them, was you? You ain't— you ain't as bad as them others?''

"I am very little better, for I killed three men in cold blood this night, and I cannot say that I regret a single one of them.''

"But one of them you killed . . . that was to save my life,'' she reminded him.

"I was in the process of saving your life at the time, but I am afraid that I killed him simply because he knew my name," he replied with disconcerting candor.

"Yes," she said. "But you . . . you never . . . that is to say—"

"What you would really like to know, I fancy, is whether the blood of some other poor girl, shed under similar circumstances, is on my hands or my conscience," he furnished graciously. "By my sacred oath, it is not."

"Well then," said the girl, "I think I'll tell the Watch that you was uncommon tall, sir, and built like a carthorse. And what I could see of your eyes and your skin, I'd say you was as dark as a Spagnard."

Behind the velvet mask, he seemed to smile. His old manner returned, at once elegant and ironic.

"You have excellent powers of description, I perceive," said Mortal Sin, taking the young prostitute's hand and bowing over it, as if she were the greatest lady in the town. "Describe me just so to the men of the Watch, madam, and I shall be infinitely obliged to you."

12.

Being of a more Lofty Disposition, perhaps, than any of the Former.

The great bronze bells in the churches of Thornburg were a source of civic pride. Ancient and melodious, they called the faithful to worship every day of the week and three times on Sundays. But Sunday morning worship at the cathedral, when five hundred wax candles burned behind the altar and the best families drove 'round in their painted and gilded carriages, was the fashionable service, and anyone with any pretension to style made a point of being there.

"Such a press . . . so tedious. One scarcely has time, these days, to do more than greet one's friends," said Clothilde Vorder, as she and her family rode up Cathedral Hill in the Vorders' lumbering coach. "I often wonder why I bother to attend."

"But morning service is always so beautiful," Elsie said, in her sweet, quiet voice. "It always makes me feel so . . . uplifted somehow . . . and as though all my troubles were so paltry. I always feel stronger after it is over, as though I could bear any trouble, any pain, so long as I have Sundays to look forward to."

"Oh, yes, the service . . ." replied Mistress Vorder, with a negligent wave of her fan. "The sermons are, I believe, superior, and the choir unquestionably divine, but I do not understand why so many *tradesmen* are admitted. So common and so pushing as they are. I vow, they quite spoil the tone of the entire proceeding."

"The nature . . . if not the desired tone . . . of divine services has perhaps escaped you," said a bored voice from a corner of the carriage. Benjamin Vorder was a large, sleepy gentleman, who found his wife tiresome, his daughter's illness wearisome, and any foray into society a positive ordeal. "There is no question of admitting people or turning them away."

Clothilde sniffed resentfully. "Perhaps not. But people ought to know their *place*, and have the good sense not to intrude where they are not wanted."

In mild weather it was customary to alight at Solingen Park and stroll through the gardens, meeting and greeting one's friends, before climbing the broad stone steps to the cathedral to attend the first service.

"Oh, dear, I fear we must be dreadfully late, for the Duchess is here before us," said Mistress Vorder, as she stepped down from the coach and looked around her.

The little Duchess of Zar-Wildungen came to meet them, splendid in diamonds and heliotrope satin, and a cartwheel-sized hat loaded with plumes enough to outfit an army of ostriches. This hat all but eclipsed her escort, a short, shabby figure in a black coat and tinted spectacles, who walked at her side bobbing his head in a thoroughly obsequious manner. Trailing behind them on a leash, looking more woebegone than ever, was the Duchess's tiny indigo ape.

"She has brought Dr. Mirabolo with her," said Mistress Vorder. "How very odd that is."

The Duchess greeted them merrily and bestowed kisses all around.

"But I hear you do not like the treatment or the doctor which I have prescribed for you," she said to Elsie, raising her eyebrows

81

with a look of playful reproach. "What a wicked ungrateful child it is who refuses to take her medicine!"

Arm in arm with Elsie, Sera felt her cousin tremble. More than one unpleasant scene had occurred in the Vorder household since Elsie had declared her decision to forgo further treatment.

"Indeed, Gracious Lady, I am not—not ungrateful," said Elsie faintly. "But the nature of the treatment . . . and so horribly public . . . I told Mama that I simply could not."

"And I must suppose," said the Duchess, a little less playful, a little more reproachful, "that Miss Sera Vorder had some part in influencing your decision?"

Elsie shook her head. "Sera encourages me to do as I think best."

"Nevertheless," said Sera, "I fail to understand how Elsie could possibly benefit from a course of treatment, the mere contemplation of which—as she will readily tell you—causes her the most acute distress."

"Perhaps you are right," said the Duchess, with a return to her former sunny good nature. "And it does not matter at all, as you shall soon see, for we have another plan which ought to suit admirably." She looked around her, affecting mild bewilderment. "Now, where did Jarl Skogsrå go—he was with us only a moment since."

As if out of nowhere—but presumably from behind a nearby boxwood hedge—the Jarl appeared, exactly on cue. *Like some demonic spirit in an opera, arising through a trap door in the stage,* thought Sera. And indeed, there was something decidedly demonic in the Jarl's appearance, for he was dressed in red satin with black laces and fringes, and his boots had pointed toes. With a flourish worthy of his flamboyant attire, he whisked off his hat and proceeded to kiss the hands of all the ladies.

As always, when he touched her, Sera felt an instinctive shrinking, a strong desire to snatch her hand away. His manners had improved considerably since their first meeting—indeed, his expressions of admiration and respect were now so warm and so . . . pressing, they made her absolutely uncomfortable—but her opinion of Jarl Skogsrå had not changed. Yet what did she know against him? She had no real reason to dislike or distrust him, could accuse him of no overt impropriety . . . There was only this odd intuitive reaction—and that Sera was staunchly determined to view as mere female vaporing, the sort of thing which any strong-minded woman must immediately dismiss. So she concealed her distaste as best she could and did not try to draw her hand back again, not until the Jarl (he was a long time in the process) had finished kissing it.

"My dear Jarl," said the Duchess, "shall *you* tell Elsie of that excellent scheme we have devised between us, or shall *I*?"

Skogsrå released Sera's hand and possessed himself of Elsie's a second time. "With the Gracious Lady's permission. My dear sweet child, it is only this: you do not care for the doctor's treatments, considering them far too public—and you are right, you are very right—they do very well for the others who have not . . . your sensitivity . . . your exquisite delicacy. But see: I am a disciple of the doctor, I am conversant with all his arts. I can come to you at your own home and administer the treatment privately.

"No, no, I can assure you, there will be no *convulsions*," he hastened to add, as Elsie blanched and averted her face. "These violent reactions . . . as the body seeks to rid itself of disease . . . are not common in cases like your own, where the only problem is an infection of the blood. For you, I promise, there will only be healthful sleep and sweet dreams, and perhaps a little medicine which I shall prescribe for you, very pleasant to the taste. Now, what do you say to that?"

Elsie hesitated. "But my dear sir, you are too kind!" said her mother. "Elsie can have no objection, no objection at all."

"But what does Elsie herself say?" insisted the Jarl, holding her cold little hand to his heart and leaning forward to listen, in that way he had, as if every word she deigned to speak were of shattering importance.

Yet still Elsie hesitated. She looked to her father for advice, but that large gentleman had allowed his attention to wander elsewhere and was staring at the sky. And when she applied to Sera, the older girl only shook her head, indicating that the decision was for Elsie to make alone.

In truth, Sera liked this scheme no better than she liked the Jarl, yet she could not explain her objection to the one without first explaining her dislike of the other, and that she could not do. Moreover, she knew that however vigorously she argued against this proposal, Cousin Clothilde and the Duchess would argue just as vigorously in favor of it, and then poor Elsie would be caught in the middle. Her recent disagreement with her mother had already cost Elsie so dearly, in terms of her peace of mind, it seemed as though any treatment which the Jarl might devise would be preferable to continued discord in the Vorder household.

"Well . . ." said Elsie, bestowing a tremulous smile on the Jarl, "it does not sound so very bad, after all. I think I would like it a good deal better than some of the other treatments I have had."

Everyone except Sera was plainly delighted. "You are a wise child and have made a wise decision," exclaimed the Duchess, giving Elsie another kiss.

But Sera thought she saw something, a glance and a slight pressure of the hand, pass between Elsie and the Jarl, and something in that gesture disturbed her. As the doctor took his obsequious leave, and the others began to stroll in the direction of the cathedral, Sera kept Elsie back and whispered in her ear:

"Dear Elsie . . . you are not falling in love with Jarl Skogsrå?"

"No, I am *not*," said Elsie, so emphatically and with such a decided nod of her head that Sera could not doubt her. "I own that I find him very attractive, but there is nothing more to it than that. And yet . . . he looks to be a man who has seen and experienced much suffering . . . and I find him utterly fascinating."

He has the look of a man who has been the cause *of much suffering.* That was how Sera wanted to reply, but she had resolved not to malign the Jarl unjustly. "He is clearly a man of exceptional parts," she admitted.

"But don't you think that his manners have improved?" Elsie said, as they hurried to catch up with the others. "He spoke to you yesterday so kindly and so considerately, that I began to wonder whether we might not have been wrong in supposing him so very rude in the first place."

Arm in arm, they climbed the broad stone steps to the cathedral and entered the dark vastness of the ancient church. They were not—as Clothilde Vorder had feared—late for the service, so they had no trouble finding an empty box pew near the front of the church.

Elsie's father took a seat at the end of the stall and promptly fell asleep under the carven figure of an owl-eyed gargoyle. Jarl Skogsrå folded his arms with the look of a man who was preparing to be bored, and Mistress Vorder and the Duchess (with the indigo ape in her lap) arranged their skirts, took out their fans, and entered into an animated conversation. But Elsie and Sera knelt down on the green plush prayer stools, folded their hands dutifully, and proceeded to pray.

Even with her head bowed and her eyes closed, Sera was acutely aware of the beauty of the cathedral. As a child, she had accompanied her grandfather to the Church of All Seasons, a lovely old

84

church that would always hold a special place in her memory. On her first visit to the cathedral, the huge building struck her as cold and rather daunting. By now, however, the cathedral and its splendid Gothic architecture had long since captured her heart and her imagination: the great stone pillars soaring upward to support a magnificent vaulted ceiling, the wonderful rose windows depicting the Seven Fates, or planetary intelligences, as glorious winged figures glowing in jewel-like colors . . . these never failed to inspire Sera to higher and better thoughts. But perhaps best of all she loved to hear the deep voice of the ancient organ competing with the joyous clamor of the bells.

When the music of the bells finally faded, the organist struck a particularly thunderous chord, and the entire congregation rose. There was a brief rustling of paper as everyone opened hymnals and leafed through them in search of the proper page, then, with one voice, the congregation burst into song.

As they sang, the bishop approached the altar, followed by a long procession of black-robed clerics and white-robed choir boys, water sprinklers and thurifers, and solemn little acolytes carrying embroidered banners. When the hymn ended the congregation fell silent again. Then the bishop raised his hands and began to recite the litany:

Then the Father of All created the Heavens and the Earth . . . and the Creator assigned the Days of the week and the Ordering of the Planets to the Seven Fates, and to the Nine Powers he assigned the Ordering of the Year and the population of the Earth . . .

And the Nine Powers (or Seasons) brought forth all the Creatures of the Earth and all the races of Rational Beings, each according to his or her own Nature. . . .

When the service ended, Sera and Elsie closed their hymnals, took up their prayerbooks, and followed Mistress Vorder and the Duchess back up the aisle. "Do look, Sera," said Elsie, pausing just inside the great oak doors and touching her cousin lightly on the arm. "That boy looks exactly like Jedidiah Braun."

Sera looked where Elsie indicated. In a low pew near the back of the church sat a party of dwarves, decent and prosperous in appearance. The only Man among them was a tall youth in a plain suit of brown wool and a cherry-colored waistcoat. His brown hair was lightly powdered, making it impossible to guess the exact shade, but he had a good face, adorned by a pair of earnest dark eyes, and his shoulders were broad and capable-looking.

Sera was amused by the resemblance. "The features are *very* like, and the pigtail, too, but . . ." Catching Sera staring at him, the boy turned pink with embarrassment. "May the Fates preserve us, it *is* Jed! But how came he here, dressed so fine, and in such unexpected company?"

"He—he looks very well," said Elsie, turning nearly as pink as Jed himself.

"Indeed he does . . . so brown and healthy. I expect that his new occupation—whatever it may be—suits him very well," Sera replied.

But Elsie shook her head. "I meant . . ." she said, in a breathless little voice, ". . . that he appears quite the gentleman."

Sera looked at her sharply, detecting something in Elsie's face and manner *now* which had *not* been there earlier when she spoke of her attraction to Jarl Skogsrå.

Heavens above, thought Sera, *this will never do!* That Jed admired Elsie was no secret; it was all perfectly proper and perfectly harmless, for Jed was a good boy who knew his place: he would never make improper advances. But if Elsie were to fall in love with Jed . . . nothing could come of that but heartbreak and disappointment for everyone concerned.

"Do you think—do you not think it would be a nice show of courtesy if we were to stop and speak to him?" asked Elsie.

"I certainly do not," replied Sera very decidedly. "We have not been introduced to any of his friends, you know, and perhaps they are not people with whom we ought to be acquainted." And, determined to do all in her power to avert disaster, she took Elsie by the arm and whisked her out of the church and down the steps.

So hastily and so heedlessly did they descend that at the foot of the steps Sera collided with a slender gentleman in apricot satin and gold lace. Blushing furiously, she disentangled herself.

"L-Lord Skelbrooke . . . I do beg your pardon."

Francis Skelbrooke bent to pick up the fan and the prayerbook which had fallen out of her hands during their collision. "Pray do not apologize. I can assure you that it was entirely a pleasure," he replied gently, and Sera blushed more painfully than before.

He handed over the fan and the prayerbook, which Sera accepted with a shaking hand. He turned his attention to Elsie. "And you, Miss Vorder . . . how do you do, this fine day?"

Elsie, still pink and breathless from the sight of Jed in all his splendor, replied faintly that she did very well.

86

"Indeed?" said Lord Skelbrooke, looking from one flushed and excited face to the other, and raising an eyebrow in well-bred astonishment. "It must have been . . . a most remarkable sermon. I regret that I was not present to hear it. Yet it is no more than I deserve, for arriving so late."

Sera tried desperately to remember the text of the sermon and failed. With an heroic effort, she struggled to compose herself. "The sermon was not particularly inspired, but the music . . . the organ and the choir . . ."

"Ah, yes . . . the music," said Lord Skelbrooke, taking her hand and raising it to his lips. "I had forgotten, madam, that you and your cousin were musically inclined. The grand old organ and the heavenly choir . . . you must tell me all about them, indeed you must."

When Jed came home that night, carrying two thick cloth-bound books under his arm, he found Uncle Caleb waiting up for him, sitting in the little rocking chair by the fire.

"You look mighty fine . . . hair powder and all," the old man said, with a snort. "I see you brung home more books. Geography and mathematics! Does that bottlemaker of yours imagine he's educating you for a gentleman?"

"He *imagines* that he's educating me to be of some use to him," said Jed. "He's expanding his business outside of Marstadtt, and I'm to be in charge of the foreign accounts. As for the hair powder . . . I been to church, and I didn't want to put Master Ule and his family to no—to *any* shame, that's all."

"Been to church? I know a thing or two about going to church—though you might not think it to look at me," said Caleb. "I been to church a time or two in my life, and I never heard yet there was any shame in a man appearing there in his own natural hair."

Jed kicked off his shoes, sat down on the edge of the lower bunk. "Well then, there isn't. But we had dinner afterwards, at Master Ule's, and he gave me a hint afore—*before* time, his old mother is awful fine and she don't sit down to the table with anyone who don't—who *doesn't* dress for it."

"Had dinner at home with dwarves?" Caleb sat up a little straighter and began to look interested. "Your Master Ule . . . he lives in one of them dwarf mansions, does he?"

In his time, Caleb had been acquainted with very few dwarves, but it was no secret they were a luxurious race. Even dwarves of modest means lived in grand houses, sometimes pooling the resources of several families to erect their lofty mansions of stone, as ornate on the inside (it was said) as they were on the outside, with elaborate pillars and pediments and balustrades, fountains of porphyry, onyx, and white marble, and cavernous high-ceilinged chambers which reminded them of their origins in the caverns of the north. Caleb had never set foot inside one, but he knew (or thought that he knew) what the mansions of the dwarves were like. "Don't hold out on me, lad—tell me everything you seen."

Jed stood up, stripped off his coat, and hung it carefully on a peg on the wall. He knew all the same tales that Caleb knew and while it was true that Master Ule's home was very old, very beautiful, and filled with fine things, there was nothing on the scale that Caleb was obviously expecting.

"It was the grandest home *I* ever been in," he allowed at last. "We must of climbed fifty stairs just to reach the second floor and old Madam Ule's parlor. There wasn't no shortage of velvet draperies, or painted china, or crystal goblets, or silver teapots— most of it real old, and been in the family for hundreds of years, I guess. Them dwarves take real good care of their things."

He pulled up one of the unreliable chairs and sat down by the fire. "It was old Madam Ule as lent me them books—they set a great store by education, all the Ules—and *you* got something against book-learning, then all I got to say: you chose a d----d strange occupation for yourself when you left the river!" Jed proclaimed defiantly.

"Aye . . . Well, I ain't got nothing against books—most books," Caleb was forced to allow. "And I guess you won't take no harm from geography and mathematics, nor working in no import house, neither. Come to think on it," he added thoughtfully, sitting back in his rocking chair, "you may rise in this world by and by—and not by any efforts of your wichtel bottlemaker." Caleb nodded emphatically. "Learn all you can while you can, that suits me just fine."

Jed, who had been in the process of poking up the fire, stopped what he was doing and glared at Caleb suspiciously. "Now, what do you mean by that? Just what do you and Gottfried Jenk think you are doing there at the bookshop?" he said, unconsciously brandishing the poker as he spoke.

"Here, now . . . you ain't lost your wits entirely and gone for to transmute lead into gold again? I thought you put all that alchemical nonsense—no use scowling at me, for you called it that

88

yourself!—I thought you put all that behind you a long time since.''

"Never you mind what we think we're doing, old Gottfried Jenk and me. We know what we're doing, never you fear," said Caleb, folding his hands piously and continuing to rock, with such a smug expression generally that a more violent man than Jed might have been tempted to use the poker in earnest. "Don't you trouble your head at all. Just do your job and please your master, and leave me to do the same.''

13.

In which the Duchess entertains Visitors.

The Duke of Zar-Wildungen's town residence was a crumbling edifice built of white stone, all but concealed by a tangle of creeping vines: ivy, owl-flower, and wild rose. Its halls and corridors were floored with cracked tiles, its windows draped with faded and fragile velvets and satins, and all its furnishings were dark, heavy, and out of date. Thus it had stood for many years, and thus it seemed likely to stand, at least during the lifetime of the present Duke, who even as a young man had displayed an absolute passion for the antique—old books, old art, old buildings—and for manners, customs, and usages hallowed by time, which as the years passed had grown to the point of obsession.

Only in a single suite of stylish rooms done in gold and ivory could anything new be seen, and in these rooms was *everything* new to be seen, for these chambers were allotted to the Duchess, and there she indulged her own taste for the fashionable, the faddish, and the fanciful. Perhaps some spark of rebellion against the mustiness of her mate, the dreary, time-worn splendor of his house, had first engendered in the Duchess this passion for all that was fresh and original. Whatever the cause, she, too, had grown obsessive with the passing years. Her gowns and her carriages, her hats, gloves, shoes, and fans, were the height of fashion— and sometimes preceded it. She redecorated her rooms on an average of twice a year. Any man with a new invention, a new philosophy, a new cure for the ills that afflict mankind; any poet, novelist, musician, or painter with a talent so progressive as to be misunderstood found in the Duchess an eager and generous patroness. Nor was she any less generous with her personal favors: her love affairs were various, passionate, and brief, and her lovers invariably many years her junior.

Like other women of fashion, she habitually slept until noon, drank chocolate with her breakfast, spent an hour in the expert hands of her hairdresser, and then—elegantly coiffeured, perfumed, and powdered, but otherwise in charming dishabille—repaired to the salon off her bedchamber, to read the letters, invitations, and calling cards that arrived daily; answer those that appealed to her; and receive early callers.

So Jarl Skogsrå found her one afternoon, sitting on a little gilt and satin sofa, sorting through a lapful of invitations with one hand, while, with the other, she absent-mindedly fed candied apricots and sugared violets to her tiny indigo ape.

"My dear Jarl," she said, impulsively rising to greet him, in a shower of scented note-paper. "I have expected you these three hours." This was not strictly true, for it was only half past two. "How wicked of you to keep me waiting."

Murmuring his apologies, he helped her gather up her correspondence, then accepted her invitation to take a seat on the sofa beside her. He looked exceedingly debonair this afternoon, in a coat of green velvet and buff smallclothes, with an emerald brooch in the lace at his throat.

"And so . . ." she said, smoothing the creamy satin folds of her dressing gown, rearranging the wide collar of blond lace which was already quite low on her shoulders, "I understand that you are to see my godchild again today. But you never told me of your last visit. In what manner did Elsie receive you?"

"She received me rather nervously, I think," said Skogsrå. "Yet she is suggestible—oh, but extremely suggestible!—and she slipped into a trance quite readily."

The Duchess put a hand on his shoulder, leaned a little closer; she was suddenly very interested, very eager. "And when she awoke?"

"She awoke feeling refreshed, expressing her surprise at finding the treatment so simple and so pleasant. Her gratitude was touching," said the Jarl, with considerable satisfaction.

"Excellent," said the Duchess, no less satisfied. "For gratitude, you know, may easily turn to love. I am convinced that she will be yours, sir—so long as you continue to go on exactly as you have begun."

The Jarl made a careless gesture, indicating that he was not so certain. "There is still the matter of the cousin who has such a strong influence over Elsie. Though I do everything in my power to ingratiate myself, Miss Sera Vorder does not like me.

"Oh, she is always so polite," said Skogsrå, "but when she looks at me . . . I think if she were a man I would feel a little threatened."

The Duchess removed her hand. "We females can be dangerous, too, and you are foolish to underestimate us. Though this one, as you have rightly guessed, is quite young and powerless—except, of course, as she is able to influence Elsie."

The Jarl smiled. "But of course. And that being so . . . I cannot help but entertain an apprehension that she may know . . . something to my disadvantage."

"Nonsense," said the Duchess, leaning back against the cushions. She took the blue ape from his perch on the back of the sofa and placed him in her lap. "How could she indeed? There is nothing for her to know, for your behavior since you came to Thornburg has been entirely respectable. As for any indiscretions you committed before . . . I do not think there is a man living who has not sown a few wild oats in his time."

Skogsrå made another wide gesture with his hands. He cleared his throat. "I do not speak of romantic entanglements. Perhaps I should have mentioned this before. When I was in Katrinsberg there were stories . . . I do not know how they began. Perhaps because people noticed certain . . . eccentricities of dress." He crossed his legs, indicated the polished leather boots which he wore on even the most formal occasions. "There were tales of deformity which, catching the public imagination—and growing more sensational as these things will—soon made my life so uncomfortable that I was obliged to leave the city much sooner than I had planned. Perhaps those stories have followed me here; perhaps Miss Sera has caught wind of them."

"Nonsense," repeated the Duchess. "If they had, I should certainly have heard of them, too." She continued, absent-mindedly, to caress the ape. "But it would not matter even if these stories of yours were the talk of Thornburg. For I can assure you that Miss Sera Vorder would be the last to credit them. She is such a practical girl, she would laugh them to scorn."

The Jarl knit his darkly penciled eyebrows thoughtfully. "Perhaps you are right. Yes, perhaps you are right."

He uncrossed his legs, leaned closer to the Duchess. "But now we come to the purpose of my visit: the medicine which I have promised to our sweet Elsie."

"But yes . . . I am glad that you remind me." The Duchess shooed her pet from her lap, rose from the sofa, and pattered across the room. She disappeared into the next chamber, reappearing a few minutes later, carrying a crystal flask about the size of her hand, encased in a delicate ormolu filigree.

"A drop or two, morning and evening, should be sufficient," she said, as she handed over the flask.

The Jarl slipped the bottle into an inside pocket of his coat. "She will not be harmed by this? I would not do anything to peril her health," he said very earnestly.

"Harm her—by the Nine Powers, no." The Duchess resumed her seat. "I want that no more than you do. If anything it will strengthen her blood. That, indeed, is the purpose for which the potion is principally used, and the other effects I mentioned are of secondary importance. You need not fear, my dear, that your bride will not be in the very best of health on the day you marry her."

The Jarl smiled thinly. "You are somewhat premature. I must first win the young woman's heart before I can aspire to her hand."

At this point, the Duchess's butler, a portly dwarf, came into the room and announced that Baron Skelbrooke was below, wishing to know if the Duchess would receive him.

"I shall be very glad to see Lord Skelbrooke," said the Duchess. "Admit him without delay."

The Jarl rose gracefully to his feet. "Then it is time for me to go. You will wish to entertain your . . . lover . . . in private."

The Duchess laughed her tinkling little laugh. "Now it is you, my dear Jarl, who are a trifle premature. Skelbrooke is not yet my lover, although I have reason to hope . . . But you must not leave so soon. It would look suspicious if you were to leave just as Skelbrooke arrives. He might imagine there was more between the two of us than there really is, and that might put an end to our little romance before it even begins."

The Jarl smiled sardonically. "That, of course, would be a great tragedy."

"It would indeed," said the Duchess. "Yes, positively, it would be a disaster . . . for someone. Take a seat, Lord Skogsrå, and attempt to make yourself look more comfortable. Besides, I have not yet told you—"

She did not finish her sentence, for just then Lord Skelbrooke entered the room, very smart in primrose-striped satin, a flowered waistcoat, and a cocked hat with a feather panache, which he promptly removed and tucked under one arm.

"My dear Francis . . . my very dear . . . how glad I am to see you," said the Duchess a little huskily, as she offered him a dainty hand to kiss. "I was just saying to Jarl Skogsrå—was I not?— that it has been an age since you called on me."

Skelbrooke kissed the palm of her hand, then the wrist, then claimed the other and repeated the process, in a manner which argued a far greater degree of intimacy between the two of them than the Duchess had admitted to the Jarl. "It was necessary for me to leave Thornburg for several days. I only returned this morning—and as you can see, I hasten to your side. But if you are determined to be cross . . . I bring a peace offering with me."

He took a slender book bound in lilac leather out of his coat pocket and presented it to her with a little flourish. "A volume of my latest poetry. No one has seen it but you, Marella. You are the very first."

"How perfectly delightful," said the Duchess, accepting the volume. Her hand trembled as their fingers touched. She opened the book and leafed through the pages, reading a line or two from each one aloud. "But this is enchanting . . . Dare I hope that *I* was the inspiration for these charming verses?"

"Regrettably no," said Skelbrooke, laying a hand on the flowered waistcoat (which was very prettily embroidered with daisies and marigolds) somewhere in the region of his heart. "It is a poem in praise of the Art of Alchemy, personified as a beautiful woman. At the time I composed these verses, I had not the privilege of your acquaintance. That will account, perhaps, for certain deficiencies which you are kind enough to overlook.

"Had *you* served as my inspiration," he continued, very low, very intimate, "I do not doubt that the poetry would have been far superior."

During this exchange, Skogsrå remained standing, with a look of growing discomfort written plain on his face. But at last he could endure no more. He cleared his throat. "I perceive that I am an intruder here. It is time for me to be on my way."

The Duchess dropped her seductive pose and shot him a fulminating glance. "Must you really?"

The Jarl inclined his head solemnly. "Alas, I must. With the Gracious Lady's permission, of course."

"Well then," said the Duchess, rising slowly to her feet. "I will see you out. You will excuse me, Francis?"

"With the greatest reluctance," said Skelbrooke. "Yet how can I deny you anything? Return as swiftly as you may, fairest of charmers, or I shall be desolate."

Outside in the corridor, the Duchess made sure to close the door behind her. "I vow you are an impatient fellow!" she said softly, linking her arm in Skogsrå's. "But I have not told you, yet, of the letter I received from Vodni."

The Jarl scowled at her. "Vodni! It was against my advice you chose to employ him. He is too fond of his own way, that one. If he troubles you now, it is no fault of mine."

"He does not trouble me in the least," said the Duchess, as they descended the long curving staircase to the ground floor. "In his capacity as Secretary to the Duke he is absolutely invaluable. Moreover, he has recently managed to uncover information which may prove to be of the greatest use . . . information so startling that . . . well, it may all come to nothing, after all. But *you* can aid me in judging the value of this information, by confirming what Vodni tells me."

The Jarl's scowl faded, to be replaced by an expression of deep interest. "I exist but to serve you," he said.

By this time, they had reached the foot of the stairs, and the Duchess rose up on tiptoe to whisper in his ear. "You may begin," she said, "by going to a certain bookshop not far from the river and asking to speak to the proprietor . . ."

Left to his own devices in the Duchess's sitting room, Francis Skelbrooke remained where he was, in the same languid pose, only so long as he heard the voices of the Duchess and Skogsrå in the corridor outside. But once their voices faded, he moved swiftly, through the connecting door and into Marella's bedchamber beyond.

He paused for a moment, just inside the door, surveying the room with an amused and appreciative eye. The Duchess's bedchamber was an intensely feminine room with a seductive look of elegant disarray which (he suspected) was more likely the result of precise calculation on her part than any carelessness on the part of her servants. The gilt and ivory bed was unmade—which was to say, that the silk comforters had been neatly turned back and the satin pillows plumped up invitingly; ruffled petticoats, lacy pantelets, and other items of intimate apparel were scattered across the floor or draped over chairs; a pair of crystal goblets and a decanter of red wine had been casually arranged on a table by the bed. Despite himself, Skelbrooke stooped to pick up a dainty embroidered glove and hold it appreciatively to his nose. Like all her possessions, Marella's glove was deliciously perfumed.

Then, conscious that he wasted valuable time, he dropped the glove and began to search the room in earnest. The dressing table was overflowing with scent bottles, pouncet boxes, and little porcelain jars containing cosmetics. A sofa by the window contained a hat, two pairs of shoes, a pair of silk stockings, and other small items. He realized the room was too large and too cluttered for him to make a thorough search before the Duchess returned. Unless . . .

He knew that he would have to risk it. He reached into his waistcoat pocket and drew out a slim metal disk attached to a short silver chain. The disk was made of lead and engraved with kabalistic symbols—it was a talisman consecrated to the Planetary Intelligence known as Sadrun, the keeper of secrets, the finder of hidden things. Holding the talisman before him like a pendulum, Skelbrooke moved slowly and methodically around the room.

At the north end of the bedchamber, the pendulum started to swing wildly. Skelbrooke took two more tentative steps, and the talisman reacted even more strongly, describing a larger arc with every swing it made. Two more steps and he was facing the wall. He gathered the disk and the chain up into his hand, spoke a word to deactivate the pendulum, slipped it back into his pocket, and began to examine the wall.

Painted in pastel shades and decorated with scrollwork and cherubs done in stucco, the north wall of Marella's bedchamber was the perfect location for a secret panel or hidden cubbyhole. Skelbrooke smiled a trifle ruefully. He did not anticipate anything along that line here—he could expect something more ingenious or original from the Duchess.

He transferred his attention to a decorative table done in ebony and gold that stood against the wall. An assortment of trinkets, fans, note-cards, and the like was scattered across the table—and one other object, in stark contrast to the rest of that frivolous room: an old prayerbook bound in pale ivory leather.

Skelbrooke stared down at the elderly volume. That Marella attended church every Sunday he knew—it was, after all, the fashionable thing to do—but that the Duchess kept a prayerbook in her bedchamber lest a sudden pious urge seize her and an overwhelming desire to say her prayers arise in the middle of the night—this possibility Skelbrooke did not seriously contemplate.

But perhaps . . . perhaps it was no common prayerbook. Knowing what he knew of the Duchess, it occurred to him that the rites this volume contained might be of a darker, more occult nature. He picked up the book and began to leaf through it.

A cursory examination convinced him that the volume was exactly what it appeared to be: a standard book of devotions such as any respectable woman in Thornburg might be expected to carry to church. He was about to close the book and put it down when he noticed that one of the pages, a leaf near the back, was thicker than the rest. With growing excitement, he carried the prayerbook over to a window and held the page up to the light. It was not one piece of paper but two, glued together along three sides, with the fourth side secured by the binding, and what might be a third piece of paper or parchment inserted in the pocket between the pages.

Aware that the Duchess might return at any moment, he removed a stickpin from his lacy neckcloth. The pin had an ornate golden head, but the body was made of hard steel, in the form of a miniature stiletto, honed to a razor sharpness. He used it to make a slit in the pocket. He slid his fingers between the two pages and extracted a frail piece of parchment, which he slipped, unread, down the front of his flowered waistcoat. Then he moved swiftly across the room and carefully placed the prayerbook, exactly as he had found it, on the little ebony and gold table.

By the time the Duchess returned to her sitting room, Skelbrooke was there before her, standing by a window, staring pensively down at the garden below.

He adjusted the golden stickpin in his exquisitely arranged neckcloth. "I am afraid I arrived at an inopportune moment. Indeed, I feel the awkwardness quite keenly and can only hope that you will accept my heartfelt—" he began, only to have his apology suppressed by a small white hand placed over his mouth.

"It is Skogsrå who is awkward. I am so glad you arrived when you did," said the Duchess. "In truth, I find him rather disagreeable, and only tolerate him for the sake of the good he may do my poor Elsie. But do not play the fop with me, Francis. It is amusing in company, I own, but in private I prefer you more natural . . . more earnest. That is your true nature, is it not? That quiet intensity I have seen from time to time . . .''

"You are very perceptive," said Skelbrooke. "You have found me out. And yet, we are not really so very well acquainted."

Taking him by the hand, she drew him over to her couch. "Then it is time we improved our acquaintance . . . past time," she said, in the same husky voice she had used before. "Tell me something about yourself . . . where you were born . . . how old you are."

Though uncomfortably aware of the stolen parchment he wore inside his waistcoat behind the daisies and the marigolds, Skelbrooke forced himself to relax. "I was born on my grandfather's estate near Lundy, some four and twenty years ago."

The Duchess raised an eyebrow. "So young as that? No, I do not really doubt your word. It is . . . difficult for people to lie to me about their ages. You certainly have the appearance of a young man, a boy even, but there is something in your eyes, a look that usually comes with age . . ."

"It is dissipation, Gracious Lady, that has made me old beyond my years," he said, with such a mournful air that the Duchess could not help laughing at him.

"But now you *are* attempting to deceive me. Everyone in Thornburg knows you to be the most temperate of men!"

Skelbrooke shrugged his shoulders. "As to that . . . I am addicted to certain vices which I do not elect to practice in the presence of . . . ladies. Hence, my frequent absences from the town."

The Duchess began to look just the tiniest bit bored. "I suppose you mean cock-fighting and other tedious masculine pastimes. We will not speak of them, if you please."

"I do not mean cock-fighting . . . or other tedious masculine pastimes," replied Skelbrooke. "That is: I must confess to an insatiable appetite for bloodshed, but the torture of brute beasts has never amused me."

"Ah," said the Duchess, her interest reviving. "You fight duels, do you? Have you killed many men?"

"I have killed scores of them," said Skelbrooke. "And there used to be a practice, among wild young men of good family, to ride the Imbrian countryside in the guise of highwaymen, and rob carriages and mail coaches . . . merely for the thrill of the thing."

The Duchess was smiling now, a warm intimate smile. He was not certain whether she believed him or not, but at least he was keeping her amused.

"Heavens above!" said the Duchess. "I believe that I have fallen into the hands of a rascal. And tell me this . . . among your other vices, have you perhaps experimented with . . . the more intricate forms of sexual dalliance?"

Skelbrooke shook his head. "You see, I am not yet five and twenty," he said apologetically. "I thought it wise to save something for later in life, lest I grow too soon bored."

"Now, that is certainly shocking," said the Duchess. She moved closer, so that she was leaning on his shoulder. "For myself, I consider such naïveté unpardonable in a young man of four and twenty. Fortunately, it is a failing we can easily remedy."

The lacy neckline of her dressing gown had slipped very low, revealing a lovely pair of shoulders and a seductive display of soft white bosom. Her lips were slightly parted, her breathing was irregular, and her perfume, as Skelbrooke bent his head to kiss her, was sweet and intoxicating. Her mouth, as he had expected, was warm and inviting.

She was utterly appealing, he thought . . . entirely desirable.

How unfortunate that he would not be able to accept her invitation . . .

14.

Containing sundry Curious matters.

Motherwell prison was a grim and lowering pile built on an island in the middle of the river Lunn, about two miles above Thornburg. It was a cold, hard, barren island, with only a narrow stretch of pebbly shore. At high tide, the beach disappeared altogether, and the water came almost up to the rusty prison gate.

So it was on Midyear's Day, when the tide was at its highest, that an elegant black barge landed on the shingle below the gate and let off two passengers: a very young gentleman in a wine-colored coat, and a lady, perhaps ten years his senior, exceedingly smart in oyster satin and a wide leghorn hat. With great diffidence, they approached the warder at the gate.

"We wish to speak with the governor," said the youth, and a small coin passed between the iron bars.

The warder grinned at them, revealing crooked black teeth. "What names?"

The lady made an agitated motion with her hands. "Is it absolutely necessary for us to tell you our names?"

" 'Tis, if you wants to speak with the governor," replied the warder, pocketing the coin. "He's a busy man, the governor, and he don't see just everybody."

The two visitors held a whispered conference. "Why not, after all?" said the young man. "You've made no secret of your intentions . . . everyone in town is already talking. You said so yourself: the only way to proceed is to conduct the entire affair openly and treat the necessity as if it were naught but a grim jest."

"Yes, yes," replied the lady impatiently. "But it is one thing to hear one's name bandied about by one's own acquaintances . . . quite another to hear it spoken in a place like this. Oh, very well. Do as you think best. The whole situation is so degrading, how could it possibly be any worse?"

They returned to the gate and peered through the iron grillwork. "Lord Vizbeck and his cousin, Lady Ursula Bowker," said the young man.

"Honored, I'm sure," said the warder, and sketched a mocking little bow as he unlocked the gate and ushered them in.

"Are you honestly determined to do this thing?" Lord Vizbeck whispered to his cousin, as the guard led them down a dank and shadowy corridor.

"I am," replied Lady Ursula. "What other choice do I have?"

The youth gave her hand an affectionate squeeze. "You might, for instance, think of marrying me."

"Impossible," said Lady Ursula. "Nor would you offer, if you had any idea of the extent of my debts. They would swallow up your entire fortune whole. Besides . . . your mama has a very good idea of my wretched circumstances, and though she has been kind to me through all my troubles, she would never consent to our marriage."

"I come of age," said Lord Vizbeck, "at the turn of the year, and then there would be no need for my mama's consent."

"Thank you," said Lady Ursula, "but I do not wish to spend the interim languishing in a debtor's prison."

The governor received them in a high, cold room, overlooking the prison yard. He was a meagre little man with parchment-colored skin, a crooked wig, and an enormous hooked nose. He offered Lady Ursula a chair and sent the warder for another to accommodate Lord Vizbeck.

"And how may I be of service to your ladyship?" he asked, resuming his own seat behind a large, cluttered desk.

Lord Vizbeck answered for her. "The lady finds herself in financial difficulties . . . I will not bore you with the details. It is enough to tell you that her creditors are growing impatient, and a writ may be issued against her at any time. Therefore, she requires a husband to assume her debts."

The governor tipped back his chair, made a steeple of his hands. "I see," he said. "Something in the felonious line, I take it—a murderer or a highwayman, on his way to an appointment with the hangman? Yes, indeed, I think I can provide just what you want. A fine young fellow with the manners of a gentleman—the sort to behave himself and not put your ladyship to any embarrassment at the wedding ceremony. He'll be executed . . . let me see . . . next Friday afternoon at one o'clock."

He tilted his chair forward, rested his elbows on the desk. "Yes, I believe that something can be arranged, but I feel obliged to warn you that even in Motherwell husbands do not come cheap. This man I am thinking of, for instance, he's a hardened rogue for all his engaging ways, and he won't consent to marry you and cheat your creditors merely for the love of your pretty blue eyes— oh, no!"

Lord Vizbeck stiffened. "Here now, my good man, there is no need to be impertinent. If you haven't the decency—"

Lady Ursula silenced him with a motion of her hand. "Let us not waste the governor's time—or our own. Perhaps, sir, you will be good enough to tell me what is the . . . the usual recompense."

The governor knit his fingers together. "A bottle of wine the night before and a whore to warm his bed. And the next day . . . a coin for the hangman, to make sure the execution is swift and painless, and your word in writing that he'll be buried decently, and not turned over to the College of Chirurgeons for their fiendish experiments." Lady Ursula shuddered visibly. "My own compensation—for allowing the thing to go forth at all, for the arrangements that have to be made—is not inconsiderable." And he named a price so high that the lady gasped in dismay.

"I think you must be aware," Lady Ursula said, in a stifled voice, "that unless you are willing to be more moderate in your demands, we won't be able to do business at all. Indeed, were

100

my circumstances not so fearfully reduced, I would not be forced to take this step in order to circumvent my creditors."

"That goes without saying," replied the governor coolly. "Yet I doubt, my lady, that you are entirely friendless. Borrow the money, if you must, for I do assure you: the thing cannot possibly be done for less."

Lady Ursula laughed bitterly. "Borrow the money . . . when it is by living beyond my means that I came to this pass! There isn't a goldsmith or a moneylender in Thornburg who would—"

Lord Vizbeck leaned down and spoke softly in her ear. "By the Nine Powers, Ursula, there can be no question of going to the dwarves. If you will not allow me to marry you myself, at least permit me to defray your . . . wedding expenses."

"I will not," hissed the lady. "Do consider my feelings. Having refused your own too generous offer, how, in all conscience, can I possibly allow you to—to buy a husband for me?"

The governor continued to rock his chair back and forth. "I should perhaps add that there has been considerable outcry against these prison weddings, against the well-born and the titled using this expedient to cheat honest tradesmen of their due. Any day now, the Prince may issue a proclamation forbidding these marriages. Then where will you be, my lady?"

"The same place that I shall be if I do not satisfy my creditors by the end of next week," said the lady. "Imprisoned for debt. . . . oh, it would be unendurable. Very well, your price is extortionate, but I suppose there must be something . . . some old silver or china that I can sell. Make the arrangements, and expect to see me on Friday week . . . my wedding day."

The lady left the prison on her cousin's arm. His lordship's mama, the dowager Lady Vizbeck, awaited them on the barge.

"And are you engaged to be married, my dear?" the older woman asked.

"I believe that I shall be, before the day is out." Lady Ursula collapsed on a velvet-cushioned bench and took out her fan. "The governor will arrange the wedding ceremony . . . he will attend to all the details. All that remains for me is to decide where the reception will be held."

"You have had a great many offers, I believe?" said Lady Vizbeck, patting her hand affectionately. "But of course . . . such a novelty as it will be, your wedding feast. Half the ladies in Thornburg would be honored to host the reception and claim credit for the sensation it will cause. Whom will you choose, do you think?''

Lady Ursula gave a weary little sigh. ''I believe that I will choose the Duchess. Who else, indeed, could do the thing as it ought to be done?''

Though Lady Ursula's upcoming wedding was the talk of the town, the Thornburg magistracy would not be hurried; they issued no writ against the lady, and the wedding went off as planned. On Friday morning, the bride, pale but composed, arrived at the prison, was introduced to her bridegroom, and was married. At one, the groom mounted the scaffold, kissed his hand to the Fates, and was hung. By sunset, carriages and sedan chairs began to arrive at the crumbling Zar-Wildungen mansion, where the bride, in a gown of figured white satin, a gauzy floor-length veil, and the Duchess's diamonds, greeted her wedding guests at the door.

The Vorders were among the earliest guests to arrive. ''So poignant,'' said Clothilde Vorder, as she, Elsie, and Sera climbed the marble steps to the door. ''So heart-rending, really, to think of the poor dear receiving her guests—and she so recently widowed!''

''She was scarcely even *acquainted* with the man,'' said Sera. ''Any emotion that the bride may display on this particular occasion can be nothing but—but the most blatant form of play-acting!''

''But of course,'' replied Mistress Vorder. ''That hardly detracts from the sentiments one must feel on viewing the young widow. I, myself, am prodigiously fond of the theatre. And I would not be as insensitive as you,'' she added severely, ''not for all the world.''

They passed through the receiving line, and down a wide, torch-lit corridor lined with faded tapestries. In the cavernous dining hall, the table was set with elegant gilt-edged china and crystal goblets, but the very finest setting (all gleaming with gold and jewels) had been placed at the head of the table in honor of the groom, who was expected to attend the reception in spirit. To this end, someone had placed a wax effigy in the bridegroom's chair and tastefully arranged a hempen noose around its neck.

Francis Skelbrooke strolled into the room, very prettily attired in white and gold, all but the black satin bow which held back his powdered curls. He carried a short malacca cane with a quizzing glass mounted on the knob at one end. He seemed especially struck by the arrangement of the table and spent several minutes minutely examining the groom's setting through his quizzing glass.

"And what—if one is permitted to inquire—is your impression of all this, Miss Vorder?" he asked.

"It seems," said Sera, in no mood to mince words this evening, "that people will do anything for a sensation these days. I think that Society has gone quite mad."

If she hoped to ruffle his composure, she did not succeed. "I have always admired your keen perceptions," said Skelbrooke, and ambled off, presumably in search of the Duchess.

When the feast was over, and the last toasts had been made—to the beauty of the bride and her improved prospects for the future— it came time for the wedding guests to see the bride and her groom upstairs to their bedchamber. Two brawny serving men lifted the chair and carried the wax effigy out of the room, the bride and her guests snatching up candlesticks and falling into place in a procession behind the chair.

Sera walked alone, without a gentleman's arm to lean on— which she accounted a blessing, for it allowed her to lag behind the others and spared her much of the conversation and unseemly jesting. Up the long curving marble staircase to the top floor of the mansion, the procession climbed, the flames of their candles like tiny sparks of light in the vast, gloomy halls. They walked through a series of rooms connected by archways, and along an echoing corridor, where the dust lay thick on the floor and cobwebs hung like tattered lace curtains from the groined ceiling. Then there was a sudden blaze of light and warmth, as someone threw open the door to the bridal chamber.

I will not go inside, Sera thought. *The whole situation is so patently obscene!* With which resolve, she turned around and headed back down the corridor. But in the rooms beyond, a draught of cold air put out her candle, and she lost her way in the dark. When she finally came out into a torch-lit corridor, she was in a totally unfamiliar wing of the mansion.

Certain that one of the doors on either side of the corridor must open on a set of stairs, Sera tried several, only to discover that each of them was locked. Then she decided to relight her candle on one of the torches and try to find her way back in the direction she had come. But through *which* door had she entered the corridor? All of them looked exactly alike.

Growing frustrated, she began turning the knobs again, searching for the unlocked door. *Perhaps I have grown disoriented . . . perhaps I should try the doors on the other side of the corridor.* A knob turned in her hand, and Sera eagerly pushed the door open.

She paused on the threshold, certain this was a room she had never seen before. It was a lofty chamber, about the size of the dining hall down below, awash in moonlight which entered the room through a kind of domed skylight in the ceiling. The vast chamber resembled nothing so much as a museum, for the variety of curious objects that were displayed in glass cabinets or mounted on marble pedestals.

I ought not to be here, Sera told herself. But the thought which immediately followed was: *the door was unlocked.* Curiosity overcame propriety, and she stepped over the threshold, closing the door softly behind her.

This room showed signs of frequent use, or at least of a recent dusting. Yet there was something heavy and stifling about the atmosphere, as though it were laden with some subtle incense which added *weight* to the air rather than fragrance.

Lifting her candle high, Sera wandered through the room, gazing at one thing and then another: a bowl of crystal fruits . . . a jeweled dagger with a blade like a crescent moon . . . a wreath of silk flowers which (or so Sera fancied) might be the source of the strange, odorless perfume.

On one wall, she discovered a gallery of oil paintings . . . portraits of men and women of some bygone age, all of them depicted with such mournful or tragic expressions that it seemed as though the artist must have caught each one in the midst of some terrible catastrophe or the grip of some lingering grief. And a display of antique costumes hung on pegs all along another wall: gauzy gowns in soft bright colors, fanciful hats loaded with jewels and plumes, and elaborately curled wigs that seemed too heavy for the heads that once carried them. There was a grey cape covered with silver spangles and lined with swansdown, and a stiff lace ruff edged with pearls, which somehow put Sera in mind of Mistress Sancreedi. But the size of these tiny, delicately made garments astonished Sera. *These are children's costumes . . . but who would dress their children so elaborately?*

There were also a number of masks, arranged on the wall around a long mirror in a gilt frame. Some of these masks were beautiful, but many of them had an ugly or an evil aspect. On an impulse,

Sera took down one of the more hideous masks and held it before her face.

When she turned to examine her reflection in the mirror, she experienced a painful jolt of surprise. The mask had transformed not only her face but everything about her. She was gazing at the image of a tiny hunchback with a twisted lip, in a tattered black gown. A soft noise behind her startled Sera so badly that she dropped the mask and whirled around, just in time to see Lord Skelbrooke enter the room by a door near the back.

Apparently as startled as she was, he stopped with his hand still on the knob, and such a scowl on his face as Sera had never seen there before.

Then the frown disappeared, and Lord Skelbrooke regained his easy composure. He closed the door behind him and made a deep bow. "There you are, Miss Vorder. I did not mean to startle you, but your cousin sent me to find you."

Sera put a hand to her heart. "Elsie . . . Elsie has sent for me?" she asked, in a strangled voice. "Has she taken ill, Lord Skelbrooke?"

"I beg your pardon," said Skelbrooke, crossing the room. "Neither did I mean to alarm you. I should have been more specific. It was not Miss Elsie who sent me to look for you, but her mother."

Sera flushed a hot shade of crimson. It was bad enough that she should encounter Lord Skelbrooke in this place where she had no business to be . . . how much more vexing that Cousin Clothilde had actually sent him in search of her, as though she were a naughty child.

Skelbrooke bent down and picked up the mask, spent a long moment examining it through his quizzing glass. Then, with a tiny, enigmatic smile, he lifted the mask to his face and examined his image in the mirror.

Sera could not stifle another gasp of surprise. Before her eyes, Skelbrooke became shorter, he grew taller, he went through a whole series of amazing transformations: man, woman, dwarf, gnome, child, adult, monster, brute . . . all in a matter of seconds. And then, just as suddenly, he was himself again, a neat little man elegantly clad in white and gold, staring back at her through the eye-holes of the ugly mask.

"It is all in knowing how to work these things," he said calmly, as he hung the mask back on the wall. But Sera felt a surge of outrage, as though he had somehow made her the victim of a vulgar jest.

When he offered her his arm, she shook her head and walked out through the door by which she had first entered the room. But she did pause and wait for him, while he took a tiny silver key out of his waistcoat pocket and slipped it into the lock.

"I should tell you, Miss Vorder, that the things in that room and the one beyond it are very old and valuable. Neither the Duke nor the Duchess wishes to expose them to public view. I cannot think how the door came to be unlocked."

"But you did not enter by this door," Sera pointed out, a trifle pettishly. "Was—was the other chamber you spoke of unlocked as well? That seems very careless."

"The door by which I entered *was* locked—but to that one also I have the key," said Skelbrooke. "And no," he said, as he pocketed the key, "I need not go back and lock it again, for I have already done so."

The purer air in the corridor did much to restore Sera's mental equilibrium. She realized that she could not easily find her way back to the dining hall unless she accepted his lordship's offer to escort her. Yet she still felt angry and obscurely insulted and would not take his arm, insisting on making the journey unsupported.

"You do not seem to appreciate the seriousness of your own situation," said Skelbrooke reprovingly, as she followed him down the corridor. "Indeed, if Marella knew that you had been in that chamber, she might be very angry. If you wish to avoid an uncomfortable scene, you will not mention to anyone that you -were in the museum, or that you and I met anywhere in the vicinity."

Sera had heard rumors before this that Francis Skelbrooke and the Duchess were lovers. That he actually had access to chambers in the ducal mansion where nobody else was allowed to go—that he even carried the keys about with him—only served to confirm those rumors. *Though I am sure I don't know why I should care, when the Duke himself always countenances these affairs of hers. How splendid it must be to be a Duchess and able to flout convention!*

Nevertheless, Sera was deeply uncomfortable contemplating Skelbrooke's intimacy with the Duchess—was it that which made her feel so keenly resentful (she wondered) or merely his mountebank's trick with the mask?

Whatever the reason, she was mightily vexed, so disturbed that

106

hours would pass before she began to wonder why on Earth Lord Skelbrooke should have gone looking for her in a suite of rooms which he had every reason to suppose would be locked and inaccessible.

15.

In which the Reader makes the Acquaintance of two new characters.

It was the afternoon of the last day of the season of Flowers. At Master Ule's bottle factory, Polydore Figg and his three young clerks were all bent over their desks, hard at work.

Tomorrow was the Festival of the Harvest and an intercalary day, when all the shops and businesses in Thornburg closed their doors and the Guildsmen paraded through the streets in their splendid ceremonial robes flaunting medals and orders with mysterious-sounding names like "The Order of the Western Horizon" and "Master of the Temple of the Star." Plays, processions, feasts, balls, and other entertainments would be the order of the day. Moreover, the moon had been shrinking for four days now, and the combination of a holiday on the morrow and a so-called safe night meant that festivities would begin before dusk this evening and outdoor revelry would continue well past midnight.

In the glasshouse, Master Ule and his men abandoned their trade for the day, to prepare for the official events of the morrow. They were building a great wicker effigy in one of the storerooms and adorning it with gaily colored ribbons and dried flowers. They intended to carry it down to the river and tip it into the water, shortly after daybreak.

But in the counting-house, work continued on as usual— perhaps a little more industriously than usual—for to the scribes and clerks of the town, the advent of a new triad of seasons meant more than an opportunity for celebration. As on the last day of any season, there were accounts to be rendered, bills to be paid, wages to be calculated—more than enough to keep Polydore and the other two dwarves in a fever of activity all morning long and well into the afternoon. Meanwhile, Jedidiah sat at a makeshift desk in a corner of the room, attending to the more usual correspondence of the firm.

Copying letters was careful, painstaking work. If Jed made a mistake, he had to take a clean sheet of paper and begin all over again, because blots and smears reflected unfavorably on his employer. But it was a sight more interesting than doing ledgers, which were all just names and figures, and Jed felt proud that Polydore had entrusted him with such a meticulous task.

To Messers Willibald, Wibblingen, and Wolfenbüttel, Jed wrote, in the firm, clear, old-fashioned hand that Jenk the bookseller had taken such pains to teach him, the knack of which Jed was slowly regaining (along with the grammar old Jenk had dinned into him). *In answer to your letter of the twenty-first . . .*

There was a great deal more, all very formal and correct—for all that Willibald, Wibblingen, and Wolfenbüttel were half a year behind in paying for a consignment of black bottles—right down to the punctilious: *Yours respectfully, I remain &c.*, which Jed finished off with a dramatic flourish and took to Polydore Figg to be signed.

Polydore and the other clerks were already clearing their desks. But Polydore stopped long enough to sign his name, sand the letter to set the ink, and hand it back to Jed. "Don't trouble the boy—you can deliver this yourself, on your way to dinner."

"Sir?" said Jed, on the impression he had missed something.

Figg readjusted the spectacles on the end of his nose. In most ways, he was a younger, rounder version of Master Ule, but he was somewhat short-sighted and he lacked the older dwarf's penetrating gaze. "You were not told? You are to dine with my uncle at two. It is half past one now, so you may as well tidy your desk and fetch your hat."

Jed went back to his desk and slipped the letter into an envelope. Then he closed his inkpot, cleaned his pen, rearranged the papers on his desk, and put on his shiny new tricorn. By that time, Polydore and the other clerks had departed, leaving the street door unlocked behind them. Jed picked up the key. He was half way across the room when the door opened and an elderly dwarf, a tall young man dressed in black like a doctor or a clergyman, and a dandified gentleman in grey velvet walked into the counting-house.

"Beg your pardon, we're closed for the day," said Jed.

"We are here to see Master Ule on a personal matter, and we

are expected," said the dwarf, with an amiable nod of his head. He wore a purple coat and a full-bottomed wig—suitable to a dwarf of his years and dignity—and he carried a hat with a round brim under one arm. "Perhaps you would be good enough to fetch him?"

"Yes, sir," said Jed. "What name shall I say?"

"Mr. Christopher Owlfeather, Mr. Hermes Budge, and a gentleman they wish to present," replied the dwarf, with another half bow. "And you, if I am not mistaken, will be Jedidiah Braun."

"Yes, sir," Jed answered, wondering why this distinguished dwarf should know his name.

He went off in search of Master Ule and found him in the other storeroom putting a few last-minute touches on the wicker man. "Mr. Owlfeather and Mr. Budge is here, sir."

"Very good," said Master Ule, removing his leather apron and reaching for his coat and hat.

The walk to Master Ule's took longer than any of them had anticipated, for the streets were already crowded with early revelers: morris dancers in flower-bedecked hats and strings of chiming bells, gnomes with their horns and their claws painted gold for the holiday, dwarf children and human children in masks and fancy dress—all jostling about with the usual peddlers and street vendors.

The bird girls were selling cabbages now, cabbages and braided onions, and crickets in little straw houses. And the foreigners hawked sweetmeats and silver horns. On some streets it became impossible to move at all; the crowd formed so effective a barrier that Master Ule and his party had to take a circuitous route. This gave Jed ample time to become acquainted with Master Ule's friends. He was a bit dazzled to find himself in such distinguished company.

Christopher Owlfeather was a prosperous and highly respected merchant—an honest businessman as well as a shrewd one—and he was related to all the better dwarf families. Mr. Hermes Budge was the tall man—not a doctor or a clergyman as he appeared, but tutor to the Owlfeather children. And the dandy in mouse-colored velvet and exquisite point lace was Francis Love Skelbrooke.

". . . Lord Skelbrooke, I should say," Mr. Budge amended himself in presenting his friend to Jed and Master Ule. "Skelbrooke and I attended the University of Lundy together, but he

109

was not so exalted in those days, and I have some difficulty remembering his present consequence." A humorous glance passed between his lordship and the tutor.

"If my consequence was less, yet I was a better man in those days," Skelbrooke replied cheerfully. "For I had then, as I recall, an idea that I might yet be of some real use in the world. Whereas now, I am as you see me: a mere ornament to Society.

"But I am very much obliged to meet you, Mr. Braun—and you, too, Master Ule," he added, with a bow. "For you look to be an honest fellow, Mr. Braun, and you have, moreover, the air of a man of great practical utility."

"I hope that Master Ule finds me so," Jed replied, bowing in return. "But I believe I know you from somewheres, my lord, though it don't—*doesn't* seem likely we've met."

"I think not," said Lord Skelbrooke. "For I have an excellent memory for faces and I am certain that I have never seen yours."

Finding the way blocked on one street, they turned down another. Master Ule fell into step beside Lord Skelbrooke. "I believe, sir, that you are a member of our lodge."

His lordship inclined his head. "I have that honor."

"Lord Skelbrooke is too modest to acknowledge his services to our Brotherhood," said Mr. Owlfeather. "It was he who brought a certain document to my attention, a document which caused no little excitement when I presented it to the Council. If I were to tell you how—and from whom—Lord Skelbrooke obtained it, I believe you would be favorably impressed by his enterprise and daring."

"You do me too much honor," said Skelbrooke, with a suggestion of a smile. "The circumstances surrounding my acquisition of the document were not so much *dangerous* as they were awkward. In short . . . I was forced to disappoint a lady."

Mr. Owlfeather laughed heartily. "A noble sacrifice on your part, I do not doubt. Let us hope it is one you are not forced to make again."

"I hope not indeed," said Skelbrooke. "For I have formed a strong impression that the Gracious Lady in question might prove to be a formidable enemy. Particularly if she imagined that I was more interested in her . . . epistolary talents . . . than in her considerable personal attractions."

Mr. Budge nodded solemnly. "I have heard a rumor of fairy blood . . . a connection with the Fees. I would tread carefully, in your place, Francis, and not give any offense if I could help it.

110

They say that the Fees are constitutionally *incapable* of forgiving an insult, and their revenge can be terrible.''

Jed had ceased to pay close attention to the conversation. "The Duchess of Zar-Wildungen," he interjected suddenly, and wondered what he had done to cause such a sensation. Skelbrooke gave a visible start and the others all turned to stare at Jed as if he had uttered something particularly disconcerting. He hoped he had not mortally offended someone by an innocent slip of the tongue.

"Someone said something as put me in mind of the Duchess, and I finally remembered where it was I seen Lord Skelbrooke before," he made haste to explain. "I seen—I saw him on Sunday after church . . . maybe two or three times . . . walking in Solingen Park with the Duchess of Zar-Wildungen and the Misses Elsie and Sera Vorder.''

The others accepted this explanation, though Skelbrooke, who had been pale a moment before, now turned faintly pink. "You are acquainted, Mr. Braun, with the Misses Vorder?''

"Yes, sir," said Jed. "That is, not well acquainted with Miss Elsie, but I grew up with Sera in a manner of speaking, and she don't—doesn't forget old friends.''

"Indeed, you do not surprise me," said his lordship. "For my judgement of Miss Sera Vorder is that she is a lady likely to prove steadfast in her affections. But speaking for yourself, Mr. Braun . . . does Miss Vorder inspire a similar loyalty on your part?''

"I guess so!" replied Jed. "As dear to me as my own sisters, meaning no disrespect to a lady of her position. There isn't much I wouldn't do for Sera, my lord, supposing she was inclined to ask.''

"Why then," said Lord Skelbrooke, "I am more obliged than ever, and I think, Mr. Braun, that you and I would both do well to further our acquaintance.''

16.

Wherein the Duchess learns Something to her Advantage.

At that very moment, Sera was climbing the steps to the Vorder residence, after a morning call on her grandfather. A footman in blue and gold livery admitted her into the lower hall, where she removed her hat and her gloves and inquired whether the other ladies of the household were planning to dine at home.

"They was dressed to go out at noon, but Miss Elsie, she took another bad turn, and they decided to stay in."

Sera felt a clutch of fear at her heart. "Elsie suffered another attack? But how is she now? Where can I find her?"

A light, aristocratic voice answered her: "She is nearly recovered and she is resting in her mother's sitting room," and Sera looked up to see the Duchess of Zar-Wildungen standing at the top of the long oak staircase to the second floor.

"I ought to have been with her—oh, I wish that I had been!" Sera dropped her hat and gloves on an octagonal table by the door and started up the steps.

"There was nothing you might have done either to prevent or to alleviate poor Elsie's fit," the Duchess replied soothingly. "Fortunately, Clothilde had the good sense to send for Jarl Skogsrå immediately. Elsie began to improve as soon as he arrived."

"I ought to have been here," Sera repeated, as she followed the Duchess into Mistress Vorder's sitting room.

There they found Elsie, still looking pale and shaken, half reclining on a rose-colored sofa, with her hand clasped tightly in the hand of Jarl Skogsrå, who sat on a little gilded stool drawn up at her feet. Cousin Clothilde sat in a chair by a window overlooking the street, fortifying herself with sherry and sugar cakes. From the level of the wine in the decanter, it appeared she had been strengthening herself in the same manner for quite some time . . . or else the Vorders had entertained morning callers.

"You have nothing to fear," Skogsrå said in honeyed tones,

112

just as Sera entered. "Never anything to fear, my heart's dearest, so long as I am with you."

Sera scowled at the Jarl. "I thought you had been called in to treat Elsie's disorder—not to trouble her with sentimental nonsense." She bent to kiss Elsie on the forehead.

"But he has treated my disorder," said Elsie. "Oh, Sera, I was absolutely terrified, I thought I should *die* of terror! But as soon as Haakon—that is . . . the Jarl—came to me and spoke a few words, I knew just how foolish I had been and that I had nothing to fear. Now or ever," she finished, with a tender glance at Skogsrå.

"And we are very grateful, my dear sir," put in Elsie's mother. "It was exceedingly kind in you to abandon your own amusements—on the eve of the holiday, too!—and come here to tend my poor ailing child."

Sera sat down at the foot of the sofa, took Elsie's other hand, and stroked it comfortingly. "These attacks of panic . . . they are a new symptom," she told Skogsrå. "Elsie was not prone to these unreasoning fits of terror before you began dosing and magnetizing her. I suspect it is something in the medicine you give her, or an unexpected effect of the magnetic treatments."

"My dear Miss Vorder," said the Duchess, "I fear that the blame is entirely mine—though indeed, I meant all for the best. Elsie's visits to Dr. Mirabolo were so upsetting to her, I believe that her nerves were seriously weakened, and these attacks are the unfortunate result."

"Nonsense," said Skogsrå, with a smile that was more a baring of his teeth. "You must not blame yourself, Gracious Lady. The explanation is simple: our poor Elsie's body is undergoing a—how should I say it?—a kind of revolution, as the disease is conquered and expelled through the pores of her skin. At the present time, her blood is full of poisons which bring on the visions and the palpitations—a temporary effect and easily treated, as we have seen. And not too high a price to pay (I think you must agree) for the total restoration of this poor child's health."

"It is true," said Elsie. "Except for these attacks, I am so much improved I can scarcely believe it. Come, Sera, you know it is so. I am never dizzy now, my appetite has improved, the numbness and the tingling in my hands and my feet no longer plague me . . ."

"None of which were symptoms of the original disease—whatever that may have been—but effects of the medicine you were taking before. I was and am convinced of that—and no, Cousin

113

Clothilde, I will not be silenced." Sera continued on bravely despite Mistress Vorder's intimidating glare. "What we have now is merely a case of a new medicine and a new set of symptoms, and where is the benefit in that?"

"Always so skeptical," said the Jarl, with another toothy smile. "Always so much wiser than any of the rest of us . . . so unwilling to entertain any opinions but her own!"

"My dear Jarl . . . my dear Miss Vorder—you must not quarrel," said the Duchess, with a warning glance at Skogsrå and a melting smile for Sera. "As you are both motivated by nothing less than a deep concern for Elsie's welfare, surely you can cry peace between you, and each continue to do for Elsie what he or she thinks best."

"That scarcely seems possible . . . so opposed as we are in our viewpoints," said the Jarl, continuing to smile that same fixed smile.

Sera said nothing, only sat there clasping Elsie's damp little hand in both of hers, scowling at Skogsrå more fiercely than before. The Duchess released an exasperated sigh.

"I wonder, Miss Vorder, if you would care for a stroll through the gardens below. The weather is delightful. I have something particular I should like to discuss with you, and I doubt I would ever find the courage to say a single word, while you and the Jarl continue to gaze at one another so ferociously."

"Yes, do go with her, Sera," Elsie urged sweetly. "I don't need you now. And you look so . . . overheated . . . I believe that a walk in the garden would do you good."

"My dear Miss Vorder," began the Duchess, when the two of them had donned their hats and descended to the garden. "I know that you want only what is best for Elsie—as indeed, we all do—but have you considered: these arguments over her course of treatment can only do dear Elsie harm."

But Sera was not ready to retract her hasty words. "I *have* thought, and I *do* think—and indeed, I try very hard to avoid any appearance of a quarrel when Elsie is present. If you only knew how often I have longed to speak, how many, many times, and yet kept silent for Elsie's sake! Yet when I balance the harm I may do by speaking out against that I may countenance by remaining silent . . . I take leave to tell you, Gracious Lady, that I do not know where Elsie's best interest truly lies."

The Duchess stopped by a rose bush and bent to inhale the

114

perfume of a pale blossom with a golden heart. She looked very small, very frail this afternoon, her gown of pale blue satin enhancing her porcelain fairness, the fragility of her hands and wrists. It amazed Sera that a woman so delicate in appearance as the Duchess should always enjoy such excellent health.

"It is difficult for any of us to be certain what is best," said the Duchess, "so long as Elsie's symptoms continue to be so varied and mysterious. But we are quite alone now, Miss Vorder, and I beg you to be frank. I have some influence over Clothilde Vorder, as you must be aware, and if you will tell me all that concerns you—who knows?—you may find in me an ally where you least expect one."

Sera experienced a sharp pang of guilt. While she always thought of this woman as chief among Elsie's tormenters, she was also convinced that the Duchess (unlike Cousin Clothilde) was motivated neither by vanity nor self-interest, but by a sincere— if somewhat misguided—desire to do good in the world. Yet so accustomed was she to the stubborn opposition of Mistress Vorder and the obstinate greed of the physicians Clothilde generally employed, that it had never occurred to her until this moment that the Duchess might actually be someone with whom she could reason.

Sera took a deep breath. "Very well, then, I will tell you what I think. Three times has Elsie suffered these attacks of panic . . . and on none of those occasions was I near. Had I been there, I believe I could have soothed her as effectively as Jarl Skogsrå. I have been caring for Elsie for many years now, and I have more influence over her than anyone—yet in every instance Cousin Clothilde sent immediately for the Jarl, and did not even bother to inform me that Elsie was ailing."

The Duchess nodded her head. "Yes, that was rude of Clothilde and inconsiderate as well. Naturally, you would want to be with Elsie at a time like that. But aside from the snub to yourself, I do not understand why this should particularly disturb you."

Sera picked a yellow rose, began to tear it apart, petal by petal. "We know that Jarl Skogsrå wishes to marry Elsie—whether because of her fortune (which is considerable), or because he has formed a sincere attachment, I do not pretend to say—and we know that Elsie's mother encourages his suit. I fear that Cousin Clothilde and the Jarl between them are using these fits of Elsie's, and his ability to bring her out of them, in order to render her emotionally dependent on him."

115

The Duchess appeared to think this over, then she nodded her head. "It might be so. Indeed, Miss Vorder, you have all but convinced me. And yet... would this be so very bad a thing? Elsie must marry someone, she must marry sometime, and I believe the Jarl to be genuinely attached to her. He would make her an excellent husband, for he is a man of culture and refinement, and harbors a tender concern for Elsie's well-being. If, then, he has allowed his ardor to get the better of him, and is unconsciously making use of the present circumstances in order to encourage Elsie's already decided preference for his company—can we find it in our hearts to deplore his behavior?"

Sera picked another rose, a red one this time. The Duchess moved down the garden path, and Sera followed obediently after her, leaving a trail of scarlet rose petals behind her. Never before had she and the Duchess spoken at such great length, never before had Sera been so long exposed to her celebrated charm. There really was something oddly appealing about the Duchess (Sera decided), something... something that made one eager to win her approval if it could possibly be done. "Or is it... I beg you will pardon me for also being frank, Miss Vorder... have you considered the possibility that what you are feeling in regard to the Jarl might be... jealousy. Can you convince me that you do not view Skogsrå so much as a danger to Elsie, but rather as a rival for her affection?"

Sera wanted to convince the Duchess, she wanted that very much—but how could she, when she doubted her own motives? "I do love Elsie, most tenderly, and she loves me; our friendship, until now, has been an exclusive one. Perhaps I *am* a little jealous that she is beginning to care for the Jarl, but that is not—I am *certain* that is not the only reason that I distrust him."

"Well, well," said the Duchess, "let us leave that subject for the time being and address another." As they started across a sunny stretch of velvety green lawn, the Duchess opened her parasol. It was an exceedingly pretty affair, as ruffled and beribboned as her gown. "You tell me," the Duchess said, "that Elsie only suffers these unfortunate attacks when you are not present."

"I do," said Sera. "And so I cannot help but suspect that the Jarl is doing... something... to induce Elsie's fits."

The Duchess stopped in her tracks, quite plainly aghast. "No, no, please do not say so," she said. "Indeed, how could he?— for if *you* were not present, than neither was *he*. I beg you to

116

consider this: except when you leave home on these visits to your grandfather, you and Elsie are virtually inseparable. Only when you are out of the house, or when she is lying drugged with sleeping potions in her bed at night, is Elsie ever truly alone.

"But she was up in her bedchamber dressing to go out, had just sent her maid off on some trifling errand, when this recent attack overcame her. And I think that you would find, if you cared to inquire, that she was also alone, at least in the beginning, on each of the previous occasions. It may be," said the Duchess, continuing on with her stroll, "that Elsie is more vulnerable at these times, and that the reassuring presence of a friend or kins-woman—even one of the servants—might enable your cousin to fight off her panic, and regain her mental balance before the fit gains a hold on her.

"If this is true, the solution is obvious," concluded the Duchess. "We have only to make certain that Elsie is never alone, that she is attended at all times. A simple solution, I think you will agree, and one that ought to appeal to your practical nature."

Sera felt a surge of gratitude. The solution did appeal to her; it struck her as both neat and practical. And why (she wondered) had she never before noticed this striking resemblance between the Duchess and the little owl-eyed apothecary, Mistress San-creedi? The same diminutive figure (though the Duchess was per-haps the taller), the same elegant bone structure, the same gentle, caressing manner. And what was it Mistress Sancreedi had said about the Duchess? Why, merely that Marella Carleon was uni-versally regarded as a great philanthropist. "You are very kind, and . . . I think . . . very wise," said Sera. "It is possible that I have seriously misjudged you in the past."

"You need not apologize," said the Duchess, with one of her delightful silvery laughs. "You would not be the first to have done so, I assure you. But do tell me—and I beg you will continue to speak plainly—is it not possible that your doubts about the benefits of the Jarl's treatment are due more to . . . the revolutionary nature of the cure, than to any distrust of him or me?"

"Say it is due to the *mystical* nature of the cure, and you would describe my feelings almost exactly," replied Sera.

"I see," said the Duchess, twirling her parasol. "But of course you are a skeptic; I knew this already. The result of your early upbringing, no doubt. But no"—she smiled one of her enchanting smiles—"your parents named you Seramarias—did they not?— which argues a mystical bent on somebody's part."

117

Sera felt herself blushing. "I know very little about either of my parents. I do not believe that either one of them had any . . . mystical leanings. But I was raised by my grandfather, Gottfried Jenk, and it was he who named me."

The Duchess gave a tiny exclamation of surprise. "Gottfried Jenk! Jenk the Alchemist!" She clapped her tiny hands together as though she had just been presented with a delightful gift. "But I had no idea, no idea at all, that this was the grandfather you go so often to visit."

"You know my grandfather?" Sera was puzzled by the Duchess's sudden enthusiasm.

"Say rather that we were acquainted . . . oh, a long time ago. It must have been fifty years," said the Duchess.

Sera tried not to stare, for she knew that was rude, yet she could scarcely help doing so. To all appearances the Duchess was not so many years older than she was herself. "Impossible," she exclaimed. "Or rather . . . I knew, of course, that you must be considerably older than you appear, but fifty years . . . !"

The Duchess dismissed the compliment with a careless wave of her hand. "Indeed, you flatter me, Miss Vorder. But yes, I passed my fiftieth birthday some time since. It is not a fact that I am able to conceal, alas, for I have so many old acquaintances in Thornburg.

"Yes, yes, at one time, your grandfather and I were very well acquainted," she continued reminiscently. "And now that I know . . . I believe I perceive a resemblance. Yes indeed, you have a look of him . . . the stubborn set of the brows, the proud tilt of the head. I hope you will not be offended when I tell you that he was considered to be the most arrogant young man! But of course he had reason, for he was also a brilliant one. Yes, I am also acquainted with his unfortunate history—and it explains a good deal."

The Duchess smiled at her. "Oh, yes, I understand you far better now, my very dear Miss Vorder." She linked her arm companionably through Sera's as they turned back toward the house. "But how pleased I am that we had this conversation. We are better acquainted now, you and I. Do you know, Sera—I may call you Sera, may I not? And you must learn to call me Marella— I feel that I have sadly neglected you in the past! Our precious Elsie has consumed so much of my time and attention, I believe

118

I never had the opportunity to get to know you as I ought.

"But now that I do know you and something of your family history," she said sweetly, "I think—yes, I am entirely convinced—that you and I are going to be the greatest of friends!"

17.

Containing a Message which was eagerly Awaited.

In the cold hour before daybreak, the people of Thornburg were already up and astir, preparing for the festival, which would begin in earnest at first light. The streets and lanes were filled with early-rising revelers—or those who had not seen their beds the night before—either making their way down to the river or jostling and shoving for a good position along one of the wider streets, the better to observe the pageants and processions as they passed by.

Among the crowd surging toward the river was one stoop-shouldered old man in a rusty black coat, a somber figure in stark contrast to the gaily dressed revelers surrounding him. Gottfried Jenk moved like one in a dream, in a state bordering on preternatural exaltation. All around him he felt the ebb and flow of mental force as the excitement of the crowd pulsed and faded. But above and beyond the energy of the crowd, there were greater forces at work, the powers of light and darkness raging in their awesome eternal struggle—Jenk knew the battle for men's souls continued at all times and in all seasons, but it was only possible for a man like himself, on an occasion such as this, when his intuitive faculties could feed on the excitement around him, to receive a faint intimation of the contending cosmic forces, an imperfect impression of their terrifying power and splendor.

With the first rosy light of dawn, the air filled with raucous music: the tootling of silver horns, the clatter of rattles and wooden clappers; from somewhere off to the east, in the vicinity of Cathedral Hill, came the thud of bass drums and the deep moan of a bull-roarer, as the people of Thornburg welcomed in the new day, the new season, and the advent of the Harvest Triad.

119

Moving as swiftly as he could through the press of bodies, Jenk followed Tidewater Lane, turned down Dank Street, pushed past a party of drunken dwarves, and emerged on Oyster Walk. A sudden movement of the crowd pressed him up against one of the buildings. Jenk knew, by the rhythmic stamp of feet moving steadily his way, that a procession was coming. He stood with his back against a damp brick wall, made himself as tall as possible in order to see over the heads in front of him, and watched the Clockmakers Guild march by.

The Masters of the Guild came first, splendid in purple robes, glittering with medals and orders. Behind them walked twelve journeymen and 'prentices robed in rainbow colors ranging from pale rose, through gold, to midnight blue, representing the hours from dawn to dusk and from dusk to dawn. Last of all came a hunched old greybeard in tattered brown: Father Time, with his flail and his winnowing sieve, and a golden sickle tucked into his belt.

No sooner had the Clockmakers passed than a burst of melody announced the approach of the Spinners, Weavers, and Fullers Guild, a lodge consisting mainly of women. Strumming on harps they came, or jingling silver sistrums, or bearing the tools of their trade: a spindle, a teasel, and a little hand loom. At the end of the procession came four who represented the phases of the moon as worshipped by the Ancients: a slender girl wearing a gown of starry black and a wreath of delicate night-blooming flowers, symbolizing the frail new moon . . . two stately women in trailing court gowns of ivory silk embroidered in intricate patterns of seed pearls and tiny seashells, symbolizing the crescent and gibbous moons . . . and waddling along, considerably behind the others, in a garish gown of orange and yellow satin extending over a hoop of enormous proportions, a grotesquely fat woman, as ugly as a troll, representing the moon in her goblin phase.

Jenk gave a gasp of dismay as the fat woman walked by; behind her like a shadow, or a drift of mist, he could just make out the form of another: a hag with a wide mouth and a distended belly that jiggled as she walked—the old Goblin herself, come to join the revels, and no one but Jenk any the wiser.

He passed a hand over his brow. He was a civilized man, he told himself, an educated man—he did not *believe* in these heathen superstitions. Like other educated men, he worshipped the Father, the Nine Seasons, and the Planetary Intelligences, Iune among

120

them. He knew her true aspect—had he not seen her image in the cathedral a thousand times at the center of one of the glorious rose windows? Serene and beautiful, she hovered on outstretched snowy wings, like the wings of a great white swan; according to the Scriptures, she was a being formed of pure light. This—this grotesque *thing* was only a figment of his imagination. If he did not believe in her, she would cease to be. And yet . . . and yet . . . the harder he tried to will her away, the solider, the more convincingly *real* the Hag became.

As the procession disappeared in the distance, Jenk slowly recovered his mental equilibrium. Then he began to move again, heading for the river. Once, a party of masked revelers, going in the opposite direction, hailed him by name, invited him to join them; recognizing none of them, he did not respond and continued on his course with single-minded determination.

Jenk arrived on the banks of the Lunn just in time to observe the approach of the Glassmakers and the Gravediggers. The two guilds came in from opposite directions carrying gargantuan wicker effigies with them. Jenk felt another surge of excitement, for this was the one event he had come to see: the Drowning of the Giants, a ritual symbolizing the destruction of the two great island empires, Panterra and Evanthum.

The Glassmakers reached the river bank first—as had doubtless been arranged in advance—and tipped their ribbon-clad and flower-bedecked wicker man into the water. The wicker giant hit the surface with a loud splash, then slowly sank. But the Gravediggers brought their giant in on a kind of a wagon; it was a monstrous figure with curling ram's horns, and sooty rags and tufts of dried grass had been tied to the wicker frame-work. At close quarters, the wagon proved to be no ordinary cart, but a wheeled catapult which launched the monster into the air and over the river. The horned giant landed with a mighty splash, sent up a fountain of white water twenty feet high, and promptly disappeared below the murky surface. With one voice, the crowd let out a roar of approval. Shouting as loudly as any of the others, Jenk felt the excitement around him rising to an almost unbearable crescendo.

Jenk returned to the bookshop in the mid-afternoon, drained of all emotion and in a subdued frame of mind. The shop windows were shuttered, the door locked, but he let himself in with a key and bolted the door behind him.

121

Inside, the lanthorns hanging from the beamed ceiling were dark; the air was as thick and black as ink. But a single ray of light pierced the gloom, and the door to the room at the back stood open.

Jenk found Caleb in the laboratory, seated on a high stool, staring intently into the crystal egg, which now contained a new homunculus. The old bookseller shook his head. Following the death of the first mannikin, he had made two more attempts using *sperma viri* obtained in the same manner as before. Both attempts failed. In a moment of weakness, he finally yielded to his old friend's repeated importunities and allowed Caleb to provide the seed for a fourth homunculus. Much to his surprise, this new creation thrived. Since the day they had first detected signs of change and growth, Caleb had hovered over the developing mandrake root like a doting nursemaid. This habit inspired in Jenk a profound uneasiness; he feared that Caleb's increasing obsession was not a healthy one.

"It's growing fast—faster nor the first un," said Caleb, by way of greeting. "I see it change a little, day by day."

"It is growing fast," Jenk acknowledged, as he hung up his coat, took his spectacles out of his waistcoat pocket, and placed them at the end of his nose. "And it will continue to grow whether you are on hand to observe or not."

"That may be," said Caleb, rubbing his hands together, like a miser contemplating his gold, "nor again it may not be. I just don't want nothing to go wrong with this one, that's all."

"We decanted the other one much too early," sighed Jenk. "Its heart and its lungs were imperfectly developed. And we were both on hand when the unfortunate creature died; there was nothing that either of us could have done to save it."

Caleb set his jaw and folded his arms. "I ain't inclined to argue the point—we been through that afore. What's done is done, and there's no going back. I just want you to come over here and take a look. When you carved the mandrake root, you was at some pains—wasn't you—to make it into a proper little man? You didn't consider any . . . changes . . . by way of variety?"

Jenk moved closer; he bent forward to peer into the egg. "No, Caleb, I made no changes. I made every effort to form this one as like to the other as I possibly could. Why do you ask?"

"Because," said Caleb, "I guess this little 'son' of mine has a fancy to become my daughter instead."

Jenk adjusted his spectacles; gazed intently at the tiny creature

122

in the glass vessel. "It is too soon to be certain," he said at last, "but I believe you are right: the homunculus seems to be taking on female characteristics. But this is most interesting, Caleb. I wonder how and why such a variation would happen to occur."

Caleb ran a work-roughened hand over his unshaven chin. "It come about the same way girl babbies always do—how else would it happen? I don't see nothing mysterious about it."

Jenk shook his head. "Ah, but you see . . . nobody *knows* how female babies come about—or male ones either. It has always been assumed, though without any proof, that sexual characteristics were the gift of the mother, the result of some condition existing in the womb at the moment of conception. But here we have no mother, no living womb, only a vessel of glass, and all conditions exactly correspond to those which existed at the time I created the other homunculi. With our failed attempts it was impossible to be certain, but surely there is no doubt that the first homunculus was a little man."

Caleb passed that off with another careless shrug. "Then they was all wrong . . . your doctors and your natural philosophers," he said. "As simple as that. It must of been something in the *sperma viri*, Gottfried, and I done fathered a dainty little daughter, without the aid of any woman."

Caleb stood up and walked across the room. He went over to the table where the coffin rested. "I reckon I forgot to tell you, when you first come in . . . there was a letter and a package arrived while you was out."

Jenk raised an eyebrow, mildly surprised. "A letter and a package . . . today? I had thought the coaches were not running."

"It come by private messenger: a gnome in Zar-Wildungen livery . . ." Caleb came back, carrying a long parchment envelope and a velvet bag tied shut with a satin cord. By the weight and the feel of it, when Jenk took it in his hands, the bag contained a considerable sum of money, all in coins.

The letter consisted of several sheets of thin paper, written over in a small but clear hand. "Not in the Duke's hand, nor in his style . . . it appears to be the work of some confidential secretary. It does, however, bear his seal," said Jenk.

" 'I turned the body of the homunculus over to my personal physician," he read out loud, "a man of the utmost integrity . . . and asked him to perform a dissection.' I am sorry, Caleb, but the creature was already dead."

Caleb hunched his shoulders, gave his grizzled pigtail a meditative tug. "Dead and past helping. But nothing like that is agoing to happen to the new one. We'll make precious certain of that."

"We shall indeed," said Jenk, thinking of two little graves in the walled garden behind the bookshop, the pitifully small body of the homunculus he had sent to the Duke. "We have learned our lesson and will proceed more cautiously this time.

"It may be," he added thoughtfully, "that others who tried the experiment before us also fell victim to their own impatience and brought forth mannikins prematurely. That would explain why so many previous attempts failed.

"But be that as it may," he continued, "the Duke (or his secretary, writing on his behalf) goes on to say: 'The internal organs, not only in their form and complexity but in their location as well, bear an amazing resemblance to human anatomy—far more than in dwarves or gnomes, though not so marked as in fays or giants—yet for all that, there was no evidence either to prove or disprove that the tissue had ever quickened—or if it had, that the creature was (as you inform me) an artificial creation and not a human fetus which had naturally aborted due to its slight internal deformities. All this, I feel obliged to point out, speaking as a scholar and a scientist. Speaking as one gentleman to another, however, and as one who knows you of old, I reject any suspicion of a deliberate deception on your part and am ready to accept the tissue you sent me as proof positive that you have indeed unlocked the mysteries of ages past and created a living creature by wholly artificial means. In earnest of further support in the future, I send you . . .' He sends me," said Jenk, "a substantial sum of money, all in gold."

He unwound a cord that had been wrapped around the mouth of the velvet bag, and emptied a shower of golden coins onto the table, where they lay in a gleaming pile. "He makes but two conditions, should I wish to obtain that future patronage: 'Whatever other experiments you may currently be engaged upon, you must not neglect this one. I am a wealthy man and have little interest in any process which purports to change lead into silver or gold, nor do I care for elixirs or precious stones. The other condition is simply this: when the present homunculus comes to term, you must send word to me at once. A few days later, as soon as traveling conditions permit, you will admit my representative—one Baron Vodni—to examine the results.'"

"Well then," said Caleb, with evident satisfaction, "you've succeeded so far: you've gained the old Duke's interest and his gold. Now you can meet Jakob's price and buy them tinctures, and there shouldn't be no more obstacles."

"I wonder . . ." said Jenk, drawing up a stool and sitting down on it. "I cannot help but wonder. Not only is the letter written in another hand, but it is scarcely like the Duke to write of sending a representative, when he might ask to view the living homunculus himself."

"The Duke is old and ailing," Caleb reminded him. "It may be that he ain't well enough to travel."

"But he might send for *me*," said Jenk. "He might inquire whether I am able to travel to the Wichtelberg, carrying the homunculus with me. And as he is an old man and in feeble health, I wonder that he expresses such a profound disinterest in *elixirs and precious stones*."

Caleb shook his head. "The letter was sealed with the Duke's seal, delivered by the Duke's man—and someone's taken it onto hisself to send you a good fair portion of the Duke's gold. You've gained yourself a generous patron, Gottfried; why not content yourself with that?"

Jenk opened his mouth to reply, but a loud, impatient pounding on the bookshop door distracted him. Caleb heaved himself to his feet and went off to answer it.

He returned a few minutes later, scratching his head. "It's that foreign gentleman, Colonel Jolerei. He seems set on speaking to you, for all I told him we was closed for the holiday."

"I will see him, then," said Jenk. Rising to his feet, he shrugged into his coat and went into the bookshop to greet his visitor.

Colonel Jolerei was a sleek-looking individual in the uniform of a Nordic cavalry officer. He wore his fair hair unpowdered and tied back in a neat queue with a plain black ribbon. He bowed stiffly when Jenk came into the room, and he immediately stated his business.

"The volumes we spoke of during my previous visit—most particularly Catalana's *Book of Silences* —you have succeeded in finding them?" The Colonel tapped a short riding whip impatiently against one highly polished boot as he spoke.

"I am sorry that I put you to the trouble of returning here," said Jenk, removing his spectacles, "for it appears that none of those books are to be had in Thornburg, or any of the towns around. I shall, of course, continue the search. So if you would be good enough to leave me your direction—"

"My address would be of no use—I do not remain in Marstadtt

much longer," the Colonel interrupted him. "My regiment, you understand, has been recalled to active duty."

"Then perhaps you have some friend or relative in the town, who would be willing to forward—"

"That will not be necessary. You do not have the book; you say it cannot be obtained at the present time. I am as likely to find the book in Nordmark, I think." The foreigner bowed curtly and turned to go; Jenk followed him to the door and bolted it behind him.

He returned to the laboratory frowning thoughtfully. "I should not like to think that the nature of our experiments were common knowledge," he told Caleb. "And yet I cannot but harbor a suspicion. It seemed to me, when the Colonel called before, that he had less interest in obtaining any books than in gauging my reaction when he named the *Book of Silences*."

"Then why did you ask him to come back for? Why did you pretend you was going to look for them books?"

"Because if I had not, I might have aroused his suspicion—as he must have feared to arouse mine, if he did not call again. I fear that we have both wasted our time, for *I* am certainly suspicious of *him*, and he appears to be equally distrustful of me."

Jenk sank down on the stool he had vacated earlier. "Is it likely," he asked, "that a man with such a pronounced limp would be recalled to active duty, even in a Nordic cavalry regiment?"

The candle in the single lanthorn hanging from the ceiling began to flicker wildly. Caleb left his own seat, took up another candle, and opened the glass case. "He had a sly and sneaking look about him, that I won't deny. But who do you reckon it was that sent him?" Caleb lit the new candle and snuffed out the old one.

"He *looked* entirely the gentleman to me," said Jenk, "and acted one, too, though his manner was somewhat abrupt. But I had the *feeling* the whole time that I was speaking to him, that I was in the presence of a serpent. As to who it was that sent him ... perhaps one of the guilds, if they somehow caught wind of our activities."

"Not the Glassmakers!" Caleb protested. "I'd swear by all the Powers, it weren't my Jed who blabbed." He slammed the glass case shut.

"I am far more inclined to suspect either Matthias or Walther," said Jenk. "And to do the Glassmakers no more than simple justice ... I doubt that a man such as Colonel Jolerei—who aroused in both of us such an instinctive mistrust—would ever be admitted

126

into the inner circles of the Glassmakers Lodge.''

"Well, whosoever he was, and whosoever it was that sent him, he didn't learn nothing from you," Caleb said. "You was as cool as ice, and I'll lay any wager he never suspected you had the book right here in the shop the whole time.''

"We must hope not," said Jenk. "But of course you are right . . . If he had gained any inkling during his previous visit and passed that information on to anyone else, then he or some other agent would have attempted to break into the shop long since and taken the book either by force or by stealth.''

He shook his head and smiled a weary smile. "Perhaps it is only that I am inclined to mistrust our current good fortune. Our luck has turned on us, so many times before . . . and now it all appears to be going our way: the books, the homunculus . . . the Duke and his gold.'' He took one of the coins into his hand, held it close to the lanthorn, so that it caught and reflected the light. "And yet . . . why should we not finally come to good fortune, after all the long years of struggle and regret?''

He came to a sudden decision. "I believe you are right, Caleb. We should not ask too many questions. I shall take a few of these coins with me on the morrow, and with them I shall purchase the tinctures. It may well be that our luck *has* turned, and that the Elixir and the stone Seramarias have finally come within our grasp.''

18.

In which Sera appears at a considerable Disadvantage.

It was Count Xebo's custom, each year, to hold a grand ball, some time early in the season of Ripening. Invitations were eagerly sought and eagerly awaited, for Count Xebo's ball was the focal point of the entire season.

This year, however, anticipation ran even higher than usual, for in addition to the customary feasting and dancing, the Count promised his guests an opportunity to view the splendid new wax statues depicting the Nine Seasons, which he had recently commissioned. Count Xebo was known to be a collector and a connoisseur of wax; moreover, it was rumored that he had spent a princely sum on these latest acquisitions, therefore an expectation grew on the part of the Thornburg elite, that the new statues would be truly extraordinary.

As might be expected, Clothilde Vorder was more than willing to accept the Count's intriguing invitation; her husband would have preferred a quiet evening at home, sequestered in his study. But the lady carried her point—in part because Jarl Skogsrå offered to escort the ladies home afterwards, offering the reluctant Benjamin an early escape. So it was arranged that the family would attend.

A pair of sedan chairs were ordered for eight, but the ladies dressed early and assembled in the downstairs sitting room at seven forty-five: Clothilde, imposing in diamonds and purple satin; Elsie, as dainty as meadowflowers and twice as sweet, in a gown consisting of layer upon layer of spangled tulle; and Sera, in one of Clothilde's cast-offs, cut down and remade to fit.

Sera sat on a loveseat by the fireplace, utterly dissatisfied with her own appearance. With a sigh, she spread out the skirts of her gown. It was an excellent wine-colored watered silk, trimmed with black lace, and still in good condition—but decidedly matronly in color and cut, manifestly unsuitable for a girl of eighteen. Compared to Elsie's youthful freshness, Sera in her heavy claret silk felt old and plain and dull.

Not that it's entirely the fault of the dress, thought Sera. *I wish I had a tenth of Elsie's beauty! Here am I with these dreadful crow-colored locks . . . and there is Elsie with her pure living gold. But I think the difference between us might not be so* very *noticeable, if only I had something attractive to wear.*

That, however, would never happen while Sera lived under Clothilde Vorder's roof. Elsie was generous, and always shared her fans and her lace mittens, her parasols and her Mawbri silk shawls—it was not her fault that Sera was too large to fit into her dresses as well. But Cousin Clothilde seemed to take a positive delight in playing up the contrast between them. *She might have given me the primrose satin—she hasn't worn it in years. It would have looked well with Elsie's white . . . but perhaps then Elsie's gown would not have displayed to such* particular *advantage.*

"Dearest Sera," said Elsie, sitting down beside her and lifting a raven lock, "your hair is so thick and glossy, and the color in

128

your cheeks so ravishing, I vow you'll be the prettiest girl at the ball.''

Sera's cheeks grew pinker still. How could she think of envying Elsie—Elsie with her ill health and a thousand other cares to plague her? *I am becoming so wicked, I scarcely know myself.*

But before she could scold herself as she deserved, the clock struck the hour and Cousin Benjamin appeared, languidly announcing that the sedan chairs were at the door. The ladies gathered up their fans and their light summer shawls and followed him out of the room.

The night was warm and the walk to Count Xebo's imposing grey mansion was not a long one, so Mistress Vorder and Elsie traveled by chair. Though no conveyance had been ordered for Sera, she was perfectly content to make the short trip on foot, leaning on Cousin Benjamin's arm.

Six footmen and two page-boys escorted them, the pages to act as linkmen and carry torches, the footmen bearing the long spiked poles known as "hobstickers" that were designed to fend off marauding hobgoblins. Even though the moon was so small and young, and there was no real danger of encountering any hobs, the Vorder servants went armed—it was a matter (Cousin Clothilde liked to say) of maintaining the family dignity.

As they climbed Thorn Hill, one of the men struck out with his pole, skewering something small and grey that squeaked and struggled at the end of the spike, then shuddered and went completely still. Sera shuddered, too, though she knew the footman had only spiked a rat. It seemed a bad beginning to the evening's entertainment.

Surrounded by gardens and high stone walls, the Xebo mansion generally gave the impression of a walled fortress. But tonight the heavy wrought-iron gates stood wide open, the grounds glowed with a thousand tiny fairy-lanthorns, and it was possible for the coaches and the chairs which brought the Count's guests to come directly up to the front steps.

A serving man carrying a lighted flambeau escorted the Vorders to the door and admitted them into the lower hall. Another led them up a curving onyx staircase and into the vast glittering ballroom.

The two girls looked around them curiously, for Elsie, at sixteen, had been out less than a year, and this was their first glimpse of the ballroom. It was a magnificent chamber, if somewhat oppressive.

The south and the east walls were all windows and gilded stucco; the other two walls had been covered with mirrors. The dance floor and the massive pillars supporting the roof were black marble veined with gold, polished to a glassy brightness. Crystal chandeliers suspended from the frescoed ceiling looked so huge and so heavy, it seemed they must shortly come crashing down by their very weight.

"It is all so beautiful," Mistress Vorder told their hostess. "I have always admired your exquisite taste, Countess."

"I have never seen anything like it," breathed Elsie, but when nobody else could hear her, she whispered in Sera's ear: "I think that it frightens me just a little."

"I'll not leave you alone for a single instant," said Sera. "That is . . . not until somebody asks you to dance."

But someone was already moving their way, and that somebody (unfortunately) was Jarl Skogsrå, impressively garbed in black velvet and snowy white lace and a red satin sash laden with foreign orders. He had powdered his hair in honor of the occasion, and he wore an enormous ruby ring on his left hand. "Fairest of charmers, I am entirely at your service—and yours as well, my dear Miss Vorder. But pray assure me, my Elsie, that you have not promised the first minuet to anyone but me."

Elsie colored prettily and offered him her hand, which he kissed and retained in that clinging way that Sera always found so particularly repulsive. Elsie, however, did not seem to mind. "But of course I have reserved the first dance for you, Haakon, that is, Lord Skogsrå."

The musicians were now striking up. Turning to look at them, Sera experienced a jolt of surprise—the players were all powered by clockwork; there was not one real man among them. Seated on a revolving platform, they all sawed away at their various viols, fiddles, and cellos, their short jerky movements quite at odds with the music. It took Sera another moment to realize they were only going through the motions; the tinkling tune issued from the gilded platform, which was really a gigantic musicbox.

Sera frowned, thinking the entire effect ludicrous. She would have much preferred live musicians.

"If you will only try to look as though you were having a good time, and *not* as though you contemplated murder, I feel certain that someone will ask you to dance. See, there is Mr. Hakluyt

130

and his friend Lord Krogan, and both of them are looking at you,'' Elsie whispered in Sera's ear, just before Skogsrå led her away.

As for the odious Lord Krogan and his equally repulsive crony, Mr. Hakluyt, they were certainly staring in Sera's direction. She favored the pair of them with a toss of her head and a glance so explosive that both men blenched and sidled out of the room.

Sera doubted that any *suitable* partner would appear, nor would it matter if one did. She was not about to stand up to be laughed at in her made-over gown. She found a seat on a sofa by an open window, and sat there for the next hour and a half, while one partner after another asked Elsie to dance.

"Oh, Sera, the gentlemen are all so agreeable, and I vow I've not spent such an enjoyable evening in all my life,'' said Elsie, during a pause between dances, as she sank down beside Sera on the black velvet cushions. "For in general, you know, I am always too ill to really enjoy a party.''

Perhaps, thought Sera, *the attentions of these other men, which she seems to enjoy, will convince Elsie to wait a little longer before accepting Jarl Skogsrå*. "You look flushed, my dear,'' she said aloud. "Do not tell me that you have been drinking wine . . . You know that it always makes your head ache.''

Elsie shook out her fan. "Only a little cherry ratafia, which Lord Vizbeck was so kind as to bring me. Now, Sera, do not scold me, for I only had a sip or two.''

"What a charming tableau the two of you do make,'' said a bell-like voice, and Sera looked up to see a dainty figure in shades of rose and cream. It was the Duchess of Zar-Wildungen, arriving fashionably late, leaning on Francis Skelbrooke's arm.

Lord Skelbrooke bowed deeply. He looked especially fine this evening, in an exquisite coat of sea-green satin trimmed with silver braid, with a fall of shimmering lace at his throat and drooping at his wrists, and a pattern of pearls and silver threads worked into the design of his embroidered waistcoat. But Sera's attention was immediately engaged by his shoes, which had crimson heels and were adorned with large satin bows the color of his coat.

"The Misses Vorder . . . as ravishing as ever, and a perfect study in dark and light,'' said Skelbrooke.

Sera tore her gaze away from the satin bows and gave him a puzzled frown; if he meant a compliment, it was an awkward one at best.

"Lord Skelbrooke—'' she began, but proceeded no further, as Elsie made a tiny, inarticulate sound of protest and clutched her

131

hand convulsively. Her attention immediately on Elsie, Sera saw that her cousin had lost all color and was trembling violently.

"What is it, my darling, are you feeling ill?"

Elsie shook her head. "N-not ill . . . no, no, not ill . . . but I see such terrible *things* crawling on the floor, and I believe that I am going to scream if I stay here much longer."

Sera sprang to her feet, looking for the nearest exit. Spotting an open door not twenty feet away, she helped Elsie to stand and move in that direction. "You have nothing to fear," Sera said soothingly. "Truly, Elsie, there is *nothing* on the floor, not anything at all . . . but I will take you into the next room, which appears to be a delightful library."

They headed toward the door, the younger girl supported on the elder's arm. Elsie's breathing was so swift and shallow, Sera feared she was about to swoon. Yet they made it into the library without any mishap, and Sera found a high-backed leather chair for Elsie to collapse into. She knelt on the floor at her cousin's feet.

"Elsie, darling Elsie, you need not fear . . . It is only an effect of the Jarl's wretched potion. There is nothing crawling on the floor . . . though perhaps one of the reflections . . . But if you would only try to regulate your breathing, I feel certain you would feel better, almost immediately."

"Sera . . ." whispered Elsie, in tones of horror. "I can feel my skin *withering* . . . and falling off the bones . . . It is . . . the most . . . terrible . . . sensation."

"No, no, your skin is just as it was," Sera protested helplessly. For once in her life, she had no idea what she might do or say to make things better. She felt an unexpected surge of relief when Jarl Skogsrå strode into the library and fell to his knees on the floor beside her.

"My darling, I am with you, and nothing will harm you," said the Jarl. The words were scarcely out of his mouth before Elsie ceased to tremble, and her color began to return. As Skogsrå continued to speak in reassuring tones, she even managed a wan smile.

"Haakon . . . yes," she said faintly. "How very strange . . . I was terrified nearly to death only a few moments ago . . . but I feel quite safe now."

Sera thought it rather *more* than strange. She could not, for the life of her, detect anything in the Jarl's speech or in his manner to account for the sudden, almost magical change in his patient.

Within minutes, Elsie's color was entirely restored, and she was laughing shyly at something the Jarl said to her.

Sera rose to her feet and dusted off her skirts. "I congratulate you, my lord," she said bitterly. "You have accomplished the miraculous."

"That being so, I make bold to claim my reward: will you not dance with me, Elsie my heart?" Skogsrå rose gracefully and offered her his arm.

To Sera's surprise and consternation, Elsie stood up and placed her hand in his. "Yes, Haakon, I believe that I will."

"But this is madness!" exclaimed Sera. "You cannot dance when . . . when you have recently been so very ill."

"But I am entirely recovered now. Indeed, I feel remarkably refreshed. And I was having such a lovely time—before that foolish attack of mine—it seems a shame to spoil it." And Elsie allowed the Jarl to lead her out of the library and onto the dance floor.

Fighting back tears—of frustration? of disappointment?—Sera collapsed into the chair her cousin had so recently vacated. *She will have him now . . . oh, she will certainly marry him now. And I shall have to let her, for it is obvious he can take better care of her than I can. But what will become of* me, *after she marries him?*

"But the Jarl has the most amazing powers of healing in his voice!" exclaimed the Duchess. "It really was a privilege to observe him."

Sera started violently. She was uncertain just when the Duchess and Lord Skelbrooke had entered the library.

"Miss Vorder," said Skelbrooke, "if you are not feeling too fatigued after your recent ordeal . . . I was about to ask you for the honor of a dance."

Sera stared up at him, wondering what had prompted him to make such an outrageous proposal. Surely he must know how poorly her made-over gown would contrast with the delicate pastels of the other ladies on the dance floor—how dark and ugly it would look beside his own sea-green satin and silver lace.

"I make it a practice, sir, never to dance at such large gatherings."

"Your accustomed good sense, Miss Vorder," he replied gravely. "For I can think of a few things more tedious than to stand up in an overheated and overcrowded chamber and attempt to dance. Were it not for the hope of the pleasure of your company

133

I would never have contemplated that folly myself.

"But if you will not dance . . . perhaps you will allow me to escort you into the long gallery? The wax statues there are said to be extremely fine."

Sera opened her mouth to refuse him, but Skelbrooke forestalled her. "I was recently so fortunate as to make the acquaintance of an old friend of yours, Miss Vorder: a Mr. Jedidiah Braun. And he charged me with an important message."

"Jedidiah!" Sera was too exhausted, emotionally and physically, to conceal her surprise. "You are acquainted with Jed, Lord Skelbrooke?"

Lord Skelbrooke bowed, indicating that he was. "I have that honor, Miss Vorder."

Sera took a long breath. "Then by all means, my lord," she said, "escort me to the long gallery."

19.

Which is largely Confidential.

The long gallery was situated in another, older wing of the Xebo mansion. To reach it, Sera and Lord Skelbrooke ascended a twisting stair and walked down a long candle-lit hallway. As they strolled along the corridor, they passed many other couples, in attitudes either confidential or amorous.

Sera blushed as they passed a particularly ardent pair wrapped in a passionate embrace. She was uncomfortably aware of Skelbrooke's arm supporting her own, of the light, firm grip of his other hand covering hers. To make matters worse, they were much of a height, and consequently, whenever he turned to speak to her, she had either to look away or else meet his gaze directly, at alarmingly close quarters.

"I dined with your friend at Master Ule's a fortnight ago," said Skelbrooke. "You will be pleased to know that he was in excellent health and spirits and that his prospects for advancement continue to improve."

134

"I am more than pleased, I am enormously relieved," said Sera, marveling at the steadiness of her own voice. "I have been endeavoring, for some time now, to communicate with Jed. But I continually find obstacles thrown in my way. I wrote and received no answer . . . I called at his lodgings only to learn that he had moved and left no direction . . . When I spoke to his uncle, Caleb Braun, last week at my grandfather's, he refused to tell me Jed's present lodging, saying it wasn't 'fitting' for me to call on him— a boy I have known all of my life. It is very frustrating!"

Skelbrooke nodded solemnly. "Mr. Braun informed me that you had expressed some concern . . . had doubts about the wisdom of some project your grandfather had undertaken along with Caleb Braun. Jedidiah wished me to tell you that he, too, is increasingly concerned, though he is very far from learning the nature of their endeavor."

"Yes." Sera released a sigh of profound exasperation. "I thought as much. I believe there is a conspiracy of sorts, to keep Jed and me from communicating, lest we compare what we know and somehow discover what those two dear, stubborn old men are doing!"

Skelbrooke cleared his throat apologetically, hesitated a moment before speaking. "I would not wish to accuse anyone in the Vorder household unjustly . . . but it would seem this conspiracy extends farther than you think. Mr. Braun informs me that he wrote several letters to *you*, yet he sincerely doubts that any were delivered."

Sera did not conceal her annoyance. "*That*, I believe, is another conspiracy of longer standing. Cousin Clothilde does not approve of my friendship with Jed, so naturally her servants have orders not to deliver his messages. How vexing that is—especially now, when it is so important for Jed and me to communicate!"

Again, his lordship cleared his throat. "I am going into the country tomorrow, and expect to be out of town for a week or more, but . . . You frown, madam. Will you tell me why that is?"

"It is only," said Sera, "that you are so seldom *in* town."

Skelbrooke made a half bow. "It is true that I visit the country a good deal. How charming of you to notice, Miss Vorder." Sera felt the heat rising in her cheeks. She had not meant to sound flirtatious.

"But as I was about to say," he continued. "When I return, Mr. Braun and I may cross paths again. Should that happen, I will of course be happy to deliver any message you might care to send . . . ?"

135

"You are very kind," said Sera. "I should have thought . . ." And then she stopped to wonder what *he* must think of *her*.

Skelbrooke inclined his head politely. "You would have thought?"

"It is no matter. I only wondered that you were so—so tolerant of a friendship which everyone else seems to disapprove. I hope . . . I hope, sir, that you do not imagine you are assisting the parties in a—a thwarted romance?"

"I imagine nothing of the sort," said Skelbrooke. "If that were so, you would have told me as much at the very beginning, and not made any pretense about it."

As he spoke, they finally reached their destination; they passed through an open set of doors, into the high-ceilinged gallery where the Count displayed his collection of wax statues.

The figures nearest the door were those which first established the Count's reputation as a collector of wax. Their fame extended far beyond the borders of Marstadtt, and indeed, they drew scores of art lovers and critics from throughout the principality of Wäldermark to view them each year. Sera, however, had never been privileged to observe the collection before.

"But these are exquisite . . . incredible," she exclaimed, pausing before a group of statues in antique costume arranged in a tableau of striking dramatic power, depicting the last Emperor of Panterra and his court. "How realistic they are—how charmingly lifelike the color!"

"I had thought you might appreciate them," replied Skelbrooke, with evident satisfaction. After a few minutes, he led her on to the next group.

The next were even better; Sera looked, exclaimed, and expressed her obligation to Lord Skelbrooke.

"Miss Vorder," he said, leaning so close that now she could feel his breath warm on her cheek, "I have a confession to make. I did not bring you here merely to view the statues . . . nor to pass on a message from Jedidiah Braun."

Sera was suddenly acutely aware that the two of them were alone in the gallery. This late in the evening it was unlikely that the collection would draw more viewers. Had she allowed his soft manners and his gentle speech to mislead her?

She forced herself to look him directly in the face. His grey eyes were fringed with dark lashes that any girl might envy; undoubtedly it was to accent those fine eyes that he always wore the little black satin star high on his cheek . . . just as a second patch

136

which he wore this evening, a tiny crimson heart, emphasized the beautiful shape of his mouth. Yet for all his fashionable affectations, he did not strike her as a dissolute young man.

"You did not, Lord Skelbrooke?" she asked frostily. "Then why . . . ?"

"I asked to speak to you alone, primarily on your cousin's behalf," he said, and smiled at Sera's audible sigh of relief.

"You may remember that I was one of the party when you first called on Dr. Mirabolo. Moreover, I have been back to his establishment since—and I was also a witness, a week or two past, when Jarl Skogsrå magnetized Miss Elsie. What I saw then, and what I have seen this evening, convinces me that Dr. Mirabolo is a quack, and Skogsrå a rascal and an adventurer!"

For a moment, Sera was speechless, flabbergasted by such plain speaking. Indeed, she hardly knew what to think, much less how to reply.

"Lord Skelbrooke . . ." she said at last. "The Jarl is an intimate friend of the Duchess. That is—I do not believe that their acquaintance is of long standing, but nevertheless . . . I suppose that you are trying to tell me that Skogsrå is imposing on her?"

"It is possible," said Skelbrooke. "A woman of the Duchess's rank and position—especially, if I may say so, a woman of her age and . . . and sentimental propensities—is apt to be imposed on by younger men, from time to time."

They continued to stroll through the gallery, pausing to view each group of statues before they passed on. When Skelbrooke leaned close to speak to her, Sera's heart gave another treacherous bound. She wondered, as she had often wondered before, what there was about this dapper little man that invariably rattled her composure.

"You might not think it to look at me, Miss Vorder," his lordship was saying, "but when I attended the University of Lundy, I had some ambition to become a doctor."

Sera opened her eyes wide in surprise. She tried to imagine Skelbrooke, his poetic affectations put aside, in the role of a physician. The exercise was not so difficult as she had supposed. "But what caused you, Lord Skelbrooke, to set that ambition aside? No, there is no need for you to say, for the answer to that question is obvious. You considered the occupation of poet more worthy of a man of your rank and position."

As she lowered her eyes, her gaze chanced to fall again on those ridiculous satin bows. The sight of them served to steady her, allowing her to collect herself and return his gaze with a tolerable imitation of well-bred disinterest.

"On the contrary," said Skelbrooke. "At that time, my uncle was still alive and I had little expectation of becoming Baron Skelbrooke or succeeding to the family estate. It was a sense of my own inadequacy that caused me to abandon my hopes. I had a burning interest in the science of medicine, but not the aptitude necessary to become a good physician."

He smiled, a small disparaging smile at his own expense. "You may not approve of my poetry, Miss Vorder . . . any more than (as I perceive) you approve of my footwear . . . but even you must concede that I had better by far have inflicted myself upon Society as a bad poet than as an incompetent physician."

"But I think you would have made a very good physician," Sera protested. Then she blushed at her own vehemence. "That is to say . . . you have a gentle manner which I should imagine that sick people would find soothing, and I believe you would be sensitive to the needs of your patients."

He placed his hand on his heart and bowed his head, as one overcome by a deep emotion. She had the impression that perhaps he was laughing at her—or at himself. "You overwhelm me, Miss Vorder. I had no idea you thought so well of me as that. As I have the greatest respect for your sagacity, I rise in my own estimation. I am vastly obliged to you!"

Sera sniffed loudly at this piece of play-acting—which did a great deal to restore her equanimity—and Lord Skelbrooke immediately grew sober. "But as I was about to say . . . having observed Miss Elsie's recent . . . discomfiture . . . I feel I ought to tell you that this kind of attack could have been brought about by no disease of the blood that I know of—nor would any medication used by a *reputable* physician affect her in that way."

"The Duchess believes that Elsie's fits are brought on by a weakening of the nerves," said Sera. "Though to be sure . . . she also said that we might prevent these attacks by making certain that Elsie is never alone."

For just a moment, Sera wondered if the Duchess had made that suggestion only to gain her confidence—then she dismissed the suspicion as unworthy.

"Miss Vorder," said Skelbrooke, "considering all that Elsie has endured at the hands of her physicians, the morbid fancies which her mother encourages, and the fact that your cousin has not yet been reduced to a permanent state of raving insanity . . . I

138

am convinced that Miss Elsie's nerves must be nearly as strong as your own!''

"Yes . . ." said Sera. She was amazed to hear her own opinions echoed so precisely. "I have often felt that Elsie must be far stronger in *all* ways than anyone supposes, or how could she endure even a small part of all she has suffered?''

They arrived before the statues of the Nine Seasons or Powers, which were arranged in a semicircle on a low dais. Neither Skelbrooke nor Sera could speak for a moment, standing side by side in rapt contemplation of the beauty of the figures.

On the far left stood Mother Snow, a regal but somehow gentle-looking old dame in a gown of white feathers and a light blue cloak fastened with a crystal brooch. A snowy owl perched on her shoulder and she carried an iron staff in one hand. Her other hand she extended in a benevolent gesture. It was easy for Sera to imagine her gathering the whole world into one great grand-motherly embrace.

"She is just as I have always pictured her . . . so noble and so wise," said Sera, around a sudden constriction in her throat. "I never . . . I never was acquainted with any of my nearer female relations, but when I was very small and my grandfather took me to the Church of All Seasons . . . I used to believe that her image on the altar always looked at me with—with a special sort of tenderness.''

"As perhaps she did," said Skelbrooke kindly. "Why should she not? I should imagine that you were the most enchanting child.''

Sera shook her head, wishing, too late, that she had not revealed her childish fancy. "I was an ugly little black-haired imp, and never could sit still to listen to the sermons.''

Skelbrooke smiled his disconcertingly beautiful smile. "I am certain I should have thought differently, had I been privileged to know you in those days. But I direct your attention to the next grouping. The lion and the lamb are especially fine, do you not think?''

Sera nodded. Yes, there was Thaw, a blustery, robust old man of gigantic stature, and with him his two companion beasts, signifying his two natures: rough and boisterous, and gentle and mild. And beyond him: the androgynous shape-changer, Showers; the spry jokester, Leaves; and the maidenly Flowers, with her fresh complexion and a garland of orange-blossoms in her hair.

Sera and Lord Skelbrooke viewed each of the other statues in turn: buxom Ripening, with her long auburn hair and her apple cheeks, her crown of golden bees; Gathering, whom the artist had depicted as a small, active, wrinkled little man, rather like a monkey, dressed all in nut-brown; his frail sister, Fading, with her pale blonde hair, her fluttering gown in the colors of dying leaves, and her companion crows and blackbirds. The last figure was Frost: a bent old man with an iron-colored beard extending nearly to his knees, and a long robe of black and grey homespun. A silver wolf, amazingly lifelike, crouched at his feet. The artist, thought Sera, had portrayed exactly the stern eyes and firm jaw of the old man, but also his underlying honesty and integrity.

"Lord Skelbrooke, I am obliged to you," she said, blinking back tears. "I beg your pardon . . . I am not usually so . . . so sentimental."

"Your emotion does you honor, for I am convinced that it springs from a natural piety, a lovely attribute in any woman," he replied. "And the statues are so beautifully done. I must confess that I, too, am moved—though I am not, in general, a deeply religious man."

They turned away from the dais and went on to another grouping of wax figures, and then another. The rest of the collection came as something of a disappointment after the beauty and significance of the Nine Seasons. As they moved on, Skelbrooke placed his hand over Sera's again, a solicitous gesture, not out of keeping with the moment and the emotions they had just shared.

Rather than look him in the face, Sera stared at that hand. It was undoubtedly the hand of a gentleman, being fair-skinned and well tended, and yet there was something about it . . . It was so small, square, and capable-looking, it seemed out of keeping with what she knew—or thought that she knew—of his character.

"My lord," said Sera, when she could trust herself to speak again, "I believe we were speaking of Elsie's magnetic treatments . . . these trances which Jarl Skogsrå induces, and which (he assures us) are calculated to free my cousin from all that ails her."

"Ah, yes." Skelbrooke knit his brows together. Like his eyelashes, they were surprisingly dark against the fairness of his skin, and they were particularly well shaped. "About the so-called magnetic treatments . . . I must confess that I continue to be uneasy. I believe there is more of—how should I say it?—a kind of mind control in the Jarl's treatments, than of animal magnetism. Of that I may say more later. But for the present I will content myself with this: I am convinced that there is something decidedly unwholesome in the medication he is giving her."

Though there was no one but Sera and the silent statues in the gallery to hear him, Lord Skelbrooke lowered his voice. "As I perhaps ought to tell you . . . though I abandoned the serious study of medicine, I have not lost interest in the art, and have since made the acquaintance of many fine physicians. In particular, I know a lady—an apothecary by trade—who is a woman of deep learning. Were you to obtain for me a small quantity of Miss Elsie's medication, I would take that sample to my friend and ask her to tell me what the potion contains. By scent, by taste, by color—by a thousand other indications which you and I would not be aware of—this lady would be able to tell us exactly what herbs or other substances go into Elsie's medicine . . . and how we might counteract their effect."

Sera hesitated before replying, uncertain whether or not to accept this surprising gentleman as an ally. She realized that she really knew very little about him, and that most of that had been founded on a false impression. And yet . . . he spoke so feelingly and with such good sense!

"I will do it," she decided. "Yes, I will, for it can do no harm, and much good may come of it."

But even as she spoke, she felt a sharp pang of guilt, a sense that she betrayed her newly minted friendship with the little Duchess. And for that reason she felt constrained to ask: "But do *you* not feel as though you were committing some . . . slight disloyalty to the Duchess? It is she who recommended Jarl Skogsrå's services, you know, and she has done everything in her power to throw the Jarl and Elsie together. Considering your—your intimacy with the Gracious Lady, I should think you would feel obliged to do everything in your power to—to promote her interests."

Now it was Skelbrooke's turn to look flustered. The color in his cheeks darkened, and he had difficulty meeting Sera's eyes. "Whatever my relationship with the Duchess, a man must follow the dictates of his own conscience. Moreover, you seem to be under some misapprehension. I have spent . . . many enjoyable hours in Marella's company, but I am not in love with her—nor, I should hasten to add, is she in love with me!

"No doubt you will think me rather cynical," he continued, releasing her hand, and making a great show of shaking out the deep silver lace at his wrists, "when I tell you that our . . . friendship is of a practical rather than a sentimental nature. As an aspiring

141

poet, I gain by association with a woman of her consequence, and she . . . well, by sponsoring me, the Duchess also adds lustre to her own position as patroness of artists and philosophers."

They had returned to the door by which they had entered the gallery, but Skelbrooke paused at the threshold. His eyes were dark with emotion, and it was evident that he was undergoing some internal struggle. "But all of this quite aside . . . it would be impossible for me to fall in love with Marella because—because my entire devotion has already been bestowed elsewhere."

The gallery had suddenly become unbearably warm. Sera shook out her fan and plied it vigorously. "I suppose . . . I must suppose you are speaking of your poetic muse. The Goddess of Hermeticism, or whoever it is to whom you address your verses."

"I do not speak of my muse," said Skelbrooke. Having arranged his laces, he was now staring down at his shoes. It seemed that he, too, found something to disturb him in the appearance of those pastel satin bows. "Far from being the product of any high-flown fancy, the lady of my affections is indisputably real."

Sera fanned herself even more vigorously, "And does this lady . . . the object of your devotion . . . is she aware that you . . . love her? And if she does—can she possibly approve of your liaison with the Duchess?"

"I have not dared to address her," said Skelbrooke, the troubled frown deepening between those expressive eyes of his. "As long as the . . . the exigencies of my present situation require me to continue my association with the Duchess, I am not worthy to approach her."

"I should think . . ." Sera began, then thought better of what she would say, shook her head, and grew silent.

Lord Skelbrooke looked up at her. "You were about to say?"

"It is no concern of mine," Sera replied, just above a whisper. It was increasingly difficult for her to speak, and her mouth was very dry. "I have said too much already. I wonder that you have endured my impertinence so long as you have."

"But I very much wish to hear what you would say. Miss Vorder, I beg you, do not think to spare my feelings."

Sera took a deep breath. "Since you would have it so . . . I was about to say that I wondered about the strength of your affection. For if you really loved . . . this lady . . . I believe you would be willing to put all considerations of—of poetry aside and put an end to your affair with the Duchess."

With a visible effort, his lordship mastered himself. "Ah, but

142

you see . . . my situation is very much more complicated than you suppose, and there is far more at stake than *poetry*. Were that not so, I would certainly do as you advise: end my association with the Duchess and lay my heart at my lady's feet.

"In truth," he added, with a wry attempt at gaiety, "there is no reason to suppose that the lady in question would see fit to accept my offer of heart and hand. Nevertheless, I do assure you that no uncertainty on my part would prevent me from making the offer."

Sera tried to match his light, bantering tone. "You were not in love, then, with—with the lady you speak of when you entered into your present . . . complicated situation?" Yet she was afraid that she had betrayed too much, when Skelbrooke instantly grew sober.

"No," he said quietly. "I was not. When I came into Marstadt I had no idea of falling in love. Indeed, it was the one thing of all things that I would have prevented had it been in my power."

20.

In which the Duchess lays her Plans.

Count Xebo's ball was the talk of Thornburg for many days: how agreeable the music (said those who had attended) . . . how bountiful the food . . . how elegant the gowns of all the ladies and witty the discourse of all the gentlemen! The Count's wax statues were pronounced perfectly exquisite, the Count and his Countess the perfect host and hostess. The ball was an unqualified success, said practically everyone, and everyone else agreed.

Yet there were those few—whatever they might have *said*—who failed to view the event in quite such an amiable light. Sera Vorder was among those few, and (rather more surprisingly) so was the Duchess of Zar-Wildungen.

Two days after the ball, the Duchess sat at her dressing table in her gilded boudoir, reviewing the event in her mind's eye. It was evident, from her stormy aspect, that the lady did not find the exercise an entertaining one.

She lifted a filigree hand mirror, frowned at her own charming reflection. She picked up a haresfoot, rubbed on a dab of rouge, and carefully applied it to her cheeks. Then she examined the effect in the mirror. "Bring me my patch box," she told her obsequious little maid.

Just then, her butler stalked into the room and announced Jarl Skogsrå. "Deny me," said the Duchess, with an impatient gesture of her hand. "My head aches and I feel so dreadfully cross . . ."

But then, as the dignified dwarf turned to carry out her instructions, she reconsidered. "No . . . after all," she said, with a sigh. "You had better admit him."

The Jarl appeared a few minutes later, in a coat of scarlet broadcloth, with a riding whip tucked under his arm. "I had intended to ask you to join me for a ride through Solingen Park," he said, bowing low over her hand. "But it appears that the Gracious Lady has already made other plans."

Though the Duchess still wore her dressing gown, her costume for the day lay spread out upon the bed: the heliotrope satin walking dress and the hat with the ostrich plumes.

"Indeed I have made plans," she said, withdrawing her hand before he had quite finished kissing it. "I have so many demands on my time, so very many obligations, that I can ill afford to linger here of an afternoon, waiting for *you* to call . . . or for Lord Skelbrooke to offer to gallant me."

From which the Jarl immediately gathered that the Duchess's cavalier had again left town without asking leave.

Skogsrå twirled his riding crop, idly wondering whether Skelbrooke was visiting another rich patroness—in Mittleheim or Ingeldorf, perhaps—or had he a taste for buxom country girls, instead?

"I cannot, of course, account for Lord Skelbrooke, but as for myself . . . I am entirely yours to command," the Jarl replied smoothly. "Surely you are aware of this."

The Duchess discarded her dressing gown, stood up in her corset and her ruffled petticoats. She lifted a lacy hem to examine her feet, which were very prettily shod in lavender kid with diamond buckles. The effect was a pleasing one, but it did not improve her temper. "Yes, yes, you are very good. You do everything that I tell you to," she said impatiently. "At least . . . you do so to the best of your somewhat limited ability."

144

The maid gathered up the voluminous skirts of the heliotrope gown and slipped it over the Duchess's head. The lady reappeared, looking flushed and irritated. She gave the satin skirt a tug, to settle it into place, and the girl arranged the pleats and folds so that the gown draped to the best advantage.

"You seem to imply some failure on my part," said the Jarl. "I wish you would tell me how I have failed to please you."

The Duchess pulled up the tight-fitting bodice, slid her arms into the sleeves.

"Your wooing of Elsie has been somewhat desultory," she said, as the maid circled around to hook her into the dress. "A fine ardent lover you are, to be sure! Not even the sense to press the advantage you gained at Count Xebo's ball . . . or do I wrong you? Have you waited these two days to tell me that my godchild has accepted you, that Elsie has finally consented to be your wife?"

"Alas, no," said the Jarl, with a stiff little bow. "That honor has yet to be mine."

"Dear me," said the Duchess. The maid brought her a pair of long lavender gloves. "I hope you do not mean to tell me that you were such a fool as to allow the opportunity to slip?" she asked, donning first one glove and then the other. "You did *ask* Elsie to marry you?"

The Jarl tapped his riding crop against his high leather boots. "Ask her to marry me? I begged her to be mine, I entreated her . . . believe me, I was the most ardent of lovers! She only smiled sadly and asked for more time to think the matter over. For my part, I believe she is much inclined to accept me, but that she is so very young and fears to make the wrong decision."

The Duchess shook her head. "I had no idea the girl was like to prove so prudent. But I suppose it is just a case of our Miss Sera putting ideas into her head . . . Either that, my dear Jarl, or you have bungled things entirely."

She picked up a diamond bracelet, handed it to Skogsrå, and gracefully extended her arm. "Oblige me by fastening the clasp."

The Jarl had smiled at the mention of Sera's name, showing his gleaming white teeth. "Miss Sera Vorder is a young woman of such forceful character, such incomparable spirit, I sometimes wonder why we bother with the other one at all. If you would allow me to—"

"You could not do it," said the Duchess. "No, positively you could not—even if I were inclined to permit it—for you aroused her dislike and her suspicion from the very beginning. That . . .

145

pleasure . . . you are thinking of, if it is to be enjoyed by anyone, must be reserved for another. It will never be yours."

She tied on her plumed bonnet, picked up her fan and her reticule, then turned back to the Jarl. "I have a call to make, of particular interest. You may accompany me, if you like—providing you will not think the pace too slow, and that great horse of yours does not frighten my sheep."

"It will be my pleasure," said Skogsrå. "But the Gracious Lady has yet to inform me where she is going."

"I am going to the Hospital of the Celestial Names, to view a demonstration of natural laws," said the Duchess. She moved toward the door. "Dear me . . . you seem rather flustered. Have you never visited a hospital before? Then by all means, you ought to accompany me. You are something of a physician yourself, are you not? So I hardly think that anything you see there will shock or dismay you.

"Or do you," she asked, with a sly smile, ". . . do you fear to find your surroundings a little too . . . attractive?"

The Jarl offered her his arm. "You are pleased to jest with me," he said coldly. "But naturally my greatest concern is for you . . . A charity hospital hardly seems the proper setting for a great lady like the Duchess of Zar-Wildungen."

"You are entirely mistaken," said the Duchess, equally cool. "A great lady like the Duchess of Zar-Wildungen can go where she pleases and do as she likes . . . the advantage of age and rank."

They left her rooms and descended the curving marble staircase to the floor below. "Perhaps you are not acquainted with my young friend, Mr. Theophilus von Eichstätt? But of course you must know him—he is so often here," said the Duchess.

"Von Eichstätt?" The Jarl took a moment to consider. "But yes . . . the ugly young man with the awkward manners . . . I have often wondered why he was such a favorite."

The Duchess glared at him. "Yes, he is terribly plain, I am afraid, and his manners lack polish, but he has been studying medicine for two years and already promises to become a brilliant physician—as well as an experimental scientist of some note. He is not, however, a young man of independent means, and so he is obliged to seek my financial assistance. It is as his patron that I attend thc demonstration today. I believe that you will find it fascinating, for it involves the circulation of the blood and the action of the heart."

The Jarl raised a delicate eyebrow, but he did not otherwise reply.

In the lower hall, they met one of the Duchess's footmen, leading the miniature ape on a leash. Skogsrå could not conceal his disgust as the Duchess took the little creature into her arms, and the ape clasped its hairy blue arms around her dainty neck. "I suppose it is necessary for this . . . this monkey to accompany us?"

"It pleases me to bring him," said the Duchess. The footman had opened the door, so she sailed on through. She paused at the top of the steps and looked back at Skogsrå. "Why should I not? He is very well behaved and undoubtedly a novelty. And he is not a monkey, you know. He is an indigo ape, very rare—oh, yes, I assure you, very rare indeed."

"The creature has a lugubrious look and I have never seen it but when it was lethargic," insisted the Jarl, as he followed her down the front steps to her carriage and watched her hand the ape up to her gnome coachman. "I am convinced this animal is diseased."

The Duchess allowed the Jarl to assist her in mounting the scallop shell carriage. "Nonsense," she said, settling herself comfortably on the plush cushions. "Sebastian cherishes a secret sorrow—and that, as you know, is inclined to depress the spirits—but otherwise, he enjoys the very best of health."

Skogsrå sneered; it was not an expression that went well with the golden lovelocks and the delicately painted eyebrows. "You speak as though the creature were human."

The Duchess smiled sweetly. "Surely that is a distinction, my dear good Jarl, over which the pair of us are singularly unqualified to quibble."

The Hospital of the Celestial Names occupied what had once been a fine large house, a sprawling structure of wood, plaster, and brick, some three or four centuries old, which was situated on the outskirts of the town. The Duchess left her grotesque little pet behind her in the carriage, in the charge of her coachman, and Skogsrå escorted her into the building.

A stench of blood and of unwashed bodies, the sickly sweet odor of rotting flesh, assailed them as soon as they stepped through the door. The Jarl pulled a scented handkerchief out of his sleeve and held it up to his nose. "This place is filthy," he said, sur-

147

veying, with marked disfavor, the dingy entry hall. "It reeks of contagion."

An ill-dressed young man, carrying a mere stub of a lighted candle, shortly appeared to show them the way. He took them down a tunnel-like corridor, up a narrow, creaking stair, and along a dark, echoing gallery, passing by many open rooms along the way. The Duchess stopped in one such doorway, peered inside, then signaled to the Jarl to do the same. Reluctantly, he complied.

It was a warm day, but the windows were closed and shuttered, the low chamber dimly lit by a single oil lamp suspended from a beam in the ceiling. On a narrow table within the circle of lamp light lay the grey-skinned figure of a young man, naked to the waist. At the patient's head stood a slatternly woman in a shapeless gown, holding a wet piece of rag over his mouth and nose. His legs and his arms—which were covered with running sores—had been secured to the table by iron bands. The patient's eyes were closed and he appeared to be unconscious, if not already dead, mercifully oblivious to the clumsy operations of the blood-stained chirurgeons who were sawing off his right arm just below the elbow.

Skogsrå gagged quietly into his handkerchief. He turned away, and found the Duchess watching him with a speculative eye.

"You find this place unappetizing?" the Duchess inquired archly.

"I abhor the very appearance of diseased flesh," Skogsrå replied, walking away from the door, as steadily as he could.

"Ah . . ." said the Duchess maliciously. "But of course, you would be particular about these things, would you not?"

The Jarl did not reply. Their escort paused to wait for them much farther along the gallery, and they hurried to catch up with him. He took them through one of the wards—past row upon row of low beds, where emaciated figures shivered with ague or tossed feverishly under ragged blankets, and the stench of the dead and the dying was stronger than before—then down another dark corridor.

At last they came into a larger and lighter chamber which had been thoroughly outfitted as a medical laboratory, with wooden vats and great brick furnaces; stills, crucibles, baths, and condensors; and long tables filled with gleaming glass beakers, aludels, retorts, and similar apparatus, all joined together by yards and yards of glass and copper tubing. The young man in the shabby

148

coat promised to summon Mr. von Eichstätt, bowed to the Duchess, and withdrew.

"But it seems that you were not expected, after all," said the Jarl. He was beginning to recover a little and was pleased to witness the Duchess at a slight disadvantage. "There is no one here to greet you . . . no one to welcome the Gracious Lady."

"I am a trifle early," she replied, dropping gracefully into a chair and unfurling her fan. "Or rather . . . I am not so late as was perhaps anticipated. Sit down, Lord Skogsrå. We apparently have the time for a little private conversation, and indeed, it was with that in mind that I asked you to accompany me."

Conscious of an undercurrent of displeasure in her words, the Jarl hastened to obey her. As the Duchess occupied the only real chair in the room, he perched, rather awkwardly, on one of a number of very high stools. "The lady has only to speak, and I am all attention."

The Duchess waved her fan. "As you know," she said, "I leave for the Wichtelberg at the end of the season. I had hoped to see things settled between you and Elsie before I set out on that journey, but that seems not to be. Perhaps I ought to take the pair of you with me, so that I may continue to oversee your affair. The country air—so notoriously salubrious!—ought to be just the thing for my poor ailing godchild."

The Jarl crumbled up his handkerchief and put it into his pocket. "If you can obtain the permission of her mama . . . who seems to regard Elsie's presence in Thornburg, with all of her so interesting afflictions, as something of a social asset."

"It is true that Clothilde must be handled very carefully," said the Duchess. "But after all, her position in Society is largely based on the consequence she derives as my friend. As reluctant as she may be to relinquish Elsie for a season or two, how much more reluctant to risk offending me?

"As for you, my dear Skogsrå, I apprehend that you are entirely at my disposal."

The Jarl slipped off his stool and bowed his assent. "That is naturally understood. And I suppose . . . But yes, of course. You will invite the other Miss Vorder as well. It is not to be thought that Elsie would think of traveling without her. She will be on hand to flout me—and to tempt me into some indiscretion—at every turn."

The Duchess snapped her fan shut. "But of course Sera must come with us—and you shall just have to control whatever gro-

149

tesque impulses she may inspire in you!" she said. "Indeed, I shall be glad of the opportunity to cultivate her friendship. Were you aware that she is the granddaughter of Jenk the bookseller? I see you were not. I do not like to leave town just when Jenk's experiments seem likely to bear such interesting fruit, but what else can I do?"

The Jarl resumed his perch. "You might, one supposes, postpone your visit to Zar-Wildungen."

"Then one supposes wrongly," said the Duchess, dropping her fan into her lap and beginning to remove the lavender gloves. "The Duke asks very little of me—only that I spend eight or ten weeks out of the year with him at the Wichtelberg—and in return for all that he gives me, his many indulgences, I am glad enough to oblige him."

"Ah, yes," said Skogsrå. "I have always thought the Duke the most admirably indulgent of husbands."

The Duchess glared at him. "More indulgent than you guess . . . and considerably less stupid than you mean to imply. The Duke knows all about me and understands my needs. Surely, you who are obsessed by your own impulses should understand as well."

The Jarl shrugged his shoulders. "It is my nature to be obsessed by my impulses, as you are pleased to call them."

"As it is also mine," said the Duchess, folding her gloves. "It is not a matter of mere inclination: I *require* passion, I *must* have gaiety, I *live for* admiration. But most of all, there must be new experiences. If (as I must confess it seems unlikely) you ever live to be as old as I am, you will understand that boredom means death."

The Jarl began to look interested. "And just how old *is* the Gracious Lady, if one is permitted to ask?"

"Older than the Duke . . . and younger," said the Duchess. "I am one hundred and eighty years old, and I confidently expect to live at least another century."

Jarl Skogsrå was visibly impressed. "Then it is true what I have heard rumored, and what you have often hinted . . . a trace of fairy blood?"

"More than a trace," said the Duchess. "My mother was a half-breed, human and Farisee; my father is a full-blooded fairy. His people are the Fees—and a strange and terrible folk they are, for all their diminutive size! I am three-quarters fairy, yes, fully three-quarters."

150

"And yet . . ." said the Jarl, "you live in Thornburg and shun the company of your own kind."

The Duchess picked up her fan. "Ah, well . . . you must understand . . . they are so very different, Men and fairies, so different in their interests, their needs, and their passions, it is a wonder that they should ever meet and mate at all. And yet it does happen, and when it does: the result is a most remarkable hybrid.

"But fairy Society," said the Duchess, "and most particularly the fairy court, is by nature so very conservative that there is no place—no place at all—for hybrids of any sort. We do much better in the society of Men, dwarves, and gnomes, which by its very nature must make room for a little variety."

They left the hospital an hour or two later, and the Jarl was not sorry to leave that place and its stifling, unwholesome atmosphere. Yet he remained a little uneasy about the Duchess's motives in asking him to accompany her.

She, on the other hand, had apparently gained considerable satisfaction from the visit. Her mood was lighter and her manner gracious as he handed her up into the carriage. "Would you care to follow me home and join me there for a little supper?"

"Alas, no," said the Jarl. "Your chosen mode of transportation—if one may say so—obliges you to travel at such a leisurely pace . . . and my poor horse appears to be growing restive."

He took up the reins and swung into the saddle. "No doubt you shall employ a swifter means of travel on your journey to Zar-Wildungen?"

"I shall travel in a coach with six horses," said the Duchess. "I and my companions . . . for I believe that I *shall* take Sera and Elsie with me. As for you . . . your presence and that of the other gentleman I have invited might make things rather crowded. You can hire your own conveyance, or ride along beside us, exactly as you choose."

The Jarl's grey gelding was indeed growing restive, and it was increasingly difficult to keep the beast standing, but the Duchess had not yet dismissed him. "I shall begin to make my preparations at once," said Skogsrå. "And this other gentleman you spoke of . . . I suppose you mean Lord Skelbrooke?"

"I do not," replied the Duchess. "It is true that I originally intended to invite him, but I have since revised my plans. He seems a shade too interested in our Miss Sera, and I would not wish to throw them too much into each other's company.''

The grey gelding dipped his head and moved sideways; the Jarl's hands tightened on the reins. "Ah, yes," said Skogsrå, with a suggestive smile. "Leave the neglectful young lover behind, to languish and reproach himself. It will teach him the lesson that he deserves."

The Duchess stiffened. "I cannot imagine what you are talking about. Skelbrooke is devoted to me . . . completely devoted. Any interest he takes in Miss Sera Vorder is an entirely fraternal one, and as for any other woman—''

"—as for any other woman . . . it is not to be thought of," the Jarl finished for her. "But of course, that goes without saying."

21.

Which ought to Confirm certain Suppositions on the part of the Reader.

On the road between Thornburg and Gdanze, in the village of Lüftmal, about ten miles from the ducal seat in Zar-Wildungen, stood a humble country inn called the Head of Cabbage. The landlord at the Cabbage kept a respectable house, but the inn was small and not a favorite among travelers, who generally preferred to stop the night at the Hanging Sword in Pfalz, which was a larger and altogether grander establishment. Yet the occasional traveler, less affluent or more frugal, did stop in.

Such, apparently, was the fresh-faced young clergyman in a neat brown wig, who rode into the village late one morning. He was dressed, as became his calling, all in sober black, except for a plain neckcloth without a bit of lace, and narrow ruffles at his wrists. He spent an hour or two wandering through the village— he seemed particularly interested in the church and the churchyard cemetery—made some inquiries as to the quality of the food served at the inn, and at last strolled into the Cabbage.

The interior was rather more prepossessing than the exterior, with gay chintz curtains and scrubbed flagstone floors and a fine display of well-polished pewter on the sideboard in the common room. The gentleman spoke at some length with Mr. Chawettys, the landlord, and ended by securing a room for a fortnight.

His name (he told the landlord) was Marcus Sylvester Crow, Doctor of Divine Philosophy. He had recently been ill. His physicians advised a visit to the country in order to hasten his recovery, and he hoped that the inn was as clean and quiet, the fare as simple and wholesome, as he had been led to believe. He spoke with a faint accent, a sort of rising inflection at the end of each sentence, which suggested he was a native of the island of Mawbri.

He ate a good dinner, served by Charlotte the ancient barmaid in a private parlor at the back, told the landlord that his baggage would arrive on the morrow, and allowed Mr. Chawettys to escort him upstairs to the best bedchamber.

He reappeared that evening and ate his supper by the fire in the common room, with a book lying open on the table before him. He appeared to be ill or depressed in his spirits, for he picked at his food and said nothing to anyone—until Tilda, the new girl, brought him a tankard of ale.

He looked up, met the girl's curious gaze, and started violently.

"Sorry, sir," said Tilda. "I know you didn't order none, but it's a good brown ale . . . and you being so recently ill and all . . ."

"I beg your pardon. You did not really startle me; it is only that my nerves are sadly weakened," said Dr. Crow. "Yes, it was a kindly thought. I am normally an abstemious man, but perhaps under the circumstances . . . yes, my physicians *have* recommended to me the benefits to be derived from a good strong, country ale."

He accepted the tankard and returned to his book. He continued in the same fashion for another hour or so, until a low-voiced conversation between two farmers attracted his attention.

". . . a pauper's grave, and you'll know what that means," said the first farmer, a big-shouldered rustic with a mop of straw-colored hair. "Seems to me the decent folk in these parts could arrange it between them, so nobody goes into the ground without some manner of an offering. If the dead of Lüftmal don't rest safe in their graves, how can the living rest easy in their beds?"

The other man, leaner and more weathered-looking, scratched his head. "A handful of copper pennies ain't sufficient; it takes gold and silver to sanctify a grave. We learned that lesson, if we didn't know it already, when that old beggar died last winter. No, and there ain't many in these parts has the means to be charitable

153

to the living, much less the dead. We offer up our gold and our silver for the sake of our neighbors, there won't be nothing left for our own kinfolk when *their* hour comes around.''

"I beg your pardon," said Dr. Crow, glancing up from his book. "I could not help overhearing . . . and naturally, as a man of the cloth, the matter is of some interest. Have you really reason to suppose that the dead do not rest as peacefully in Lüftmal as they do elsewhere?''

The two farmers squirmed in their seats. They had arrived after the incident with the ale and had not noticed the stranger reading so quietly by the fire.

"Don't you pay no mind to what you just heard, for there ain't nothing in it," said the lean, leathery man. He gestured toward his stocky companion. "My friend here, he's a cautious man, always aworrying what will happen when things ain't done proper . . . particular when the doing things right means dipping a hand into his neighbor's purse.'' And he glared fiercely at the other farmer.

"That's right . . . he has the right of it," the big man agreed, perhaps a little too heartily. "Speculation, that's all it was. We've a fine churchyard here . . . a grand old graveyard with lovely old stones. Scholarly gentlemen from the town come down to look at 'em all the time. You might want to take a look yourself, Parson.''

Dr. Crow realized he had hit on a topic the locals did not care to discuss with outsiders. It was also plain that the subject of the antique stones in the churchyard had been introduced by way of a distraction.

"Thank you," he said, "I have already seen the graveyard. The older stones are indeed a fine example of the funerary arts as they were practiced in the thirteenth and fourteenth centuries— you are fortunate in being located on rising ground and so far from the river, else your graveyard had not survived so long. When I had my health, I traveled extensively and always made a particular point of stopping to look at cemeteries along the way. I find yours of great interest.''

He took a sip of ale and cleared his throat. "However, I also take a deep interest in the history of these places, and especially in local traditions and superstitions relating to graveyards. I have heard some disturbing tales in my time, as you may well imagine. And I find there is often a direct relationship between a wave of . . . well, we can scarcely call them grave-robberies, for those who lie in unhallowed graves do not possess anything to attract the

154

ordinary scoundrel . . . let us say, then, a relationship between a wave of *clandestine exhumations* and an increase in black witch-craft in the country around. It seems that practitioners of the dark arts make use of the bodies in some of their more appalling rituals. The Hand of Glory, for instance . . . I do crave your pardon," he said, looking around him, at the sullen faces of his listeners. "I did not mean to bore you or to make you uneasy by this somewhat grisly hobby-horse of mine. I can see very plainly that nothing of the sort is happening here."

And so saying, Dr. Crow returned to his book. For all that he sat so near the fire, he was aware of a pronounced chill in the common room. Yet he had learned much more than any of them realized: in his experience most villagers were all too willing to regale inquisitive outsiders with hair-raising tales of local horrors, so long as the ghosts and ghouls were purely imaginary—it was only when the horrors were genuine that everyone in the vicinity began to clam up.

Certainly, no one approached him or spoke to him after that, except for Tilda, when she came to remove the empty pewter tankard. "I had a fancy, sir, when I first saw you, that I met you somewheres afore."

The clergyman turned a page before looking up. Tilda was a remarkably pretty girl, no more than seventeen or eighteen, with long, silky, corn-colored hair, which she wore in a single plait. "Had you indeed? That hardly seems possible. I have never been here before."

"No, sir," said Tilda respectfully. "It was only a resemblance, like as not. You have a look of a gentleman . . . a gentleman who lent me a hand up out of the gutter and reformed my way of life . . . in a manner of speaking."

Dr. Crow smiled faintly. "Ah . . . a clergyman, like myself, I apprehend."

"Well, sir," said the girl, with an answering smile. "He appeared to be some kind of a religious, anyways."

The next morning, Tilda volunteered to carry Dr. Crow's breakfast upstairs. "No reason Charlotte should do it . . . all them stairs. Let me look after the Reverend, after this."

Balancing the tray, she climbed two flights to the attic, knocked on the Reverend Doctor's door, and announced herself. A voice on the other side invited her to enter. The chamber under the eaves ran the whole length of the attic. It was a bright, airy room, with

155

two large dormer windows, floors of bleached oak, and an enormous old-fashioned bed with velvet curtains that dwarfed the other, plainer furnishings.

Dr. Crow had not yet donned his coat, but he was otherwise dressed as he had been the day before, in a dark waistcoat and breeches, and immaculate white linen. He sat in a ladderback chair by an open window, with his feet propped up on a stool and his black-stockinged ankles crossed, buffing his nails with a handkerchief.

"I trust you slept well, sir."

"I seldom have difficulty sleeping, my dear." He reached into his waistcoat pocket and extracted a tiny box (it might have been a snuffbox, but Tilda knew that it was not) with an inlay of pearl and ivory. "There is no need for you to pretend that you do not recognize me, or that you do not remember what this box contains," he chided her gently. "We both of us know that you do."

Tilda carried the tray over to a table by the other window. "I'm sorry about that down below. I should of held my tongue. I hope you don't think, sir, that I would ever betray you?"

"How could I, indeed?" he said. "But of course you could not know: the constables of Thornburg are still combing the streets for a gigantic one-eyed Spagnard."

Dr. Crow had both his eyes; and very fine eyes they were, too (as Tilda was not slow to notice), being a sober grey, fringed with extravagant dark lashes. He was not above average height, and his build was slender.

He waved a hand in the direction of the bed. "Sit down and chat with me awhile. In truth, I am glad to find a friend here, where I had expected none. It seems that the Fates smile on me . . . or is there more here than mere coincidence? I was sent here by certain . . . associates of mine . . . to investigate a report of witchcraft in the district. But who was it that alerted *them* —do you know?"

Tilda sat down on the edge of the bed and folded her hands in her lap. "Well, sir . . . you've guessed it. It happened this way: I did as you told me, sir, and left Thornburg real quick. I was on my way to Pfalz, but I stopped in here. They was looking for a barmaid and this seemed . . . a quiet little village, sir, a safe sort of place. And I wasn't eager to take up my old way of life, after . . . after the risks involved was brought home to me as they were. So when Mr. Chawettys offered me the job, I was glad to take it. And I like it here, sir, and I had met a young man, afore I

156

heard . . . what strangers to these parts don't generally hear . . . and discovered the village wasn't near so safe as I thought.''

She shook her head, released a long, heartfelt sigh. ''Well, there it was . . . I was scared to stay, but I hated to leave my young man—he's a good man, is 'Zekiel, and he treats me real good, in spite of I told him I used to be a whore—and I was in a rare taking, you may believe me, until I thought of you. I said to myself, if there's mischief of *that* sort afoot, perhaps Mr. Carstares would like to hear of it.''

''Just by the way of information,'' he said quietly, ''my name is not actually Carstares.''

''No, sir, I didn't suppose that it was,'' said Tilda, spreading out her skirts. ''Nor I don't suppose it's Dr. Crow, neither.''

''It is not,'' he said, replacing the snuffbox and tucking his handkerchief into a pocket in his breeches. He rose gracefully to his feet and began to pace the room. ''At least . . . I am all but certain that it is not. I do experience some difficulty, now and again, remembering exactly who and what I am, but I am generally able to recall my own name.''

She smiled uncertainly. ''Your little joke, sir?''

He paused by the fireplace, rested an elbow on the mantel. ''Perhaps. Perhaps not.'' He smiled back at her, but the smile did not reach his eyes. ''But I must apologize for interrupting— you were telling me, I believe, that you felt I might be interested . . . ?''

''Yes, sir. But I didn't feel right contacting you direct. I thought . . . I thought if I sent a message with your name on it, mentioning where I met you, you might think the Knights was involved and that I was in danger . . . and you might be angry, sir, if you come to help me, and found out that it weren't so, having—having more *important* affairs to occupy you.

''So what I did, I asked 'Zekiel to write it out for me: that the village of Lüftmal weren't a proper place to live no more . . . everyone walking in fear of witches, and the dead not safe in their graves . . . and he took it into Thornburg, where he left it in the shop of a glazier, a bottlemaker, and a man who sold trinkets of blown glass.''

He nodded approvingly. ''You are a young woman of considerable resource—as indeed, I suspected when first we met—and your friend Ezekiel sounds like an excellent young man. My own friends were not slow in passing the information on to me, you may be sure, nor did I consider the matter beneath my attention.''

157

He removed his elbow from the mantel, put up a hand to straighten his neckcloth. "And so . . . I am here. But your neighbors do not confide in me. Not an unusual state of affairs, to be sure. It is common practice to hush these things up . . . the innocent fearing to arouse the wrath of the guilty. Yet it is a definite inconvenience. I could attend to this matter far more expeditiously if I had a friend here . . . someone . . . not a newcomer like yourself . . . but a trusted and knowledgeable member of the community, who was willing to assist me. You have no clergyman, as I suppose?"

Tilda shook her head. "No, sir. Dr. Ulfson rides over from Pfalz every Sunday, if the weather ain't bad."

"And what of your swain . . . the resourceful Ezekiel—would he be willing to conspire with me for the good of his neighbors?"

Tilda twisted her hands together. "He may be willing . . . I don't know. He's done so much already—more than anybody else in the village would of done. I'll ask him, anyways. But . . . if it ain't impertinent for me to ask, I'd like to know something more about—about your friends who sent you here."

He turned to face the window. "I understand perfectly that you desire reassurance . . . but I am bound in honor not to reveal their names. I am—as you seem to have guessed—a kind of . . . agent . . . assigned to sniff out practices of black magic and put an end to them if I may."

"An agent . . . of the Grand Duke, sir? But no . . ." said Tilda. "You wouldn't be here in Zar-Wildungen, would you? Of the Prince, then?"

He turned back to look at her. "Perhaps I have chosen the wrong word. It may be too much to dignify my calling with the name of agent . . . or of spy, either. I represent no government, but rather an organization of well-meaning but self-appointed citizens . . . what our cousins in the New World would call a Vigilance Committee. Yes, I suppose I must admit to being a vigilante. It is a lowering reflection, to be sure, but it is always best to face the facts."

He heaved a great sigh. "Yes, I am a witch-hunter and a vigilante. And something of a magician on my own account, as well. I wonder if this recitation of my . . . rank and titles . . . offers you any reassurance at all?"

Tilda unclasped her hands. "You said enough to satisfy me. I hope it will be enough for 'Zekiel. It may be—I don't know.

Anyways, I'll speak to him this very day, and if he's agreeable, I'll arrange for him to meet you in the churchyard this evening.''

"Thank you," said the self-styled vigilante. "Somehow, I have every confidence that you will be able to persuade him."

22.

Wherein the Wickedness of the Lüftmal Witches is more fully Revealed.

Dr. Crow spent the afternoon in the ancient Lüftmal cemetery, studying the gravestones. Tilda's young man arrived at sunset. He was a rangy youth with a shock of flaming red hair, and a huge bouquet of meadowflowers clutched in one hand.

" 'Zekiel Karl, your worship," he said, offering his other hand to the supposed clergyman in a forthright manner. "I come here pretty regular, for to lay flowers on my granny's grave, so I reckon there's none will wonder at our meeting here."

Dr. Crow sat back on his heels—he had been down on his knees and his elbows in the long green grass, examining the lettering on one of the stones—and placed his own well-kept hand in Eze-kiel's big meaty palm. "I am obliged to you for agreeing to meet me."

"I'm willing to do more than that, sir," said the young farmer. "If it pleases your worship, I can take you to see them witches at their mischief. They always holds a Sabbat in old Matt Wood-ruff's barn at the full of the moon, and that's coming up real soon."

Dr. Crow raised a shapely dark eyebrow, for this was plain speaking indeed. He rose gracefully to his feet, adjusted the narrow ruffles at his wrists, took out a handkerchief, and dusted the knees of his breeches. "Their habits and their meeting place are known, then? And yet nothing has been done to bring any of them to justice? This dwarf (as I must suppose by the name), Matt Wood-ruff . . . ?"

"Dead sir, these twenty years. Nobody lives over to Woodruff's

159

anymore. He weren't much of a farmer (them wichtel never are, they just don't seem to take to it) and they say he bought the place because it were so lonely and secret-like . . . him being a black warlock, as the story goes.''

Ezekiel lowered his voice impressively. "They say, also, that his ghost still walks, but I don't know. We do know they meet there, sir, but what's that to the purpose? Nobody knows who any of them are—though I guess most of us got our suspicions.''

"And do not dare to act on them," said Dr. Crow, leaning up against a towering granite slab. "The Circle, I take it, is a large one—twice or thrice the usual thirteen?''

"Yes, sir, I reckon so, though nobody seems to know exactly how large. It don't do to inquire too close, there being so many and all so spiteful," said Ezekiel, balancing back on his heels. "A man says or does anything that one of them decides to take amiss, the next thing he knows his cows are dry and his sheep got the staggers and . . . and sometimes worse things as well. There's been children died, and nobody rightly knew what ailed them. But the worst of it is, it ain't always something that some-body's *done* to rile 'em—sometimes they'll ruin folks just for pure wickedness. Maybe you don't know this, sir, being city-bred, but a farmer or a herdsman living off the land . . . you kill his crops and his stock, 'tis the same as killing him, it ain't no different, excepting he dies so slow. And once it's known they've got it in for a family, there's not hardly anybody who dares to lend a hand.''

"And the local authorities?" asked Dr. Crow. "They, too, are powerless?''

Ezekiel clenched and unclenched a big fist. "Three years ago, before them witches grew so bold, the magistrate over to Pfalz sent some of his men. They caught Hagen Jansen with a wax doll stuck full of pins in his pocket, and they . . . they tried to beat the names of the other witches out of him. It didn't do no good, though, and maybe it made things worse. There was a spell on Hagen, and he *couldn't* betray the others, not if them constables had tortured him to death. They finally left off beating him, and tried him and hung him. But after that . . . them witches got real busy, and things ain't been the same since. You won't do anything, sir, to stir them up?''

The flowers in Ezekiel's hands grew limp, due to the tightening and squeezing of his enormous hands. Apparently, the young farmer was entertaining second thoughts. "Tilda said, if you set out to stop them, they'd *be* stopped. She said you was a match

160

for the whole lot of them. She said you could bust up any Coven, any Magic Circle or Secret Society that ever was. But I don't know . . .''

"I have enjoyed considerable success in the past . . . and against more sophisticated sorcerers than your local Circle. Yet it is unlikely that I am infallible," said Dr. Crow, smiling faintly at Tilda's exaggerated opinion of his capabilities. "But succeed or fail, I shall make very sure that nothing I do appears to be the work of any mortal agency.

"I intend," said Dr. Crow, "to put the fear of the Divine into your Lüftmal witches."

Midnight found Dr. Crow and Ezekiel Karl on the road to Woodruff's farm. *"It would be wise,"* the good doctor had said, *"to learn the lay of the land in advance, and plan our campaign carefully."* They made the journey on foot, and Ezekiel carried a covered lanthorn—they would want a light later, but did not wish to attract attention, if anyone passed by on the road.

The waxing moon was still high and bright when they arrived at the abandoned farm. The barn was a sturdy structure, standing weathered but firmly upright, its boards gleaming silver in the moonlight. The huge double doors were closed and barred.

Dr. Crow stepped forward to lift the bar, but Ezekiel stopped him with a hand on his shoulder. "Look up, sir . . . this ain't no way for the likes of you and me to enter."

The supposed clergyman raised his eyes. Suspended from a beam over the door dangled what first appeared to be a dirty scrap of tattered cloth; when Dr. Crow stepped sideways, to view it with the moon at his back, he discovered that it was a crudely fashioned rag-doll, of uncertain sex, hanging like a felon from a noose.

"An unpleasant piece of business, to be sure," said Dr. Crow, frowning up at the fetish. "But we need not fear so awkward and crude a device. Indeed, it were child's play for me to—"

An uneasy movement on the part of his companion caused him to look around. Ezekiel's rusty hair was bleached by the moonlight to a commonplace straw, but it was not the moonlight that drained his face of all color or drew his features into a mask of apprehension.

"Ah, well, as you say, it would perhaps be better not to tempt the Fates," Dr. Crow decided. "We can come back tomorrow with the proper tools and loosen one of the boards."

"There's a loose board at the back," said Ezekiel. "Fact is, that's why I brung you here . . . I knowed about the poppet already. If you'll just follow me, sir, I'll show you what I mean."

They circled around to the back of the barn, where Ezekiel counted five planks from the northwestern corner. "This'll be the one." A single wooden peg held the board in place, allowing him to rotate the plank and reveal a narrow entry into the barn.

"I would not wish to appear suspicious," said Dr. Crow, "but how did you come to know this?"

Ezekiel allowed the board to fall back into place. "I told you old Matt had a bad reputation . . . that some folks say his ghost still walks? There was many a night my friends and me spent in this barn when we was boys, just hoping to catch a glimpse of Woodruff's ghost.

"There was no reason, in them days, we couldn't of entered by the door," he added, with an embarrassed grin, "but once we knew about this loose board . . . it just seemed more romantical, somehow, to enter by 'the secret way.'"

"But of course . . . I understand perfectly," said Dr. Crow. He lifted the plank and passed sideways through the gap, into the barn. There was ample width to accommodate his slender frame, but it made a tight squeeze for Ezekiel, who had clearly added to his bulk since his ghost-hunting days.

Once inside, the young farmer rotated the metal covering on his lanthorn, allowing the light to shine out on one side. He held it high, to reveal the vast, empty interior of the barn. "I see no stalls, no grain bins," said Dr. Crow.

"Guess they tore them down to make room for . . . for whatever it is they does here. Then they used the wood to feed their fire." Ezekiel indicated a large heap of blackened boards in a kind of firepit at the center of the building. He lifted the lanthorn again. "The loft's still there . . . Hope they didn't burn the ladder."

A lengthy tour of the premises did not yield the ladder. "No matter," said Dr. Crow. "I can bring a rope ladder with me on the night of the Sabbat and draw it up behind me."

Ezekiel shrugged his shoulders. "I don't know, sir, as I can come up with one. At least . . . not the kind with grappling hooks on the end, which I reckon is what you're after."

"Do not trouble yourself," said Dr. Crow. "I can provide the ladder. You might be surprised by the variety of things I carry about in my baggage."

He had been carrying the light, but he passed it back to Ezekiel.

162

"I have seen enough. This place (though you may not think so) offers ample possibilities, sufficient scope for my talents. I shall arrive here early on the appointed evening and make my preparations. You may come with me, if you like. There will be considerable danger involved, but I believe the entertainment I provide will be well worth the risk."

While Dr. Crow returned to the Head of Cabbage, Ezekiel went home to his own small farm. The next two days passed quietly and they did not communicate again until the night of the full moon, when they met behind the inn an hour after sunset.

Though the night was a sultry one, they were both wrapped in long, dark, concealing cloaks, and wore their tricorns pulled low to shadow their faces. Ezekiel again carried the covered lanthorn, while Dr. Crow brought with him a leather satchel, resembling a physician's handbag.

"You got a rope ladder with grappling hooks in there?" asked Ezekiel, eyeing the leather bag doubtfully.

"I have," came the soft reply. A chance movement caused the cloak to fall open, revealing the paler-colored garments below. For whatever reason, "Dr. Crow" had apparently abandoned the clerical pose for the night.

"It is very light, but exceedingly strong, for it was woven of the roots of a stone, the hair of a virtuous woman, the shadow of . . . but I wax fanciful. It was not, in truth, made of any of those things—neither was it woven of any common hemp. I carry, besides, everything else that we are likely to require . . . including these." And he opened his cloak and his coat to reveal a brace of pistols in a belt around his hips.

The walk to Woodruff's farm took about an hour. When they reached the barn, the doors were still closed and barred, but Dr. Crow insisted on a stealthy circuit of the building, just to make certain that he and Ezekiel were the first to arrive. Then they entered again by way of the loose board at the back.

Ezekiel uncovered the lanthorn, set it down on the floor, and opened his coat. "I reckon I ought to tell you that I brung a pistol, too."

"I expected nothing less," replied Dr. Crow. His face, by lanthorn light, was uncharacteristically grim. He opened the satchel and extracted a small clay pot covered with a thin skin of leather. "This contains an explosive."

Then he took out another object, about the size and shape of a

163

pomegranate. "This, also, is an incendiary device . . . a kind of grenado. You are a big man, but you appear agile. I assume, therefore, that you have an accurate eye and a good throwing arm. Yes? Then you will oblige me by taking this device into your keeping, and throwing it onto the witches' fire at the appropriate moment."

"Yes, sir," said Ezekiel, gingerly accepting the explosive. "But how will I know the appropriate moment?"

"You have revealed yourself as a man of some wit and imagination," said Dr. Crow. "I believe you will recognize the moment when it comes."

He knelt down beside the firepit, removed several blackened boards, and scraped away the ashes underneath. He produced a trowel out of his satchel, dug a hole, and buried the covered pot about ten inches deep. Then he rearranged the wood and the ashes, so that everything looked undisturbed.

He stood up and dusted off his hands. "The hour is growing late. We had best climb up to the loft."

With the help of the "uncommon" rope ladder they ascended to the half-floor above. Dr. Crow pulled up the ladder after them, depositing it, along with the satchel, in a corner of the loft. Then he took the lanthorn and examined the floor minutely, until he found a large split in the wood, wide enough for him and his companion—if they knelt on the floor and lowered their heads—to view most of the floor below. "Now we can only wait," said Dr. Crow, as he extinguished the light.

How long they remained in the dark before they heard voices and a fumbling at the bar at the barn door, it was impossible to tell. There was nothing furtive about the approach of the Lüftmal witches. Those who arrived first spoke in loud, slightly tipsy voices, as though they had fortified themselves with ordinary spirits, for their meeting with the supernatural.

A creaking of hinges and a draught of fresher air announced the opening of the doors; there was a flicker of torch light, and two men and three women, cloaked and hooded, entered the barn. Once inside, they lowered their hoods.

Up in the loft, Dr. Crow heard Ezekiel draw in a sudden sharp breath, as though he had recognized someone and received an unpleasant surprise.

One of the men carried in an arm load of twiggy wood, which he proceeded to place on top of the remains of the previous fire.

He stepped back and allowed the other man to kindle the blaze with his torch.

The next to arrive was an ancient dame in a black shawl and a dirty yellow dress, an ugly, lumbering old woman with a twisted lip and pendulous breasts. From under her shawl she drew a thick book bound in crumbling black leather.

"That will be the book in which new members of the Circle are required to write their names," whispered Dr. Crow. The witches were making so much noise down below that he and Ezekiel might have spoken aloud without fear of discovery, but the Reverend remained cautious. "The act binds them as no spoken vow could. There is many a poor man in Thornburg, unable to make a living for his very illiteracy, who would cut off his arm for this same skill with which your neighbors, fortunate in the attentions of some honest country parson, sign their miserable souls away."

Ezekiel nodded grimly. "Mr. Ulfson . . . I guess he'd break his heart, if he knew some of the names in that Black Book."

Members of the Circle continued to arrive: a woman and four men; and close on their heels, a sweet-faced girl and a handsome, swaggering youth, who came in hand in hand. "Isabel Winkleriss! I knowed she'd suffer through that scoundrel Martin Bergen, but I never thought he'd lead her into nothing so bad as this!"

About a dozen more came in, and then one of the men pulled the doors shut.

"I make the count six and twenty . . . something less than I had feared," said Dr. Crow.

Ezekiel shook his head mournfully. "Less than I reckoned. But most of them, I never suspected. Old Granny Hügel (that's the dirty old hag), I ain't surprised about her—but as for some others . . ."

"It is possible," said Dr. Crow, "that some are here merely because they feel safer within the Circle than without."

"But hush," he said, "I believe they are about to begin."

The witches continued to be as rackety as ever, but the good doctor wished to pay full attention to the scene down below. Several of the women carried baskets or covered wooden pails, which they now began to open. Out of these baskets came chickens and rabbits, which the Circle proceeded to sacrifice in a series of rituals so lewd and bloody, they shocked poor Ezekiel to the very core of his honest being. Dr. Crow, however, watched impassively.

With the ceremonies and the sacrifices completed, Granny Hügel reached up under her ragged skirts and drew out a long, slender object like a spindle. It gleamed faintly yellow in the firelight, like a piece of well-polished bone or ivory.

"A carrier," hissed Dr. Crow. "This explains, at least in part, the depredations on your graveyard." He already knew something of these spindles: how they were usually carved from an arm or a leg bone, and nourished (for the carrier had a kind of unnatural life of its own) on the witch's own blood, sucked out through a raised bump, not unlike a nipple, inside the witch's thigh. "If any of your more honest neighbors are storing bags of wool in their barns . . ."

As Ezekiel and Dr. Crow looked on, the old woman put the piece of bone, point down, in a spot where the earth was particularly hard and smooth. She gave it a spin, as though it were a top, then withdrew her hand, squatting back on her heels to watch the carrier work.

It continued to spin, much faster than a top . . . faster and faster still . . . with a loud, unpleasant hum very awful to hear. The area around the carrier began to glow and shimmer, as if by some disturbance in the fabric of existence. And then, quite suddenly, the spindle began to fill with a thick, creamy thread . . . drawing it out of the very air, until the carrier grew so full that it overbalanced and fell to the ground of its own weight.

Very calmly, the hag picked up the spindle and began to unwind the wool. Another woman produced a large cloth sack, into which she began to stuff the stolen yarn, as fast as Granny Hügel could pull it from the spindle.

When all the yarn was in the sack, the process began again. The carrier spun around and around, magically transporting the wool. It fell to the floor, the hag stripped off the yarn, and then set it spinning once more.

Meanwhile, some of the other witches were busy elsewhere. One of them, a man with brown skin and a sour face—whom Dr. Crow had no difficulty recognizing as one of the two farmers he had overheard talking at the inn—took a long knife out of his belt and thrust it into the north wall of the barn. He spoke a few guttural words and made some magical passes over the knife. Then he picked up a bucket and held it below the knife. A thin stream of milk came out of the hole in the wall and poured into the pail. When the bucket was full, the farmer took it down, and a woman brought him another pail.

"In the morning, one of your neighbor's cows, normally a good milker, will be unaccountably dry," said Dr. Crow. "Possibly, her udder will be inflamed, for the process is not a gentle one."

Milk continued to stream into the second bucket, until it, too, was overflowing. But this time, when the farmer withdrew the pail, nobody brought him another. The flow of milk went on for several minutes, soaking into the ground. Then it turned scarlet, like fresh-flowing blood.

"They mean to kill the cow," said Dr. Crow. "Do not fear, Ezekiel, we shall act very soon."

23.

Being most Regrettably Violent in its Character.

"I believe," said Dr. Crow, "that we have seen all that is necessary." Standing up, he removed his cloak and his hat. He was just shrugging out of his coat when the double doors of the barn flew dramatically open, and a draught of cooler air blew in. Dr. Crow stooped low again.

"Hark!" cried Granny Hügel. "Our Lord and Master is come to join our revels." The other witches immediately left off what they had been doing and formed a nervous semicircle around the fire, facing the doors.

A tall, elegant figure, in a full-skirted coat of crimson velvet with a vast quantity of gold braid on the wide cuffs, strolled into the barn. He wore his plumed tricorn pulled low, to shadow his face, so that it was impossible (at least from the vantage point of the loft) to make out his features.

Ezekiel drew in his breath. "It's the Dark One . . . Old Mezztopholeez hisself," he hissed in Dr. Crow's ear.

"I think not," came the whispered reply. "Neither the Prince of Darkness nor any other demon of the earth . . . Else why should he need to enter by way of the door?"

With a languid grace, the newcomer moved across the floor, raising black-gloved hands, as if in benediction. Granny Hügel

167

threw herself, groveling, at his feet. "Give us a sign . . . reveal a wonder."

For answer, the figure in red stripped off a glove, flourishing . . . but it wasn't a hand beneath the glove—it was a scaly yellow *claw* with hooked talons.

Now it was Dr. Crow's turn to draw in a sharp breath. "Troll! That explains why fresh corpses disappear from your churchyard. But I had never expected to meet one so far south."

"Troll?" echoed Ezekiel. "But I always heard tell they was ugly and misshapen . . . That is—"

"Some are more obviously misshapen than others," replied Dr. Crow, speaking directly in Ezekiel's ear. "Many have only a single deformity, which they may conceal or disguise. That he chooses to reveal his, argues that he has some exceptional hold over those poor deluded fools down below."

The old woman, after wallowing in the dirt for some time— and receiving whatever curse or blessing the troll had to bestow— rose to her feet and waddled over to join the others. Someone produced a silver goblet, and somebody else provided a long sharp pin.

The cup and the bodkin passed slowly from hand to hand. Each member of the Circle, as the cup came around, used the bodkin to pierce a vein in his or her wrist, and the goblet to catch the sudden, unnatural gush of blood.

When the cup was full, Granny Hügel presented it to the waiting troll. "Payment offered for favors given," rasped the hag.

The troll did not answer, but he took the stem of the cup between his talons, lifted it, and drank all the blood in a single draught. Then he extended the goblet to Granny Hügel. "It is not enough. I require more."

At his words, several of the women began to tremble. The troll raised his talon and pointed at one of the more comely females. "That one," he said.

With a faltering step, with eyes rolling back in her head as if she were about to swoon, the chosen victim advanced.

But now Dr. Crow was ready to take action. He removed his waistcoat, stood up in his full-sleeved white shirt and breeches. A large metallic medallion, suspended from a silver chain, glittered on his breast. He slipped a hand up his left sleeve and pulled a dagger out of some hidden sheath. "Come with me to the edge of the loft, Ezekiel, but stand a little back. It is not likely they will notice you, considering the distraction I am going to provide."

With the dagger in one hand and the medallion clutched in the other, he advanced to the edge of the loft. After a moment of hesitation, Ezekiel followed, bringing the grenado with him.

Down on the floor, they were all entranced by the drama of the woman and the troll. Up in the loft, Ezekiel was equally entranced by his companion's startling transformation.

Before the young farmer's astonished eyes, Dr. Crow's slender figure seemed to change and grow . . . taller . . . wider . . . brighter . . . so bright that the light dazzled Ezekiel's eyes. Dr. Crow was gone—in his place stood a shining figure wrapped in garments of light, spanning the distance from the floor of the barn, all the way up to the roof. Where Dr. Crow had carried a dagger, his gigantic counterpart wielded a tremendous jeweled sword.

The sudden blaze of light and heat finally drew the attention of the witches . . . that, and the thunderous beating of mighty rainbow wings. Granny Hügel gasped and staggered toward the fire. All of the women (and most of the men) shrieked in terror. Then people began falling to their knees, in abject submission. Only the troll remained standing.

Radiant Martos, the avenging Fate, brandished his gleaming sword. "Repent ye who would do wrong to the innocent," he roared, in a deep, stormy voice, like lightning and thunder, like the fury of the wind on a wild night. "Repent ye who do wrong to your neighbors."

It was then that Ezekiel, sensing that the proper moment had indeed come, flung the grenado into the fire.

There was a brilliant flash and a loud explosion, followed an instant later by a second, more violent blast as the firepot in the earth ignited. This second blast caught many of the witches and flung them into the air. They came back to earth again with so many sickening thuds. Some of them did not move again.

With shrieks and cries, all those who could scrambled to their feet and ran out of the barn. The troll—his elegant crimson velvet blackened by the blast—led the exodus.

The barn caught fire in two places, but mighty Martos pointed his sword and spoke the words, and the fires were instantly extinguished.

Dr. Crow sat on the edge of the loft, dangling his legs. By the light of Ezekiel's uncovered lanthorn, he looked ill as well as weary.

"Do not stare at me in that fashion, my good Ezekiel, I do

169

implore you," he said. "I am not Great Martos incarnate. It was an illusion, nothing more."

Ezekiel grinned sheepishly. "It were a mighty impressive illusion, that's certain. Said you'd put the fear of the Divine into the lot of 'em and that's just what you did."

He brought the satchel and the rope ladder over to the edge. He was about to attach the hooks and toss the ladder down, but then he stopped. "We use the ladder, we can't take it with us. We leave it behind—"

"If we leave it behind, the whole elaborate illusion will come to naught," said Dr. Crow. "If demons of the earth do not enter by way of the door, neither do wingéd Fates require the use of a rope ladder. Well, after all, it is not too great a distance . . . If we lower ourselves from the edge by our hands, we ought to be able to drop the rest of the way without any harm."

Ezekiel eyed his companion doubtfully. "Begging your pardon, sir, but you look done in. Do you really reckon you could manage that? Why don't *you* use the ladder? I can throw it down after you and then drop down myself."

"Yes, if you please," said Dr. Crow. "Undoubtedly that would be best."

Following this plan, they both reached the floor of the barn without sustaining any injury. "I suppose," said Dr. Crow, "that we are obligated to look at the bodies—one of them may yet live."

He bent down to examine the first corpse. "Granny Hügel—I am pleased to count her among the dead." The hag lay in an awkward tangle of arms and legs, in a pool of her own blood.

"Isabel Winkleriss . . . that I regret," he said over the next. "And her swain, Martin Bergen . . . that I shall have to consider."

As the need for action was past, he was rapidly undergoing a change in identity, from vigilante-saboteur to a man of compassion and compunction—he had not spoken frivolously when he assured Tilda that he was far more likely to remember his name than who and what he was—it was one of the less comfortable features of his chameleon-like nature, this tendency on the part of his more ruthless personas to beat a hasty retreat once they had done their dirty work, and leave one of the gentler spirits to deal with the consequences.

He turned over the body of an old man. All the hair had been singed off the head, and the face was as black as soot.

"Rudolf Bormann . . ." offered Ezekiel. "He were a bad one—

170

beat his wife and starved his children. Tell you what, though: I'm mortal sorry we didn't get the troll.''

"As am I," said Dr. Crow. "For I feel certain he was responsible for much that we saw here. More often than not, these Circles never rise above the level of petty mischief—some of them, indeed, work their magic for the benefit of the neighborhood—but with a gentleman troll of some learning to instruct them in the darker, more potent magics—''

"But why?" asked Ezekiel. "Why did he want to stir them up for? Why did he set them to robbing and tormenting their friends and neighbors?''

"To gain power over them," said Dr. Crow. "To gain power, by apparently bestowing power.

"They are a strange race," he continued reflectively, "and their origins are a mystery, for none of the ancient texts credit any of the Nine Powers with their creation. Some believe them a mongrel race . . . others, a breed of Men altered by their own evil magic."

He walked over and picked up the silver goblet. "If that is so, then they are cannibals . . . but rather curious cannibals. They relish no meat so much as the flesh of Men, but as for drink . . . the males prefer, above all else, to drink the blood of living maidens. Moreover, when the blood a he-troll drinks has been obtained from a girl who has been sealed to him in a species of matrimony, the troll is said to derive some special benefit. A troll superstition, perhaps, yet one in which they firmly believe. The male will often go to great lengths to find a girl and persuade her to marry him . . . usually a dairymaid or shepherdess: a big, healthy country girl, in whom the life force runs strong. But an unattached troll, as we have seen, can live equally well on blood obtained by other means . . . and of course on the flesh of the recently deceased.''

Ezekiel shook his head. "Don't seem likely he'd find enough meat on the bones of a beggar . . . Don't seem like what there was would be very sweet.''

"But paupers are buried without silver or gold to hallow the grave," said Dr. Crow.

Bending down, he scooped up Granny Hügel's Black Book. The cover was scorched around the edges, but it was otherwise undamaged. He opened the book and leafed through the pages, and Ezekiel came up behind him and peered over his shoulder.

Though most of the book consisted of blank pages, it still contained many more names than either of them had expected. The first names—written in ink so old that it had faded to brown—

were Matthias Woodruff, Rebeckah Hügel, and Rudolf Bormann.

Dr. Crow frowned, shaking his head. "It would appear, then, that the Circle is older than we suspected. Not white witches in the beginning, certainly, but perhaps comparatively harmless and discreet in their activities, until they fell under the influence of the troll."

A few more pages, and the ink appeared fresher. Ezekiel read the names with ever-mounting dismay. "Seems half the families between here and Pfalz was touched by this filth. Some of these people is dead . . . starved out by the witches or victims of the Eye. Or so the rest of us thought, anyways."

"Perhaps they were, in some sense, victims," said Dr. Crow. "It is easy to be drawn into these things, as I have reason to know, but difficult to get out. In most secret societies, death is the penalty for a lapse in loyalty."

He studied the volume for several minutes more. "Were I a hard-hearted man, I should certainly turn the entire volume over to the magistrate at Pfalz. But what you have told me and what I have seen convinces me that there was more criminal *weakness* here than genuine wickedness—and so I am inclined to be merciful."

He tore out the last three written pages. "The earliest names will be those of the most culpable; those that live shall suffer the full penalty of the law. Granny Hügel and Rudolf Bormann were undoubtedly the ringleaders, but they are dead. As for the names on these later pages: the fright they received this night may incline them to mend their ways. I should like to give them that chance . . . to live and to work hard to expiate their sins, as I—as others have done before them. But if they will not . . ."

He handed the torn pages over to Ezekiel. "I shall entrust these pages to you. Bury them in a safe place—your grandmother's grave perhaps—or secrete them in the church, for they are dangerous to keep by you. Observe the behavior of your neighbors . . . If you have reason to suspect even a single instance of black witchcraft in the neighborhood, turn these over to the magistrate at Pfalz. I can rely on you to do this . . . you will not falter, for the sake of old friendships?"

"No, sir, I won't falter," said Ezekiel, with a stubborn thrust of his jaw. "I've got to live here, don't I? I'm going to marry Tilda and raise a family, and I'll be d----d if I don't do everything in my power to make it a safe place to live!"

"Very good," said Dr. Crow, closing the book and tucking it into some inner pocket in his cloak. "I am content to leave the matter in your capable hands."

24.

Wherein Jedidiah improves on his Acquaintance with Mr. Budge.

All through the season of Ripening, Jedidiah worked hard, both in the counting-house and at the other new tasks Master Ule assigned him. He was determined to learn as much as he could about the glass trade, to aid the good old dwarf (as much as it was humanly possible) in the expansion of his business, and so justify his benefactor's faith.

That Master Ule was pleased with his progress, that he was now a vital part of the enterprise, Jed had no doubt. The dwarf was generous in his praise and he demonstrated his approval in other ways as well. Several evenings spent in company at the Ule mansion introduced Jed into dwarf Society, where he rapidly gained favor, for the dwarves valued industry and honest ambition, and were quick to recognize and encourage those qualities wherever they found them. Soon, Jedidiah was receiving invitations not only from the Ules and the Owlfeathers but from all the best dwarf families. In addition, he dined twice with Hermes Budge, the Owlfeather tutor.

So it came as no surprise, near the end of the season, when Jed looked up from his work at the close of one day, to find the tall, solemn tutor waiting to speak to him.

"Mr. Braun, your servant!" Mr. Budge made a low bow. "I wondered if I might have the honor of your company for the evening? I am on my way to the Cat and the Crown, an excellent chop-house, and I thought you might care to accompany me."

Jed stood up and returned the bow. These friendly attentions on the part of a man of such superior education flattered him, but

173

he knew the tutor's means were nearly as limited as his own. "Mr. Budge, I am obliged to you. But I'd rather . . . that is . . . I beg you will allow me to play the host. It is only a step to my new lodgings. Let me buy the supper and a bottle of wine; I'd consider it a kindness on your part."

"As you wish," said Budge, replacing his hat.

Jed sealed his inkwell and wiped his pen. He slipped into his coat and picked up his hat. He took leave of Polydore Figg, who was also clearing his desk, and followed the tutor out to the street.

The day had been hot, but the evening was foggy; they walked out the door into a chill, swirling mist. Jed reached into his coat pocket and pulled out a woolen muffler, which he wrapped around his neck. His companion also produced a long scarf and a pair of white gloves.

"I wonder, Mr. Braun," said Budge, as they walked to the chop-house, "how much do you know . . . about the aims and the activities of the Glassmakers Lodge?"

So here it was, thought Jed, the thing Uncle Caleb had warned him against time and time again. *"They'll be after you for information . . . mark my words . . . asking you to join them, hoping you'll blab . . . Don't you trust them, boy, don't you tell them nothing!"* Yet even so, Jed could not quite believe there was anything sinister, either in Mr. Budge's question or in his motives.

"I know . . . I know they ain't all of them interested just in making glass," he said slowly. "I heard about ceremonies . . . and rituals . . . and secret vows. I guess everyone knows that much."

"Indeed," said Hermes Budge, striding upright and dignified beside him—looking not at all like a man who was privy to dark secrets and even darker deeds. "And yet I should have thought that the grandnephew of Caleb Braun would know considerably more."

Jed sucked in a mouthful of the misty air and slowly released it. "It would seem I have surprised you, Mr. Braun—have I surprised you?" asked Budge. "But you mention your granduncle often, and also Jenk the bookseller . . . You make no attempt to conceal your association with either of them, though surely you must know that either name is bound to attract attention from members of the Guild.

"No one wishes to place you in an uncomfortable position, or to urge you to do anything against your inclination," said the tutor. "Indeed, it was just because we feared some . . . I believe

174

grudge would be too strong a word, for there was never any harm done on either side, so far as I am aware . . . some predisposition against the lodge on the part of your granduncle, which he may have passed on to you . . . It was partly because of this that we hesitated so long in approaching you."

They came to a corner and turned down another, narrower street. The lamps were farther apart here, the mist thicker and more clinging. Jed had difficulty making out his companion's face.

"Seems to me," said Jedidiah, "it's an odd sort of thing you should approach me at all. Supposing, of course, this is all leading up to an invitation for me to join your lodge. Who am I that you should want me, if you don't mind my asking?"

"I do not mind you asking at all," said Mr. Budge. "Indeed, I should expect no less. Because you are quite right: our mysteries are not for everyone. The quest for knowledge, particularly the quest for occult knowledge, carries many risks. These risks are increased when the seeker is frivolous or dull of mind, so we are exceedingly particular in choosing our candidates. I might add," said Budge, "that there are many men who have served in glass-houses all of their lives and never been invited to join the . . . the speculative branch of the lodge.

"As to why we should take an interest in you, and not in the others . . ." said Mr. Budge. "Your name was first advanced by master Ule as just the sort of bright, decent, honest young fellow that we are always looking to recruit. His recommendation alone carries great weight, but nevertheless there are procedures which must be observed. I hope you will not be offended, Mr. Braun, when I tell you that my original reasons for cultivating your friendship were in accordance with those procedures. As an educator, I have gained an ability to assess the capacity of young minds, and in like manner I was called upon to evaluate you."

By this time, they had reached the chop-house, but Jed held back at the door. A warm glow of firelight issued through the mullioned windows; bits of conversation drifted through the door; there was the sizzle of steaks and chops cooking over an open fire—all these invited him to come in out of the dark and the damp. But he lingered on the street, determined to have this out with the tutor before he ventured inside.

"And what . . . what did this evaluation tell you?" he asked warily.

Mr. Budge smiled. "If I may say so, Mr. Braun, you lack the quickness which all too often passes for brilliance, but you are

175

steady, studious, and thoughtful, and I believe that you possess an excellent mind. You protest . . . you are all modesty . . . but you must allow that I am something of an expert in these matters and ought to know whereof I speak. Moreover, I admire your efforts to better yourself, and if you decline to join our brotherhood, I would still like to think that our friendship could continue.

"I do sincerely believe," the tutor went on earnestly, "that if you were to join our lodge you would learn much that would amaze you, much that would broaden and expand your intellect, and that you would not only benefit from the exercise, but find it the source of deep and enduring pleasure in its own right."

Mr. Budge sighed. "You continue to frown . . . you look uneasy . . . It is evident you have inherited your kinsman's distrust of the guild. I understand, and will say no more."

Jedidiah shook his head, shifted uneasily from one foot to the other. " 'Tisn't that so much. It's true that Uncle Caleb don't think highly of your guild, but I guess I'm a man now and able to make my own decisions. The fact is, they never did my people any good . . . mysteries and magic books and all the rest. They did my Uncle Caleb a good deal of harm, and he's not a *frivolous* man, nor yet a dull one. And as for Gottfried Jenk . . . he's been called a madman—many and many is the time—but never a fool.

"I guess," said Jed, "I guess me and Sera Vorder got this much in common: we've developed a natural aversion to your occult knowledge, all on our own."

"I understand completely," said Mr. Budge. "Pray do not feel obligated to explain any further. And do not fear that this will affect your position or your advancement at Master Ule's glasshouse. I assure you that it will not."

They went inside the chop-house, where Jed purchased two nicely grilled steaks, a pot of gravy, and some roasted potatoes. A stop at the tavern next door provided them with liquid refreshment. Then, with the steaks, and the potatoes wrapped up in brown paper and divided between them, a bottle of good wine under Mr. Budge's arm, they continued on their way.

"I will say only this much, and then we shall abandon the subject entirely," said Mr. Budge, as they walked down Tidewater Lane. "If you should change your mind at any time, please feel free to approach me. Or if you should experience a change of heart while I am out of town, you may speak to Mr. Owlfeather or Master Ule."

"Very well," said Jed. He put his hands into his pockets along with the potatoes to keep them warm. "I guess . . . I guess maybe I'll give it some thought, anyway. Was—are you thinking of leaving town, Mr. Budge? Not permanent, I hope?"

"For a matter of eight or ten weeks . . . perhaps a little more. I shall be visiting a famous scholar and antiquarian, who leads a very secluded life in the country. I suppose, Mr. Braun," he added politely, "that you have never been out of Thornburg yourself?"

"I've never been anywhere," said Jed. "I've never been anywhere, and I've never seen anything. But I mean to travel, by and by."

"I hope that you may one day do so," said Mr. Budge. And he proceeded to regale his companion with tales of his journey from Imbria into Marstadtt, until they reached the shabby (but eminently respectable) old house where Jed and his Uncle Caleb had recently taken lodgings.

This boarding house had obviously seen better days, but still managed to retain a genteel atmosphere of faded grandeur by virtue of an imposing portico, some worn carpets of oriental design, and a number of still elegant fireplaces. The fireplace in Jed's attic sitting room was tiny, but it was solid marble, and boasted a decorative molding consisting of two miniature Fates, a garland of crumbling roses, and numerous fantastical birds.

Uncle Caleb was not in, as a quick peek inside the two adjoining bedchambers confirmed. Jed knit his brow and gnawed on his lower lip. It seemed that Caleb and his employer were keeping later and later hours. When Caleb did come home, he always looked so old and frail it made Jed's heart ache just to gaze on him. Nor would Caleb deign to eat so much as a scrap of food, declaring he had supped at the bookshop and lacked the appetite. For all that, the expression he wore was not of a man who had eaten well . . . it was the look of a man who was dying of some insatiable hunger.

"I beg your pardon, Mr. Braun . . . I do not mean to intrude . . . but has something disturbed you?" asked Budge, coming up behind him.

Reminded of his guest, Jed smoothed out his frown. "Nothing. That is . . . nothing much, I don't reckon." He dropped his parcels on a table by the fire. He brought a three-branched candlestick and some of the finer plates and cups, and pulled up two battered but sturdy chairs.

The two men sat down, unwrapped their suppers, and prepared to eat. But their previous conversation, along with his concern for

Uncle Caleb, put Jed in mind of another source of worry.

He cleared his throat. "I would be obliged, Mr. Budge—that is, if you wouldn't consider it a violation of confidence—if you would tell me something about your friend Lord Skelbrooke."

The tutor paused in the act of pouring the wine into a willow pattern cup. "What do you wish to know?"

Jed felt himself blushing. "I know . . . I know that it isn't the custom, among gentlemen of good breeding, to—to freely discuss the *respectable* young women they happen to know. But Lord Skelbrooke being an old friend of yours, well, I reckon he speaks a little more openly, and that you've a fair idea what goes on in his mind."

Mr. Budge put down the wine bottle. "There is, I believe, a degree of confidence between us."

"Well then," said Jed, all in a rush. "That day that I first met him, I took it into my head that he had maybe formed an attachment to my very good friend—my all but sister—Miss Sera Vorder."

Mr. Budge nodded thoughtfully. "Yes, I remember the conversation. The more so, because it struck me as uncharacteristic. I would not have you misunderstand me: Lord Skelbrooke is all that is gentle and courteous in the company of ladies, and I believe they consider him the most gallant of men. But in private, he has expressed himself on the theme of romance in such shocking terms . . . I would not offend you by repeating them. And indeed, if you knew what I know of his history, you would not be surprised to find him something of a misogynist."

Mr. Budge lifted his cup and took a sip of wine. He sat back in his chair and frowned at the ceiling. It seemed as though Jed's statement had troubled him deeply. "Since the lady is a friend of yours (almost a sister, you say), I take it that you wish to know if Skelbrooke's interest in her is . . . a wholesome one. I wish that I could say that it was, but I really do not know."

Jed's fork dropped on the table with a clatter. He pushed his plate away. Suddenly, he had no appetite at all. "He don't speak of her when you're together?" he ventured.

"Only on that one occasion, when you also were present," said Budge. "I confess that it has been many years since I last heard my poor Francis speak so warmly of any woman. And it is evident that he admires and respects the young lady . . . which is a remarkable thing in itself. But if he has actually formed an attachment, I am not absolutely certain that would be an altogether fortunate thing for your Miss Vorder. He is generally capable of achieving anything that he wants, and if he set out to win her regard . . ."

Jed sprang to his feet, images of rape and abduction crowding into his mind. "Here now . . . you don't mean to tell me that this friend of yours is a rogue? One of those arrogant noblemen who takes a fancy to a girl and thinks nothing of ruining her?"

"No, no, nothing of the kind," said Budge. "Heaven forbid that I, who have known him so long and so well, should imply anything of the sort. I believe his essential generosity, his sense of fair play, would prevent him from victimizing any woman in that way. Yet he is undoubtedly a dangerous man, and capable of terrible deeds when the mood is on him. But as to the peril to your Miss Vorder; I believe that would principally pertain to her peace of mind. He would never harm her, not physically . . . I am virtually certain of that." The tutor shook his head sadly. "But to love a man so troubled as Francis Skelbrooke, that would be a heavy burden for any woman to carry."

Jed scowled ferociously. "Sounds like you're talking about two different men."

"Two men . . . a dozen men . . . yet in each of them I still see something of my old friend," said Budge, picking up his knife and fork.

Jed resumed his seat, slumped down in his chair. "And I've been encouraging her to see him. Using him to carry notes back and forth. D--n and blister me for a short-sighted fool! He was so soft-spoken and polite, I thought he was perfectly safe."

Mr. Budge skewered a piece of potato with his fork. "You have been employing *Lord Skelbrooke* as a go-between?"

Jed nodded glumly. "Twice he carried messages from me to her, and once from her to me. I reckon he thought it a fine way to gain her confidence. But what do I do now? Send her a letter, warning her to stay clear of him? That doesn't seem right, somehow, and I guess he might open it, anyway."

The tutor took another sip of wine. "He is capable, under certain circumstances, of not only opening a letter entrusted to his keeping but of altering the contents as well. I doubt, however, that he would be moved to open any letter written by you. Among honorable people, he is himself the soul of honor. By all means, warn the lady, if you believe she will heed your advice."

Jed drummed his fingers on the table. "Well, there . . . I reckon you've put your finger on it. She never takes advice, not Sera— not my advice, anyway. Or so seldom, it doesn't hardly matter. More likely, if I warned her against him, she'd fall in love with

179

the fellow out of sheer perversity. Guess I won't write again at all.''

"No," said Mr. Budge. "You ought not to send her any more letters by way of Francis Skelbrooke. You must not do anything more to encourage their friendship.''

25.

Which promises to be Brief.

The day was hot, sticky, and oppressive, with a taste of thunder in the air. Throughout the town, along the dirty meandering lanes and alleys down by the river, along the wide, well-paved streets where the wealthy lived in mansions on the heights, the people of Thornburg cast open their doors and window casements, in the hope of attracting any vagrant breeze, any breath of cooler air rising up from the water.

Sera left the Vorder mansion at noon and set off on foot to visit her grandfather at the bookshop. Despite the dark clouds piling up on the horizon, the sky overhead was a clear eggshell blue. Surely, she told herself, she had ample time to walk to the bookshop, have a good long visit with her grandfather, and walk home again before the storm struck.

But when she arrived at the bookshop, her grandfather and Caleb Braun both looked so old, dusty, and frail, the little suite of rooms up in the attic was so cluttered and disorganized . . . Sera spent the entire afternoon cooking, cleaning, and mending, fussing over the two elderly men. It was little wonder that she overstayed her time. She was just putting on her hat and her gloves when she heard the first scattered drops of rain hitting the roof.

"I shall send Caleb to hire you a chair," said Jenk.

"You must do nothing of the kind," said Sera. She knew there were no sedan chairs to be hailed in this part of the town and that Caleb would have to walk a long way in the rain before he spotted one. She was of no mind to send the old man out into the wet simply because she lacked the foresight to hire a chair in advance.

"Only lend me an umbrella, Grandfather, and I shall set out at once. If I walk swiftly, I can reach the Cathedral in a matter of minutes, and there I should have no difficulty hailing a chair."

Jenk protested, but Sera was adamant. In the end, he did as she requested, and lent her his rusty black umbrella. Sera dropped a kiss on his forehead, picked up her reticule, and ran downstairs. Out on the street, she unfurled the umbrella and set out at a brisk pace.

She did very well at first. The rain was light and seemed to evaporate the moment it hit the steaming cobblestones. But then it began to pour, and the streets became slick and dangerous. Nevertheless, she continued on hopefully for another half a mile until she reached Church Street.

There, she stopped and looked hopelessly around her. The street was all but deserted, save for a few improvident foot travelers like herself; there was not a sedan chair or a goat cart in sight. A gust of wind spattered the bottle-green gown with rain. The big black umbrella would offer scant protection if the wind continued to rise.

"Miss Vorder, your servant," said a soft, familiar voice. Sera tipped up the umbrella to see who had addressed her. A small man in a voluminous coat with many capes and a wide-brimmed hat like a buccaneer peered back at her.

"Pray do not take offense," said Francis Skelbrooke "if I tell you that you seem to be getting very wet. Please allow me to procure for you some suitable conveyance."

Sera scowled at him. "If there were any suitable conveyance to be had between here and the river, be sure, my lord, that I should have hailed it myself!"

Lord Skelbrooke made her a very pretty bow (though he did not, Sera noticed, imperil his exquisite powdered curls by removing his hat). "But of course . . . how dull of me to imagine otherwise. Allow me, then, to escort you to a place of shelter. It happens that I know a house not far from here . . ."

And before Sera could either consent or refuse, he had taken her by the arm and was leading her, gently but firmly, around a corner, down a broad street, and through the narrow door of a little shop with a blue slate roof.

The interior of this shop was crowded with tables and chairs, and men of all ages: talking, smoking long pipes, or sipping a

181

steaming brown liquid out of brittle white cups. There were only two women present so far as Sera could see: an overdressed young beauty surrounded by a circle of admiring youths, and an elderly dwarf sharing a plate of sugared biscuits with a small boy.

Sera hesitated by the door. "This is a respectable house," said Lord Skelbrooke, with a reassuring smile, "and it is entirely proper for you to come here with me."

Sera bit her lip. Was there something just the least bit patronizing in his tone? Contempt for her obvious lack of sophistication? She straightened her spine and lifted her chin, and followed him through the maze of tables and chairs.

A rotund gnome woman in a clean white apron came to meet them, her claws clicking on the planks of the floor. "I wonder," said Lord Skelbrooke, "if we might have a room upstairs?"

Sera opened her mouth to protest. "Trust me, Miss Vorder," said Skelbrooke. The brim of his flamboyant hat shaded his face; it was impossible to guess his expression; but there was a dangerous edge to his voice. "If the day ever comes that I attempt a seduction, I shall not conduct the affair in a Chocolate House." Sera blushed, closed her mouth, and meekly followed him up the stairs and down a short corridor.

The gnome ushered them into a cozy room at the end of the hall. This room, Sera saw, was built like a box at the theatre, open on one side to the floor below, offering the illusion of privacy but no real concealment. The walls were paneled in dark oak, and there was a round window made of wavy panes of leaded glass overlooking the rainy street. A glass oil lamp fashioned in the shape of a spouting whale hung by a brass chain. There were two chairs and a table covered with a flowered cloth. Lord Skelbrooke ordered a pot of chocolate and a plate of gingerbread, and the gnome withdrew.

Skelbrooke offered Sera a chair facing the round window. He hung his oversized hat on a peg by the door and removed his dashing caped overcoat. In apricot velvet and cream lace he looked more like the man she knew; small, neat, and delicately scented. Why had he seemed so threatening, only a moment before?

"You are very kind," said Sera, as he took a seat on the other side of the table. She folded her hands primly in her lap. "But the storm will only grow worse . . . and if I do not return home by nightfall my cousins will be dreadfully upset."

"The storm is likely to continue for some time," agreed Skelbrooke. "But once you have had the opportunity to dry off and

182

to drink a cup of chocolate I shall send a boy to hire you a chair.

"You have nothing to fear," he added, with a smile. "I am aware that you never accept invitations to ride or to dine . . . that you do not allow gentlemen to escort you to the play or to the museum. Though you make an exception in the present instance, it is not a circumstance which I am likely to allow to go to my head."

This speech, far from offering reassurance, only served to disturb Sera. How had he learned so much about her? "Lord Skelbrooke . . ." she said with a frown. "Lord Skelbrooke, is it the custom among the gentlemen of Thornburg—Mr. Hakluyt and Lord Krogan in particular—to discuss my habits."

"Not when I am present. They would not dare to," said Skelbrooke, and continued to smile so amiably that she did not immediately take his meaning.

Then she blushed and looked away. "I see," she said, in a stifled voice. "Then . . . I believe that I ought to thank you."

"Why is that, Miss Vorder?" he asked politely.

"For . . . for defending my good name, as I suppose," she said, and forced herself to meet his eyes.

The smile faded from his face, and he leaned forward in his chair, suddenly very serious. "Your name and your honor require no defense. It is merely a matter of personal distaste, an aversion on my part, to hearing your name mentioned by those who are unworthy."

The room was quiet, save for the drumming of rain on the window and her own irregular breathing. Lord Skelbrooke sat back in his seat; he crossed one leg over the other and tipped back his chair. "Mr. Hakluyt and Lord Krogan . . . I thank you for bringing their names to my attention."

The rosy-cheeked little gnome woman came in then bearing a pot of steaming chocolate, two cups, and a dish of ginger cakes.

By the time the gnome departed Sera had not only composed herself but had remembered what she carried in her reticule. She unfastened the drawstrings, drew out a tiny glass vial, and placed it on the table between them.

"Miss Elsie's medication?" said Skelbrooke.

"I have carried it with me everywhere, these last three days," said Sera, fastening her gaze on the little star-shaped patch on his left cheek, rather than looking him directly in the eye. "As I told you earlier in the week, when—when you were so obliging as to deliver Jedidiah's letter, the bottle disappeared after Count Xebo's ball, though I had reason to suppose Elsie continued to take the medication. It appears now that Elsie did not hide the bottle—which, to be sure, seemed like very odd behavior on her part—but had turned the medicine over to her mother for safekeeping. It was only by good fortune that I discovered the bottle in Cousin Clothilde's sitting room when no one else was there.

"I was beginning to fear," she added, "that I would not have the opportunity to give you this, before we leave for Zar-Wildungen."

Lord Skelbrooke put down his cup of chocolate. "I beg your pardon . . . I knew nothing of this. To Zar-Wildungen, you say? You will be traveling with the Duchess to her country house?"

"With the Duchess . . . yes," said Sera, in some confusion. "I hoped . . . that is . . . are you not also to be a member of the party?"

"No," said Skelbrooke. "I was not invited. I had assumed the Duke's poor health was the reason for her visit. And now I discover she is taking a party with her . . ."

He made a steeple of his hands, rested his chin on the tips of his fingers. "I begin to fear that I have fallen from favor."

He spoke the words lightly, but a frown creased his forehead, and the grey eyes went dark as if in pain. *He does care for her . . . She has hurt him deeply,* Sera thought, with a sinking sensation. *It is the Duchess he loves, and not the woman he mentioned at Count Xebo's ball.*

"Miss Vorder," said his lordship, continuing to frown. "I wonder if this journey is really advisable? We are not, after all, entirely certain as to the state of your cousin's health."

"The decision was not mine to make," said Sera. "Elsie and her mother are both determined that she should go. I tried to dissuade her, but she would not listen. All that remained for *me* was to decide whether I should accompany Elsie or not. Naturally, I could not allow her to make the journey without me."

Skelbrooke unfolded his hands. "In that case, there is nothing more to be said." He picked up the vial containing Elsie's medication and slipped it into a pocket. "I shall deliver this to my friend the apothecary on the morrow . . . but we can hardly expect to learn anything immediately."

He picked up his cup, took another sip of chocolate. "If I do learn anything of particular interest, I shall write to you at once. But perhaps . . . perhaps, as the letter will pass through so many hands . . . With your permission, Miss Vorder, I shall write to you under an assumed name . . . the name of some friend, unknown to the Duchess.''

But Sera did not like this suggestion at all. Surely, she thought, there was something dishonorable about staying in the Duchess's house and accepting clandestine messages from the Duchess's lover . . . whether he currently stood high in her favor or not. And what an odd, unpredictable man Lord Skelbrooke was! Only a moment ago, it had seemed that he was totally devoted to the Duchess . . . a few weeks past, he had spoken wistfully of another woman . . . and now he seemed bent on initiating an intrigue (no matter how unromantic) with Sera herself.

"Lord Skelbrooke," she said aloud. "I think that I should tell you that I despise subterfuge.''

"Who could know you and believe otherwise?" said Skelbrooke. He reached into a waistcoat pocket and brought out a gilded snuffbox. "But if I may say so, you have already been guilty of an innocent deception, when you secretly obtained a sample of Elsie's medicine.''

Sera felt herself blushing, remembering other actions she had taken in order to circumvent Cousin Clothilde.

"For your cousin's sake," said Lord Skelbrooke, "I beg you to accept my word that concealment of my part in this matter is absolutely necessary.''

Sera knotted the drawstrings on her reticule. She was hardly in a position to impose conditions. "Very well, Lord Skelbrooke. I shall expect a letter, ostensibly from this friend of yours. What name shall I look for?''

Lord Skelbrooke shook back a lace ruffle, dropped a pinch of snuff on the back of his wrist. "Carstares," he said, over his hand. He inhaled, and sneezed delicately. "I shall write to you under the name of Robin Carstares.''

26.

The storm continued through the night, passing on in the early morning. The cobbles were still wet when Jenk opened the shutters in his attic sitting room and looked down the street. Water dripped from the eaves of the slope-roofed old houses and shops.

Near the foot of the hill, a familiar stoop-shouldered form began the short climb. He cut an odd, hobgoblin sort of figure these days, did Caleb Braun, his back so crooked and his movements so stiff, and his clothes all mismatched bits and pieces. Very fine he was as to his striped satin waistcoat, brass shoe buckles, and shiny new tricorn; very shabby as to his faded blue coat and scarlet breeches, his patched stockings, and the knotted kerchief he wore in place of a neckcloth. Jed had provided him with a new suit of clothes, had outfitted him properly from head to toe, but Caleb steadfastly refused to wear everything at once, preferring to eke out his new wardrobe two or three pieces at a time.

Jenk drew in his head. He put on his snuff-colored coat and sidled down the stairs to the bookshop. He unlocked the door and opened it just as Caleb arrived, and stood on the threshold, a figure nearly as bent as Caleb himself, impatiently waving his henchman inside.

"You have interrupted my breakfast. There was no need for you to come so early. I told you—did I not?—that I did not intend to open the shop before mid-morning."

"Aye . . . you told me," said Caleb, limping in through the door. "But I had a hankering for to see her. Now, if I had a set of keys: one for the bookshop and one for the laboratory . . . it would set my mind at rest, Gottfried, it would ease my heart. I can't bear to be locked away from her, you know that."

Yes, Jenk knew that. These last few weeks had wrought a terrible change in Caleb. His skin was grey and hung loose on his bones; his eyes had a hollow, sunken look. Jenk gave him a weary little pat on the shoulder as he passed. But when he spoke, the bookseller's voice was stern.

"I begin to regret that I ever yielded to your pleas, that I ever allowed you to play so important a role in creating the little creature. This obsession you have developed: I fear it is not a healthy one, my old friend."

"That may be," said Caleb, bristling up. "But who are you to say so? Least I got my heart set on something I can see . . ."

"I cannot deny it," said Jenk, with a heavy sigh. "If you are obsessed with the growing homunculus, am I not equally obsessed by my search for the Stone?"

He made a fumbling search of his coat pockets, at last produced the key to the room at the back. "I do not suppose there is any use asking you to join me upstairs? Very well, then. I shall meet you in the laboratory, very shortly. We have much to discuss, Caleb . . . It is time that we took some thought for the future."

Only the stubby candle incubating the crystal egg, and a pale silvery glow issuing from the vessel itself illuminated the inner room. Caleb limped across the laboratory and peered eagerly into the clouded fluid.

The tiny creature at the center of the egg had not shifted position since the night before; she was still huddled in a tight little ball, with her knees drawn up to her narrow chest and her arms wrapped around her legs. But her pale green eyes were wide open, and her gaze curiously intent.

Caleb pulled up a stool and sat down, with his elbows on the table, and his face close to the crystal egg. Only when Jenk came into the room, almost an hour later, did he shift his position, slowly and stiffly.

"She's awake, Gottfried. Just you come here and look at her. She's awake again, and staring at me with them big tragic eyes."

Jenk hardly spared a glance; he was too occupied lighting the lanthorn suspended from the ceiling. "I see that her eyes are open, but whether she is actually awake and conscious remains to be seen . . . I believe that we allowed ourselves to be fooled by an *appearance* of intelligence in the first one." He closed the glass door of the lanthorn. "In any case, she will soon go dormant again."

Caleb glanced back over his shoulder. "She were awake for a long time yesterday . . . moving about. She beat her tiny little fists against the glass, like she wanted out. I don't reckon she's happy in there no more.''

"Nonsense," said Jenk. "Her movements are random; you deceive yourself if you attach any meaning to them. And your 'long time,' as I recall, was not above twenty minutes—if as much. Then she closed her eyes, and the gills on the side of her neck ceased to flutter. And she lost color, as though her heart had ceased to beat and circulate her blood. We have seen this happen a dozen times—she is still more dead than alive.''

Caleb shifted impatiently on his stool. "She's bigger nor the other one was . . . bigger and livelier. She wants to get born, I know she does.''

"Nonsense," Jenk repeated, moving toward the other table. "She will lose whatever degree of animation she has attained if we decant her too soon—just as the first one did. We must not allow our impatience (nor our misplaced compassion) to get the better of us a second time. We must wait another three or four days.''

Jenk lifted the lid of the coffin. Even after so many seasons it still came as a shock to him, each time that he looked inside. The perfect preservation of the body, the lifelike color beneath the clear, waxy skin, the half-smile on the face of the sorcerer—as though he were only sleeping, and his dreams were sweet.

Jenk wondered (as he had wondered so many times before) . . . if he gathered the courage to cut the threads that stitched the eyelids closed . . . would the eyes open . . . would the magician awake? Almost, Jenk believed that he would, yet he feared to make the experiment, to tamper with the body, lest even so tiny an alteration cause the preservation spell to fail, the corpse to disintegrate.

He turned away from the coffin, shuffled across the room, and opened the iron door of the furnace. He inspected the glass vessel he had been gently heating in a bed of hot sand for four and twenty days now. An oily black sediment was still forming on the walls of the flask, but otherwise there had been no change.

With a shaking hand, Jenk placed the vessel back in its bed of sand. He had followed the formula so carefully . . . the early results had been encouraging . . . he knew that the process was necessarily a slow one . . . yet he was beginning to wonder whether it was time to abandon this attempt and begin anew.

He put a hand to his chest, felt the slow, painful thud of his heartbeat, a buzzing and rattling in his lungs. Time . . . time was the very thing that he lacked. Indeed, with every passing day, he

188

grew more acutely conscious of his own mortality.

"It ain't going well," said Caleb.

"No," said Jenk. "I believe that this attempt has failed, also."

Caleb waved his hand dismissively. "What does it matter, then? Ain't we done a great thing in creating the homunculus? Seems to me the time was that would've been glory enough and more than enough for you."

But Jenk shook his head. It was not enough, it was not nearly enough. Yes . . . the creation of the living homunculus must gain him some measure of fame . . . it had already served a useful purpose in attracting the interest and the patronage of the Duke. But it was the stone Seramarias and nothing less that would bring Jenk all the wealth and all the power that he craved.

"I must begin again," said Jenk, sinking wearily down on a stool beside the copper still. "It will be very expensive, very time-consuming, but I must begin again. And I am weary, Caleb . . . I am most unutterably weary.

"It has been difficult, has it not?" he asked, with a heartfelt sigh. "Maintaining the illusion . . . for Sera's sake and for Jed's . . . that it is still the book trade that principally occupies us. But now that Sera is leaving town (not to return for so many long weeks), now that Jedidiah's new duties, his new friends, keep him so thoroughly occupied . . . I do not see why we should not close the bookshop and take an extended holiday, you and I."

"Aye . . ." Caleb gave a tug at his kerchief, as though he found it tight around his throat. "It's been a burden on my conscience, lying and deceiving the lad that way that I been. Less need for that now, when he don't have time to ask so many questions—and all for his own good, I keep telling myself, but sometimes it troubles me . . ."

"As I, also, am similarly troubled," said Jenk. "Yet I am convinced that we act for the best in keeping the pair of them as innocent as possible. Less worry for them now, less chance of disappointment later.

"It has occurred to me, Caleb, that when we do decant the homunculus, someone must be on hand to care for her at all hours."

Caleb took a deep breath and released it slowly. "That case, I'll have to move in, here at the bookshop."

"Yes," said Jenk. "I had already considered that. You may have Sera's old room. Tell Jedidiah . . . tell him whatever story he is most likely to believe. That I am ill—or that you are. You

189

must be entirely convincing, he must not suspect a thing . . . lest he communicate his concern to those new friends of his.''

"He'll think what I tell him to think . . . believe anything I say,'' insisted Caleb. "He's just a boy, Gottfried, for all he's growed so big.''

As they spoke, the homunculus closed her eyes, apparently went dormant again. Caleb left his stool and began to move restlessly around the laboratory. His eyes chanced to fall on the crudely made garments, the tiny shirt, breeches, and full-skirted coat Jenk had stitched together for the first homunculus. "When the time does come . . . she can't wear these. 'Twouldn't be fitting nor proper.''

Jenk felt a surge of annoyance. "I do not see why not. I wish you would not fidget so, Caleb. It makes me uneasy. Oh, very well . . .'' Eager to get his henchman out of the shop and out of his sight, if only for a quarter of an hour, he reached into a pocket in his breeches and extracted one of the Duke's gold coins. "There is a shop at the foot of the hill. Purchase a doll, to forestall any questions, and have it dressed. One or two gowns at the very most, Caleb. There is no need to provide the little creature with an entire wardrobe.''

The doll shop was a low white-washed building with bay windows, a thatched roof, and a red door. According to a sign nailed up over that door, Jenny Sattinflower was the proprietor.

Caleb knew her by sight: a stout young dwarf with a shrewd face and a sharp manner. He had encountered her moving briskly through the streets of the town, greeting her neighbors with a clipped word or a curt nod of her head. Something of an anomaly she was: a solitary dwarf, living alone and owning nothing of great value, an independent, bustling little person who cared more for her work than the money it might bring her. Nor had she any time for idle chatter. Six days a week she could be found in her shop, morning to night, sitting at her low work table, sewing gowns for dolls, or painting uniforms on toy soldiers, by the light of a single oil lamp.

When Caleb walked into the shop, a wooden rattle suspended from the door frame clattered to announce his entry. The dwarf immediately put aside her bits and pieces of sewing and came to meet him, lamp in hand.

"I give ye good day, Mistress Sattinflower, and I come to buy a poppet—nigh about this size.'' Caleb dipped his head sheepishly

190

and indicated a span of perhaps eight inches with his hands.

"Hmmmmph!" replied the gruff little thing—and that was all the greeting that he got from her. "Cloth or kidskin? China, bisque, or porcelain? Composition, paper-paste, wood, or wax? We've a good many dolls here, Mr. Braun, made of just about any material you might care to name. You'll have to be more specific."

Caleb removed his hat and scratched his head; he was new to this business of buying dolls and had never imagined he would be offered such a bewildering array of choices. "Wax'll do, I reckon."

Holding the lamp before her, she led him to the back of the shop, and a glassed-in cabinet filled with dainty wax figures dressed in the latest fashions. "They are rather dear, I am afraid," said Jenny.

"It don't matter . . . I can pay," said Caleb. He had already set his heart on a delicate little lady in a gown of flowered silk. "I'll take that one—the lass with the flaxen curls."

Without comment, the dwarf opened the glass case, removed the doll, and placed her in Caleb's unsteady hands. Then she escorted him to the counter where she kept her cashbox.

"Three days," said Jenny Sattinflower, after he paid for the doll, described the kind of garments that he wanted for her, and paid for those, too. "I've a number of other commissions to perform first." And she indicated the scraps of shimmering silk, the bits of lace and ribbon on her workbench.

"Three days it is, then," said Caleb, bobbing his head. With the wax doll in his hands, he felt easier in his mind, more settled in spirit. It no longer seemed such a long time to wait.

27.

Containing scenes of Travel. Also, a "blessed" event.

It was noon on the last day of the season when the Duchess's heavy berlin rumbled down Thorn Hill, followed by Jarl Skogsrå's light cabriolet and a humbler conveyance carrying baggage and servants.

Out through the Great North Gate lurched the coach and the two smaller carriages, with outriders escorting them before and behind. Along the Prince's highway they traveled, bowling along at a great rate, farther into the green countryside than Sera and Elsie had ever gone before.

The country just north of Thornburg was a pleasant, settled region, sprinkled with neat little farms and picturesque ancient villages. Late wildflowers, goldenrod, milkweed, and fennel, bloomed in all the fields, and sheep and cattle grazed in large peaceful herds. The land was gently rolling, mostly open country, with an occasional short stretch of forest—mixed beech and oak and pine, or willow and alder where a stream ran through—so that the journey progressed as a series of pleasant vistas viewed from the top of one hill after another, with every now and then a fleeting glimpse of the river Lunn shining in the distance.

The Duchess had entered the coach in a state of ill humor, but the enthusiasm of the two girls was contagious. They kept her tolerably well amused for most of the afternoon, with their questions, their innocent observations, and their continued exclamations of wonder and delight.

As they had started late, they could not expect to reach the hotel at Mittleheim (where rooms had been reserved for them) before nightfall; therefore, they stopped for an early supper at a country inn. They rumbled into the innyard at about five o'clock, with the Jarl's cabriolet right behind them. But the carriage with the servants and the baggage, which had been delegated to go on ahead to Mittleheim, continued down the broad highway and was soon lost to view.

The Jarl was out of his carriage in an instant, and on hand to assist the ladies as they emerged from the berlin. His traveling companion—the Duchess's other guest, Mr. Hermes Budge—stood quietly at his elbow, courteous and gentleman-like. Jarl Skogsrå claimed the honor of escorting the Duchess into the inn. Much to his relief, she left Sebastian the ape behind in the coach. But it was not Sebastian who had incurred the Jarl's displeasure today.

"This companion you have saddled me with . . . so solemn, so virtuous. Why do we bring him? Is this your idea of a joke?" he asked in a low voice.

The Duchess glanced up at him, through the cobwebby veil of her enchanting bonnet. "I don't deny that Mr. Budge is decidedly lacking when it comes to *amusing* conversation, but I do not regard that—for he has an interesting mind and speaks quite well on any *serious* topic. And no," she added, with an impatient gesture, "I did not invite him for the purpose of tormenting you! I bring him along as a favor to the Duke, who will, I believe, find his company stimulating."

After they had eaten, the Duchess and the young ladies decided on an after-supper stroll through the tiny village surrounding the inn. There was a feeble attempt at a country fair on the village green: a juggler, a handful of ramshackle booths selling tawdry half-penny trinkets, and a man hawking gingerbread. The girls were eager to look over the booths, and Mr. Budge offered to accompany them, but the Duchess was troubled by the late afternoon heat and had left her fan and her parasol back in the coach. Jarl Skogsrå declared that he would be delighted to escort her down the High Street and into a pleasant little wood bordering the village.

"The Gracious Lady is rather pale and low in spirits," said the Jarl, as they entered the shade of the trees and the Duchess lifted her veil. "Is it possible that this journey does not agree with her?"

"I thrive on travel," said the Duchess. "No, it is not the journey that afflicts me, but something I learned quite recently, which has depressed my spirits. Something shocking . . . incredible. I have been robbed, my dear Skogsrå, deprived of something valuable and irreplaceable. And what is immeasurably worse: I cannot escape the conclusion that it was almost certainly stolen by somebody close to me."

The Jarl was the picture of sympathetic curiosity. "But who could have betrayed you in this infamous fashion . . . and what exactly was it they took?"

"I do not know *who* or even *when*," said the Duchess, sitting down on the mossy trunk of a fallen oak and spreading out the skirt of her grey satin polanaise. "You wonder how that might be? Well, I will tell you. I had hidden this valuable object in my bedchamber, in what I supposed a very good hiding place. Indeed, it had rested there unmolested for more years than I care to count. And I had grown complacent, I suppose, and had fallen out of the habit of checking on this . . . document . . . to make certain that I still kept it safe. It must have been half a year since I last handled it—perhaps even longer—and I only thought to examine it again, two days ago, when I meant to pack it along with my other personal effects and carry it with me to Zar-Wildungen."

The Jarl took out his fan—it was nearly as pretty as the one the Duchess had left in her coach. Made of chickenskin, it was painted with a delicate design of funerary urns, cypress wreaths, and drooping willow trees. He opened the fan and began to wave it idly. "You say, then, that this valuable object may have disappeared anytime in the last half a year—and therefore, might have been carried away by any one of a number of people who had access to your private chambers during that time? But of course you are distressed—how could you not be? It is a terrible thing, not knowing whom you may trust.

"I must suppose," the Jarl added, after another moment of thought, "that I, also, am among those suspected."

The Duchess favored him with an irritable glance. "If you were, do you suppose that I would be confiding in you now?"

"I cannot be certain," said Skogsrå, with a low bow. He looked particularly dandified today. He wore a tiny, dagger-shaped patch at the corner of one eye, and another, shaped like a crescent moon, on the opposite cheek. "For the subtlety and wit of the Gracious Lady are so often beyond my poor comprehension."

"Yes," said the Duchess, still a bit snappishly, "you are exceedingly single-minded. But it is just that narrowness of vision that absolves you now. I cannot think you would have the necessary knowledge to recognize the value of the object if you stumbled on it, or to understand its potential uses." She removed her white net gloves and dropped them in her lap, then untied the ribbons of her bonnet. "It was . . . is . . . a magic parchment, inscribed with secret signs and figures, created under extraordinary

194

circumstances. One would have to know something of its history to realize that it was anything more than an ordinary charm of protection.

"Now, if your friend Vodni had visited me during that time . . . him I should surely suspect," said the Duchess, removing her hat and placing it carefully on the log beside her. "For *he* would know its value in an instant."

"Please . . . he is no friend of mine, this Vodni," the Jarl protested. "My compatriot, if you will, but never my friend!"

"Of course," said the Duchess, with her sweetest smile. "It is natural, I suppose, that you should envy Vodni, for his youth and his energy if for nothing else."

This was, undoubtedly, a provocative remark, when spoken by a woman of nearly two centuries, to a forty-year-old dandy. But the Jarl knew he was still a fine figure of a man, and that women still sighed over his handsome face and his golden lovelocks. He was willing to let the remark pass.

"I dislike Baron Vodni for his inflated self-opinion, his insufferable . . . ah, well, it is an old grudge, and has nothing to do with the matter at hand," said Skogsrå, snapping shut his funereal little fan. "And so I am absolved by virtue of my dullness, and Vodni by his absence during the time in question. Whom does that leave?" The Jarl started counting the fingers of one hand. "Lord Vizbeck . . . Mr. von Eichstätt . . . Dr. Mirabolo . . . the good Mr. Budge . . . Lord Skelbrooke—"

"It need not have been a man," the Duchess interrupted sharply. "I have women friends as well, you know. What makes you so certain that it was not one of them?"

The Jarl took her soft little hand and kissed it. "The Gracious Lady is so very formidable a personality, it would take extraordinary nerve to contemplate crossing her in such a manner. Surely a woman would lack—"

"You are forgetting," the Duchess said, with a frosty glare, "that I, also, am a woman."

"But no ordinary woman," the Jarl replied smoothly.

"Nevertheless," said the Duchess, withdrawing her hand, "you cannot flatter me by denigrating my own sex. It might have been a woman, just as easily as a man. It might have been . . . Ursula Bowker, for instance. I am sure that *she* has effrontery enough for anything!"

"That is true," said the Jarl. "Well then . . . say that it was a female. Why not as soon suspect Miss Sera Vorder . . . Miss *Ser-*

amarias Vorder, the granddaughter of the alchemist, who (we may safely assume) has the very knowledge I lack, and would recognize your artifact on sight."

"And would wish to avoid it, on that very account," said the Duchess, with a little gurgle of laughter. "Or have you forgotten Miss Vorder's well-known distaste for anything which smacks of mysticism?"

"I have not forgotten," replied Skogsrå. "I am merely wondering if I actually believe in this . . . distaste, as you call it. Perhaps it has only been a pose, all along."

The Duchess stared at him in patent disbelief. "My dear Jarl . . . what an imagination you do have! I had not thought it of you, I declare that I had not. My felicitations! But do you actually mean to suggest that Sera Vorder could possibly be so—so clever and so bold as to maintain this . . . this incredible pose . . . for all of these years, merely in order to spy on me and to rob me?"

"Most assuredly I do," said the Jarl. "For I am convinced that the young woman, like your friend Lady Ursula, has sufficient effrontery for any enterprise she might choose to undertake."

Three days to the very hour, and Caleb reappeared at Jenny Sattinflower's shop to claim his purchases. The dwarf wrapped up the dresses in brown paper, and the old man returned to the bookshop with the package under his arm.

As Caleb entered the laboratory, his eyes went immediately to the crystal egg on the iron tripod. But the tripod was empty for the first time in many weeks. The egg lay in two empty halves upon the table. The homunculus was gone.

In a panic, Caleb looked around him. Then he spotted a doll-like figure lying under a ragged scrap of blanket, in a basket on the floor between the furnace and the still.

He looked at Jenk reproachfully. "You give birth to her while I was out!"

Jenk, who was much occupied with his flasks and his vials and his evil-smelling tinctures, barely glanced up from his work. "My dear Caleb . . . her transition from the liquid element to the aerial seemed likely to be a traumatic one. Indeed, she screeched and struggled so when I removed her from the egg: she sounded like a blackbird in the jaws of a cat. It would have done you no good to witness her distress, and your own apprehension would only have served to increase hers.

"She is resting now," he added calmly. "I fear she exhausted

196

herself, reacting so strongly, but she appears to be slumbering naturally. There is no doubt that she possesses a fully developed set of lungs.''

With an angry sense that he had been cheated, Caleb limped over to the basket to take a closer look at his tiny sleeping ''daughter.'' Her grey-green hair was still damp—it had an odd, feathery appearance, like moss or fern—and her skin was pale, with a creamy tint. The gills on the side of her neck had closed, and she appeared to be breathing easily. And suddenly . . . Caleb did not feel cheated any longer, but humble and grateful, and slightly in awe of the miracle that he and Jenk had created between them.

He cleared his throat. ''She's . . . she's real pretty, ain't she? Daintier than a little wax doll.''

''Indeed,'' said Jenk, with an indulgent smile. ''And that reminds me . . . you might as well show me the garments you had made for her.''

But when he saw the elegant little gowns Caleb had commissioned, the smile changed to a frown. ''I perceive that you mean to spoil her. You will turn her head with all this finery!'' He turned back to his flasks and his chemicals. ''Never mind . . . you can hardly return them. You may dress her when she awakes.''

''Dress her . . . me?'' said Caleb. He lifted the little blanket, looked doubtfully down at the tiny female creature. Neither child nor woman, as yet, she appeared to be something in between, her figure immature but developing.

''We can hardly bring a woman in here to do it,'' said Jenk. ''Yes, of course, you are the one to dress her. Have you not already promised to play the role of nursemaid?

''She must be perfect in every respect before I publish her existence abroad,'' added Jenk. ''She must know how to speak . . . to read and to write . . . she must have elegant manners. There must be no doubt in anyone's mind that she is indeed intelligent and self-aware . . . not a brute beast to perform a series of actions on command or to parrot certain phrases. Were she anything less than perfect, so, too, would my triumph be less than perfect. I shall supervise her education, when the time comes,'' the bookseller went on, with mounting enthusiasm. ''But for now . . . she must learn what every other infant learns: to walk about, to feed herself, and to communicate her needs. I leave her in your hands, Caleb, for the time being. When you have taught her to behave tolerably well, we shall send word to the Duke, and he will undoubtedly send his man out to observe her.''

197

Caleb experienced a sharp pang of apprehension. "The Duke ... he won't be expecting us to hand her over, will he? She's ours, Gottfried ... she don't belong to him. You promised we'd be able to keep her for ourselfs."

"But of course," said Jenk. "I would not think of parting with her, my miraculous creation. The Duke must be satisfied with the formula. He *will* be satisfied with the formula—you need have no fear on that account."

"And later on ... if you should be offered money—a circus or a traveling exhibition—what then?" Caleb persisted.

"She is not for sale ... she is positively not for sale. I grieve, my dear Caleb, that you should think me capable of any such thing," replied Jenk, with his hand on his heart.

"That's all right, then," said Caleb. "That's as it should be.

"Because I tell you straight out," he added fiercely, "there ain't no one going to part us, my little daughter and me ... not while I'm alive and breathing!"

28.

In which Francis Skelbrooke experiences a Revelation.

Not far from Capricorn Street was another dark and narrow lane, where the sun did not shine until mid-day and evening shadows came early. Yet Blue Phoenix Lane was a street less dirty and degraded in character, being the abode of the "working" poor, and lined with old houses and humble businesses: chandlers, printers, ropemakers, and coopers; old-clothes men, cobblers, and rag merchants; purveyors of ink, quills, paper, pins, and needles.

Along Blue Phoenix Lane, one evening, slouched a sinister figure in a frieze coat. He wore his dirty blond hair in a greasy pigtail, and a battered tricorn pulled low to shadow his features. Just where the lane began to climb Fishwife Hill, a green lanthorn suspended from an overhang cast a beam of light on the door of a neat little apothecary shop.

After a moment of hesitation, he entered the shop.

It was a typical apothecary shop, cluttered and homely, smelling of herbs and unguents, soaps, perfumes, and essential oils. The walls were lined with shelves and cabinets crowded with china jars and earthen pots, bottles, bags, and boxes, containing pills, powders, syrups, elixirs, cordials, drops, essences, and tonics. A stuffed fish hung suspended from the ceiling, among strings of poppy-heads and strings of rose-hips, and bunches of catnip, fennel, and madder hung up to dry. There was a fire burning on a little hearth at the back, a pot of boiling lye, to be made into soap, and a hypocaust brewing hydromel for drops and confections.

The proprietor was a little white-haired lady, who sat in a rocking chair behind the counter, writing labels for bottles in a thin spidery hand. Finding that he and the woman were alone in the shop, the man—he appeared to be either a gaoler or a particularly low sort of bargeman—closed and barred the door behind him.

He removed his hat and executed a low bow. "Your most obedient servant, Mistress Sancreedi."

"Lord Skelbrooke . . . what a turn you gave me," said the little apothecary, but a mischievous twinkle indicated that she had seen through his disguise immediately. "Might one ask what this . . . astounding costume . . . is supposed to portend?"

"Bad men, ill deeds, and (if I am successful) vengeance of no mean order," said Skelbrooke. Evidently much at home, he perched on the counter and set his battered tricorn down beside him. "I had your note, yesterday, promising extraordinary revelations. And I should have come last evening, but I was otherwise engaged."

Mistress Sancreedi shook her head. "*Unexpected* information . . . I believe that was the sense of my message. I must say, it was quite a puzzle you set me. It has taken me these many days to determine the contents of that vial you brought me."

"And . . . ?" asked Skelbrooke, swinging his legs.

Mistress Sancreedi put down her pen. "It contains, principally, the essence of a rare plant which grows only in the mountains on the continent of Orania. You were correct in supposing this medicine is the cause of Elsie Vorder's panics and visions—but I must tell you it is often used as a tonic to strengthen the blood, and may have been innocently prescribed with that purpose in mind. You told me—did you not?—that Dr. Mirabolo had diagnosed an infection of the blood."

"That is true," agreed Skelbrooke. "But my own observations—"

199

"Your own observations agree with mine. At least when I knew her, Elsie Vorder was suffering from a poor circulation of the blood due to insufficient exercise, irregular hours, and an improper diet. Her *original* problem, as I believe, was nothing more than the growing pains and dizzy spells which are so common among young girls of twelve or thirteen years. Had she been left alone to recover naturally, she would be as healthy as her cousin Sera is today. But that is quite beside the point," said Mistress Sancreedi. "We both know that it is not uncommon for physicians to disagree—and indeed, Dr. Mirabolo was not the first of Elsie's doctors to diagnose a disease of the blood. Even I must admit that a girl who regularly breakfasts on vinegar and biscuits might well benefit from a blood-building tonic. As for the other, unfortunate, effects of the potion . . . they are less well known, and indeed may be easily avoided. The visions and the rising sense of panic only occur when a large dose of the tonic is followed soon after by the ingestion of sugar and alcohol . . . as in a cordial, or cakes and sweet wine, or—"

"—or cherry ratafia," said Lord Skelbrooke.

"Did Elsie drink ratafia at Count Xebo's ball? Yes, that would certainly have brought on an attack, if she had taken her medicine earlier that same evening." Mistress Sancreedi went back to labeling her bottles. "It is altogether possible that Elsie's problems are only the result of honest ignorance on the part of Dr. Mirabolo and Jarl Skogsrå, who perhaps did not know to warn her against these undesirable effects of the medication."

Skelbrooke slipped down from the counter. "A convenient mistake for Jarl Skogsrå, who uses these fits of Elsie's, and his ability to bring her out of them, in order to gain an emotional hold on her and press his suit. The entire situation seems so very contrived, and his methods so sinister—"

"His methods do not seem altogether sinister to me." The apothecary dipped her pen in an inkwell on a shelf beside her. "This animal magnetism—or mind control as you have called it in the past—it is not so very different from a method that *I* employ to soothe my patients, to calm unquiet minds. Fairy glamour, they used to call it in the old days, for it comes quite naturally to those of us with a hint of the blood."

She looked up from her work. "It is, I believe, a very important part of the Duchess's famous charm, and may also be closely akin to those spells *you* employ in creating your illusions. The face

200

you wore when you came in the door, for instance . . . that was very convincing."

"With all due respect, dear lady, I do not think so," said Skelbrooke. He began to pace around the shop. "The ability of which you speak is (I take it) a natural talent, a species of intuition. Whereas the magic I practice is a discipline of the mind, the application of a trained will, the—"

"Yes, yes," said Mistress Sancreedi, with a humorous sigh. "We have discussed this before. No doubt it is just as you say . . . yet this applied will may also be aided by a natural aptitude on your part. I have often wondered, dear Francis, if you might not be one of us, and never know it."

Lord Skelbrooke stiffened. "I can assure you that my ancestry is solidly human on both sides of the family. The genealogies I was taught to recite as a boy, at my grandfather's behest—"

"Not a recent ancestor, certainly," said the lady. "Else you would certainly know. Fairy . . . gifts . . . do not always take an attractive form, but they are virtually unmistakable. Do stop and gaze at yourself in a mirror some time, Francis. But I stray from the point . . .

"I know that you are ready and more than ready to suspect evil motives on the part of the Duchess, yet you have no idea what those motives might be. My dear boy," she asked, with a look of pain, "how long must all women suffer in your regard, for the wickedness of the one?"

"I believe," said Skelbrooke, beginning again to move restlessly around the shop, "that in my more lucid moments I can tell the difference between a good woman like yourself . . . and the other sort. Nevertheless, I do not consider the Duchess a virtuous woman. You will tell me, no doubt, that she is generous . . . that she endows hospitals, schools, and other charitable institutions—all with the Duke's money. But I will tell you that her private habits are perverse, and her knowledge of the Black Arts varied and extensive."

Mistress Sancreedi corked her inkwell and her gluepot. "Yet to study these arts is not necessarily to practice them—else how would good folk like you and I know to recognize them? No, I should not go so far as to term the Duchess a woman of virtue, but I can assure you of this: Marella Carleon is not one to act out of *idle* malice. It is not in her nature; it is not in any fairy's nature, be she Fee or Farisee. That being so, and under the circumstances, I cannot believe that she means Elsie any harm.

201

"It would be different," she added, "if we knew of anything that Elsie had done to offend the Duchess. They are an unforgiving lot, the Fees, and their vengeance can be . . . exaggerated. It would not even have to be something that Elsie had done intentionally. But indeed, the girl is so very inoffensive, I find it hard to imagine even an unintended insult."

"As do I," said Skelbrooke, with a slight shake of his head.

It was a very different Francis Skelbrooke who ate supper at the Guildhall with his lodge brothers, later that same evening: freshly bathed and barbered, powdered, scented, and patched, in pastel satin and snowy point lace, and a waistcoat embroidered with roses and pansies. The members of the guild ate a very good meal and lingered long over their brandy.

"My dear Lord Skelbrooke . . . pray tell us something of your recent exploits," said a pale young fellow in a grey wig, another of the "bookish gentlemen" attached to the speculative branch of the guild. "I daresay that you are presently engaged in something particularly dangerous and exciting."

Lord Skelbrooke took out his pocket watch. It was shaped like an egg: a very pretty trinket, if a bit outsized, it had been coated with a shell of fine white porcelain and painted with tiny flowers. "I am presently endeavoring to put an end to the white-slave trade as it is practiced in Thornburg and neighboring towns. Decent young girls . . . and sometimes young boys as well," he said, lifting the upper half of the egg and studying the watch face beneath. "Kidnapped and spirited away—sometimes in wagons over the Alps, but more often in ships by way of Spagne—and sold in Ynde to serve as concubines, or even common prostitutes."

"A shocking practice, no doubt," said the pale young gentleman. "Though why it should merit your concern, I do not precisely comprehend. Your purpose—indeed, the purpose which we all share in common—is to seek out instances of the misuse of magic, and see that the offenders are punished."

Skelbrooke smiled his sweetest and blandest smile. "But of course, Lord Mallekin, it is just as you say. And that being so . . . perhaps it would be in order for you to share with this assembly your own (no doubt considerable) exploits in the pursuit of that goal?"

There followed an uncomfortable silence, during which Lord Mallekin and some of the other gentlemen exchanged uneasy glances. Lord Mallekin cleared his throat. "I beg your pardon. I did not mean to criticize . . . I am well aware—''

"You are well aware," said Skelbrooke, closing his watch, and still smiling that same amiable smile, "that it is only my presence among you, and my willingness to take on risks which none of the rest of you dare to even contemplate, that extends this chapter any credibility at all. You are also aware that until I arrived in Thornburg and presented my credentials to the Grand Preceptor"—here he gave a respectful nod of the head in the direction of Mr. Christopher Owlfeather—"and was duly admitted into the chapter, you and your fellow members could no more claim an active pursuit of that particular purpose than . . . I beg your pardon, I do not mean to imply that the other goals of the Glassmakers were neglected, that the poor were not fed or that widows and orphans were not given aid, or that my own contribution is in any way more important than the charitable works of this institution . . . but in regard to the oath that all of us take *to seek out the guilty and to render justice*, nothing at all was done, beyond a great deal of talk and the performance of endless rituals. Even now—''

"Even now," put in Mr. Owlfeather, from his place at the head of the table, "only you, my good Francis, have the courage, the daring, and the expertise necessary to take an active role. For which reason," he added, with a significant glance in Lord Mallekin's direction, "I have taken the position that it is not for the guild to dictate Lord Skelbrooke's activities, so much as to sponsor them. And where and when he chooses to act must be left entirely to his own discretion.''

"I thank you," said Skelbrooke, with another nod. "I am perfectly convinced that insofar as you are concerned, Mr. Owlfeather, no explanation is necessary. But for the sake of the other gentlemen here present I will say this much: there is evidence that these white slavers make some use of magic in snaring their victims and rendering them docile. These spells, so very minor in themselves, would hardly merit my attention, were it not for the purpose to which they have been addressed.''

"Nevertheless," the young man in the grey wig insisted, "from what I know of your previous activities, this project does not appear to be precisely in line with your usual endeavors.''

"My dear Lord Mallekin . . ." Skelbrooke's voice took on a steely edge, and his smile lost some of its sweetness. "I oppose myself to anything which tends toward the rape of innocence.''

• • •

The Glassmakers conducted their more private ceremonies in a vault beneath the Guildhall: a vast octagonal chamber built of stone, purposely constructed to resemble a glassblower's furnace, with arched apertures on every wall, except at the east, where the heavy iron doors were located.

There were seven arches, and twice seven pillars, and seven marble statues of the winged Fates. The floor was tiled in an elaborate mosaic pattern depicting the ascent of the soul through the seven spheres. At the center of the vault was a raised dais, reached by nine shallow steps.

On this particular evening, only lodge members of the sixth rank and higher were present, for this was a ceremony of elevation to that rank and title: Exalted Commander of the Burning Water.

There were two Wardens at the door, south and north, Francis Skelbrooke and Master Ule, both of them attired in purple robes emblazoned with suns and stars. They wore sharp-edged scimitars with golden handles, tucked into their belts. Mr. Owlfeather, as the Grand Preceptor, waited on the dais.

The iron doors opened; the Wardens drew their scimitars. And two members, acting as Chaplains, appeared on the threshold, escorting the blindfolded Candidate between them. His eyes were bandaged and his wrists manacled with wide cuffs joined by a stout chain—symbolizing the heavy weight which those who live in ignorance must bear through the world. The Chaplains led him to the dais, and Mr. Owlfeather, descending, removed the blindfold.

In his place by the door, Francis Skelbrooke was experiencing the greatest difficulty concentrating on the action by the altar. His thoughts kept straying back to the apothecary shop and the puzzling revelations of Mistress Sancreedi. Every instinct he possessed assured him that Skogsrå and the Duchess presented a threat to the health and well-being of Elsie Vorder, yet the nature of that threat continued to elude him. Something was missing, he told himself, some clue, some word, some perception, lacking which he was incapable of making the right connections.

Up on the dais, the ritual continued. The Preceptor produced a poniard and placed it ceremoniously at the initiate's throat. On receiving the correct response, he removed the blade and freed the Candidate of his shackles. The initiate crossed his arms, palms up, offering his wrists to Mr. Owlfeather, who carefully made a shallow, ritual scar on each one.

With a violent start, Skelbrooke dropped his scimitar. It fell clattering on the tile floor, drawing all eyes in his direction. With an embarrassed word of apology, he stooped to recover his weapon.

In one brief flash of intuition, all the facts had fallen into a neat, comprehensible pattern in Skelbrooke's mind. Yet the puzzle revealed was so fantastic, the whole thing so wildly improbable, that he was not absolutely positive that he believed any of it himself.

Certainly, thought Skelbrooke (as he slipped the blade back through his belt and strove to regain his composure), certainly none of this was anything he might communicate to Sera Vorder in a letter—not if he expected her to credit a single word. No, he decided, he would have to travel to Zar-Wildungen in person and arrange to speak to Sera privately. Once he had convinced her, it would be up to Sera, in her turn, to convince Elsie that a plot existed against her.

Yet his present perilous business still demanded his immediate attention. He could not leave Thornburg until that was finished, lest the prey he had marked for himself slip right through the net he was so carefully weaving, and escape altogether.

But . . . three days to complete his business, four at most . . . and then two days on the road to Zar-Wildungen, if he traveled swiftly and encountered no delays along the way. He would be there inside a week. And Elsie and the Jarl were not even betrothed, therefore, Elsie Vorder was not in any *immediate* danger.

Skelbrooke felt confident that he would reach the Duke's estate with ample time to spare—in plenty of time to prevent a wedding . . . and a blood-letting.

29.

In which Skogsrå learns more of the Duchess's Intentions.

The road between Lüftmal and the larger town of Pfalz was well maintained, and the Duchess and her party traveled along at a steady clip for perhaps five miles. But then the road divided, and the coach, and the lighter carriage following behind, deserted the broad and easy way for a winding country lane, leading toward the Duke of Zar-Wildungen's country estate.

The lane soon became rutted and bumpy, heavy going for the big berlin, which jounced and bounced in such a way that the ladies inside were much shaken. But Jarl Skogsrå, in his well-sprung cabriolet, and his companion Mr. Budge, took the bumps lightly and arrived at the iron gates of the Wichtelberg still comparatively fresh.

From there on, the way was smoother; a gravel-covered drive wound through the park in wide, leisurely loops. The Duchess shook out her skirts and righted her bonnet, took a reviving whiff of hartshorn, and opened her fan. The two girls, recovering more swiftly, each took a window.

The drive continued on for almost a mile through wooded country, then past a lake and down an avenue lined with ash trees, before Sera and Elsie caught their first glimpse of the house.

Located on rising ground above the lake, the manor was a great rambling dwarf-built structure of whitewashed stone, reached by a series of marble terraces. The coach pulled up before a flight of low steps, and the Duchess was the first to alight, followed by Sera, and then Elsie.

A broad-shouldered young man in an exquisitely tailored coat of blue superfine appeared on the terrace above. He ran down the steps and presented himself to the Duchess with a very pretty bow.

"My dear boy, how delightful to see you again," said the Duchess. "Allow me to present you to my companions. Miss

Seramarias and Miss Elsie Vorder: this gentleman is Baron Vodni.''

The Baron had an open countenance and a fresh complexion. He wore his own hair, carelessly tied back, with one dark lock straying romantically across his brow. He looked, thought Sera, like a man who lived in the country and liked it. He had an easy, graceful way about him, as he took first Elsie's hand and then Sera's, each time executing an elegant bow.

Then he turned to greet Jarl Skogsrå, who was just dismounting from his carriage. "My old friend . . . you look fagged to death. The journey was undoubtedly a difficult one. But you must not exhaust yourself . . . really you must not," said Vodni, with a wide grin. "For the sake of your friends, my dear Skogsrå, you must make every effort to guard your health."

"I thank you," said the Jarl, with a characteristic grimace, "my health remains excellent—you young popinjay—and I am not so many years your senior."

Baron Vodni continued to smile brightly. "But of course . . . a decade or two—what is that? I meant no disrespect. Do not disturb yourself, I beg you."

It was evident, at least to Sera, that the two men disliked each other heartily, and the Baron rose in her estimation accordingly. Certainly there was nothing mocking or objectionable in his manner when the Duchess introduced him to Hermes Budge. "The Duke sent me down to welcome you, sir. He is resting at the moment, but he hopes to entertain you in his study this evening."

The baron fell into step with Sera as they crossed the marble terrace. "Seramarias . . . it is a charming name. The mythical gemstone of incalculable price. *Radiant Seramarias, which men have sought* . . . I fear that I have forgotten the rest of the verse, but perhaps it will return to me."

"Are you a poet, my lord?" asked Sera, with a frown. She was not eager to make the acquaintance of any more poetical young noblemen.

"Alas, no," said Vodni, with unimpaired good nature. "Though I once had aspirations along those lines. Not a poet, Miss Vorder, but the Duke of Zar-Wildungen's secretary."

"The Duke's . . ." Sera experienced a momentary confusion. "Perhaps I misheard the Duchess. It is . . . it is *Baron* Vodni, is it not?"

"Baron Nicolai Vodni . . . but the title is little more than a courtesy," he replied. "In my family, we are all barons and

207

baronesses . . . It is the custom of our country, where titles are more easily come by than gold. My uncle does own a fine estate, near Katrinsberg, which he inherited from my grandfather . . . but in Ruska, as elsewhere, the younger son of a younger son is often obliged to work for his living.

"You must not think that I am complaining," he added cheerfully. "Apart from my blighted poetic ambitions, my situation suits me very well. And I believe that a man as energetic as I am requires a profession, to keep him out of mischief."

The Duchess's personal attendants, along with the house servants, were lined up to greet her in the great marble entry hall. She assigned a maid to Sera and Elsie and delegated a footman to the Jarl and Mr. Budge.

"I believe," she told her guests, as she handed Sebastian the ape over to her butler, "there is time for you all to take a brief rest before dressing for dinner. For myself . . . I am eager to visit the Duke. You will accompany me, Vodni?"

"It will be my pleasure," said the Baron, offering her his arm.

"I have no desire to rest," said Skogsrå. "I find myself . . . restless, not tired at all. With the Gracious Lady's permission, I will accompany her as well."

The Gracious Lady lifted an eyebrow, but made no demur, not even when Skogsrå followed her and Vodni out of the hall and down a broad corridor lined with suits of armor and ancient portraits in gilded frames.

"And what do you think of the young ladies . . . my guests?" the Duchess asked the Baron, as they moved in the direction of the east wing, where the Duke's rooms were located overlooking the lake. "Are they not both of them delightful young women?"

"Always remembering . . ." Jarl Skogsrå put in, with a slight baring of his teeth, "that Miss Elsie Vorder is reserved for me."

Baron Vodni made a dismissive gesture. "And you are entirely welcome to her, so far as I am concerned. I hasten to assure you, she is not to my taste. The other, however—so handsome and spirited as she appears to be—I find myself enchanted, thoroughly enchanted. With the Gracious Lady's permission, I should like very much to become better acquainted with Miss Seramarias Vorder."

"And so you shall," said the Duchess, obviously pleased. "So you must. I confess that I had hoped a mutual attraction might develop. By all means, become friends with her, win her trust if

208

you can. Perhaps then she will confide in you.

"Although I must warn you," she added, with a mischievous sidelong glance at the Jarl, and a gurgle of laughter, "that our friend Skogsrå would have us believe the girl a monster of iniquity. A kind of agent sent to spy on us, and to rob me of all that I own. That being so, you might wish to tread carefully. The girl is clearly much deeper than you or I would ever suspect."

The Duchess and Vodni had time for a good laugh at Skogsrå's expense before they reached the Duke's rooms. There, the Duchess dismissed them both and disappeared inside the Duke's bedchamber. Skogsrå stood in the corridor, glaring at the door she had just closed behind her.

"Now, what occasions this black look?" asked Vodni. "Is it possible that you have designs on both of these girls—that you intend to woo them both at the same time?"

"I intend nothing of the sort. I intend only to obey the instructions of the Gracious Lady," the Jarl replied, with an air of great injury. "I do all as she instructs me . . . I am entirely at her service, and yet she continually mocks me. *A monster of iniquity*, she says . . . And what is the Duchess herself—requiring you to gain the young woman's confidence—and all this time you are both doing your utmost to steal the secrets of her grandfather?"

Vodni only laughed again. "Steal the secrets of her grandfather? But how unjust of you to say so! The information we have so far obtained was all bought and paid for . . . and this Gottfried Jenk has been living on the Duchess's bounty these many weeks. I will admit that some deception has been necessary, and the alchemist has been led to believe that it is the Duke who is his benefactor . . . but as for stealing—"

"And is it not stealing to publish the startling results of his experiments before the man Jenk is able to do so?" said Skogsrå. "The Duchess wishes to claim all of the credit for herself. You open your eyes . . . you feign surprise. Do you pretend that her motives are not exactly as I have described them?"

"Pretend?" said Vodni, with another annoying laugh. "I pretend nothing. The Duchess's motives are purer than you guess. She does not intend to publish the results of Jenk's experiments; she wishes to duplicate them. She wishes, my dear Skogsrå . . . to become a mother."

The Jarl's amazement was written on his face. "But yes, I promise you that this is so," said Vodni. He turned away from the door and started briskly down the corridor, forcing the Jarl, who wished to hear more, to lengthen his own limping gait in order to keep up with him. "These half-blood fairies—even three-quarter fays like the Duchess—they generally have difficulty producing children of their own. Some families are more fortunate than others: their children are few but the line breeds true. But for the less fortunate . . . conception is easy . . . they are as prolific as rabbits . . . but their offspring are often so poorly made, they die in the womb—or emerge so grotesquely deformed, so wildly eccentric in their appearance, they bear no resemblance to either parent.

"It is because they are so very much worse than barren that some of these hybrid fairies take a burning interest in such matters as childbirth, infants, and naming ceremonies," he added. "It is the reason they are so eager to offer themselves as godparents."

The Jarl sneered nastily. "And arrange such marriages for their godchildren as the Duchess wishes to arrange for Elsie Vorder? It is a wonder that the mothers and fathers of these infants should be so gullible."

Vodni gave a slight shake of his head. "The Duchess is no one's godmother—certainly not Miss Elsie Vorder's. I do not perfectly understand why she pretends that she is. Nor has the Gracious Lady any living children—not by the Duke, or by any of the other Men, fairies, gnomes, or dwarves she has taken as her lovers over the years—I beg your pardon: not any children that she is prepared to acknowledge. And so she is obsessed, obsessed with this idea that, though she cannot bear a child, she can at least play a part in creating a homunculus . . . a tiny child, but otherwise perfect."

The Jarl continued to sneer. "Very affecting. Yes, you spin an affecting tale, my dear Vodni. But I am not so certain that I am ready to believe it."

"Believe what you please," Lord Vodni invited him cordially. "But do not be hasty in drawing your conclusions, particularly where the Gracious Lady is concerned. She is considerably more complex, my friend, than you seem to think."

30.

In which Our hitherto Resourceful hero finds his Powers severely Taxed.

The Sultan's Jewelbox was a high-class brothel and bagnio on the eastern bank of the Lunn, catering to a large clientele. The girls were comely, clean, and amiable, the oriental baths luxurious, and the suppers served there both elegant and cheap. The riverside location was particularly advantageous, allowing the proprietor to run a lucrative business on the side: a traffic in opium, illegal spirits, and other contraband goods. And his girls were discreet—he made very certain of that—those who gave evidence of seeing or saying too much had a habit of disappearing.

Of the origins of the man, little was known: he dressed like a gentleman, swore like a sailor, drank like a fish, whored like . . . in brief, his appearance was good but his habits deplorable. He went by the name of Mr. Jagst.

To the Jewelbox one warm evening came a man with a nautical gait, a hard-looking rascal with a number of scars seaming his face, though he dressed like a man of considerable means. He presented himself at the door, giving his name as Captain Melville, and was promptly escorted to a boxlike room at the top of the house, a room of bare boards and broken-down furniture.

Mr. Jagst greeted him, thin-lipped and grey-eyed, and coldly invited him to take a seat on a low settle located next to the door. Mr. Jagst was seated in a spindle-legged chair by the fireplace, with a decanter of brandy and two glasses on a table beside him.

"I do not believe we have met before, though word of your exploits precedes you through our mutual acquaintance," said Mr. Jagst. "But I am interested to hear rather more about your ship."

Captain Melville removed his tricorn and held it to his breast. "*Fancy's Fool*, your worship . . . as trim a sloop as you could wish for to see. A hundred tons with a shallow draught and—"

"And accordingly very fast . . . I see," said Mr. Jagst. "But can she fight—as in the instance of an encounter with excise men? How many cannon does she boast?''

"She prefers to run, not fight, sir—that's cheaper in the end—but she's equipped with six cannon and four swivels guns," the Captain replied earnestly. "She could carry more, but 'twould slow her down. I makes my money delivering goods cheap, fast, and secret."

"Yes . . ." said the pimp, looking him over very carefully and comparing his rough way of speaking with his prosperous appearance. "And apparently successfully. But the goods I ship are often quite expensive; they require a certain amount of care. And the young women, in particular . . . their value depends on whether they reach their destination intact—they are examined before they are bought and paid for. Will you be able to discipline your men?''

Captain Melville grinned, displaying strong yellow teeth. "Trust me for that, your worship."

Mr. Jagst poured a glass of brandy and handed it to his visitor. "That sounds satisfactory, so far as it goes. But are they discreet . . . can you depend on the lot of them not to talk too much while they are in port?''

"Better than discreet," said the Captain, his grin broadening. "My whole crew is men from the Isle of Mawbri—they don't speak a word of your local lingo. Not a single word."

Mr. Jagst looked gratified. He poured a glass of brandy for himself. "I believe, Captain Melville, that we can do business."

They spent an hour in negotiations, during which time Captain Melville made rather free with the liquor, and they hammered out a deal rather more advantageous to Mr. Jagst than might have been the case had the Captain been sober.

Pleased by these arrangements, Jagst unbent sufficiently to escort his new associate to the top of the stairs. "A pleasure to do business with you, sir," said the Captain.

"And with you," replied the pimp. "I have an idea we may be about to embark on a very lucrative association."

"It won't be my fault if it ain't!" said the Captain, with a rather boozy grin. "*Fancy's Fool* shall prove our fortune, Mr. Jagst, I warrent you!"

Mr. Jagst watched his visitor's unsteady progress down the stairs, standing in the hall at the top of the steps. "Well, well," said a jocular voice. "Quite a surprise . . . yes, quite a surprise."

Mr. Jagst glanced down to the end of the hall. A decidedly disheveled Lord Krogan stood there in his breeches and his shirt sleeves, leaning against a door frame. "Now, what did you and his lily-white lordship find to talk about?"

"I beg your pardon," said Mr. Jagst. "I do not quite understand . . . ?"

"The fellow was here just a moment past, the man you spoke to a minute since," said Krogan.

His wig had slipped down over one ear, the back of his shirt was hanging out behind, and one of his stockings drooped down around his ankles. Mr. Jagst regarded him with ill-disguised disdain. "You are referring, I take it, to my late visitor, Captain Melville?"

Lord Krogan began to chuckle. "Captain Melville . . . was that what he told you? Blister me! His bleeding lordship's a liar as well as a hypocrite."

Mr. Jagst frowned at him. "You are telling me that the man who was just here was . . . not exactly as he presented himself to be?" Mr. Jagst narrowed his eyes. "But you are perhaps a little tipsy, Lord Krogan. Is it possible that you have mistaken the Captain for somebody else?"

"Not likely," said Krogan, all his good humor gone in an instant. "I grant you there was something queer about his face and his manner of speaking, but I knew the voice—I couldn't be mistaken about the voice."

He took several steps down the narrow hallway, and Mr. Jagst was forced to conclude that he was probably not so very drunk as it might appear. "You tell me . . ." said Lord Krogan. "Supposing you found yourself, one fine night, on a dark, deserted lane, with the point of a rapier pricking your throat, and the man behind it very white and very grim, threatening to hamstring and geld you if you ever again put your tongue to the name of a certain young woman . . . would *you* be inclined, thereafter, to forget or mistake his voice?"

Mr. Jagst considered very carefully before he answered. "No, Lord Krogan, I am under the impression that I would not.

"But if not captain of the sloop *Fancy's Fool*—then who is this man, and how does he occupy himself when not lurking in the dark, championing nameless young women, and making horrid threats? His lordship, you said . . . Lord Melville perhaps?"

Lord Krogan adjusted his wig. "Thought I told you his name before: 'twas Francis Love Skelbrooke, the Imbrian poet."

• • •

213

Two nights later, according to their agreement, "Captain Melville" returned to the Jewelbox to make the final arrangements. But when the servant ushered him into the attic room, he found Mr. Jagst awaiting him with a brace of pistols in his hands, and two rough-looking seamen flanking the door.

Though expressing some surprise at this irregular reception, the visitor nevertheless made no resistance when one of the sailors pulled his arms behind him and bound them with a short length of rope.

"Good evening, Lord Skelbrooke," said Mr. Jagst. "It is so very kind of you to visit me . . . for it spared me the trouble of having you brought."

"Guess you've made some sort of a mistake," said the prisoner. "Don't reckon I know who you've taken me for, but—"

"Spare me these protests," said Mr. Jagst, "I am informed that the face you are wearing is in fact not your own. Having some experience in these matters, I am aware that these spells can seldom be maintained when the magician is subjected to great pain or distress."

Though the evening was sultry, a small fire was smoking on the hearth. Mr. Jagst picked up a poker and thrust it into the heart of the flames. "Call it morbid curiosity if you will, but I have conceived a strong desire to see what you actually look like . . ." He spoke curtly to the two sailors. "Remove his shoes and his stockings."

This, however was only accomplished after a long and furious struggle. But eventually it was done, and Jagst's seagoing minions bound the still resisting prisoner to the chair, then tipped it back and held it in place.

By that time, the tip of the iron was glowing red. "I must say . . . you are very good at this. The mere prospect would be sufficient to make most men lose their concentration." Mr. Jagst spoke softly as he moved in closer, poker in hand. "Almost . . . you have me convinced."

The room filled with the stench of sizzling flesh, and the prisoner clenched his teeth against the pain. A cry of agony ripped out of him, and the spell slipped, revealing his own face, pale and anguished.

"Pointless heroics," said Mr. Jagst, as he removed the poker, and motioned the sailor to tip the chair forward, allowing his lordship to assume a more dignified position. "Did you really think your concentration would not fail you?"

"I thought I would try it," Francis Skelbrooke replied, as steadily as he could.

Mr. Jagst regarded him briefly. "You were obviously sent here in order to spy on me. But who sent you? Will it be necessary for me to apply the poker again, or will you tell me the names of your associates?"

"It won't be necessary at all," said Skelbrooke. Beads of perspiration stood out on his brow. "I have no associates and nobody sent me. I am an adventurer and an inveterate meddler." He managed a weak smile. "I do these things to obtain a thrill. But I feel that I have had quite enough excitement for one evening, and I would be obliged to you if you would allow me to depart."

"Though you are a trifle eager to provide this information, nevertheless I am inclined to believe you. It is in line," said Jagst, "with what I have already learned about you. But of course I cannot possibly allow you to go . . . at least, not in the way that I suppose you mean."

He paused, as if waiting for Skelbrooke to ask for further enlightenment, but his lordship was silent, not giving him the satisfaction.

Mr. Jagst smiled broadly and told him, anyway. "I am told, Lord Skelbrooke, that you are something of a poet. For that reason, I have an idea that you will appreciate the poetic irony of your fate. There is a ship sailing for Ynde with the morning tide. You will be on that ship, part of the consignment I have promised to traders in the East.

"You are a very pretty fellow," Mr. Jagst added, shaking his head. "And a few years past, would have certainly found favor with our eastern clients . . . but you are just a bit old now, to serve as a catamite. No, it seems more likely that you will end up as a eunuch in a harem . . . a turn of events which our friend Lord Krogan would surely appreciate."

Skelbrooke awoke with an aching head and his left foot still agonizingly on fire. He lay in a dim, rolling place, on a bed of straw . . . the only light a few pale beams that came in through an overhead grating about a dozen yards away.

With an effort, he pulled himself up into a sitting position. Though his head spun after the crack it had received, he knew that was not the cause of the rolling motion or the vibration. He was in the hold of a ship. He heard the slap of waves against the hull and guessed that the vibration came from a mast overhead.

Jagst had made good on the first part of his threat, and Lord Skelbrooke was on his way to Ynde.

The straw that made up his bed was damp, and the hold reeked of bilge and other, less immediately identifiable odors. He wrinkled his nose distastefully. Somewhere, not very far off, he could hear chickens clucking and pigs grunting.

"Had a lovely sleep, did you?" said a voice in the darkness. A shadowy figure near the grating moved his way, and his lordship could just make out the features of one of the sailors from the brothel. "Must of been a good one—you was out all last night and most of today. Was a time there, we thought you was a dead un."

"Thank you," said Skelbrooke, between his teeth. "I believe I am tolerably well rested. But it seems that no one has bandaged my foot, or returned my stockings or my boots. I wonder . . . is there a chirurgeon on board this ship?"

The sailor hooted derisively. "You're a high and mighty one . . . demanding to see a doctor."

"I assume," said Skelbrooke, with a great effort, "that as I am still *alive*, I am accounted of some value. That value will be substantially diminished if this wound goes bad and I lose the foot."

The sailor shrugged. "That may be . . . You're a sharp one you are. But we ain't got no doctor. I could send the quartermaster down . . . He usually sees to them things, but I warn you: his hand's inclined to be a bit shaky, when he's using the knife."

At the word "knife" Skelbrooke flinched. "Never mind, then, I thank you."

There were heavy manacles on his wrists, joined together by a stout chain, which was joined to a longer chain and fastened to a beam by an iron ring. He leaned against the beam for support. "I have some training as a physician, and would prefer to treat myself. Could you possibly provide me with a length of clean cloth . . . and whatever salves and medicaments the quartermaster is accustomed to use?"

The sailor thought that over, then he shrugged again. "I might . . . if the First Mate give permission. In the meantime, I brung your breakfast." He deposited a mug, a bowl, and a piece of biscuit, down on the damp and dirty straw.

Skelbrooke shook his head wearily. The motion of the ship did not much bother him, but the pain in his head, and especially the throbbing torment of his foot, made his stomach feel weak. He closed his eyes and tried to collect his thoughts. His situation could hardly be worse. He was on his way to a fate which did not bear thinking about, and he had no idea how to save himself.

"You don't eat it now . . . the rats'll get it," said the sailor. He moved back through the shadows in the direction of the light. "You might want to keep them weak and feeble-like . . . They get too big, they might eat you alive."

On consideration, his lordship decided he might try the food. He opened his eyes and examined what the sailor offered him. The mug was half full of water . . . fortunately fresh . . . the bowl contained the burned scrapings from the bottom of a stewpot. The biscuit smelled so vile and tasted so unwholesome, he immediately spat out the first mouthful.

Yet if he was going to find a way to win his freedom and avoid castration, he would require all his resources of mind and body. With a grim resolution, he ate the stew and swallowed the water. Neither sat well on his stomach.

31.

Containing a great deal of Conversation.

The gardens at the Wichtelberg boasted few flowers, for they had been originally designed by dwarves. Follies, pavilions, and gazebos there were in plenty; fountains, reflecting pools, and tiny meandering streams; there was an occasional expanse of green lawn checkered with stone pathways, and a number of sculptured hedges; such flowers as there were had been rooted in marble urns. These were gardens of water and stone, not gardens devoted to growing things.

To explore the grounds of the Wichtelberg took Sera and Elsie several days. The gardens, alone, were as full of surprises as they were of stone. To one side of the mansion, opposite the lake, there was an enormous iron cage, dome-shaped and arising about two stories, which served as an aviary, where Sebastian the indigo ape was allowed to run free. Beyond that there was a brief expanse of manicured turf, and then a sort of orchard, with statues of onyx and green bronze serving in place of fruit trees.

By starting at the lake, one day, and moving upstream along the brook which fed it, the girls arrived at the entrance of a cave, which led them to a vast, torch-lit grotto under the house, and a complex of underground waterways. From the grotto, a long flight of damp stone steps led back up to the interior of the mansion.

There was also the wood begging to be explored (it yielded a little ruined chapel), and farther on an open meadow . . . The girls took long morning walks and came back exhausted, then spent the hot afternoons with the Duchess and her gentlemen guests in the cool marble salons of the mansion, or picnicking in the gardens in the shade of the house.

Elsie was flourishing, so full of energy and good spirits, Sera could hardly believe she was the same girl who had been a pale and nervous invalid only weeks before. Whether it was the country air or the Jarl's magnetic treatments or merely this respite from the ministrations of her other physicians remained to be seen, but however it came about, Elsie grew in strength and vigor with every passing day.

As for Sera: her attitude more nearly approached resignation. Though pleased by Elsie's progress, she was not certain she trusted these changes and lived in fear that one day Elsie would do too much and bring about a relapse. And Jarl Skogsrå was always so much in evidence, up at the house and in the gardens, tending to monopolize Elsie's time and attention. It pained Sera to see the attachment growing between her cousin and the Jarl, but she had long since voiced all her objections to Elsie, and now found herself without anything new to say.

About ten days after their arrival, deciding that her houseguests were growing a little stale of each other's company, the Duchess arranged a more elaborate al fresco luncheon in the gardens and invited the country gentry.

It was a fine day, and the Duke's neighbors arrived in great numbers, to feast on crab cakes and lobster patties; lark's tongues and boiled snails; whole roasted peacock and swans; cold soup flavored with fennel; pastries, cakes, chantillies, and fruit ices; along with an assortment of the candied flowers which the Duchess served on every occasion.

It apparently served the Duchess's whim to bring Sera into fashion; accordingly, she kept Sera by her and took pains to introduce her "dear Miss Vorder" to each of her afternoon guests.

218

Distracted by these attentions, Sera failed to keep a close eye on Elsie, with the result that the two girls did not speak together until late in the afternoon, when Sera, escaping at last from the Duchess, was horrified to discover her cousin drinking a second (or was it a third?) glass of sweet wine.

"My dear . . . what *are* you doing? Your head will ache and you will be miserable all evening."

"I never have headaches anymore!" said Elsie, with a defiant toss of her head. "I wish you wouldn't fuss so, Sera. You've grown quite as bad as Mama!" And she strolled off on Jarl Skogs-rå's arm, taking the wineglass with her.

Sera was speechless. She had always regarded herself as Elsie's champion, the one who encouraged her to lead as normal a life as possible. To be told that she fussed—worse, to be compared with Clothilde Vorder and her odious smothering attentions—that was a new and unpleasant experience.

"Miss Vorder, you look uncommonly warm. May I bring you a glass of lemonade?" said a voice behind her. And Sera, turning, found Hermes Budge watching her with a sympathetic look in his calm brown eyes.

"Mr. Budge," she asked bluntly, "do you think me overprotective of my cousin Elsie?"

"I do not," said Mr. Budge. "But surely my opinion is of little account, and it is what Miss Elsie herself thinks that ought to concern you."

Sera bit her lip. "You advise me, then, to hold my tongue and allow my cousin to make her own mistakes?"

Mr. Budge permitted himself a faint smile. "Madam, acquit me! I would never say anything so rude. But if I cannot convince you to drink some lemonade, perhaps you will consent to walk with me as far as the aviary."

"Perhaps I will," said Sera, accepting his offer of an arm to lean on. There was something reassuring about the tutor, so solemn, so sensible, so wholesome. Though he was years older and immeasurably better educated, he reminded her strongly of Jedidiah.

"Mr. Budge," said Sera, "you are an educated man and—I believe—well traveled." The tutor bowed an acknowledgement. "I wonder if you might answer a question which has been puzzling me of late?"

Mr. Budge bowed again. "It has recently been brought to my attention—I believe that I knew it once, but had somehow forgotten,'' said Sera, ''that the system of inheritance in foreign countries is not the same as it is here in Wäldermark. For instance, Lord Vodni informs me that it is the custom in Ruska for all the sons of a nobleman to inherit his title, though only the eldest inherits his estate. Would you—would you happen to know if a similar custom pertains in Nordmark?''

Mr. Budge shook his head. ''No . . . I believe that inheritance in Nordmark descends exactly as it does here—and indeed in my native Imbria as well. A titled Nordic gentleman . . . let us suppose him a jarl . . . might well be short of ready cash, but he would almost certainly own a house and land—perhaps some heirloom jewelry—which he had inherited along with the title but was forbidden to sell.''

Sera could not repress a sigh of disappointment. Cousin Clothilde was such a snob that even an encumbered estate, when coupled with a title, would undoubtedly be enough to satisfy *her*. After all, Elsie had no need to marry for money, but a grand house and the rank of Countess might serve to gratify her mother's ambitions.

''You would prefer it otherwise,'' said Mr. Budge. ''I must presume that the gentleman in question is Jarl Skogsrå, whom you wish to think impoverished and a fortune-hunter.''

Sera blushed. Were her motives truly that transparent, or was Budge merely uncomfortably clever? ''If Elsie were your cousin . . . would you wish her to marry a man so vain and selfish as Jarl Skogsrå?''

Mr. Budge, who was generally a thoughtful man, answered promptly. ''No, I would not. Believe me, Miss Vorder, I am entirely sympathetic. Your cousin appears to blind herself to those faults in the Jarl which to you and me appear so evident—therefore, you wish to produce something more substantial against him. We both know that a well-born bachelor may maintain himself in fine style, passing himself off as a man of wealth as well as position, living on credit for a long time before the tradesmen he frequents become too demanding and his poverty becomes evident to all. Indeed, it may well be so with Jarl Skogsrå.''

''Yes,'' said Sera. ''But even so . . . a house and land, you said, which he could not have sold or gambled away, no matter how profligate his style of living, because of the entail—''

''Excuse me,'' said Mr. Budge, ''but have you never considered that the title itself—and therefore any accompanying inheritance— might be a sham? Many hundreds of miles lie between Thornburg and Nordmark, and Jarl Skogsrå would not be the first foreigner

220

to maintain an imposture for many seasons."

Sera took a deep breath. No, this had never occurred to her . . . but it sounded plausible, entirely plausible. "Have you . . . have you, Mr. Budge, reason to believe that the Jarl is not what he claims to be, but a penniless adventurer?"

"No," said the tutor. "I have no just cause to think so. Like yourself, I merely *wish* to consider Lord Skogsrå an imposter. Nevertheless, some careful inquiries might yield gratifying results."

They passed the aviary and moved on in the direction of the statue orchard. "Yes . . . perhaps," said Sera. "But as you said: Nordmark is such a great distance away, and I know no one, no one who has ever even been there, except for Lord Skogsrå himself. I would not even know where or how to begin to make those discreet inquiries."

"Then allow me to assist you," said Budge. "I do have a friend in Nordmark, a fellow student from my days at the university, now serving as a language professor in Ghyll. And another friend, now that I come to think of it, who spent two years in Katrinsberg, which as you may know lies on the border between Ruska and Nordmark. Were I to write to these old school-fellows of mine, we might learn something to Miss Elsie's advantage."

They walked on in silence for some time after that. "Mr. Budge," Sera said at last, "you are very obliging. I scarcely know how to thank you."

"Not at all," said Budge. "I am happy to assist you. And after all, it is no great thing for me to write to my friends.

"I must confess," he added, "that I do not like the Jarl any better than you do. There is something in his presence . . . I cannot put a name to it . . . which invariably causes my skin to crawl."

Sera stopped and stared at him. "My dear sir, do you actually *believe* in intuition?"

The tutor inclined his head. "I do, Miss Vorder, most emphatically. Do I suffer in your opinion on that account?"

Sera hardly knew what to think. "You are so wise and sensible, sir, and your education so superior, I cannot help but wonder—seeing as we are so totally in disagreement on this one issue—if my own views on the matter might possibly require revision."

They had circled the orchard and were heading back toward the gardens, when Sera chanced to catch sight of Elsie. Pale and trembling, Elsie was obviously in the grip of another attack of panic—her first since leaving Thornburg.

"I beg your pardon," said Sera, dropping Budge's arm and rushing off to offer her assistance.

But by the time Sera arrived, the attack had already passed. Elsie was sitting on a marble bench beside Jarl Skogsrå, with a weary little smile on her face and an expression of deep contentment in her eyes. That contentment quickly faded, however, when Sera knelt down beside her.

"I am perfectly well. You are fussing again, and it is very tiresome. Haakon takes excellent care of me, as you ought to know by now. He can soothe my fears with a word and a smile."

Sera stood up again, blinking back tears. That Elsie should speak to her so reproachfully, and before Lord Skogsrå, too! She felt bitterly mortified.

Mr. Budge had followed her across the garden. "I think," said the tutor, "that you would benefit from that glass of lemonade that I offered you earlier."

"Yes," said Sera, as steadily as she could, and allowed him to lead her over to the refreshment table.

"How very extraordinary," said Budge, as Sera sipped her lemonade. "This is the first time that I ever witnessed one of Miss Elsie's attacks . . . though I have heard them described. Perhaps you can tell me . . . is Jarl Skogsrå actually able to bring her out of them with a few spoken words?"

"Always," said Sera, with a catch in her voice. "He is always able to do so . . . while I, who have cared for her all of these years, am totally helpless."

"How very extraordinary," the tutor repeated thoughtfully. He stood in silent contemplation for several minutes. "Miss Vorder," he said at last, "perhaps you would be kind enough to tell me . . . have you received any communication from your . . . friends in Thornburg, since you arrived here?"

"No, I have not," Sera said, more sharply than she had intended. The question, coming when it did, had surprised her. It sounded almost . . . almost as though he knew of her arrangement with Lord Skelbrooke. But that was highly unlikely; certainly, *she* had said nothing to anyone, and (at least so far as she knew) Skelbrooke and the tutor were not even acquainted.

Yet why else should Budge have asked with such a look of interest? And why, in any case, should he frown and shake his head, as though he found her denial so particularly disturbing?

• • •

222

It was the following afternoon—when Elsie and Skogsrå were walking in the gardens, the Duchess was upstairs in her bedchamber resting, and Hermes Budge had gone into Pfalz on some unnamed errand—that Sera, feeling at loose ends, wandered into the vast library in the west wing in search of amusement. There were a great many rooms in the mansion devoted solely to books—for in addition to inheriting many volumes from his ancestors, the Duke was a great collector of scholarly tomes—but only in this room had Sera found any of the plays or the histories which were her particular delight.

Lord Vodni was in the library when she arrived, seated in a comfortable armchair, with a volume of poetry lying open in his lap. "Miss Vorder," he said, putting his books aside and immediately rising to his feet. He had been out riding earlier that day, and he still wore buckskins and a scarlet coat, a pair of highly polished black boots—a costume vastly becoming to a man with his fine figure and his restless, romantic appearance.

"I wonder, sir," said Sera, "if there was a letter for me today?" It was Vodni, as the Duke's secretary, to whom the butler brought all of the mail to be sorted.

"That is the second time this week you have asked me that question," said Vodni. "I begin to suspect some secret attachment. I believe that I am growing jealous."

Sera felt the hot blood rising in her face. "I can assure you, my lord, that it is nothing of the sort," she answered sharply.

"I beg your pardon," said the secretary, growing suddenly very earnest. "I am wrong to tease you. Your correspondence is no business of mine." Seeing that Sera showed no disposition to take a seat, he sat down again.

Sera turned her back on him and began to examine the nearest bookshelf. She located a volume of ancient history, took a seat opposite the Baron, and opened her book.

"You have not yet paid a visit to the Duke," Lord Vodni commented. "He lives so very retired in his own apartments, and many days he is not well enough to receive visitors. Yet he has expressed a desire to meet you—motivated, it seems, by a previous acquaintance with your grandfather."

Sera looked up from her book.

"Perhaps you would be willing to visit him some day soon," said Vodni. "I fear that His Excellency is not always lucid, but when he is . . . he can be a fascinating companion. Yes, he is really a most interesting old man."

223

"I should like very much to become acquainted with the Duke," said Sera.

The Baron rose to his feet. "Then come with me, now. This is one of his better days, and we might do well to seize the opportunity."

Sera accepted readily, very eager to meet the learned old man.

"I daresay," ventured Vodni, as they left the library, "that you have not yet explored the entire house. The Wichtelberg has a long and fascinating history . . . Do you know when and how it was built?"

"I know that it was built by dwarves, many hundreds of years ago," said Sera. "That, of course, explains the name."

"It passed through many hands—many, many hands—before it came to the ancestors of the Duke. And every new owner made extensive modifications. Some of these modifications did not survive, and it is principally the dwarf work which you see now . . . Stone endures, and the wichtel are meticulous craftsmen. The frescoes on the third floor are accounted very fine, and the chandeliers in the dining hall . . . I beg your pardon, I do not mean to lecture you. It is just that I have such enthusiasm for this fine old house."

"But please continue," said Sera, who had been listening with pleasure. "Your enthusiasm is contagious."

They walked down a long corridor. All along the walls, ancient weapons were displayed, and the stuffed heads of exotic beasts, many of them long extinct.

"I will show you a curiosity," said Vodni, pausing before an expanse of unadorned wall. There was a decorative molding near the ceiling and another near the floor, but the wall was otherwise blank. The Baron bent down and pressed one of the carved rosettes on the molding, and a section of wall slid aside, to reveal a hidden staircase. "It is a pity that I did not think to bring a light, for then you might have inspected the mechanism, which is very elaborate—rather more elaborate, I believe, than is strictly necessary to perform such a simple task—but very ingenious, oh, remarkably ingenious.

"We believe that the Wichtelberg was once occupied by gnomes, for (as you may know) they have a fondness for these devices." He pressed another rosette to close the panel, but the section of wall refused to slide back into place.

Vodni aimed a kick at the secret door, as if by doing so he hoped to jog something loose. But when the panel still refused to move, he kicked it again and yet again much harder, with increasing violence, evidently angry because the mechanism did not appear so impressive as he wanted Sera to think. Then, with a visible effort, he regained his composure.

"We will leave it open . . . it scarcely matters. I beg your pardon," he said, with an apologetic laugh. "As you can see: I possess a wicked temper, a vile disposition. I do not doubt that you are shocked."

Sera, who so often felt the urge to vent her rage in the same fashion, was not at all shocked. "Pray kick the wall again, Lord Vodni, if it affords you any satisfaction. I find myself in complete sympathy with you. I can assure you, sir, that my own temper is a match for yours."

Vodni laughed again. "And yet, Miss Vorder, you contrive to control that temper. You invariably display an admirable self-restraint."

"Ah . . . but I have so very many opportunities to practice that self-restraint," said Sera, "that it is little wonder I have mastered the art."

They continued on toward the Duke's chambers, both of them in high good humor. Sera realized that she was enjoying herself—she, who rarely cared for the company of young men. Oh, to be sure, she was fond of Jedidiah—but he was only a boy, and not at all fashionable—and Hermes Budge was old beyond his years. As for Francis Skelbrooke . . . no, she could not say that she *liked* Lord Skelbrooke; the effect he exerted on her was far too disturbing. Yet here was Lord Vodni, fully as handsome and quite as courteous, and she found that she liked him exceedingly.

After much navigation of marble halls, Sera and the Baron reached their destination. "I will go inside and announce you to the Duke," said Vodni, opening a door and disappearing inside.

He reappeared a few moments later. "His Excellency is delighted to receive you," said Vodni, ushering her through the door.

Sera, who had spent a good part of her life in the company of her elders, discovered that the Duke was considerably older than she had anticipated: a frail wisp of an elderly gentleman in an antique periwig and a brocade dressing gown. He sat in an oak armchair of medieval design, by an open window.

"Miss Vorder, your servant. I am informed by Lord Vodni that you are the granddaughter of Gottfried Jenk. Yes, indeed . . . indeed you do have a great look of him. I like the way that you

225

hold yourself," he said, with an approving nod. "And am I to assume that your grandfather, Mr. Jenk, took an active interest in educating you?"

Sera sat up a little straighter. "When I was younger he educated me himself. But I have lived with my father's relations these last five years, and they do not approve of . . . of scholarly young women. My Cousin Benjamin, however, possesses an excellent library, and I continue my studies as best I can."

The Duke directed a mischievous glance in Vodni's direction. "And how old is she now, d'you think?"

The Baron made a humorous face. "I would not presume to guess. Why do we not ask the young lady herself?"

"I am eighteen," said Sera. "I shall be nineteen at the turn of the year."

"Eighteen years old . . . and five years in the house of your cousins," said the Duke. "And I do not doubt that your grandfather was educating you in your cradle. That would make thirteen years as Jenk's pupil. I am pleased to make your acquaintance, Miss . . . I do crave your pardon. I have forgotten your name."

"Miss Seramarias Vorder," said his secretary.

The Duke bobbed his head. "Miss Vorder . . . yes. It is not often that I am so fortunate as to encounter an educated woman. The Duchess, of course, is a notable exception. I am pleased to make your acquaintance, Miss Jenk. Pray stay awhile and visit me."

•

32.

Which transports the Reader to the High Seas, and then Back again to Thornburg.

Skelbrooke soon lost track of the days he spent in the dark hold of the ship. It was all ceaseless motion, and foul smells, and the endless throbbing of his left foot. He tossed and turned, alternately burning with fever and shivering with an ague. They had robbed him of the Sleep Dust to which he was addicted, and without the

226

drug in his system true rest eluded him. He spent his nights and his days, too, in a kind of waking nightmare, the victim of terrifying hallucinations and agonizing sensations.

At length his mind cleared and his senses returned to him. His appetite revived and with it came a raging thirst. As the days passed, the water they gave him began to taste bad. And when he wanted to eat a piece of the ship's biscuit, he had to tap it against one of the beams to encourage the black-headed weevil maggots to crawl out.

Sometimes, he felt strong enough to speak to the sailor who brought him his meals and emptied his chamber pot. It was rarely the same man; two or three times it was the cabin boy, a skinny, toothless lad, slightly more garrulous than his mates, who told Skelbrooke about the other prisoners on board: two girls from the country, very young, very pretty, and exceedingly frightened. They were locked in a cabin up above, where the captain could keep an eye on them and prevent the men from molesting them. "Though why we shouldn't have our chance at 'em before the black men gets 'em . . . it don't seem right to me," said the boy.

"Merchandise," said Skelbrooke wearily. "The ladies are valuable merchandise . . . but you, my lad, are nothing. If it is any comfort to you, those poor girls would undoubtedly prefer to be in your place now, rather than their own."

The boy grinned toothlessly. "Guess *you'd* like to trade places, right enough. I may be nothing now, yet I'll grow to be a man. But you—"

"As you say," said Skelbrooke, leaning back on his bed of straw and closing his eyes.

It was the cabin boy, too, who told him the name of the ship. She was a small bark, the *Black Bear*, and the captain was Troilus Diamond. "A hard man, the Captain," said the boy, and Skelbrooke believed him. The youth was emaciated; he bore marks of ill treatment: bruises and cuts and scars . . . and he dropped mysterious hints as to the fates of his predecessors.

My lord had better hopes of the First Mate, a quiet man who had come to speak with him once. His name was Kassien, formerly an honest trader (said the cabin boy) and the captain of his own sloop, fallen on hard times due to an overfondness for the bottle and the machinations of enemies in "high places." Mr. Kassien, Skelbrooke decided, was a man to whose principles he might possibly appeal . . . supposing he could find a way to make it worth the Mate's while to act on them.

227

It was on this Mr. Kassien's authority that Skelbrooke finally left the hold, escorted by two sailors. His boots and his stockings had not been returned to him, but another pair of boots, split at the toes and much too large, were provided. As his left foot was still bandaged, he donned only the right boot and rose shakily to his feet. The ceiling was low, not more than five feet under the beams, so he bent his head as he limped toward the ladder. He went up through the crew's quarters on the lower deck, past hammocks and sea-chests, and a group of sailors gambling by lanthorn light. He climbed a steep staircase and finally emerged into the sunlight and salt air.

For the first time—in how many days or weeks?—he was introduced to the Captain. Troilus Diamond glanced over him briefly. Skelbrooke had an idea that his appearance was not prepossessing; he was dirty and unkempt, he stank like a horse, and he still wore the costume he had affected in the persona of Captain Melville, expensive but somewhat gaudy: a blue coat and a crimson waistcoat, and a pair of striped trousers, all very wrinkled. Perhaps the bright colors served to enhance his pallor. "You look a mite peaky. Don't know if you're worth your keep. Even gelded, you're not like to fetch much."

"The crewmen who brought him in assure me that he is considerably stronger than he appears," said Mr. Kassien. "And in any case . . . Jagst made it quite clear that he expects this man to be delivered to his eastern clients exactly as arranged."

The Captain, after a little more thought, agreed that a healthful turn around the deck, every day or two, was probably in order.

Skelbrooke limped over to the rail and gazed out across the water. There was no land in sight, but this was scarcely surprising. A ship carrying contraband, a ship that did not wish to make contact with official vessels, would not hug the coastline. Moreover, if there were any chance of swimming to shore, they would not have permitted him to approach the rail, even with his chains and manacles.

He left the rail and sat down on a barrel by the mainmast. Captain Diamond, grinning broadly, reached into his waistcoat and withdrew a pocket watch . . . a very pretty affair, shaped like an egg and covered with a shell of painted white porcelain. Skelbrooke immediately recognized it as his own.

The Captain flipped open the lid and glanced at the watch face. "Real pretty, ain't it?" he said archly.

"Indeed," said Skelbrooke. "But if you will listen to a word

228

of advice . . . the mechanism is rather delicate. You might wish to handle it with extreme care.''

Captain Diamond snapped the watch shut and thrust it back into his pocket. Skelbrooke opened his mouth to warn him. This watch had been especially designed; it had a hidden chamber in the upper half, which contained an explosive based on picric acid, many, many times more powerful than gunpowder; there was also a percussive device, to detonate the charge.

But then he changed his mind. So long as the device had not been set, it would take more than a jolt or a bump to cause an explosion. And though the day must certainly come when some careless action on the part of Captain Diamond caused the charge to go off, it seemed unlikely that Skelbrooke himself would be on hand to share the consequences. That being so, there was really no reason for him to speak up.

His lordship leaned back against the mast, closed his eyes, and contemplated, with considerable satisfaction, the Captain's explosive demise.

It was the cold hour before dawn. In Jenk's laboratory behind the bookshop, the two old men were nearing the limits of their strength after a long, sleepless night spent in fruitless experimentation.

The appearance of the laboratory had changed during the last several weeks, had become quite cluttered, for Jenk had been spending heavily to acquire new equipment. There was a second and more elaborate still, a number of vats in graduated sizes, a new set of scales with precisely measured brass weights, and all manner of funnels, flasks, tongs, irons, and crucibles recently purchased. Yet Jenk was no closer to compounding the Stone than he had been two seasons past.

The bookseller sighed and seated himself on one of the stools. He was keenly aware of his years, of late. He felt old and heavy and bent, weighed down by disappointment. And the fact he was exhausted almost to the point of illness did nothing to lighten the load.

"Our funds are dwindling," he said. "Soon, the Duke's gold will all be spent. The Duke's gold . . . and all my savings."

"Write another letter, asking for more," said Caleb, who was busy stoking the furnace. "Seems to me that's simple enough."

But Jenk shook his head. "If I were to write and beg the Duke's indulgence, he would insist that we receive his man and allow him to observe Eirena. That I am not prepared to do. I must confess

229

that I am disappointed with her lack of progress.''

Caleb slammed the door of the furnace shut. "Lack of progress? How do you mean her lack of *progress!*" he asked indignantly. "Don't she dress herself, and feed herself, and tend to her own private needs? Don't she walk about as easy and natural as you and I? And ain't she entertained us, time and again, with all her pretty little gestures and her dainty little ways?''

"Yes, yes," said Jenk, beginning to fuss impatiently with the equipment on the table. "In some areas her progress has been amazing. A natural child of the same age could not do any of the things that you mention. But it is all mimicry . . . She has only to see a thing done once or twice, in order to copy it exactly. It is the *quality* of her intelligence that I question. She does nothing that an ape or a hobgoblin could not do fully as well—given the time for proper training—and still she refuses to speak.

"It is speech," said Jenk, brushing a flask aside with an irritated wave of his hand, "that separates the sentient races from brute beasts. I recall when Sera was an infant . . . she made charming little cooing sounds, babbled to herself incessantly . . . She seemed to demonstrate a natural desire for expression, even though the concept of *words* had not yet occurred to her. If Eirena did the same, I would be considerably more optimistic.''

Caleb snorted. "What if she's mute? Maybe she'd like to talk, but her voice don't work.''

"My dear Caleb," said Jenk, with a sneer. "Your Eirena is very far from mute. She made noise enough on the day she was 'born', but she has refused to utter a sound since. Moreover, I sincerely doubt—''

He was interrupted by a frantic banging sound, which came from a wooden chest on the floor by the furnace. With a reproachful glance over his shoulder, Caleb limped over to pick up the box. The lid, which was fastened by a catch but not with a lock, had been drilled full of holes, and something was thumping wildly about inside the chest. Caleb placed the box atop the table and lifted the lid.

The little female homunculus climbed out, looking rumpled and indignant. Her face had a greenish cast, from so much exertion, her feathery hair was tangled, and her gauzy gown creased.

"Think she don't understand you?" said the proud father. "She knowed you was talking about her . . . and that was why she started in to raise a ruckus.''

The bookseller sniffed disdainfully. "Nonsense. She woke and wished to come out of the box, that is all. And I daresay that she wants her breakfast.''

The little creature sat down cross-legged on the table, glaring up at them. ''And that's another thing I don't like,'' said Caleb. ''Keeping her shut up in the dark, the way we do. It ain't right . . . 'tis downright cruel.''

Jenk passed a weary hand across his brow. ''It is done for her own protection. She is so small and active, and we cannot always be watching where we place our steps, for fear of treading on her. It would be different if she would speak, if she could cry out a warning to protect herself. But I nearly crushed her, just yesterday, and she never made a sound. No, except when you are able to attend to her, it is necessary to keep her safely stowed away.''

Caleb clenched a fist. ''Like she was a parcel or a piece of baggage! It ain't right. She ain't done nothing wrong . . . We got no call to keep her a prisoner, just because *we're* inclined to be careless. Just you look at her, the pretty little thing,'' he added tenderly, ''asitting there with the tears running down her cheeks. She knows what you're saying, I tell you she knows, and she don't never want to go back in that box again.''

''If she could understand our speech,'' said Jenk, rising and beginning to pace around the room, ''she would make some attempt to duplicate it.''

''Maybe she hurt herself, squawking and struggling when you took her out of her egg. Maybe she could of spoke, but she busted something, you was so rough with her,'' Caleb said, with an accusing glare.

The bookseller gave him back glare for glare. ''Given a suitably unpleasant stimulus, perchance she would cry out again. Shall we make the experiment?'' And without waiting for Caleb to answer, Jenk moved with uncharacteristic violence and energy, snatching up Eirena and a candle off the table, and holding the flame close to one of her wildly flailing tiny hands.

The homunculus shrieked in pain and struggled in his grip. With a grim smile, Jenk replaced her on the table. For a moment, Caleb was too shocked to take any action. Then he swept her up into his arms and held the little wailing creature against his chest.

''Don't you never hurt her again,'' he shouted. ''I warn you . . . don't you never hurt her again.''

Jenk sat down again, suddenly infuriatingly calm. ''It is not a deep burn—the flame barely touched her. See . . . her hand has

231

barely turned green. I did not mean to be cruel, but it was a necessary experiment."

"It weren't necessary . . . there weren't no need at all," insisted Caleb, stroking the feathery little head in a futile attempt to soothe her. "And even if'n you thought it was . . . you should of asked me first, afore you tried anything like that. Ain't I her father—don't she belong to me?"

"Belong to you?" the bookseller asked, with a nasty smile. "You presume too much. You did no more than provide the seed, but I was the one who made her. She is my creation and mine alone. And that being so . . . I shall use her in any way that suits me."

"No, you won't, then," said Caleb, breathing hard. "I won't stand by and watch you abuse her. Think you're so high I can't bring you down. I could ruin you, Gottfried, I had a mind to. I know what you been doing here . . . Folks is already suspicious. A word from me, and—"

"My good Caleb . . . there is no need for you to threaten me." Jenk was startled by this unexpected display of spirit on the part of his hitherto faithful henchman. "Indeed, I am appalled . . . yes, appalled, that you should find it necessary to do so. I mean the little creature no harm."

He took a handkerchief out of his pocket and used it to wipe his face. "Perhaps I have allowed my impatience . . . my zeal for exact, scientific knowledge, to get the better of me. Yes, I fancy that I did. Do not look at me so . . . You have given me quite a turn, my old friend. I promise that I will be more gentle in my methods after this."

"Aye . . . you will be," said Caleb, very far from mollified. "You'll be more gentle with her—or I won't answer for the consequences!"

33.

The *Black Bear* continued to run south until she reached the Gulf of Spagne. There she lay becalmed for many days in the warm southern waters, until the wind freshened. Then, with billowing sail, she was once more under weigh, heading for the exotic shores of Ynde.

For Francis Skelbrooke, under the circumstances, the mysteries of the Fabled East did not precisely beckon. Yet he felt that he had more chance of escaping on land than he had at sea. Indeed, he had already considered and discarded a dozen daring (and highly improbable) plans—from stealing a lifeboat to holding a pistol to the Captain's head—and his invention was beginning to flag. He could only hope that further possibilities would present themselves as soon as he landed in Ynde.

Meanwhile, he was allowed to stroll the upper decks almost every day. Only once did he catch a glimpse of the other two prisoners, when pale and wobbling with a combination of sea-sickness and apprehension, the girls were escorted above the hatches for a brief constitutional of their own. The older of the two was tall and dark and fiercely protective of her younger companion. With a pang, Skelbrooke was reminded of Sera Vorder. Not for his own sake only was it necessary for him to escape.

Though not allowed to approach the girls, he nevertheless gave them an encouraging smile. But as he was standing chained to one of the masts at the time, was dirty, unkempt, and unshaven—more nearly resembling a crewman under discipline than an erstwhile rescuer of maidens—it was unlikely that the young women derived any considerable reassurance.

He was now wearing both boots (though his foot still pained him), which added greatly to his sense of personal dignity, but the Captain had denied him the use of a razor, apparently considering him a possible suicide. Fortunately the physical effects of withdrawal from the Sleep Dust were fading, and he was beginning to recover his strength. But his nights were restless and plagued by unreasoning panics and bad dreams, and the craving was still strong—the more so because he had learned that the First Mate was also addicted, and therefore must have a considerable cache hidden somewhere on board.

Whether Mr. Kassien had appropriated the snuffbox in which Skelbrooke formerly carried the Dust, his lordship had yet to discover, but the First Mate did wear a heavy gold ring last seen gracing the hand of "Captain Melville." Troilus Diamond wore the stiletto stickpin, as well as carrying the watch, and the talisman pendulum was also missing. But Skelbrooke still had a number of small useful items sewn into the lining of his coat, including a vial of deadly poison—for this reason, Captain Diamond might just as well have loaned him a razor . . . my lord had planned a tidier exit, should all else fail him.

They were off the coast of Mallahari, two days from their destination, the slave markets of Ranpuhar, when one of the lookouts up in the crow's-nest called down that another vessel had just been spotted and was rapidly approaching on the port side. Skelbrooke and Kassien moved to the rail, along with some of the others, to get a good look as the other ship hove into view.

She was a brigantine, flying the flag of Grall in the Polar Isles; her sails were patched and dark with much use, but she appeared otherwise clean and well maintained. She was evidently a trading ship: no guns or cannons could be seen, except for a pair of demi-culverins on the forecastle, and the upper deck was loaded with crates and bales. Still, Captain Diamond was wary, watching her approach through a spyglass.

"What do you make of her?" he asked, handing the glass over to Kassien.

The First Mate took the telescope and peered through it. The figurehead of the approaching brigantine depicted a woman of voluptuous proportions, scantily clad. Her face had been freshly painted in garish colors. Mr. Kassien gave an exclamation of dismay. "It's *Busty Margaret,* sir, that disappeared off the coast of Llyria two years ago. They've renamed her the *Hag's Belly*!"

The Captain let out a hissing breath. "Corsairs! Tell the men to prepare for battle, Mr. Kassien, but see they do it quiet and orderly . . . no need to let them pirates know we've guessed their intentions."

From his place by the rail, Skelbrooke observed the preparations

234

of the crew. Muskets, blunderbusses, and pistols were swiftly loaded and primed; barrels full of cutlasses, boarding axes, and pistols hidden behind the port bulwarks, along with pikes, cartridges, and loads of grapeshot. Crewmen unfastened the tarpaulins over the swivel guns, but did not yet remove them. The best marksmen were delegated to sling on muskets, bags of powder and shot, and prepare to climb the rigging to the platforms on the masts.

All this time, the brigantine had continued to approach and was now within hailing distance. Captain Diamond, still pretending that no alarm had been given, picked up a speaking trumpet and demanded that she identify herself and her business.

The captain of the *Hag* claimed to be carrying a cargo of oranges, but the wind did not carry the smell of fruit.

Suddenly the decks of the brigantine began to seethe with activity, as armed men swarmed up from below, and tarpaulins and empty crates were whisked aside to reveal a battery of large guns. The flag of Grall came down, and the pirates ran up another in its place: a bleeding heart on a white field, pierced by a cutlass. The Captain of the *Hag* took up his trumpet again, demanding that the *Bear* surrender. "Not bloody likely!" Captain Diamond muttered.

"It would appear," said his lordship, "that he has you outgunned and outmanned."

"We'll go down fighting . . . I ain't heading for no slave market, that's certain," said the Captain.

"Then allow me to fight at your side," said Skelbrooke. "Instruct Mr. Kassien to unlock my manacles and—"

Captain Diamond gave a snort of derision. "Fight for me, would you? And why would you want to be doing that for?"

"In return for your promise to set me free on shore afterwards, if we both survive this engagement. Why should you not?" asked Skelbrooke. "You've already been paid to take me out of Marstadtt. And I may prove to be valuable in the coming engagement . . . more valuable than you know."

Captain Diamond snorted again. "As like to strike a bargain with them pirates, I fancy."

"Not at all," said Skelbrooke. "I'm in no position to do so— for what could I possibly offer them? *Their* captain has no shortage of men."

The Captain turned his back. "Take this young fool down below," he instructed one of the sailors. "We don't want him underfoot."

The sailor did as he was instructed, taking Skelbrooke roughly by the shoulder and steering him toward the hatch.

From his below-decks vantage point, Skelbrooke saw little of the battle. He could, however, hear a great deal: the deep roar of cannons and bombards, the sharper explosions of the smaller culverins and swivel guns, a rending and creaking of timbers as the grappling hooks caught and slowly pulled the two vessels together.

The truth was, his fate would be much the same whoever won this engagement—supposing that he did not catch a stray cannon ball in the meantime, or fall victim to an overzealous boarder who failed to take notice of his chains and manacles. Therefore, he had no stake in the outcome.

All that remained to him, when a handful of boarders brought the battle below decks and the crew fought desperately to repel them, was to sort through his somewhat bewildering array of personalities, and select and assume the one least likely to be affected by the carnage. Fortunately or unfortunately, that particular Francis Skelbrooke was decidedly unstable, the man who was wont to bury explosive charges in the earth and let the bodies fall where they may. He sat on the bunk in the Captain's cabin with his knees drawn up and his chin resting on his folded hands, whistling a tune under his breath, and watched unmoved as a pirate with a pike skewered the cabin boy like a rat at the end of a hobsticker, and the unfortunate youth thrashed and shrieked for almost a minute before expiring. By that time, the pikeman had been virtually decapitated by one of the crewmen and lay in a pool of blood at the end of the bunk.

Yet he felt some slight flicker of interest a short while later, when two seamen came in, carrying the bleeding and barely conscious Mr. Kassien. My lord rose from the bunk and pushed the dead pirate out of the way, making room for the sailors to deposit the First Mate.

"Heard you was some sort of a chirurgeon," one of the seamen shouted over all the noise.

Skelbrooke rapidly assumed the role that was needed. "A physician . . . but I can stop the bleeding." And suiting his actions to his words, he snatched up a cloth off the Captain's table.

Kassien revived while Skelbrooke was knotting the tourniquet.

"The Captain's dead on the forecastle . . . picked off by a sniper on the mainmast."

As he had not yet heard anything spectacular in the way of an explosion, Skelbrooke concluded that the dying Captain Diamond had slid to the deck, rather than toppled. "You are in command, then."

Mr. Kassien nodded. "Aye . . . and may remain so. There have been few boarders and we've killed them all. Looks like the battle may yet go our way." He reached into a pocket and drew out a key. "In which case, we shall undoubtedly have need of your services, 'Doctor' Skelbrooke."

Skelbrooke accepted the key and unlocked his irons. "I may be of greater service as a gunner, supposing I can reach Mr. Diamond's body in time," he said. And pausing only long enough to snatch up a cutlass and a pistol from the fallen pirate, he raced above.

He was climbing the narrow stairs when the *Hag* discharged a three-gun salvo which punched through the gun deck. The blast knocked him off of the stairs, and he lay stunned for several moments before recovering. Then he rose painfully to his feet and scrambled up the stairs again.

It appeared that the tide of battle had turned since Mr. Kassien made his optimistic assessment. The pirates were beginning to swarm on board. A gigantic corsair wearing a red scarf around his head bore down on Skelbrooke, waving a pistol and a long knife. My lord swung his cutlass, slashing the fellow across the belly, effectively gutting him. The pirate screamed, discharged his pistol, and fell back. The ball whistled past Skelbrooke's head, leaving a powder burn on the side of his face.

All around him, men fought with pikes and boarding axes; the air was full of smoke and reeking of gunpowder; the deck ran with blood. As Skelbrooke made his way to the forecastle, he was engaged by a beefy pirate who aimed a wild overhand cut at his head. Moving to block, Skelbrooke slipped in a puddle of blood and fell to his knees. The pirate raised his blade again . . . only to stagger back and fall down dead as an axe flew though the air and clove through his skull.

Captain Diamond lay atop a heap of bodies, piled up out of the way of the action. My lord knelt down and searched through his pockets. Finding the watch, he pulled the timepiece out by its heavy gold chain.

There were two keys on that chain: one to wind the watch, the other to arm it. He unscrewed the ring that fastened the chain to the timepiece and inserted the appropriate key in the hole thus revealed. He turned the key three times, then made his way to one of the swivel guns, where he enlisted the aid of the gunner.

The gun had a relatively narrow bore and was designed to shoot stones and odd bits of iron shrapnel when the grapeshot ran out. They primed the gun and loaded it, inserting the watch along with a handful of rocks. Skelbrooke took a slow-burning match from the gunner, trained the gun at the mainmast of the pirate ship, and touched the match to the vent.

There was a loud explosion and the base of the mast vanished in a burst of flame and smoke. Many of the pirates were hurled to the deck by the force of the blast, others were pierced by flying splinters. The mast crashed down, crushing a dozen or more beneath it, and causing the brigantine to heel strongly to port. Meanwhile, several fires simultaneously broke out on deck.

Lord Skelbrooke viewed the destruction with characteristic detachment. "If I am needed again . . . you may find me down below, tending to the wounded." And straightening the kerchief he wore in place of a neckcloth, he sauntered toward the hatch.

34.

Wherein Sera receives Information and Knows not how to Take it.

Sera was climbing the stairs to her bedchamber on the third floor, after an afternoon spent sipping tea and sherry with the old Duke, when she met Hermes Budge descending the staircase with uncharacteristic haste.

"Miss Vorder . . . I have been looking for you everywhere. Can you spare me a moment of your time? Would you be so obliging as to join me in the library?"

Sera was heading upstairs to dress for supper, intending to change the gown of black bombazine for the more appropriate wine-colored watered silk, but more than an hour remained before the meal would be served. She turned around and followed the tutor down the stairs and into the library.

Mr. Budge closed the door behind him and silently motioned her to a window seat in the wall opposite. This was very mysterious . . . so unlike the sober and sensible Budge that Sera was intrigued.

"I received a letter this afternoon from my friend Mr. Gumley . . . you will recall that he spent some years in Katrinsberg?" said the tutor, lowering his voice. "He knows nothing of any man going by the name of Skogsrå, but—and this is really most intriguing—he does mention a man exactly answering the Jarl's description: a Colonel Jolerei as he was called, who lived for some time in Katrinsberg, where he acquired a reputation for . . . well, I will pass over the details—they are hardly proper for you to hear. Let me just say that he was not the sort of man that it would be seemly for you or your cousin to know."

Budge reached inside his coat pocket and withdrew a letter. He looked through it, selected a page, and handed it over to Sera. She accepted the paper and read carefully through the description it contained, once, and then a second time.

"It certainly sounds like the same man," she said. Then, turning the page over, she read aloud, " 'Half trolls as they are called—though indeed they are no more mongrelized than the race as a whole—more nearly resemble the race of Men, and most of them sport but a single deformity: a snout like a pig, a tail like a cow, a birdlike claw in place of a hand. . . . ' My dear sir, what *is* this about?"

"A discourse on Nordic folklore. Mr. Gumley's style, as you may observe, is inclined to be incoherent. I do not perfectly understand why he began his letter with an account of these superstitions," said Budge. "They do not appear to be in any way relevant to the subject of Jarl Skogsrå. I believe that the race of trolls—if not absolutely mythical—has at any rate been proven extinct."

"I have heard the same," said Sera, though she added with a smile, "but only think, Mr. Budge . . . if this were to provide an explanation for Lord Skogsrå's lameness. Dear me . . . the Jarl might have feet like a goat!"

"I believe," said Mr. Budge, somewhat sternly, "that cloven hooves would be comparatively rare. According to Mr. Gumley's account, a solid hoof like a horse is rather more common, with the lower limb correspondingly deformed."

Sera grew sober once more. "Your friend has certainly provided

239

us with disturbing information . . . but nothing that I can possibly repeat to Elsie. She has far too generous a mind to give any credit to malicious gossip . . . and I fear that is how she would view Mr. Gumley's account.''

''I quite understand,'' said Mr. Budge. ''But surely the fact that he has changed his name since arriving in Marstadtt, in some sense supports our suspicions that Skogsrå is an adventurer.''

''Indeed it does,'' said Sera, with a sigh. ''But Elsie would not accept that, either, not on the basis of what may well be a chance resemblance.''

Yet she was remembering that Lord Vodni had also mentioned the city of Katrinsberg, and between the Baron and the Jarl there appeared to be some ancient enmity. This being so, Sera resolved to question Lord Vodni at the first opportunity.

Not until the following morning did Sera find that opportunity to speak with Lord Vodni in private. And then it was necessary to preface her questions with an explanation of her conversation with Budge on the day of the picnic, and to produce the letter containing so perfect a description of the Jarl, though the name was not the same.

Lord Vodni was again dressed for riding. Sera had encountered him outside the stables, which were located at some distance from the house, between the lake and the woods. ''I knew him some years back in Katrinsberg,'' said Vodni, turning over the paper which Sera handed to him. ''And he was then known as Haakon Jolerei . . . but there is nothing sinister in that, I can assure you. Jolerei is the family name, and his older brother (who was then the Jarl) was still alive. Whatever else I might be tempted to say concerning Lord Skogsrå, he is certainly no imposter. His family is well known in Katrinsberg, and indeed, I believe there is even a distant connection with my own.''

Sera did not know whether she ought to be relieved or disappointed. ''But these rumors of wicked deeds and immoral habits . . . perhaps no more than idle gossip—''

''Those I am inclined to take rather more seriously,'' said Vodni. ''Though I never actually heard anything against him, I have never liked this Skogsrå. I could scarcely tell you how, but I have always entertained an impression that he was somehow . . . an unwholesome man to know.''

He glanced over the writing on the back of the page. ''You needn't pay any heed to that,'' said Sera. ''As you can see, it has nothing to do with Lord Skogsrå.''

"You think not?" said Vodni. "But I think that it may have a great deal to do with Lord Skogsrå. You have, Miss Vorder, as I must suppose, led a sheltered life. You would not know that there are actually men who—at least in a metaphoric sense—might be said to devour young women alive. Haakon Skogsrå may be one of them.''

He frowned thoughtfully. "I believe that I should speak to the Duchess. Yes, she must certainly be informed. And I shall write to my cousins in Katrinsberg and ask them what they know. In the meantime, madam, you must say nothing to anyone, certainly not to Miss Elsie, who would not believe you, and moreover, would almost certainly repeat the story to the Jarl himself. If Skogsrå had reason to suspect that we know these things . . . there is no telling what rash action he might take.''

Sera was utterly appalled. "But my dear sir! While we wait to learn more concerning these rumors, Elsie may well marry Lord Skogsrå!''

But Vodni shook his head. "There can be no danger of that. A promise to wed, perhaps—but a promise can be easily broken. Such, indeed, may already exist privately between them. But your cousin is not of age, and she cannot marry without her father's consent.

"We must assume that she is safe for this time,'' he said, with a reassuring smile. "They cannot wed until Elsie returns to Thornburg.''

35.

Containing much Speculation as to the history of the Sorcerer in the Coffin.

Jenk woke in the middle of the night, sweating and trembling in his bed under the eaves, staring up at the peaked ceiling. He knew that the moon was waning, was shriveling away to a tiny splinter of light—there was no cause, no cause that he knew to account for his present agitation.

The hours went crawling by. Try as he might to relax, sleep continued to elude him. At dawn he rose and left his bed, dressed by candle light, and sidled down the stairs.

Jenk slipped the key into the lock on the laboratory door. Something . . . something was stirring at the back of his mind. He turned the knob, opened the door, and went into the room. He set his candle down on the table by the coffin.

Slowly, he lifted the lid of the casket, stood staring down at the face of the sorcerer. Dead or dreaming? he wondered, not for the first time. With a sigh, Jenk reached for one of the books: a thick volume bound in faded red leather, with the sign of the Scolos, the two-headed serpent, stamped on the cover. He placed it carefully on the sorcerer's breast.

This particular volume inevitably fell open at the same page, as though the information written there were of particular interest to some previous scholar. Jenk had read the book through, but until tonight, he had scarcely given a thought to its contents . . . it bore no relevance to his search for the Stone. But now—now that he had all but abandoned hope of bringing his experiments to a successful conclusion, now that he was desperately seeking some new interest, some new quest to enlighten and occupy him— one passage from this book kept running in his mind. He scanned the page, looking for that passage.

" . . . *but of the Island of Evanthum, and of the People, and most particularly of her Priests who were also Great Adepts*," Jenk read aloud, "*much has been preserved in Secret records. They built a great Temple to the Moon Goddess, encircled by three Walls: the first of Brass, the second of Tin, and the innermost of Orichalcum. And they Erected there a Statue in her Likeness, ninety feet high, and Adorned with ornaments of Nacre, Sea-ivory, and Pearl, being the gifts of the Sea, with which they identified her. Many other Wonders they wrought besides.*"

Jenk shook his head; this was not what he was looking for. He skipped on ahead. "*Their Astrologers knew the movements of the Planets and of the Stars and could predict their Courses for a Thousand years. Their Alchemists had discovered the secrets of Transmutation, and of Immortality. They were a Proud and Mighty Race.*

"*Yet they were Dissatisfied. For the Empire of Panterra also flourished, and her Adepts rivaled the Adepts of Evanthum, and her Astrologers rivaled their Astrologers . . . and in All Things of which the Magicians of Evanthum had gained the Mastery, so, too, were the Panterran Magicians also Masters, save only in those Matters which they had Determined were not Meet or Wholesome for Men to meddle with.*"

Jenk skipped over another long paragraph. He knew what it contained—a lengthy explanation of the dispute between the Rival Adepts, in which the Panterrans had scolded the adepts of Evanthum for presumption, and the Evanthians mocked the Panterrans' cowardice. The Panterrans ended by warning their rivals of the dangers of that presumption, which the magician-priests of Evanthum had taken for a threat.

He turned over another page. "*Accordingly, they set out to Destroy Panterra utterly, with Spells both Mighty and Terrible, and the Panterrans, being men of Honor and Reason themselves, and expecting a like Virtue in others, were not Prepared for Treachery. Taken by Surprise, they were Helpless to avert their Doom. A great Wave overwhelmed the Island, and Panterra vanished beneath the Waters.*

"*Yet though the Land was lost and many Thousands of Lives, a very few were Saved, and they were Men skilled in Magic, though not among the Men of Highest Good Will—for all the Priests and Great Philosophers had Perished in a futile effort to Rescue as many of their Countrymen as possible. Thus it was proven that Virtue is no protection and the Mighty will always have their Way. The men who had escaped were Vengeful men and determined to Destroy Evanthum in the same Manner that Panterra had met her End.*"

While Jenk read, Caleb came quietly into the room, carrying tiny Eirena on his shoulder. The bookseller glanced up. They were an odd pair to be sure: Caleb so grizzled, gnarled, and worn-looking, Eirena so small and dainty . . . yet some deep sympathy existed between them, a sympathy which Jenk could not begin to fathom.

Caleb moved around the laboratory, tidying the clutter on the long table, picking up a broom and sweeping the floor. When he chanced to come too near to Jenk, the homunculus made a fearful sound deep in her throat. Since the incident of the candle flame, Eirena had conceived a terror of Jenk, a terror which the intervening weeks had not diminished.

Jenk went on with his reading. "*Yet the Priests of Evanthum, expecting Vengeance, were Prepared. They had taken measures to ensure their own Survival. And though they were willing to Sacrifice the lives of their Lesser Countrymen, yet they had Re-*

243

solved to preserve all the Wonders and the Riches which they had Gathered. Therefore, when the Wave came to Overwhelm the Island, the Priests of her Temples had already taken Ship for other Lands, and they had set a Spell upon the Island that though it Sink beneath the Waters, yet it should Rise again in three-hundred Days. But this Spell, being performed in Haste, went somehow Awry."

There was an undercurrent of excitement in the bookseller's voice. Caleb stopped sweeping and listened to Jenk read.

"In the Nations of Euterpe the Story spread and so it has Come Down to the Present day, that the Land of Evanthum was Lost indeed, Never to Rise again. Yet in Ynde and Llyria they tell the tale Differently, saying that Evanthum did Rise and Continues to Rise, every three-hundred years, whereupon it Remains above the Water for the space of Seven Days. And they say, also, that any man arriving by Chance or Design, in good Time to See the island Arise, might land his Boat and Walk the Streets of Ivory and of Pearl, exactly as Men did of Old, and marvel at the Wonders so miraculously Preserved, and perhaps even Discover the Secrets of her Adepts, which were carved on Ivory tablets in the Temple of the Moon. But whether this story be True, no man has Proven, for even among Scholars and Philosophers, there is no agreement as to the Year and the Season when Evanthum sank into the sea, and as for the location of the Sunken Kingdom, it is not to be found on any Map."

"That's an old story," said Caleb. "Nothing there I ain't heard afore, and in nigh the same words. Nor you, neither, I reckon."

"The gift of the sea, and not of the river," Jenk said softly. "Those were my words, on the night you brought the coffin to me. An unconscious echo of this old story? Yet it seemed to me then, I did not know why, that any connection between this coffin and the sea was vastly important. Then, too, there is the little piece of narwhal ivory . . . sea-ivory . . . which our departed friend holds so closely between his fingers."

Caleb rubbed the back of his neck with a knotted hand. "I did wonder, the night we brung the coffin in, whether it were buried in the ground proper to begin with and only come out when the earth shook and the river flooded, or only a sea burial come in on the tide."

He shook his head. "But the look of the box is against that notion—they don't build them near so fine, just to tip them into the sea. No, and they don't float, neither, them shipboard coffins.

244

They're weighted so they sink right down to the bottom."

"But mayhap . . . perchance this one was meant to float," said Jenk. He turned back to the page he had been reading. "The exact date when Evanthum shall rise again from the sea is unknown, yet one might attempt to fix it within a decade or so. By my calculation, the next Emergence may be expected some time around the end of the present century. That is . . . supposing that we choose to believe the story at all."

Jenk stood silently for a time, turning the matter over in his mind. He felt as though he were poised on the brink of some revelation. "We are old men, Caleb, and do not expect to live until the end of the century . . . yet it is not impossible, not entirely impossible. But let us imagine that we had both of us been born a hundred years earlier. Let us imagine that we had some special knowledge which allowed us to calculate the exact time and place of the next Emergence—more than a century in the future."

Caleb scratched his chin. "Guess we might gain some satisfaction, anyways, from passing the knowledge on, from knowing that the thing we knew might be of some use to some great-grandchild of my Jed or your Sera."

"Indeed," said Jenk, closing the book. He felt a rising excitement, as though he drew nearer and nearer to some hidden truth. A secret . . . greater than the spell which had enabled them to create the homunculus, perhaps even greater than the stone Seramarias. Was it possible that, in his failure to compound the Stone, he was about to make a discovery of even more profundity?

"But imagine," he said, continuing to choose his words carefully—for he always took great care in everything he said to Caleb these days, never knowing what chance word or expression would send the old river man off into a rage, or set him sulking and glaring suspiciously—"imagine in your own place, or in mine, a different sort of man . . . a man estranged from all his kin, a man who knew nothing of natural ties of blood or affection. For a man of that sort, even such cold satisfaction as you describe would be denied him. Unless . . . unless he could cheat death somehow, spend the next century in a dreaming oblivion . . . remote from the flesh yet not permanently sundered from it . . . neither dead nor alive."

As Jenk spoke, a picture began to form in his mind. He saw the sorcerer in his laboratory, making his preparations, casting a mighty spell, falling down in a semblance of death. But the body, though tenantless, remained uncorrupted. He saw the magician's assistants prepare the corpse, sew the eyelids shut, give their master

245

a proper laying out, so that no questions should be asked later. Jenk imagined them, when the time came for burial, placing the magician in a splendid casket along with his books, and taking that coffin secretly down to the sea. He saw the coffin launched into the water . . . there to ride for a hundred years or more, while the little piece of narwhal ivory in the sorcerer's hand acted as a kind of talisman to bring the body to the proper place at the proper time.

"It explains much which I have been unable to explain in any other way," Jenk mused out loud. "And if the tale of Evanthum itself be not true, yet it is still possible that this man, this magician as he appears to have been, nevertheless believed it to be true, and cast such a spell as I have described in order to be present at the next Emergence, and *Walk the Streets of Ivory and of Pearl, exactly as Men did of Old, and marvel at the Wonders so miraculously Preserved.* Nor should we forget those secrets carved on tablets of ivory in the temple, which I am persuaded would be of the greatest interest to such a man as I have described."

Caleb goggled at him in patent disbelief. "But to do that . . . to do what you said he done . . . why, he'd have to know more of the secrets of life and death than any man living."

"Indeed," said Jenk, just above a whisper. "Indeed he would. And I wonder, I cannot help but wonder, if it might be possible to communicate with this man, in spirit at least. We possess his body, which must form a vital link . . . his books, his medallion, all lending power to our invocation."

Caleb took a deep breath. "That's Necromancy you're thinking of . . . that's a dangerous art, and one we never reckoned to dabble in."

"We never attempted it before, certainly, but speaking for myself . . . I have thought of many things these last few seasons, which I had never previously considered. And we have the spells, Caleb . . . in Catalana's *Book of Silences,* which lies here in this very coffin."

"Aye . . . but if'n we did conjure him up . . . what then?" Caleb asked uneasily. "Who's to say he'd want to help us? Who's to say he'd take kindly to us for disturbing his rest afore time? Guess he wouldn't tell us nothing!"

"Ah," said Jenk, "but I believe that he would. I think he would be prepared to do great things, reveal marvelous secrets to the men who had his body in their keeping . . . who had the power to destroy that body, and by doing so bring all his spells to naught."

Caleb began to catch a little of his excitement. "You could be right, Gottfried. I'll not deny . . . you could be right. But it's a risk, that's certain. You sure you want to take it?"

"I have never been more certain of anything," said Jenk. "I am prepared to take any risk. But you . . ." he said, suddenly remembering the coldness that still existed between them, on Eirena's account, "you must not think, Caleb, that I would ask you to do anything against your will."

But Caleb was well and truly caught, too intrigued by the possibilities to back out now. "Guess I would be interested in helping you out, at that. Reckon it's not an opportunity I'd be wise to pass by."

"Why then," said Jenk, closing the lid of the coffin, "I believe that we shall attempt the conjuration at the dark of the moon, five nights hence."

36.

Containing further Stratagems of the Duchess.

The season of Gathering was advancing, and down in the little wood below the Wichtelberg the leaves on the oaks and the beeches were turning gold. Though the days grew shorter, the weather continued sultry, and the Duchess and her guests had taken up boating, rowing out on the lake in tiny skiffs shaped like walnut shells, or exploring the mysterious waterways of the grotto.

On the twenty-third day of the season, a baggage-laden coach came rattling up the drive and deposited a man and two women below the house. The Duchess, who was just returning from an outing on the lake, was there to greet them on the lower terrace.

"My dear Lady Ursula . . . and you Lady Vizbeck, how very pleased I am that you were able to come," said the Duchess, in her high sweet voice. "Lord Vizbeck . . . a pleasure. And I understand that congratulations are in order."

"Indeed," replied Lady Ursula, removing her hat and her gloves. "We are to marry as soon as the bridegroom comes of

age. And I—can you believe it? but I assure you that it is true—
I have promised to practice habits of economy.''

"I confess that I find it difficult.'' The Duchess's smile lost
none of its sweetness. She turned toward Lord Vizbeck. "What
a very sanguine young man you must be!''

The Jarl and Elsie, who were also present, sensed a certain
hostility between Lady Ursula and the Duchess. Elsie was too well
bred to mention this circumstance, but not so Skogsrå, who
broached the subject that same evening, as he escorted the Duchess
up to her bedchamber after supper.

"Why is she here . . . this woman whom you so obviously
loathe? Why do you invite her? And you suspect her, too, of
stealing your so valuable magic parchment.''

"I invited her—along with her callow bridegroom-to-be and
his rather more amusing mother—in order to get at the truth,''
said the Duchess. "How am I to learn whether she has taken my
parchment when she is in Marstadtt and I in Zar-Wildungen?''

The Jarl raised a single painted eyebrow. "The truth. It seems
that we are all here that you may learn the truth. But what have
you learned? Miss Sera Vorder—''

"Remains silent about her grandfather's activities. She has been
up to visit the Duke a half a dozen times, and always in Vodni's
company, but of Jenk's homunculus or my lord's supposed patronage, not a single word does she say.'' The Duchess shook her
head disapprovingly. "I cannot believe that she is really so ignorant, and so I redouble my efforts to gain her confidence. Meanwhile, she makes herself exceedingly tiresome—she and Mr.
Budge, with all of their snooping and asking questions. I must
admit,'' she added reflectively, "that I am sadly disappointed in
Hermes Budge.''

The Jarl made an impatient gesture. "Then send him away.''

"And direct Sera's suspicions toward myself?'' asked the Duchess. "Now, that would be extremely foolish. For now, she is
willing to believe that you are imposing on my good nature—if
she ever learns otherwise . . .'' The Duchess tilted her head, and
a tiny sigh escaped her. "She will cease to be of potential use to
me, and then I shall have to take steps I had rather avoid.''

"It always comes to this,'' said Skogsrå. "All gives way before
the Gracious Lady's consuming interest in Jenk the alchemist and
his experiments. And this, I suppose, is the reason you have sent
Lord Vodni into Thornburg?''

"That is so,'' said the Duchess, "but as Jenk himself did not

248

send for him, I have no way of knowing what sort of welcome Vodni will receive there."

Vodni returned two days later. The Duchess received him in an elegant salon on the second floor, which was known as the Clock Room, for it housed a large and varied collection of curious old timepieces. There were mantelpiece clocks and long-case grandfather clocks; clocks driven by falling weights, pendulums, and springs; clocks made of wood, metal, crystal . . . indeed, of every conceivable material. And a glassed-in cabinet at one end of the room housed a number of china figurines, each concealing an internal timepiece. The Duchess, so dainty and porcelain fair, seated on a little gilded sofa, looked rather like a part of the collection herself.

She rose from her seat and greeted the Baron with a glad little cry. "Did Jenk admit you—did you see the child? Pray tell me everything at once!"

Vodni took her hand by the fingertips and raised it to his lips. "I have seen the homunculus and she is truly amazing . . . physically perfect, although of course very small, and possessing a certain unusual cast of coloring which some might even find attractive. Her appearance is that of a tiny woman, and her only real defect, so far as I could discover, is her continued inability to speak."

The Duchess resumed her seat, fussing and arranging the folds of her skirt in an agitated manner, though her face and her voice remained calm. "She cannot speak . . . I am scarcely surprised. It is not so very great a failing, after all, in one so young . . . so long—so long, my dear Vodni—as she appears otherwise intelligent?"

Vodni replied by enumerating Eirena's accomplishments. "But Jenk himself is inclined to regard her failure to speak as a serious defect. It is for that reason (he tells me) that he was reluctant to receive me. And I understood," he concluded earnestly, "that the Gracious Lady requires a child that is perfect in every respect."

The Duchess smiled brightly, determined to make light of this supposed shortcoming. "Perfect . . . Yes, the child must be without any defect. I have suffered so much through the children in the past. But after all, this Eirena of Jenk's, she is virtually an infant!"

Since she had not yet offered him a seat, Vodni began to move restlessly around the room. "But of course, you are correct. From the moment of her conception it is not above thirteen weeks. It is only because she appears physically mature and behaves so, too, that one expects so much of her.''

"But the formula," said the Duchess, growing impatient once more. "Were you able to obtain the formula?''

Vodni paused beside a large and elaborate timepiece with three different faces, marking the hours, the seasons of the year, and the movements of the planets. The clock-case was constructed entirely of glass revealing a multitude of springs and wheels and whirling gears inside. "Alas," said the Baron, "he denied me the formula, declaring that he will deliver it into the hands of the Duke himself . . . or not at all. His manner was odd, and (I thought) full of suspicion."

"How very inconvenient," said the Duchess. "How very tiresome. But it is rather too late for me to confide in the Duke. I suppose we shall be forced to resort to less direct means . . . that I will have to arrange for the theft of the formula on my return to Thornburg.

"Not that I am not entitled to the information, and perfectly justified in using any means to obtain it," she added, with a self-righteous toss of her head. "I have already paid a handsome price, and I do not take kindly to those who would cheat me!''

The Dowager Lady Vizbeck was an energetic woman, with a penchant for long walks whenever she visited the country. Accordingly, she soon attached herself to Sera and Elsie, and insisted on accompanying them on their morning rambles. Sera, for one, was glad of her presence, for Jarl Skogsrå, in spite of his bad leg, had become a regular feature on these walks, and the sight of Elsie leaning so confidingly on Skogsrå's arm was a sight that was increasingly difficult for her to bear. It was becoming more and more difficult, too, for Sera to address Lord Skogsrå with even the appearance of civility, so she welcomed the opportunity to walk on ahead with the Dowager, while Elsie and the Jarl trailed behind.

"Miss Vorder, I am delighted to find your cousin in such excellent health," Lady Vizbeck exclaimed, one morning as they strolled through the wood in the direction of the ruined chapel. "So rosy, so blooming, so full of vigor as she appears to be. I vow that her recovery has been truly amazing."

"Yes," said Sera, who could not help being pleased by Elsie's rapid recovery—whatever she might think of Jarl Skogsrå and his methods. "Elsie is nearly as strong now as I am myself. And if it were not for her occasional *spells*, I would have nothing more to wish for."

The chapel in the wood was wanting a roof, and the stained-glass windows had long since been removed. But the stonework was still very fine, though considerably weathered, and late-flowering vines wreathed the statues of the Seasons behind the altar.

"I think it exceedingly romantic," said Elsie, and an intimate glance passed between her and the Jarl. "I am so glad that the Duke refused to tear it down."

"Yes indeed," said the Dowager, "it is a very pretty spot. It reminds me, just a little, of the Chapel of the Seasons at the cathedral—after it burned down and before they rebuilt it. I daresay you don't remember the original chapel, for it was destroyed . . . Let me see, it must have been the same year you were born. It *can't* have been earlier, for you were named in the original chapel . . . I remember the occasion very well."

"Did you attend the ceremony, Lady Vizbeck?" Elsie asked politely. "And the Duchess . . . I suppose she was there when I was named, as well. It is the reason that she likes to think of me as her godchild."

"The Duchess?" Lady Vizbeck gave a surprised little laugh. "But of course she was *not* there, and that was the cause of all the fuss."

Sera who had not really been listening to this conversation, began to attend with great interest, for she had often wondered about the circumstances surrounding Elsie's naming, and how, against all custom, Elsie had acquired an "unlucky" thirteenth godparent. "I had no idea," said Sera, sitting down on a slab of mossy stone by the altar, "that the ceremony did not go smoothly."

"It was all because of the Duchess," Lady Vizbeck explained, sitting down beside Sera and opening her fan. "She had been originally chosen as one of the sponsors, but she arrived over two hours late. You can easily imagine what a flutter poor Clothilde was in . . . the guests all waiting . . . the bishop growing impatient . . . to say nothing of the other eleven who had other engagements that same day. In the end, Clothilde grew desperate and persuaded Lady Wurzbach to stand up as the twelfth. Marella arrived just as Clothilde and the baby were leaving the chapel, and she went into a terrible rage!"

The Dowager turned to Elsie. "You have never, I suppose, seen the Duchess in a rage? It does not happen often, for in general she is the soul of good nature—then, too, being that she is the Duchess, people are always so eager to oblige her.

"Well . . . she was angry enough on this occasion," Lady Vizbeck went on, delighted to have such an interested audience. Even the Jarl, who was leaning against the ruined altar, bent a little forward, as if intent on hearing every word she uttered. "Of course I am late. I always come late!" said Marella. "And I think you might have taken that into account and made your arrangements accordingly!" And that was certainly true.

"You will not remember this," she added, "but the Duchess and your mama were polite but distant for many years afterwards. I do not perfectly recall when it was that the Duchess and Clothilde mended their quarrel."

"But I remember," said Elsie. "I was ten years old, and Mama and I met the Duchess at the cathedral. She embraced me and called me her goddaughter—I admit that I was very much surprised. I suppose," she added reflectively, "that the Duchess derives some consolation for her disappointment, by pretending that it is actually so."

But Sera shook her head. "Yet *I* find it very strange. Were I in the same position as the Duchess, I do not think that I would care to be reminded of an occasion when I had felt so dreadfully insulted."

"Indeed," said Lady Vizbeck, "I am inclined to agree with you. But there is never any accounting for the Duchess and her whims!"

The season was drawing to a close, and soon the Duchess and her houseguests would return to Marstadt. Determined to end her sojourn in the country with some spectacular display, some magnificent entertainment that would leave the Duke's neighbors marveling at her ingenuity, she eventually decided on a masked ball, to be held on the night of the next full moon. She had ten days to make the arrangements: to write up the invitations and send them out to the neighboring gentry and the Zar-Wildungen nobility, to plan the menu and conceive the decorations . . . but the Duchess (being, as Lady Vizbeck had so rightly characterized her, a creature of whim and caprice) was used to arranging festivities on such short notice and she took up the challenge with considerable relish.

252

She was also arranging another, smaller affair to take place on the same evening, but for that her plans (of necessity) were attended by a certain amount of secrecy. Only Jarl Skogsrå was in her confidence. They discussed the matter one afternoon, while the Duchess sat by the great iron aviary in the garden, watching the antics of the ape Sebastian, as he cavorted among the trees and the vines and teased the birds of bright plumage.

"It is a pity that the chapel is so unsuitable . . . considering that Elsie has taken such a fancy to the place. But the nights are growing colder, and I am afraid we must be practical."

"Elsie," said Skogsrå, "need not be considered. She is scarcely like to notice her surroundings . . . She will not have eyes or ears for anyone but me . . . You may count on me, Gracious Lady, to make certain of that."

"Very true," said the Duchess. "Well . . . then, we must give some thought to the witnesses. I shall be Elsie's, of course, and for you, the Duke—"

"I do not want the Duke," said Skogsrå. "With all due respect to His Excellency, I had far rather have Vodni."

The Duchess was surprised. "Vodni? But between you and Lord Vodni there is—"

"—no love . . . There is no love between us. But there are other bonds," said the Jarl. "And Vodni is the one that I choose."

But the Duchess shook her head. "Vodni will be occupied elsewhere."

"That is true," said Skogsrå, showing his teeth. "But he has such energy, this Nicolai Vodni, surely he can do all in one night."

The Duchess rose from her seat, picking up her parasol and slipping her arm through his. "As you wish, then. You must please yourself in this matter."

They wandered through the gardens for some time, among the statues and the fountains. The Duchess was in good spirits, but the Jarl felt uneasy. "I cannot help but wonder," he said at last, "why it is that you are so eager to assist me to my heart's desire. Do not think me ungrateful, for my gratitude in this matter must naturally be commensurate with the intensity of my craving . . . but so long as I fail to understand the Gracious Lady's interest in this matter . . . I cannot help feeling as though I were no more than a pawn in some deeper game of her own."

He stopped and fixed the Duchess with an intent stare. "Why have you chosen Elsie, so gentle and inoffensive as she is? You have some quarrel, as I have heard, with her mother . . . but as for the girl herself: what has she ever done to harm or insult you?''

The Duchess opened her parasol, spent several long moments adjusting the ruffles and the ribbons before she answered him. ''She has never harmed me, but she was the *occasion* for an insult, and by all the laws and customs of the Fees, that is every bit as bad. I am not so much my father's daughter that I am able to explain that, but I am fairy enough to feel it instinctively.''

She took up his arm again, with a weary little sigh. ''And it is not that I feel no regret, for indeed—indeed Lord Skogsrå, I do. Just as (I must suppose), though in an entirely different way, your own peculiar instincts exact an equally peculiar penalty.

''We are as we were made,'' said the Duchess, as they headed in the direction of the house. ''And if we must suffer for that, in our separate ways . . . then so must Elsie.''

37.

Which takes the Reader back Several days to the night of the Dark of the Moon.

The moon-faced clock in the bookshop was chiming half past ten, when Gottfried Jenk and Caleb Braun stepped out onto the cobblestone street and locked the door behind them.

Caleb carried a covered lanthorn, Jenk a basket, a crowbar, and a roll of papers. The bookseller had spent much of the previous day enscribing mysterious-looking characters and sonorous passages from Catalana's *Book of Silences* and the rest gathering together the paraphernalia he needed to effect the conjuration.

Clouds covered the sky, swallowing up the stars. A light, damp breeze blew in off the water. The two old men were heading for the cemetery behind the cathedral. Caleb felt a bit put out; he saw no reason to go so far. ''Don't see no point in going to no grave-yard, when the body's back there at the bookshop. Tomfoolery, just plain *tom*foolery, that's what I call it! And supposing we conjure up the wrong ghost?''

254

"The spells specify a graveyard." Jenk spoke tensely. They had argued again about Eirena on the day the Duke's man came to see her, and he and Caleb had been eyeing each other warily ever since. But they were both in too deep . . . far too deep, to seriously consider dissolving their partnership now.

"In Necromancy, as in every species of magic," he went on, "it is essential to observe the correct forms. And I bring the medallion with me, and a scrap of cloth from his robe . . . Yes, it did begin to disintegrate the moment it left the coffin, but even a handful of dust will serve our purpose. There is no possibility of summoning up the wrong ghost."

"Aye . . . maybe," Caleb sniffed. "I guess you'd know all that better'n me. But if we've got to go to a graveyard, ain't there a perfectly good boneyard on Fishwife Hill . . . and no one like to take any notice—supposing they catch sight of us, poking about?"

But Jenk was set on the cathedral graveyard. "This is a mighty conjuration that we hope to perform, and it were best accomplished in suitably impressive surroundings."

Ominous sounds filled the night . . . a stifled cry followed by a splash down by the river . . . a skittering and a squeaking of rats in the shadows . . . With the moon dark, there was no danger of an encounter with hobs, but when Caleb thought he heard furtive footsteps following behind him, he pulled out a long knife he kept tucked in his belt, and allowed the blade to flash in the light of a street lamp as he walked by. Beside him, Jenk tightened his grip on the crowbar.

"We ought to go quick," Caleb muttered. "I ain't easy in my mind, leaving her all on her own at the shop . . . sommat might happen to her."

"She cannot get into any mischief shut up in her box," said Jenk, "so long as you made certain to close the catch."

"Aye," replied Caleb. "But that ain't what worries me. *She* can't cause no mischief, that's certain sure—but what if some mischief comes to her?"

Jenk shook his head. "Sometimes, your concern for that unnatural little daughter of yours becomes tiresome."

The gates of the ancient graveyard were closed but not locked. Jenk pushed one open slowly, lest the rusty hinges creak. Then he and Caleb moved silently among the old monuments and the tilted gravestones until they came to one of the larger mausoleums.

As they were now some distance from the lighted street, Caleb uncovered his lanthorn.

A high fence of iron pickets surrounded the tomb. Jenk broke the lock on the elaborate wrought-iron gate with his crowbar, but it was a noisy business.

"My dear Caleb, I believe you are trembling," whispered Jenk. "But who are you to fear the dead?"

"Guess I'm as easy with the dead as any man," Caleb hissed back at him. "But my nerves ain't what they once was, and I don't care for all this racket."

The marble mausoleum gleamed white in the moonlight. One section of the wall, not far from the sealed door, had collapsed. Jenk dropped his crowbar and, passing the basket and the papers over to Caleb, he bent down and crept through the opening. Then Caleb handed the lanthorn through.

"As I had hoped." Jenk's voice drifted out of the tomb. "There is a narrow ledge between here and the stairs . . . and the steps appear to be sound."

Caleb stuck his head through the opening and crawled through. Jenk had already reached the head of the stairs. He held the lanthorn in one hand and offered the other to Caleb. Disdaining his assistance, Caleb edged cautiously along the ledge, until he reached the wider place at the top of the steps. Then, together, they descended into the vault.

The bones of the dead lay neatly arranged on marble slabs. Weird frescoes and carvings were on the walls, stylized figures from another age which Caleb found oddly disturbing. Had the men of the past truly seen themselves and the world they inhabited with a vision so skewed and distorted . . . or had the world changed and the races mutated since then, achieving their present forms?

But Jenk was impelled by an odd sense of urgency. Without so much as a glance at the frescoes, he set the lanthorn down on a slab, opened his basket, and began to lay out the contents: a piece of chalk and some black candles; a dagger with a long, wicked blade; a tinder box and a little charcoal brazier. There was also a crudely made wooden doll, about twelve inches high, and something stiff and furry, loosely wrapped in a piece of old cloth.

"What's that lot?" Caleb asked, indicating the last two items.

"The corpse of a grey cat, and a wooden man to house the spirit, when he comes," said Jenk. "There is a little chamber inside, containing a mummified human heart."

Taking the chalk, he drew a five-pointed star upon the stones at his feet. He lit five black candles, setting each one on a separate point of the pentagram. Then he unwrapped the scrawny little corpse of the cat, with its awkward, rigid limbs and its staring green eyes, and placed it near the center of the figure.

Jenk drew out the medallion, from a pocket in his waistcoat, and a little bag containing the crumbling remains of the cloth from the coffin. He wrapped them both around the doll. "Now we are ready to begin," he said, standing the wooden man up at the center of the pentagram, propped up by the corpse of the cat.

He handed the roll of papers to Caleb. "Hold these up near the light . . . beginning with the first page . . . so that I may read them."

"It ain't too late to change our minds," said Caleb, shifting uneasily away from the dagger in Jenk's hand.

"I have no desire to change my mind . . . and do not flinch so . . . I have no intention of using this dagger on *you*," said Jenk, with dry humor. "Now, how does the spell run?" he asked, as Caleb held up the first paper. "Ah, yes!"

And with the words impressed more firmly on his mind, he turned, skewered the cat, and began to chant the invocation.

Dawn was staining the eastern sky when Jenk and Caleb left the tomb and trudged wearily toward the bookshop. A fog came rolling in from the river, and the two old men shivered in the early morning chill.

"Guess we can try again at the full moon," Caleb said. "Pay Matthias and Walther to help us cart the coffin up to the boneyard on Fishwife Hill. I told you it weren't likely to do no good, your spells and conjurations, without we had the corpse along with us at the time."

"Yes . . . you warned me," said Jenk, in a hard, bitter voice. "You were on hand to nay-say me on this occasion, as indeed on so many others."

Caleb, startled, turned to look at him. "Here, now . . . you ain't blaming *me*? It weren't no way my fault your spells was too weak."

"Was it not?" said Jenk. "But I think it was . . . You with your reluctance and your disbelief, draining the spells of their power. I am determined to try again when the moon is full, but without your assistance, Caleb—without your interference."

They continued on to the bookshop, each entertaining his own angry thoughts. The street lamps were burning low by the time they arrived at the door, and Jenk spent several minutes fumbling about in the misty darkness before he was able to fit the key in the lock.

As soon as they entered the shop, they both knew that something was wrong. A thumping and a banging and a high-pitched wailing issued from the room at the back.

"I *knowed* she'd come to some harm, we kept leaving her alone in that box!" exclaimed Caleb, rushing heedlessly into the darkened shop and crashing into a bookshelf along the way. Recovering, he felt his way to the laboratory door, where he rattled the lock and shook the door in a helpless rage, until Jenk, following more cautiously, produced the key.

The door opened on a scene of destruction. Rather than leave Eirena totally in the dark, Caleb had left a burning oil lamp hanging from a beam in the ceiling. The oil was nearly gone, the flame growing dim, but it provided enough illumination for the two old men to see the broken flasks and vials scattered across the table, the overturned vats, the chaos of bent copper tubing, the sand and the water poured out upon the floor—and the staggering figure of a man wreaking havoc in all directions as he groped blindly about the laboratory, knocking over the equipment and clawing at his face in a panicked attempt to tear the stitches from his eyes.

Eirena's box lay open on the floor, and the tiny creature ran frantically around the room, in her efforts to avoid being stepped on. At the sight of Caleb, she flung herself at his leg, wailing and scratching, trying to climb up into the safety of his arms.

Caleb reached down and snatched her up, cradling her protectively against his chest, and headed out of the room as fast as he could go. Jenk was only a step behind him, slamming the door shut and throwing his body against it.

"Guess we done better than we thought," Caleb said, in a shaken voice. "But what—what do you reckon we ought to do now?"

"I believe the choice is clear," said Jenk. He tried to speak firmly but his voice wavered. "We must either calm him . . . and convince him to allow us to cut the stitches from his eyes . . . or else find a wooden stake and drive it through his heart!"

38.

Which the Reader may Choose to regard as the Calm before the Storm.

With typical generosity, the Duchess insisted that she, and she alone, should provide costumes for Elsie and Sera. "The Wichtelberg lumber rooms contain any number of chests and boxes filled with old gowns and cloaks and wigs. And there is a clever little seamstress down in Pfalz who shall come up and see to the alterations."

Accordingly, Sera and Elsie followed their hostess up a narrow, twisting flight to the attics. As Marella had promised, there were trunks and wardrobes and boxes all stuffed full of ancient clothing, most of it still in excellent condition. And besides that, there were the accessories: shoes with rhinestone buckles; kidskin gloves scented with civet and ambergis; amazing hats, hoods, and veils; and vials of gold and silver dust—"An invention of the dwarves, I believe," said the Duchess—to be worn on the hair instead of powder.

They found also a number of masks, some quite elaborate, others very plain. "We used to wear these black velvet masks whenever we ventured out of the house," said the Duchess. "Oh, yes, I assure you, it wasn't thought decent for a well-born woman to appear in public without her mask . . . though the gowns we wore were often rather daring, and our shoulders and bosoms were shockingly bare, however we covered our faces."

There was a lovely old gown of white brocade that seemed just right for Elsie. (*Of course*, thought Sera, *it would be white . . . it is always white for Elsie!*) "With the 'diamond' stomacher and the rhinestone buckles," said the Duchess, "and the spangled scarf, it will do very well for . . . I'm not yet certain, but something allegorical."

For Sera, she found an old court costume of midnight-blue velvet, with slashed sleeves, a jeweled bodice, and an underskirt

259

of heavy bronze-colored satin. (*And of course*, thought Sera, *it is something as dark and as heavy as sin for me!*) "Lady Nemesis, the daughter of Night," said the Duchess. "I know just what is needed to complete the effect."

They went down to the Duchess's bedchamber to try on the gowns, and the little seamstress came, too, to pin them into the dresses as needed, and make note of the necessary alterations. But the Duchess would not allow the girls to look into a mirror. "You must not see yourselves in these dresses before the night of the ball, and then you will receive a delightful surprise."

Elsie looked sweet and pretty in her white brocade. And in the sunlit bedchamber, Sera realized that her own deep blue velvet was not so dark and ugly as she had feared. But the gown was obviously one of the daring ones, with a low, square neckline that put Sera to the blush.

"It does rather *gape*," said the Duchess, "but that may be easily fixed. It is nothing to take a gown *in*."

"I think that it rather suits you," said Elsie.

"But naturally it suits her," the Duchess exclaimed, "Sera is a young woman with a great deal of presence, and she carries these darker colors very well. Another girl would only look insipid."

Then she laughed at Sera's expression of surprise. "Yes, I know . . . you wish to dress like the other young ladies, and that is perfectly natural. And it does not help that Clothilde's gowns lack even a particle of style. But really, Sera, pastel satins are not for you. This dress is absolutely ravishing."

This was a new thought—one that had never occurred to Sera before—that she might look anything but hideous in her made-over gowns. She looked from Elsie to the Duchess a little warily, wondering if they were teasing.

But Elsie smiled and shook her head, and said with some of the old warmth in her voice, "Dear Sera, I have tried to convince you of this before. You always look so dramatic in Mama's old gowns. Like a princess in disguise!"

It was the fortieth day of the season of gathering, and in the counting-house at Master Ule's it was the usual hustle and bustle of letters to be written and accounts to be rendered before the turn of the season.

"Mr. Braun," said a voice at Jedidiah's elbow. Jed looked up from his ledgers to find one of the journeyman glassblowers stand-

260

ing by his desk. "Mr. Braun . . . that lot of crystal flasks as the gentleman ordered from Vien . . . it don't look like we'll finish in time to ship them out. That last load of barilla, the salts was very poor."

"Aye, very well," sighed Jed. "A letter to the gentleman in Vien, begging his indulgence . . . and a stiff note to the merchant who sent the glasswort . . . I'll see to them both, first thing in the morning."

"Mr. Braun," said the boy who swept up the offices, "you're wanted in the warehouse."

Jed pushed back his chair, reached into his waistcoat pocket, and pulled out his watch. It still lacked an hour 'til four o'clock, he noted with relief . . . he might yet make it in time for tea at the bookshop with Uncle Caleb.

"My dear Jedidiah, I thought I had given you the afternoon off," said Master Ule, when Jed returned to his desk.

"Guess I haven't had time," said Jed. "I'll just tot up these figures and—"

"You will do nothing of the kind," said Master Ule. "You are a conscientious lad, but you are working much too hard. A pleasant visit with your granduncle is precisely what you need."

Jed nodded glumly. "Guess it won't be so pleasant as all that . . . Uncle Caleb hardly makes me feel welcome anymore. And him and Mr. Jenk, they're both so queer and . . . and skittish, I don't exactly know what to make of it."

"I do not wish to pry," said Master Ule. "Particularly knowing, as I do, that interference from this particular quarter might prove unwelcome . . . but Jedidiah, I hope you know that if you should ever require any *assistance* or advice, Mr. Owlfeather and myself are entirely at your service."

"Aye." Jed reached for his hat and jammed it on his head. "I know that well enough. But I reckon this is something I've got to handle on my own."

The bookshop was locked and shuttered, but Caleb came down to admit Jed, then locked and bolted the door again.

"Thought you wasn't coming," said Caleb, as he hobbled up the steps, lighting the way with the stub of a candle. "Mayhap that would of been best . . . I don't feel much like entertaining, and that's the solemn truth."

"*I'll* make the tea," said Jed. "I'll set the table. I'm not too proud, nor yet too grand. And I brought gingerbread and a pork

261

pie . . . You don't have to do anything but tell me how you've been.''

Caleb pushed open the door at the top of the steps. ''I been tired . . . not surprising, a man of my years.'' He limped over to a chair in the little sitting room and sat down heavily. ''But I do well enough . . . I do well enough. You ain't got no cause for concern.''

Jed looked around him. The room had recently been tidied . . . rather surprising with Sera out of town and Caleb looking so peaked. And Gottfried Jenk had never been fastidious; he was always too absorbed in his books and his musty old documents to pay any heed to mundane things like dust and dirty dishes. ''Where *is* Mr. Jenk? Seems he's generally out, these evenings when I come around.''

''He's took to his bed,'' said Caleb, shifting his eyes in an odd sort of way. ''No, you can't look in on him . . . he don't want no visitors . . . Likely he's sleeping, anyways.''

Jed filled the teakettle and hung it over the fire. Then he took a seat opposite his granduncle. ''Just how long has Gottfried Jenk been ill?''

Caleb shrugged. ''Must be five or six days now. I don't rightly remember. And don't you go for to tell me I ought to of sent for a doctor—there ain't no doctor yet come up with a cure for old age . . . and I reckon that's all that it is.''

''If it's the doctor's fee you're worried about . . . I guess I could help out,'' Jed offered.

Caleb reacted with surprising vehemence. ''High and mighty, high and mighty . . . You think you're such a swell—tell the old folks how to go on, and throw your money about! But we don't want no interference from you, old Gottfried Jenk and me, nor yet none of your charity!''

He glared at Jed resentfully. ''No, and there ain't no need for you to keep coming around, neither . . . with your fancy new clothes and your high-toned ways! You got new friends, a decent job . . . why should you bother with us at all?''

Jed heaved a sigh and slumped back in his chair. He had thought it might be something like this, the cause of Uncle Caleb's growing coldness. ''So that's it . . . you think I'm getting above myself. I could—I could quit my job,'' he said wearily. ''If that's the thing that's come between us.''

''Now, now,'' said Caleb, shaking his head, softening considerably. ''There ain't no call for you to talk like that. I'm pleased

262

to see how well you done for yourself. But—but the fact is, lad, your old Uncle Caleb, he's got no place in this new life of yours . . . You're a rising man, you're—''

Jed felt a hard lump forming in his throat. "If I've worked hard to raise myself," he said, "I always intended to raise you up with me. Do you think it was all done for my own gratification? You took care of me when I was small, and now it's my turn—nay, it's my pleasure and my privilege—to do for you."

"You can't raise me up," said Caleb. "Truth is . . . I'm much more likely to bring you down. Fact is, I ain't no credit to you."

"It's not a fact," said Jed stubbornly. "It's not anything at all like a fact." He pounded his fist on the arm of his chair. "I have no cause to be ashamed of you. You've some education, and you know how to go on in polite company . . . Weren't you once a footman in the house of a jarl?"

"I used to know how to go on . . . no more," said Caleb, tugging meditatively at his pigtail. "Used to be, I could talk near as good as you do now . . . but that were a long time ago. I been down too long . . . and it's the solemn truth: I just ain't got the strength to climb up again.

"But you . . ." The old man smiled at the recollection. "You was always the bright one. Yes, and you had all them good instincts, too: *the sensibilities of a gentleman,* that's what Gottfried Jenk once told me, and I never forget it, neither."

Caleb heaved a mighty sigh. "I know I was inclined to be rough on you . . ." he said. "Acted like I wasn't pleased when you read your books and learned your lessons . . . told you it weren't your place to be so particular about where the money come from or what we had to do to get it . . . wanted to toughen you up, reckoned it wouldn't do you no good to be so finicking, the life you was going to lead. But now it turns out . . . you had the right of it all along: you was fated to be a gentleman from the day you was born.

"If you're looking about for someone to raise up along of you," he added, "look to your ma and the girls."

Jed sat up a little straighter in his chair. "I don't forget my mother nor yet my sisters . . . I've sent them money, and I mean to do more. But it was always you and me, Uncle Caleb," he added wistfully, pleadingly. "The two of us always partners. That hasn't changed, and it never will."

Caleb's face had hardened again, and his voice, when he answered, was gruff. "It has changed . . . we ain't partners no more! And it's past time you learned to accept it."

Caleb escorted him down the stairs, muttering under his breath the whole while. If it hadn't been evident before, Jed thought, it was clear enough now: he was no longer welcome at the bookshop.

They stood by the door and Caleb was bringing out the key when somebody knocked.

"Do you intend to open it, or shall I?" asked Jed peevishly, when the old man made no move to do so.

With a fierce glare, Caleb unlocked the lock, shot the bolt, and opened the door. Matthias Vogel and Walther Bergen walked into the shop. "You're early," snapped Caleb. "You wasn't expected so soon."

And rather precipitously, he shoved poor Jed out through the door and slammed it behind him.

Jed did not *mean* to eavesdrop . . . it was just that he was so shaken by Caleb's treatment, he needed a moment to recover before proceeding down the street. He leaned up against the wall of the building, and that was how he happened to overhear Matthias speaking.

"Expect us long about two . . . maybe three in the morning. We can't come no sooner nor that."

Jed cocked his hat over his brow, thrust his hands into the pockets of his coat. There was something mysterious going on at the bookshop . . . he had known that for quite some time . . . but he was just now beginning to realize how seriously *bad* that something might be. He knew it was serious, if only by the measures Caleb was taking in order to conceal the truth.

"But I mean to find out, all the same," he muttered, as he walked down the street. "I've had just about enough of this asking questions and getting crooked answers. Guess it's time I started searching out some answers for myself!"

At one o'clock, the street outside the bookshop was deserted. At two, a rickety old cart came creaking up the hill, pulled by the two burly Watchmen.

Jedidiah stood watching from the shadows at the foot of a building on the other side of the lane. Matthias and Walther he had expected, but the presence of the cart came as a considerable surprise. He shifted his position silently, growing more puzzled and uneasy by the minute. The more so when the two constables

264

disappeared inside the bookshop and returned shortly thereafter with Uncle Caleb, carrying an ebonwood casket between them.

With great difficulty, because it was really too large and unwieldy for three men to handle, they managed to load the coffin onto the cart. Then they began the slow and cautious descent of the sloping street.

Keeping to the shadows as much as possible, Jedidiah followed them . . . all the way to the old boatmen's cemetery on Fishwife Hill. He crouched outside the graveyard, peered over the low stone wall, watching as Caleb and the two constables, working by lanthorn light, dug a shallow grave and lowered the casket into the hole. But when they picked up their shovels again and began to throw clods of dirt back in over the coffin, Jed decided he had seen enough.

He walked slowly home through the dark streets of the town, turning the matter over in his mind. How ever he looked at the facts, they just made no sense: After all these seasons, after all this time, to bury the coffin from the river—and so secretive, too!—when it had never contained anything but a big wax doll in fancy dress and a parcel of old books . . .

And then Jed had a thought that was not pleasant at all. He stopped under a street lamp and caught his breath. Oh, yes, he knew well enough what the coffin had contained five seasons past . . . but he had no way of knowing what it was that Uncle Caleb and the constables had buried tonight.

"D-------n!" he said aloud. He knew now that he needed advice, the advice of men he respected and trusted. "Time to do what I should have done a long time since, if I hadn't been so willing to believe Uncle Caleb, and turn my back on those wise good men: tell Master Ule and Mr. Owlfeather everything I know, and see what the Glassmakers Guild can make of it all."

39.

In which Few things are Quite what they Seem.

When the day of the masked ball finally arrived, the Wichtelberg became a hive of activity. The Duchess was everywhere: in the kitchens supervising the cooks . . . in the ballroom overseeing the maids and the footmen who hung the decorations . . . making certain there were lanthorns and torches to light her guests' progress up the stairs and the terraces. She insisted that Sera and Elsie take their morning stroll as usual, then sent them upstairs in the afternoon with instructions to nap if they could. "You will want to be fresh for the festivities tonight."

Elsie was far too excited to rest, so the Duchess sent up a sleeping draught. Sera watched her drink it down, tucked her cousin into bed, and then went up to her own room to read a book until evening.

At sunset, the maid brought in Sera's gown. Sera eyed it warily. "It looks rather small . . . I hope there was no mistake in the measurements." But the Duchess had sent her an odd sort of corset known as a busk, evidently contemporary with the gown.

With the corset on and tightly laced, Sera could scarcely breath, but at least it was possible for the maid to hook up the back of the velvet bodice.

The Duchess came in to personally supervise the dressing of Sera's hair: in long loose ringlets without too much height at the top. Marella was already in costume, in another old-fashioned gown, crimson velvet worked with tiny seed pearls, and a wide cartwheel ruff. Her hair was powdered and she wore a tiny diamond-shaped black patch at the corner of her mouth.

"I will *not* be painted!" Sera exclaimed, as the maid produced a haresfoot and a pot of rouge. And she steadfastly refused the patch box, for all of the Duchess's attempts to persuade her.

A standing collar of stiffened white lace attached to the bodice

266

at the shoulders, and the Duchess provided a pair of high-heeled satin slippers with jeweled buckles. As a final touch the maid sprinkled gold dust on Sera's hair. Finally, she was allowed to examine her reflection in a mirror.

Sera frowned at her own image, not at all certain that she liked what she saw. The gown was certainly beautiful, but she felt awkward in such finery, particularly in the high-heeled slippers, which made her feel a giantess. And the neckline no longer gaped, but it was still exceedingly low, revealing more white bosom than she cared to expose.

"Nonsense," said the Duchess, when Sera said as much. "You look perfectly delightful. Besides, there is a mask, and no one will recognize you."

The mask in question was a midnight velvet vizard mounted on a stick—it offered little or nothing in the way of disguise. But there was no time now to further alter the gown.

"I daresay Lord Vodni will much approve," the Duchess added archly.

Sera felt herself blushing. It was true that the Baron had been very attentive . . . so very attentive of late that the thought had actually sometimes occurred: he might have serious intentions. *But of course I know better*, thought Sera. *Vodni is as poor as I am. He must marry a woman with money, or else marry no one at all.*

The Duchess steered her out of the bedchamber and toward the stairs. "It is really time that we went down. Already, I can hear the carriages arriving."

"But I ought first to see if Elsie has need—" Sera began. But the Duchess interrupted her.

"Elsie had a lovely nap and awoke refreshed. She dressed an hour ago and went downstairs. No doubt she is waiting for you in the ballroom."

The ballroom was a vast echoing chamber with a marble floor and tapestried walls. Instead of chandeliers, there were great standing candelabra of wrought iron, in which the servants had arranged enormous candles the size of lamp posts. By the time that Sera wobbled in on her ridiculously high heels, several guests had already arrived, but Elsie was nowhere to be seen . . . nor anyone who might possibly be mistaken for Elsie in her gown of white brocade.

The first person Sera met was a youthful cavalier with brown lovelocks, who bowed very low, soliciting her hand for the first minuet.

The voice was familiar, and Sera immediately recognized the young man behind the grey velvet half-mask. "Lord Vizbeck," she said, "you are very kind. But I make it a practice never to dance at these large gatherings. And what of Lady Ursula? Surely you ought to stand up with *her* at the beginning of the ball?"

Lord Vizbeck gestured toward the far end of the ballroom, and a lady in flowing Eastern garb. "Lady Ursula is feeling rather independent tonight, I fear. She says I am not to suppose, simply because we are soon to marry, that she will spend the entire evening dancing with me."

It was true that Lady Ursula's temper had been somewhat uncertain of late, perhaps due to an unresolved quarrel between herself and the Duchess, after Lady Ursula caught one of the Duke's servants searching through her drawers and promptly labeled the girl a thief.

Though Sera refused to make a fool of herself by attempting to dance in her heavy velvet gown and ridiculous slippers, she relented just a little. "Lord Vizbeck . . . if you would be so kind as to procure me a glass of ratafia, and perhaps sit and talk while the others dance . . . ?" Lord Vizbeck bowed and hastened off in search of refreshments, and Sera sat down in a little alcove to await his return.

She sat out the dance with Lord Vizbeck, and another with another gentleman. The ballroom was very crowded by now, but nowhere in the throng could Sera spot Elsie.

When the second gentleman had tired of begging her to dance—and beat a welcome retreat—Sera rose also. She wove a path through the masked and dominoed revelers, the gigantic candelabra, and the huge dripping tapers, searching for her cousin.

She did not find Elsie, but she did meet Hermes Budge—immediately recognizable on account of his height, for all that his face was masked and his hair powdered. The tutor looked unusually elegant in a coat of sapphire velvet trimmed with silver braid.

"Mr. Budge, have you seen Elsie? I have looked and I have looked but I cannot find her."

"I believe I have not," said the tutor, with a low bow. "But of course it is difficult to be certain. But here comes Lord Vodni . . . Perhaps he may be able to enlighten you."

Lord Vodni, also, looked particularly well, in a scarlet coat of

268

military cut, with the inevitable lock of dark hair falling carelessly across his brow. Like Sera, he carried his mask in his hand.

"You are very kind, sir," said Sera, when Vodni kissed her fingers and requested the next country dance. "But I cannot find Elsie. I am very much afraid that she has taken ill and has gone back upstairs to rest."

"Then I am pleased to reassure you," said Vodni. "I saw your cousin but a few minutes since, on the arm of Jarl Skogsrå. I believe I heard something about the grotto . . . The Duchess has arranged for colored lanthorns, and also for musicians, as an entertainment for those who wish to escape the heat of the ballroom.

"If you wish to go down there in search of Miss Elsie," he added, with a bow and a flourish, "perhaps you will permit me to escort you?"

Sera was pleased to accept this offer, as well as the support of his arm. "You look enchanting, Miss Vorder," said the Baron, as they moved through the crowd. He spoke with undisguised admiration. Perhaps after all, thought Sera, the gown was not so dreadful.

But in the corridor outside, they passed a slight, pale gentleman rather flamboyantly costumed as a pirate, who stared at Sera in such a way that she felt herself blushing once more.

"Impertinent fellow!" commented Vodni.

"Yes indeed," said Sera. "He is perfectly odious."

A torch-lit stone staircase led from the cellars down to the grotto. Even before they reached the foot of the steps, Sera knew that Vodni had been mistaken. Though the colored lanthorns were there as promised, shining gaily on the water and on the little gilded cockleshell boats moored by the side of the lake, the great cavern was silent and empty.

"It would appear," said the Baron, "that the musicians have not yet arrived."

"Nor have Elsie and the Jarl," said Sera, peering into the darkness, taking careful note of the number of boats.

"It is possible," replied Vodni, "that they are in the tunnel, following the stream out to the gardens. Shall we walk in that direction and listen for their voices?"

"Yes," Sera decided, after a moment of thought. "I suppose that we should. I think it very odd that Elsie should disappear in this fashion, and in company with the Jarl, too. My dear sir, you do not suppose that she is in any . . . danger?"

269

Vodni's hand tightened reassuringly on hers. "If he dares to harm her, he will have me to deal with!"

They skirted the underground lake, along the paved rim, until they came to the tunnel, where they stood looking and listening for several minutes. Exotic fish lived in the waters of the grotto, bulb-eyed, flashing silver and gold in the cold and the dark. "The tunnel echoes so," said Sera. "If Elsie and the Jarl were there, I am persuaded we should hear their footsteps, if not their voices."

"If they have not already arrived at the gardens," said Vodni.

Sera shook her head, gave an impatient twitch to the midnight-blue folds of her skirt. "It is not a warm night . . . they would hardly be so foolish as to go for a walk in the gardens. Please take me back upstairs to the ballroom, Lord Vodni. Undoubtedly, we shall find Elsie there."

As they proceeded in the direction of the stone staircase, the earth began to rumble and shake. Sera clutched the Baron by the arm. "You must not worry," he said soothingly. "These tremors are common here . . . We are quite accustomed to them, when the moon is full."

Sera was ashamed of herself, for being so weak-spirited. "As we are also accustomed to them in Thornburg," she said, as steadily as she could. "But never so strong as this."

The rumbling gradually died away, and the Baron smiled brightly. "You see . . . it is nothing. We may yet feel a stronger one, but you need have no fear . . . the Wichtelberg was built to withstand these shakes. When we go upstairs you will see that no one regards the earthquake . . . It is the merest commonplace."

Sera tried to return his smile. *It is only that I am already in such a pother over Elsie* . . . But as they continued on toward the steps, the earth began to shake once more, flinging her forcibly into the Baron's arms.

"I *beg* your pardon," said Sera, when the ground grew quiet again, and she disentangled herself from Vodni's embrace.

"But no . . ." said the Baron, pressing her hand, growing very excited and very foreign. "I believe that this is fated. I have longed to speak, but never until now did I have the courage. Yet here are we alone, and you so recently in my arms . . . I am encouraged to ask you to be my wife."

He was so very handsome and so very much in earnest; Sera felt her heart begin to flutter. *He is an agreeable man. I like him very much . . . This may well be the only offer that I ever receive.*

Yet try as she might to answer him "yes," the word simply

270

refused to come. "You are much too kind, Lord Vodni," she finally managed to say in a stifled voice. "But I find . . . I find that I cannot accept your very obliging offer."

The Baron was thunderstruck. It had evidently not occurred to him that her affections might already be engaged. "Cannot, Miss Vorder? But what does this mean? Is it possible that you have formed another attachment?"

"No," said Sera, recovering her voice. "There is no one else. At least . . . no, there is no one else. I do beg your pardon," she added miserably, "I believe that I may be guilty of . . . of encouraging your attentions. But I never thought that you had any serious intentions, and I am exceedingly sorry if anything I have said or done has caused you unnecessary pain."

In the dim light of the colored lanthorns, Vodni had gone quite pale. "But I shall not take no for an answer," he said. And without any more warning than that, he swept her back into his arms and began to kiss her.

This was a new experience for Sera, and not altogether an unpleasant one. She found that she rather enjoyed being kissed by Lord Vodni . . . until his grip on her waist began to tighten, and his kisses became so unbearably rough. "Lord Vodni," she gasped, averting her face. "I demand that you release me at once!"

"I will not," said Vodni, against her ear. "You are toying with my affections, Sera. You have aroused my passions and now you are going to have to satisfy them!"

Sera was forced to acknowledge a certain justice in his complaint—but for all that, she was not going to stand there and allow him to maul her any further. Particularly as he was now kissing her neck in a manner that she found terribly disagreeable, and he had become quite appallingly free with his hands. She stepped on his foot, grinding in the pointed heel of her jeweled slipper just as hard as she could.

With an angry cry, he relaxed his hold, and Sera was able to squirm out of his grip. By now, they were both breathless and trembling with outrage. "I beg your pardon," she said, struggling to maintain her dignity, "but I really cannot permit—"

When Vodni reached out to embrace her again, Sera put her hands on his chest and pushed with all of her strength. The Baron took a step backward and tumbled into the underground lake.

He landed in the water with a loud splash, soaking Sera in the process. He disappeared for a moment below the surface. Then he bobbed up again, made a grab at the pavement along the edge, and pulled himself up.

Sera had not intended so ignominious a fate for him—had not even known they stood so near the edge—but she determined at once to improve on the circumstances.

"Lord Vodni," Sera said sternly, as he sat dripping and bedraggled at her feet. "I do hope that this will be a lesson to you!"

Vodni curled his lips in a snarl of pure rage. And then he did something strange and terrible. He reached into his sleeve, under the wide ruffle of lace, gave an odd little tug, and began stripping the *skin* off of his hand. As Sera watched in horror, he peeled off the glove of flesh, uncovering a scaly birdlike claw.

Good heavens above . . . Lord Vodni is a troll! Sera had less than a moment to absorb this amazing fact, before Vodni reached out with that horrible taloned claw and made a furious swipe at the velvet skirt.

Sera turned and ran toward the stairs. A moment later, she heard the troll's footsteps hitting the paved walkway behind her. Fear lent speed to her flight, but Vodni's legs were longer, the high-heeled slippers hampered her, and she soon lost her initial advantage. Sera was half way up the staircase, and Vodni only a dozen feet behind her, when the earth rocked, and she fell to her hands and knees on the stone steps.

Entangled in her heavy velvet skirts, there was no time for her to regain her footing. Sera sat back on the stairs, just as the troll caught up with her. Managing to get her feet free of the skirts, she aimed a well-placed kick, knocking one of Vodni's legs out from under him. With a startled cry, he lost his balance, tumbled backward, and rolled down the stairs all the way to the bottom.

Vodni lay very still for a moment, and Sera sat on the steps, too bruised and breathless to move, certain that she had killed him. Then the troll raised his head and sat up.

Sera rose painfully and turned to run up the stairs. But then she heard something . . . a gentle voice down below, warning Lord Vodni not to follow her. Sera knew that voice. She hesitated, took a step upward, stopped . . . She turned and stared down at the foot of the stairs. The troll stood facing a slight young man dressed like a pirate, who was flourishing an unconvincing gilt-edged cutlass, seemingly a part of his costume.

"If you attempt to pursue the lady," said Francis Skelbrooke, as he reached up and removed his mask, "I shall be obliged to kill you."

Vodni only sneered at him. "Am I to be frightened by that toy?" Apparently considering the man as negligible as his weapon, the troll turned and started up the stairs.

He had climbed no further than the second step when Skelbrooke reached into his sash, pulled out a large pistol, and shot him in the back at point-blank range.

The ball came out through Vodni's chest, spattering the stone staircase with his blood. The troll cried out, dropped to his knees, and crumbled to the steps. A dark stain spread rapidly across the back of his scarlet coat.

Sera sat down again, rather suddenly. *I will not swoon . . . I never swoon!* But nevertheless, the world went dark just for a moment. Only a few minutes past, she had been firmly convinced that Vodni was the best and most amiable of men, and she had hardly been granted the leisure to adjust her attitude before witnessing his violent demise.

She sat there numbly and watched as Lord Skelbrooke stooped to examine the body. Then he stood up, opened one of the powder horns he wore as part of his costume, and calmly proceeded to reload his pistol.

"I must learn to curb these impulses and correct the habit of firing at close range," said Skelbrooke. "This shattering of flesh and bone is so very far from pleasing."

He slipped the reloaded pistol back into his sash and climbed the stairs. Sera tried to think what she ought to say, but her mind still moved slowly.

"I—I believe that I ought to thank you, sir, for saving my life," she managed to say.

"Not at all," replied Skelbrooke, sitting down beside her. "You seemed, if I may say so, to be handling the situation quite capably. Indeed, I almost hated to interfere. Had you been matched against any ordinary man, I would have been pleased to stand back and watch . . . but trolls being trolls, I chose to err on the side of caution."

He was gazing at her in such a way that Sera—who was already rather flushed—began to feel warm all over. "How very beautiful you do look tonight," he said. And lifting her chin, he kissed her gently but firmly on the mouth. The kiss lasted a long time.

"L-Lord Skelbrooke," she said, when he finally drew away. "Whatever are you *doing* here?"

"I should think that the answer to that was rather obvious," said Skelbrooke, sliding an arm around her waist. "I am kissing you, Miss Vorder."

"Lord Skelbrooke," she said, more firmly this time. "I mean to say . . . why are you here at the Wichtelberg . . . here in this grotto?"

"I came to stop Elsie from marrying Lord Skogsrå," said Skelbrooke. "He is a troll and a cannibal and—I am perfectly persuaded—wishes to drink her blood."

"Yes," said Sera. If Vodni was a troll, why should Skogsrå not be one as well? And it was then that she remembered what first brought her down to the grotto. "I fear that there is something terrible about to happen tonight," she exclaimed, surging to her feet. "I can't find Elsie or Jarl Skogsrå."

"We will each take a different direction and look for them," said Skelbrooke, offering her his hand. "Do not speak to the Duchess, for she is not to be trusted. But if you should encounter Mr. Budge, by all means enlist his aid."

So it appeared, after all, that the two men were acquainted. This was certainly a night for surprises, but Sera was too tired to ask any more questions. Hand in hand they climbed the staircase, until they reached the top and went their separate ways.

40.

Wherein all Masks are finally Discarded.

Sera searched frantically, through corridors and galleries, libraries, salons, and dining rooms. She went back to the ballroom and looked there once more. She could not find Elsie, she could not find Skogsrå, and she could not find the Duchess.

They have all disappeared . . . it is very ominous. Two trolls . . . they were both of them trolls . . . How could they both be trolls and the Duchess not know of it? thought Sera. *Lord Skelbrooke is right, she is not to be trusted. She only pretended to be so kind . . .*

Sera searched the entire first floor without success. The Wich-

telberg was so vast . . . she knew only a small part of it—and
supposing that Elsie was not even there . . . supposing the Jarl,
with the Duchess's connivance, had spirited Elsie away?

*And sooner or later, someone will go down to the grotto and
find Lord Vodni . . . and what an uproar there will be then!*

She was running up a long marble staircase to the second floor
when she met Lady Ursula and Lord Vizbeck coming down.
"Lady Ursula . . . have you seen my cousin Elsie?"

Lady Ursula and her companion exchanged a glance. "But yes
. . . only a few minutes past," said Lady Ursula. "And very sweet
she looked, in her gown and her veil, rather like a bride on the
way to her wedding."

Sera gave a little gasp of surprise. "You—you saw her, Lady
Ursula, Lord Vizbeck—where?"

The lady made a vague gesture upward. "I must say it was
very mysterious and rather secretive . . . the way Lord Skogsrå
took her by the hand and whisked her away . . . almost as though—
but you want to know *where.*" She turned a puzzled frown on
Lord Vizbeck. "Do you know, I don't quite remember . . ."

"They were going into the little salon . . . what is it called? The
Clock Room," Lord Vizbeck supplied.

Sera rushed past them, the midnight-blue velvet skirt trailing
behind her. She reached the top of the stairs, before she thought
to turn back and call down. "Lady Ursula, Lord Vizbeck, it is
very important. If you encounter Lord Skelbrooke or Mr. Budge,
please tell them where they may find me. If something is not done
to stop Elsie from marrying Lord Skogsrå tonight, the results will
be tragic."

Without waiting for an answer, she turned and hurried toward
the Clock Room. But when she came to the door, she paused in
the corridor, under one of the old oil portraits, to catch her breath
and collect her wits. *Yet what if Elsie refuses to listen to me? Oh,
but she will . . . she must . . . as soon as she sees that I am in
earnest.* And with that thought, Sera threw open the door and ran
into the room.

A candle-light wedding was in progress, among the ticking clocks
and the wagging pendulums. Mr. Ulfson, the clergyman from
Pfalz presided, with his book already open and his hands up-raised
for the first blessing.

When Sera burst into the room, everyone turned to look: the
Duchess in her scarlet gown . . . Lord Skogsrå, all satin and lace

275

and fringes . . . the old Duke with his silver-headed cane. . . . Mr. Ulfson with his hands in the air . . . everyone turned to look but the bride. Elsie stood perfectly still, in her gown of white brocade, her spangled veil, and her wreath of pansies and lilies—Elsie stood like a statue or a figure made of wax, gazing steadfastly up at the clergyman.

"This wedding," said Sera, "must not take place."

The Duchess stepped forward and addressed her calmly. "But of course dear Elsie shall marry the Jarl. Why should she not?"

"Because . . ." Sera did not know how she could possibly tell the good old Duke and the innocent parson this terrible, incredible thing.

"Because . . . she is not of age. Elsie cannot marry because she is still too young, and her parents have not consented."

The Duchess laughed her tinkling little laugh. "Consent? But of course they have consented. I have the letter right here . . . signed by Benjamin and Clothilde Vorder. Mr. Ulfson has already examined it, but if you wish to look as well . . ." And the Duchess displayed the letter for Sera to see.

Sera pushed it aside. "It is . . . it must be a forgery," she said, though without much conviction. The Duchess only laughed, as though she must be joking, and the clergyman looked at her askance.

And all of this time, the clocks went on ticking, the pendulums wagging, the gears and the wheels whirling, and Elsie continued to stand like one in a dream or a trance.

"This wedding cannot take place," said Sera, searching her mind for a suitable objection, "because the bride—is sleep-walking."

"Dear heart," said the bridegroom, taking Elsie by the hand, "you must say a few words to our good Mr. Ulfson, to His Excellency the Duke, lest they feel any cause for concern. There is nothing wrong with you . . . you are feeling very well . . . what could possibly ail you?"

"There is nothing wrong with me . . . I feel very well . . . what could possibly ail me?" came the dutiful little echo.

Mr. Ulfson looked down at his book, preparing to read the service, and Sera was reduced, in her desperation, to blurting out the truth, as wild as it might sound. "This wedding cannot take place . . . because the bridegroom is a troll!"

Perhaps Sera was as surprised as anyone when the clergyman closed his book. He turned to Lord Skogsrå with an apologetic

276

smile. "You are not to suppose, sir, that I accuse you of anything, that I give any credence to this wild accusation. But it happens that I am privy to information . . . deathbed ramblings . . . a hastily gabbled prayer . . . strange things have been happening, strange things, indeed, though I do not seriously believe they have anything to do with you. Nevertheless, in all conscience, before I can perform this service . . . I must ask to examine your hands."

"But it is not his hand," said Sera, feeling rather foolish. "You must ask him to remove his boots. He always wears boots and walks with a limp, because . . . because he has a great hoof exactly like a horse, in place of one of his feet!"

Except for the ticking clocks, the room was utterly silent. Then: "A hoof like a horse?" Mr. Ulfson repeated. "My dear young woman . . . that sounds rather bizarre."

"Bizarre," said the Jarl, growing indignant. "It is very much worse than bizarre. It is infamous . . . shocking . . . that this young woman should come here to mock my infirmity before my bride . . . scandalize you all with this vicious fiction.

"Moreover," he added, with heavy scorn, though it could be seen that his hand trembled on Elsie's arm, and drops of perspiration appeared on his brow. "I will not remove my boots or suffer this indignity, all to indulge an hysterical girl."

How Mr. Ulfson might have answered, Sera was not to learn. For it was then that Francis Skelbrooke appeared on the threshold.

There was a moment of silence, then Lord Skogsrå pulled out a small pistol and pointed it at the parson. "These interruptions are growing tiresome. We will continue with the wedding, if you please."

"I think not," said Skelbrooke, stepping away from the door, so that Mr. Budge could come in after him. Mr. Budge was armed with a brace of enormous pistols, and he wore a handkerchief over the lower part of his face, rather as though he were a highwayman holding up a coach.

"At best . . . you have achieved a stalemate," said the Duchess, still all sweetness and reason, despite this dramatic turn of events. "And the Jarl . . . he is not quite himself. So near to achieving his desire, to assuaging his hunger, he might do any foolish thing. Do not tempt him, Francis . . . do not tempt him, Hermes. For the sake of this poor Mr. Ulfson."

For answer, Lord Skelbrooke opened his hand—it contained nothing more dangerous than a tiny box like a snuffbox, inlaid

277

with pearls and ivory. He flicked open the lid with a motion of his thumb.

As Skelbrooke blew the Sleep Dust into the air, one by one, they began to fall: the Duchess . . . Elsie . . . Lord Skogsrå . . . the Duke. With a faint smile on his face, Skelbrooke crossed the room. The last thing that Sera remembered, before she lost consciousness, was his lordship's supporting arm.

Sera woke slowly, breathing a pungent but not unpleasant fragrance. Gradually, she became aware of her surroundings. She sat in an upright chair, beside a fire, in a place she did not know. Hermes Budge was leaning solicitously over her, waving a stem of burning herbs under her nose.

Sera sneezed and looked around her. The chair was a wooden armchair, the room appeared to be a rustic but cozy parlor, with a display of pewter plates arranged on the mantelpiece and some faded landscapes pinned up against the flowered wallpaper. On an oak settle built against one wall, Elsie lay with her head on a cushion, while Lord Skelbrooke and a strange young woman with corn-colored hair bent over her, burning herbs and patting her hands, in an apparent effort to revive her.

"What—what is this place?" asked Sera. She was still wearing the blue velvet gown—which was quite absurd in this rustic setting—but someone had thoughtfully thrown a grey wool shawl over her shoulders. "And how did we come here?"

Lord Skelbrooke answered, leaving Elsie's side and coming to kneel at Sera's feet. There were purple shadows under his eyes and a white shade around his mouth; Sera thought he looked ill and exhausted. "You are at the farm of a friend of mine, about three miles out of Lüftmal. You came here in a wagon."

"Oh," said Sera, on a sigh. It was still very difficult for her to keep her eyes open. "Elsie . . . is Elsie—?"

"We are having some difficulty reviving your cousin . . . the effect of the Sleep Dust combined with whatever drug the Duchess and Skogsrå used to render her more suggestible . . . but I have taken her pulse and listened to her breathing and I am convinced she will awake eventually, none the worse for inhaling the Dust. I shall try to remain here until she does."

Sera sat up a little straighter. "Stay here until . . . are you leaving us, sir?"

He shifted position, sitting back on his heels. "I must leave before daybreak (which is fast approaching) and contact certain friends of mine, as well as arrange a false trail for the Duchess and Jarl Skogsrå to follow. As soon as Elsie is well enough to travel—probably this evening—Mr. Budge will escort you both to Thornburg."

Sera put a hand to her head; she felt so dull and stupid. She looked up at the tutor, trying to remember: "Mr. Budge . . . I do not recall that you ever told me that you and Lord Skelbrooke were acquainted."

Mr. Budge looked troubled. "Yes . . . I fear I was not as open with you as I might have been, but I was not certain to what degree you and Francis were in each other's confidence. And at any rate, I continually expected that we would both receive word from him soon."

"I intended to come and speak with you both personally, rather than send a letter," said Skelbrooke. "I should have arrived some weeks sooner, but I was—most unfortunately, and quite against my will—required to take a sea voyage. It is likely that I would be in Ynde now, had the Captain of the ship not been killed, and the First Mate (at one time a man of some consequence in Ingledorf, but fallen on hard times), finding himself in possession of a ship, and therefore with an opportunity to mend his fortunes, decided to turn honest. He began by freeing me, and two other passengers who were also on board against their will."

Mr. Kassien had also, in a burst of gratitude, and under the impression that his new ship's chirurgeon had not only saved his ship but his leg, offered to divide the cache of Sleep Dust. But of this—and of his own addiction to the powder—Skelbrooke chose to say nothing.

"The new Captain was in no hurry to return to Marstadtt," Skelbrooke continued, "but I was able to earn my passage north by securing a position (on the strength of Captain Kassien's recommendation) as ship's doctor on another vessel. I stopped briefly in Thornburg to consult my friends—and to discover if you and your cousin had returned from Zar-Wildungen—and then came on here as swiftly as I could."

He looked so pale and haggard, Sera thought that he must have made that last journey without stopping to rest along the way. "I should thank you, sir, for—"

"You may thank me later—but for now there is still a great deal for me to tell you, and the time is growing short," said Skelbrooke. "When you reach Thornburg, Mr. Budge will escort you to the home of his employer, Mr. Owlfeather. Mr. Owlfeather

279

is a highly respectable dwarf, and a friend, moreover, of your friend Jedidiah Braun. You may trust him implicitly. You must not, by any means, go home—we have reason to believe that things are seriously amiss there. Mr. Owlfeather will arrange for you and your cousin to go into hiding. You must do exactly as he says, Sera, for the Duchess must return to Thornburg eventually, no matter how long and merry a chase I lead her. And if she finds the two of you there . . . She does not take kindly to having her schemes thwarted, and I believe that she will be absolutely merciless. Moreover, she is a powerful woman, and I fear that not even Mr. Owlfeather could protect you.''

"I understand,'' said Sera. She wrapped the soft wool shawl around her and tried to stand up.

But Lord Skelbrooke pushed her gently back into the chair. "Do not try to walk yet.''

"But I must see Elsie,'' said Sera. "Really, Lord Skelbrooke, I must insist—''

"As I, also, must insist,'' said his lordship. "You can see from here that Elsie's color is beginning to return. I believe she will shortly awake.'' He spoke to the young woman with the yellow hair. "Tilda, perhaps you could prepare a little nourishment for these ladies . . . some broth if you have it.''

"Aye, Mr. Carstares, sir. And perhaps some toasted bread, as well?''

"Yes, toast would serve admirably,'' said Lord Skelbrooke.

"Mr. Budge,'' said Sera, making an effort to collect her thoughts. "I am exceedingly puzzled. Lord Vodni . . . it is still so very hard to believe it . . . Lord Vodni was a troll! Do you remember a conversation we had on—on the subject of intuition? But it seems that our intuitive faculties were very much at fault. We both knew that there was something very bad, very wrong about Jarl Skogsrå, but Nicolai Vodni had us both completely fooled.''

"Yes,'' said the tutor. "I have given that matter some thought in the last few hours, and I believe I can offer some explanation. The Jarl was a creature of appetite, entirely obsessed with his impulses. Whereas Lord Vodni . . . I would not venture to say that he was not so *hungry* as Skogsrå, but merely that his hunger did not occupy him so completely. He had so many other interests . . . his books, and his horses . . . his fascination with the old house . . . and I believe a genuine attachment to the Duke. All these served to mask his true nature as effectively as the glove he wore concealed his deformity."

"If that is so," Sera said, a trifle severely, "then I do not think very much of this intuition . . . it is so very unreliable."

The parlor door opened, and a large young man with a shock of red hair came into the room. "Horses are ready, Dr. Crow, as soon as you've a mind to go."

"Yes, I thank you, Ezekiel," said Lord Skelbrooke. "Sera, the time is short, and I still have a number of things to say to you." He leaned a little closer; his manner became urgent. "I daresay you will not care for my speaking out before all of these people, and the more so because you have already received one proposal tonight already—but it may be a long, long time before we meet again." He took one of her hands in both of his, grown suddenly, desperately earnest. "Sera . . . I want you to be my wife. Will you consent to marry me?"

Sera found that she could not breathe, much less speak, she was so very surprised. And this was scarcely the time or the place . . . Everyone in the room seemed to be looking at her, waiting for her to reply.

"Lord Skelbrooke—if that is *indeed* who you are," she said crossly, "how can I possibly consent to marry you when—when I scarcely know you. It is true that we have been acquainted for some time, but really, you are so odd and changeable that I hardly know what to make of you. Why, I am not even certain of your name!"

Lord Skelbrooke released her hand. If he had been pale before, he was several shades whiter now. "Mr. Budge can confirm that the name is my own . . . as well as furnish you with abundant details concerning my character and the early years of my life. The recital, however, is likely to be long and not particularly edifying." He rose heavily to his feet. "I confess, I had hoped you would take me on faith. But perhaps, after all, that was too much to ask." He started moving toward the door.

"Lord Skelbrooke . . ." said Sera.

He paused with his hand on the door, turned back to gaze at her with a look of weary resignation. "Yes, Miss Vorder?"

Sera shook her head. "I don't . . . I beg your pardon, it was nothing, really. I only meant to say, sir, that I hoped we might speak of this again."

The ghost of a smile came into his eyes as he crossed the room and knelt by her side once more. "We shall, Miss Vorder, you may be certain of that. I do not know whether it will be soon or late, but discuss it we shall.'' He lifted her hand, brushed it softly with his lips. ''Until then, I shall have to possess myself in patience.''

41.

In which Sera's Homecoming is not what she Expects.

At Mittleheim, Hermes Budge and the young ladies boarded a pleasure barge moving down the Lunn to Thornburg. Sera and Elsie had abandoned their ball gowns for something a bit more functional: dresses of flowered chintz, provided by Tilda, and wide brimmed hats of chip straw. Mr. Budge had also changed out of his finery; yet he appeared as sober and gentlemanly as ever, in Ezekiel Karl's Sunday suit. They spent a long quiet day on the river, then part of another, and reached their destination the following afternoon.

While Mr. Budge was occupied trying to procure sedan chairs, Sera took Elsie by the hand, and the two girls, moving swiftly along the docks, disappeared into a crowd of bustling humanity.

''But Sera,'' Elsie protested, as they left the river behind and proceeded down a narrow lane. ''I don't understand. I thought that we could *trust* Mr. Budge.''

''It is not that I do not trust Mr. Budge . . . or his friends, either,'' said Sera. ''But I have misplaced my confidence so many times already. I no longer feel as though I can trust my own judgement. And really . . . we don't know anything about these people; this Mr. Owlfeather or any of the others. Lord Skelbrooke *said* they were friends of Jedidiah, but what to make of Lord Skelbrooke, himself, I really do not know!''

''Except,'' said Elsie, who was panting by now. ''Except that you are madly in love with him.''

''Madness certainly has something to do with it,'' Sera agreed, as they dove down another twisting lane.

Two seasons had turned since Sera and Elsie last strolled the streets of Thornburg. The peddlers were still there, hawking roasted apples, strings of hazelnuts, and lanthorns made out of dried gourds. The country girls were selling caged field mice for pets and blackbirds for pies.

"But Sera," said Elsie. "If Francis Skelbrooke were not our friend . . . if he hadn't our best interests at heart . . . why should he have come to rescue me from Lord Skogsrå . . . or warned us about the Duchess . . . or made arrangements to keep us safe?"

"I don't know," said Sera. "But Lord Vodni also warned me against Jarl Skogsrå—and for that I was willing to give him my confidence. I trusted Vodni . . . we both trusted the Duchess . . . and *you* were actually falling in love with Skogsrå!"

They paused for a moment, by a lamp post, to catch their breath. "No," said Elsie, "I don't believe that I was. But I felt safe with him, and I thought he would always take care of me. And I thought, if I couldn't marry . . . Well, if I couldn't marry someone that I loved, Lord Skogsrå would do as well as anyone.

"But you cannot imagine what it was like at the end," she added, with a shudder, "standing there so helplessly, doing everything he told me to do, hearing myself speak exactly as he instructed me . . . and all the while some part of me knew that something was very, very wrong."

"It must have been dreadful," said Sera, as they set out again. "And of course we have no way of knowing how much of a hold the Duchess has on Cousin Clothilde or Cousin Benjamin—even if we *could* trust them, I must suppose we would only succeed in drawing the Duchess's wrath down on them as well . . . so we must not go home. Lord Skelbrooke said that we must not, and on that point, at least, I am willing to trust him."

"You don't think . . . you don't think he might have been warning you not to go back to your grandfather's?" Elsie asked.

"My dear . . . neither you nor I live with my grandfather. And Lord Skelbrooke has never *been* to the bookshop. I don't even know that he knows where it is. And we cannot go away without speaking to *anyone*.

"If there is anyone in all this whom I know we can trust . . ." she added, "that someone is Jedidiah. If the Glassmakers *are* his friends, and Jed is in their confidence . . . he will know in an instant where we have gone, and he will come there to find us."

They arrived at the bookshop half an hour later, only to discover that the shop was closed. Sera surveyed, with considerable sur-

prise, the shuttered windows above and below. Then she gave
another tug at the door.

"How very odd . . . he is always open for business at this time
of the day," she said. "I wonder if Grandfather is ill?"

She knocked on the door, waited a long time for an answer,
and then she knocked again. Finally, the two girls heard shuffling
footsteps moving toward the door. There was the sound of a bolt
moving, and the door opened by perhaps six inches.

Caleb Braun peered cautiously out through the narrow opening.
"Burn me . . . if it ain't Miss Sera!" He did not appear overly
pleased to see her.

"Do let me inside, Caleb," said Sera, trying to peer into the
shop, over his head. "I have come to visit my grandfather."

"Well, you can't," said Caleb, shaking his head. "He ain't
. . . he ain't in. And I got my instructions: no visitors!"

"But that surely does not apply to me," said Sera, pushing her
way past Caleb and into the shop, and Elsie slipped in behind her.

Hand in hand, the two girls went up the steep stairs, with Caleb
following more slowly, muttering under his breath. In the little
sitting room under the eaves, Elsie took a seat by the fire. But
Sera insisted on opening the shutters, before plunking herself down
in a chair by the window.

Caleb seated himself on a stool and sat there glaring at her.
Then, suddenly, all the stiffness and stubbornness went out of
him. "There ain't no use you sitting there waiting," he said
wearily. "Fact is, he ain't acoming back, your grandpa. He's gone
for good, Miss Sera. Wish I could tell you otherwise, but that's
the truth."

Sera stared at him disbelievingly. Her grandfather to leave the
bookshop after all of these years—and without even telling her?
"But then . . . *where* has he gone? Where can he possibly have
gone? Give me his direction and I—"

"He ain't left no direction," said Caleb, with another shake of
his head. "He left real sudden and I'm certain sure . . . he don't
want you following him, not where he's gone!"

Sera continued to stare at him incredulously. "Caleb Braun,"
she said at last. "Either you are telling me an outright lie, or else
you have gone completely mad!"

It was then that they all heard the footsteps and the creaking,
the steady progress of someone climbing the stairs. Someone who
had let himself in with a key down below . . . or had been in the

284

bookshop all along. Sera shot a triumphant glance at Caleb and headed for the door.

But she was only half way across the room when the door opened and a stranger came in: a dark-haired man with a greying beard and a curiously waxen complexion. Sera drew back in surprise.

The stranger favored her with a cold and haughty glare, then transferred his gaze to Elsie. "And who might these young women be?"

Caleb stared at his hands, grown suddenly meek. "Miss Sera and Miss Elsie," he said slowly and heavily. "Guess I told you about Miss Sera. She's Jenk's granddaughter."

The stranger smiled at Sera, but without any warmth. "Then we are cousins, I find. An unexpected pleasure. How do you do?"

Sera frowned at him. She did not like his looks or his manner, and he did not sound at all like any cousin of hers—he sounded much more like a foreigner. "I don't do very well at all, I am afraid. This is much too puzzling and mysterious! And I demand to know what has happened to my grandfather."

The stranger turned his dark, colorless gaze on Caleb. It was not so much that his eyes were hard, Sera decided, as that they lacked any spark of expression. "You have not told her, then?"

"I told her . . . told her he was gone, but she don't seem inclined to believe me," said Caleb, gazing down at the attic floor.

The stranger moved across the room and placed a cold hand in Sera's. He bowed, almost imperceptibly. "Your grandfather left Thornburg several weeks past. He does not intend to return, and so he has left this establishment in my charge. As it happens, I am (in some sense) already a partner in the business, for it was my father who started him out, so many years ago, and the money was never repaid."

Sera frowned at him, withdrawing her hand. She felt there was something very wrong here, but she was not certain what. "You claim to be the son of Bartholomew Penn . . . my grandfather's cousin?"

"I am the son of Bartholomew Penn," he answered. "I am your Cousin Thomas."

Sera shook her head. She did not remember much about Bartholomew Penn, but surely . . . surely she had heard that he died a bachelor? "I do not believe a word of this. What is more, I think that the Chief Constable will be exceedingly interested to hear of . . . of my grandfather's disappearance. And as for you,

285

Caleb Braun, whom I have always thought my grandfather's friend—''

She stopped speaking, because someone was knocking loudly at the door of the bookshop down below. Caleb limped to the window and looked out.

"It's Jed . . ." he said, in a trembling voice. "Don't know what he's doing here, this time of day." Inexplicably, he turned a pleading look on the stranger. "This ain't my doing. I told him not to come no more. I told him—"

"I fancy," said Sera, with a toss of her head, because she did not understand what any of this was about, "I fancy that Jed has come here looking for Elsie and me."

"It is of no consequence how he comes to be here. You are not to admit him," the mysterious Thomas told Caleb. "And these young women—"

But this was all too much for Sera—whoever this man was, whatever he was doing here, he had no right to give orders in her grandfather's house! "But of course Jed is coming up," she said, striding toward the door.

Caleb gave a strangled cry and rushed after her. "Don't let him come up . . . Miss Sera, don't let him. You ain't got no idea who this man is . . . what he might do if somebody crosses him."

"Yet she will soon discover," hissed Thomas, reaching for Sera at the same time, moving so swiftly that she had no time to draw away. "Thanks to your indiscretion."

Sera intended to pull out of his grasp, but the moment he had her by the wrist, the moment he looked into her startled brown eyes with his own cold, dull black ones, she began to feel exceedingly odd. She could not stir, a cold sensation crept up her arm . . . the room began to spin . . . and when she tried to scream, she found that she could not force out any sound at all.

It was Elsie who screamed, at the top of her lungs. And Caleb—moving with surprising agility—snatched up an iron from beside the fireplace and brought it down hard on the stranger's head.

As Thomas crumbled to the floor, the room around Sera slowly settled back into place. Elsie was at the window, calling down to Jed—Sera had not seen her leave the chair by the hearth, but there she was. And Caleb knelt on the floor by the stranger, searching through his pockets.

Sera finally found her voice. "Caleb Braun, I demand to know—"

"No time for that now," said Caleb, rising stiffly to his feet.

In his hand, he held a large iron key. "Don't know how long he'll be out. You young ladies come along of me; I got something to show you. We'll let Jed in as we go."

There was a battering and crashing sound coming up from the street. "Guess we won't have to," said Caleb, as he headed for the stairs. "Reckon Jed'll have the door busted down by the time we get there."

"Caleb . . ." said Sera, as she and Elsie followed him down the two flights of narrow stairs. "Caleb . . . are you certain he isn't dead—you struck him rather hard. And what was it that he *did* to me . . . it was the most extraordinary sensation."

"Guess he was trying to do to you what he done to Gottfried." Caleb paused for a moment at the first landing, and his voice choked up for a moment. "Sera . . . your grandpa's dead. I would of said sommat afore, but I wanted to protect you . . . wanted to protect Jed and the little un, too! Guess I was afraid for myself as well."

Sera stumbled and almost fell. "My grandfather is *dead*?" Yet somehow, she felt, she had already guessed it, in that terrible moment when she was in the stranger's grip.

"Wish I could of broke it to you more gentle," said Caleb, as they proceeded down the stairs. "But we got to hurry. That wicked man . . . Thomas Kelly he calls hisself . . . he may come around again any time. I wish I could of killed him with that poker . . . but he don't die so easy . . . the Powers know I tried to kill him often enough! I—I poisoned his tea, Miss Sera, and set his bed on fire. But none of it did no good."

They reached the bookshop just as Jed crashed through the door. "Don't ask no questions, there ain't no time," Caleb forestalled him. "Just you come along of us and I'll tell you what I can."

He led them all between the crowded bookshelves to the room at the back, talking as he went. "It weren't a wax figure in the coffin . . . it was a man and he weren't dead. A dangerous man . . . and Gottfried and I didn't have no more sense than to wake him up!" Jed opened his mouth as if to say something, then thought better of it and remained silent. Caleb continued on, as he fitted the key in the door. "He murdered Gottfried just the same way he would of killed Sera just now, rather than you come up and recognize him. He'll kill us all, we're still here when he come downstairs."

Caleb paused with his hand on the door, looked back at Sera with a pleading look. "Guess it was partly my fault he done for

287

your grandpa. We wasn't . . . we wasn't such good friends, there at the end, Gottfried and me . . . too suspicious of each other to pay enough mind to the real danger, and that's how this Thomas got at him. Then he kept *me* on, because he needed someone to help him pretend that things was all as they should be.''

Inside the laboratory, Caleb moved swiftly, snatching up a little wicker cage from one of the long tables. In the dim illumination of a single lanthorn, Sera could not see what the cage contained . . . but there was something moving about inside . . . a bird or a small animal.

"Here now," said Jed, looking around him in considerable surprise. His gaze fell on a pile of books on one of the tables. "You say we shouldn't ask questions, but I want to know—''

"Guess you seen them books afore—don't have to tell you where they come from," said Caleb, as he sidled out of the room. "You can explain to the young ladies. But we got to go now . . . we got to go. Them books is proof of that. Reckon they'd all be crumbling away to dust, if I'd finally killed him. But they ain't . . . so he's still alive.''

Caleb disappeared through the door, but the others did not immediately follow him. They were still too stunned by all they had seen and heard, still trying to make sense of it all.

Then Jed crossed the room and gathered up an armful of books. "Guess Mr. Owlfeather and the Guild would be pleased to take a look at these!'' he said. With the books under one arm, he grabbed Elsie by the hand and started to pull her out of the room. "Come along, Sera, we don't know if Uncle Caleb was telling the truth, but maybe it's not so safe to stay and find out.''

They were still in the bookshop when they heard footsteps, rapidly descending the stairs. Without pausing to look up the steps as they passed, Jed and Elsie ran out the door and into the street, and Sera was only a step behind them.

42.

In which one Adventure ends, and a New one begins.

The city of Ilben at the mouth of the river Lunn was a thriving seaport: a collection of upright, salt-scoured buildings; exotic little shops selling curios from distant lands; shipyards, warehouses, seamen's boarding houses—all very clean and breezy—separated from the ocean and her restless tides, by a stout seawall and a broad mud flat. Built out upon that dark expanse was a network of piers and boardwalks bleached bone-white by the sun and the wind, all leading down to a deep water harbor, where fishing scows, pleasure boats, merchantmen, and navy ships rode side by side with passenger vessels bound for all the ports of Euterpe, Orania, and the New World.

On the tenth day of Fading, on the outskirts of the town, a particularly large but otherwise plain and undistinguished coach came clattering down the road from Thornburg and proceeded toward the Ilben harbor. Inside this coach were Sera, Elsie, and Jed—bound for the New World—Mr. Hermes Budge and the dwarves Mr. Owlfeather and Master Ule, who had come to see them off.

"This man . . . Thomas Penn or Thomas Kelly," Mr. Owlfeather was saying, "has apparently disappeared. And so has Caleb Braun, who was last seen leaving Thornburg in great haste, with some sort of a small animal that he carried in a cage. Yet even without Mr. Braun to confirm them, we have been able to reach certain conclusions. The man who killed your grandfather, Miss Vorder, is apparently the same Thomas Kelly who made such a stir in alchemical circles on the island of Mawbri one hundred and fifty years ago! As he was known then to be a wicked and powerful man, it now becomes apparent that you and Miss Elsie have *two* dangerous enemies to flee from instead of the Duchess only. And that (among many other reasons) is why we have arranged for you to travel such a distance."

289

Elsie gave a tiny sigh and spoke in a small voice. "Nova Imbria . . . it is the other side of the world. And to leave without even saying good-bye to Mama and Papa . . . it is very hard. I do not think I could bear it, if my dear Sera were not coming with me—and Jedidiah, too!"

"Indeed," said Sera, "this all comes about so suddenly and so strangely. I understand the necessity, of course—and the necessity, too, of a gentleman as escort—yet it seems rather hard on poor Jed, who is leaving an excellent position behind, and all his prospects for the future.

"There is no need for you to glare at me so, Jedidiah," she added, in response to a smoldering glance. "I know very well if you had not been asked you would certainly have put yourself forward—but the fact remains you are coming along out of a sense of duty, and not for your own advantage. I merely wished to point out that I wished it were otherwise, and you were not forced to give up so much for my sake and for Elsie's."

"In fact," said Mr. Owlfeather, "it is not so bad as you think. Mr. Braun is now in my employ, and he will be working for me and earning wages (put by with a goldsmith against his return) all the time that he is in the New World. I wish to know more about the glass and the porcelain trade as they are now conducted on the continent of Calliope. Accordingly I have commissioned Jedidiah to explore the matter thoroughly . . . to visit manufactories in Nova Imbria, make observations as to quantity and quality, and send all the information that he can gather, back to me in Thornburg. If he serves me so well and industriously as he has served Master Ule this last year, be sure that his prospects will not suffer."

The coach lurched as it hit a rut in the road. "Yes," said Sera, straightening her hat. "But nevertheless . . . !"

"Moreover," said Master Ule, "he will also serve the Glassmakers Guild by looking after those items—the books once belonging to Thomas Kelly, and the magic parchment formerly in the hands of the Duchess—which we are now sending to our brother Glassmakers in Nova Imbria for safe-keeping. Now that Francis Skelbrooke has revealed himself, in a manner of speaking, to the Duchess, it will not take her long to realize—if indeed she has not realized already—that it was he who stole the document from her. From Skelbrooke to ourselves is not so great a step. Once she begins to suspect that his association with the lodge was not so innocent a thing as she once supposed, the parchment will no longer be safe in our hands. We could not send either the books or the parchment such a distance, except in the hands of a trustworthy messenger like young Jedidiah.''

''We might have considered sending Mr. Budge,'' added Mr. Owlfeather, ''were it not for the fact that he has such a particular reason for wishing to stay—if not in Thornburg, which is now too dangerous for him as well—at least on the continent. To be brief: he is engaged to be married to my niece, Miss Garnet Winterberry.''

''*Are* you, Mr. Budge?'' Sera exchanged a fascinated glance with Elsie. It was difficult to imagine the solemn and sensible tutor in love with anyone, let alone entering into anything as daring and romantic as a mixed marriage.

''I have that honor,'' said Mr. Budge, turning slightly pink.

''Fortunately,'' went on Mr. Owlfeather, ''young Mr. Braun bears a superficial resemblence to you, Miss Sera, which lends credibility to the roles you will be assuming: those of brother and sister. Of course, his manners still lack polish (though much improved, my boy, marvelously improved!) and his speech is still just a little rough. But it is not at all uncommon for boys of his age to be . . . somewhat less elegant than their female relations.''

By this time, they had reached the harbor. The coach came to a halt, and everyone climbed out. The gentlemen stayed to attend to the baggage—hastily bought and even more hastily packed— while the girls walked ahead, out onto the windy boardwalks.

''Jed *has* changed,'' Elsie said, when they had walked some little distance. ''He truly does speak and behave in—in quite a respectable fashion.''

Sera sniffed loudly. ''There is nothing in that. Jed always could speak perfectly decently when he cared to make the effort. Didn't he and I take lessons together when we were small? But he was always one to hide his light under a bushel . . . lest the other boys and men who worked on the river get the idea that he supposed himself better than they. He has a great deal of natural modesty,'' she added, with a sigh. ''Even now, I rather suspect he would get on much faster, if he weren't so mortally afraid of appearing presumptuous!''

She gave Elsie's hand a reassuring squeeze. ''But we shall have sufficient opportunity to polish him up on shipboard. By the time we land in Nova Imbria, Jed will be a perfect gentleman. And then we shall see . . . what we shall see.''

• • •

"Miss Vorder . . . a word with you, if I may," said Mr. Budge, catching up with Sera, just as she and Elsie and Jed were about to ascend the narrow gangplank to the big merchant vessel which would take them across the sea. "We have not had the opportunity to speak alone since Lord Skelbrooke took leave of us, and I feel there are many things which I ought to tell you."

"Yes," said Sera, a little nervously, as she allowed him to lead her aside from the others, past bales, and boxes and trunks, and along the pier. "Perhaps you might begin by telling me whether . . . whether you think it likely that Lord Skelbrooke will be able to keep his promise. We are going so dreadfully far away, you know, and we shall be covering our tracks as we go—so that even Mr. Owlfeather will not know exactly where we are or where we are heading—it hardly seems possible that Lord Skelbrooke will be able to find us and demand an answer to—to the question he asked me."

"Nevertheless," said Mr. Budge, "I am persuaded that he shall. He is a man of great resource and determination, and obstacles are as nothing to him. And that is precisely why I think it is necessary for me to inform you . . . of certain unfortunate traits in Lord Skelbrooke's character."

He shook his head sadly. "You are, perhaps, already aware of a number of these—among them, his regrettable tendency to be secretive and independent, as when he failed to confide in Mr. Owlfeather or any of his friends before his disappearance. Had he told any one of them what he had guessed concerning Jarl Skogsrå . . . then Mr. Owlfeather would have sent word to me, and your cousin should not have suffered so very narrow an escape." The tutor heaved a sigh. "But it is all of a piece with his usual behavior, and I should tell you that, though the Glassmakers do employ him as a kind of an agent, his methods are sometimes so ruthless as to cause considerable consternation among them."

"Yes," said Sera, standing there above the bright water with the wind blowing her skirts against her, the ribbons on her hat fluttering. "I have seen Lord Skelbrooke when he was . . . very cold and very ruthless. But do you mean to tell me, Mr. Budge, that these defects of character are irreparable?"

"By no means," said Mr. Budge. "There is also much goodness . . . much generosity, decency, and compassion in Francis Skelbrooke. I do not consider him a wicked man, so much as a man . . . divided in his nature. And I have some hope that the love of a good woman, such as yourself, might do much to heal that division."

Sera felt an odd lightening of her spirits, though why this should be so she was not entirely certain. "Mr. Budge, I thank you. I believe that you have done me a great service, and Lord Skelbrooke as well."

Budge inclined his head solemnly. "I shall rest easier for knowing that. Farewell, Miss Vorder, and a safe voyage. I hope that we may meet again, and under happier circumstances."

Sera took leave of Master Ule and Mr. Owlfeather, and climbed the gangplank to the ship. She discovered Elsie and Jed standing at the rail, gazing out across the blue water, in the direction they would be sailing.

Elsie slipped her hand into Sera's. "How very strange it seems . . . Only a few days ago, we thought we knew everything that would happen to us for the rest of our lives . . . and now, here we are, quite unexpectedly, sailing to the New World. It seems I ought to be frightened, but instead . . . I feel rather brave and adventurous."

It was very curious, thought Sera, but she felt exactly the same. The future she saw before her was nothing at all like the life she had imagined for herself, the safe, and sober, and sensible existence; her grandfather was dead (she had not yet been given the time to mourn for him but she knew that the tears would come); she did not think that she would ever see Thornburg again—yet here were Elsie and Jedidiah beside her; Francis Skelbrooke would be following in his own good time; and a new life in a new land beckoned.

"Indeed," said Sera, with a toss of her head. "I am perfectly convinced we are about to embark on a grand adventure!"